PRICK

DL Hammons

For Gerry "Never Give Up" Sage

Prologue

The city of New Haven, Georgia, smelled like money. That's the impression Samantha McGill had as she hesitated on the final bus step, inhaling another deep breath to confirm the perception she'd formed on their ride in.

She was immediately uncomfortable.

Taking extra care with the sleeping child against her shoulder, Samantha stepped down onto the pavement and glanced at the hand-carved sign hanging from the terminal building.

New Haven--Population 22,037

A row of benches lined against the building's brick wall beckoned her weary body, drawing her toward the first unoccupied one.

It wasn't so much a specific smell that led Samantha to conclude that New Haven had more than its fair share of well-to-do residents, but rather the absence of smells. Missing was the smorgasbord of revolting aromas usually found lingering around your run-of-the-mill bus stop. God knew she was familiar with those—she could probably still list them off in order of most pungent to barely offensive. The late-afternoon sun had set almost an hour ago, still the temperature hovered in the low 80s and the ground remained damp from a midday shower—perfect conditions for a blooming stench-fest, but that wasn't the case here. The only odor Samantha could detect was a vague whiff of exhaust fumes, and even that had begun to rapidly disappear. No sir, she could tell right away this was a town that didn't sweep its dirt under the rug and paid attention to even the darkest of corners. To do that, they needed diligent caretakers … and money.

She laid the small boy on the bench, using her jacket as a combination pillow and blanket. No sooner had his head touched the makeshift pillow when he sat up and jammed his tiny fists into his eyes, doing his best to rub away the sleep.

"I didn't mean to wake you, honey. You should try to go back to sleep."

The boy dropped his arms to his side and shook his head. "Grandma?" he asked, looking around.

Samantha half-smiled and sat down beside him on the bench. At the same time, an older woman, wearing a lilac fleece sweat suit with a white knit collar, maneuvered into a seat at the opposite end of the bench. She plopped a tan overnight bag next to her. The boy edged closer to Samantha and took hold of her upper arm, his eyes turning away from the older woman.

"We're not at Grandma's yet, honey. We're almost halfway." If the boy was disappointed, he didn't show it. Instead, he began wiggling side-to-side.

"Gotta go pee," he half-whispered, eliciting a chuckle from the old woman.

"Me too, honey," Samantha answered in the same hushed tone. "We need to find where the bathrooms are."

The older woman glanced up from rummaging in her bag. "I don't mean to eavesdrop, but even though my eyes are useless," she said motioning to the thick glasses hanging from a chain around her neck, "I can still hear a flea hiccup a hundred yards away. The restrooms are inside the building to the left. There's quite a line now I'm afraid, but they're very clean—at least that's what my nose tells me."

Samantha wasn't surprised to hear about the cleanliness. "Thank you."

"And who is that trying to hide behind you?"

"This is Taggart."

"How old is he?" the woman continued.

Taggart inched even closer to Samantha, doing his best to disappear behind her.

Samantha smiled and leaned back, pinching Taggart on the dimpled chin that matched her own. "He just turned four."

"He's adorable."

"Thank you, I think so too."

"Young ones on long bus rides like this can try everyone's patience. I should know, I've been on this bus lots of times going down to visit my daughter and her family in Fort Lauderdale. It's not that I'm afraid of flying or anything, no I'm happy to fly, but my son-in-law is a bit of a tightwad and won't pay for my ticket, and being on a fixed income and all, I can't afford it myself. But no… he says the bus should be just fine. I'd like to see his backside after sitting in those seats for thirteen hours. Are you two headed to Florida to see family of your own?"

Samantha paused before answering, wishing she had chosen a bench further away. The questions were beginning to make her nervous. "My mother."

"That's nice," the old woman said. She closed her bag and shifted slightly so she was facing directly toward Samantha, adopting a more serious expression. "I hope you don't mind me butting in… you look like you haven't eaten in a week and if those bags under your eyes get any bigger, they're going to charge you for extra luggage."

Samantha's hand went to her hair, which she was sure was going on its third day unwashed.

"I'm just getting over a bad case of the flu, but I'm fine now. In fact, that's why we're heading to my mom's house, to recuperate."

The woman nodded, the worry in her face easing. "Moms and chicken soup… no better combination. Is your husband with you?"

Samantha fought the urge to grab Taggart and get away. Instead, she wrapped him in her arms and squeezed, giving the woman her best impression of a blissful smile. "It's just the two of us."

"GOTTA PEE!" Taggart exclaimed, his shyness abandoned and sense of timing as perfect as ever.

"Okay, okay, let's go."

Samantha set Taggart on the ground, took him by the hand, and the two of them walked purposefully toward the entrance, navigating the crowd of fellow bus passengers in front of the building. Through the glass windows of the bus depot, she could see the entrance to the woman's restroom to the left near the front of the building, just as the old woman had indicated.

As she reached the door leading inside, it opened and a man she recognized as their bus driver emerged, his head turned back toward the room he was exiting.

"…in ten minutes," the driver finished saying. He then focused his attention on the people standing outside, placing his hands around his mouth like a megaphone. "Bus departs in ten minutes, folks. Start making your way back to your seats."

Everyone began moving at once, people exiting the depot for the bus, others attempting to make their way into the building for some last-minute business. Samantha picked up Taggart when the crowd seemed to converge on them, making her nervous and fearful of losing hold of him. She reached for the door when there was a disturbance behind her, people pushing and jostling back and forth, seemingly caused by someone losing their balance, resulting in her being shoved from the back and causing her to almost fall over.

Samantha held Taggart tightly to her chest as she managed to steady herself. Although she heard a man's voice muttering an apology behind her, she didn't bother to turn around. Instead, she kept moving into the depot. Inside she found a line of women waiting for the restroom that backed all the way out into the waiting area.

Desperate for another option, she briefly considered using the toilet on the bus but remembered someone mumbling something about a flushing malfunction, so she turned around and surveyed the street outside. The bus, now idling as it waited for its imminent departure, took up most of her view. Directly past the front of the bus, on the other side of the street, she could make out a gasoline pump sitting underneath a metal overhang.

A gas station … gas stations had bathrooms.

"I GOTTA PEE!" Taggart reminded her, putting her feet into motion.

Samantha hustled out of the building, past the front of the bus and across an empty street -- into the parking lot of what she now recognized as a Quick-Serve. Above a pair of doors on the right side of the building were the signs for bathrooms.

She sighed a bit of relief when she turned the door handle and it opened easily, giving way to a pitch-black room. Reaching in she felt along the wall to find the light switch, which was already in the "on" position.

"Wouldn't you know it." She dug into her front pocket and pulled out her phone. After activating the flashlight, her phone illuminated a pair of dingy sinks and two stalls. She closed the door behind her and made sure to lock the deadbolt before she lowered Taggart to the ground and led him with the light into the gray metal stall nearest the wall.

Placing her phone on the top of the toilet tank, the shone light straight up, where it bounced off the white ceiling and cast just enough of an eerie glow for her to see what she was doing. She bent over, slid down the boy's loose-fitting pants, and lifted him onto the toilet seat. It took him a few seconds to get rolling, but when he did, it was with a stream so forceful she realized she had been *that close* to finding him some new jeans. When he was finished, she placed him back on the ground, pulled up his pants, and instructed him to wait near the stall door. Samantha then took care of her own business, hovering centimeters above the toilet seat. An itch swiftly flared up on the back of her right calf. Contorting her upper-body so she could look at the area, all she could see was a tiny red inflammation.

While this was going on, Taggart busied himself by using his hands to create shadowy images on the stall door.

"I'm hungry," the small boy said without turning around.

"I know, honey. I am, too. But we'll have to wait until we get to Grandma's."

Taggart didn't seem to hear and continued to play with the light.

Finished, Samantha put herself back in order, then knelt down and took Taggart by his shoulders, turning him around. The boy's teary blue eyes looked back at her, nearly ripping Samantha's already sad heart in half. It was a couple of moments before she trusted her voice enough to speak.

"You remember our adventure, right?"

Taggart nodded his small head.

"Just focus on that and our rules, okay? We'll be eating ice cream and cookies in no time. Deal?"

"Deal."

Samantha hugged the boy, kissing him on the top of his head. When she stood up she experienced a head rush of such intensity it caused her to squeeze her eyes shut. She started to lean to one side like a ship taking on water until she felt the slap of cool metal as she made contact with the stall wall. *This isn't right,* she thought. She had experienced something like this before. The memory of it made her heart race and skin turn clammy. She hadn't taken anything…not for a long time…*so why was this happening?* The old feelings … the yearning … the desperation … the blissful release … came rushing back to her. Surely it was just muscle memory. Nausea gripped her stomach, but she managed to stay calm. She knew the spinning room would soon pass and things would return to normal. But something was different. The dizziness wasn't going away; it was getting worse. She was mistaken, this wasn't the same as before. Something was seriously wrong.

Opening her eyes, she almost fell forward. Pain took over. It was as if somebody had taken a string, tied a slipknot around her brain, and was pulling as hard as they could. Samantha closed her eyes again, placing her hands on her temples. An involuntary moan escaped her as a second, more intense wave of pain washed over her.

"Taggart?" Samantha managed to whisper, but the boy had backed into the corner and was covering his eyes.

Samantha forced her eyes open, to pain was so intense it blinded her. She felt something sticky and wet flowing out of her nose and rolling across her lips.

There was only one thought Samantha could focus on.

"Honey, you need to…"

Samantha crumbled to the ground.

One

There was no doubt about it, Taggart McGill was the bane of my existence.

The thought popped into my head out of the blue while I was sitting in my car parked just outside school. I shifted in my seat car and tried to push the thought from my mind. Turning my head towards the open window I could feel the ocean breeze gently flowing through our small town of New Haven and across the school parking lot. The moist air lifted the hair off my shoulders and to a lesser degree my spirits. Our high school was a short four miles from the Georgia coast, and it was a rare day when a light wind didn't blow across campus, keeping temperatures bearable even during the most trying heat waves, like today's. At that moment, it was keeping my irritation under control, barely.

I wondered where the expression *bane of existence* came from, so I looked it up on my phone. The first definition I came across said it was a person or thing who was a constant irritant or source of misery, and the phrase first appeared in print in the 1590's. However old it was, the meaning certainly fit Taggert to a tee.

I'd never given much thought to which of the seven heavenly virtues I exhibited most, but the one I struggled with was easy to pick out...patience. I had very little. Especially when forced to wait around because of other people's poor planning. I wasn't good at it. I tended to sulk and think non-productive thoughts. Not a good quality—but the truth I'm ashamed to admit. Take this afternoon for example. I could be on my way with my girlfriend, Delta, to watch my boyfriend, Jason, play football, and then afterwards, all of us would head to the shore for a post-game bonfire. Instead, here I was sitting in the school parking lot waiting for my younger sister, Becca. And why was that?

Taggart Friggin' McGill.

Bane. Existence.

An unproductive thought if there ever was one.

How could he not be? I could trace almost every negative event in my life back to him. It was almost as if the jerk bag was put on this earth for the sole purpose of making my life miserable. It didn't matter that I hadn't said a dozen words to him in the last fourteen years.

If I was being technical about it, I was waiting on Becca because her own car was in the shop getting its transmission rebuilt. But the reason it was in the shop was because of all the added miles her already suspect transmission was forced to absorb driving Taggart everywhere – since his own car had broken down and the loser didn't have money to fix it. It was during one of Taggart's useless errands that the transmission finally gave out. With Becca without a car, it became my responsibility as the *"older sister"* to take her to and from school, as well as any of her recitals when Mom or Dad were tied up, which I had a feeling would be all of them. It didn't matter that I might have had plans of my own. Oh no... I was the older sister and it fell to me to take care of my younger sibling.

Sure, life could be unfair sometimes, but to me, it sure seemed that fairness tended to skew towards little sisters.

I glanced at my phone again, still nothing from my best friend, Delta. That was something else contributing to my sour mood. She had become more and more distant since she began going out with Jason's best friend, Kevin Steuer, or Stooch as everyone called him. Strictly speaking, the cold shoulder started after I tried to talk her out of dating him. She didn't take that so well and our relationship had been going downhill ever since. Sadly, it looked like we may have bottomed out. Jason, Stooch, and the others we usually hung out with were at an away game up the coast and their respective girlfriends, except me of course, followed them. Delta would normally be making my phone sound like it was receiving Morse code from her constant texts, but not today. I sighed as I laid my phone down on the seat beside me.

I guessed I shouldn't have been surprised. Delta rarely listened to any of the advice I gave her. Maybe I should have suggested she and Stooch hook up. That would have guaranteed she'd stay away from him.

As much as I moaned about not being able to go with them, it wasn't like I had been looking forward to the game or spending time at the beach house anyway. Well, maybe a little. I enjoyed the beach and was sure that good times would happen, but I really needed to start thinking long-term and figure out how I was going to handle my own situation with Jason.

We had both been freshman when we first started going out. I was a wide-eyed dweeb who'd spent most of the time with my head stuck in books, and Jason was putting a twinkle in all the coaches' eyes with his natural athleticism. For me to start dating him was the equivalent of a minor-league baseball player moving up to the majors, thrilling... but scary. I wondered sometimes what it was that had caused Jason to set his sights on an awkward library rat like me. It wasn't long before he'd bloomed into an all-star athlete. By the start of our senior year, he was the all-conference quarterback and captain of the basketball team. With that came popularity, something I've always struggled with. I began noticing more and more how my priorities were so different than a lot of the kids in our circle, particularly Stooch. The older Stooch got, the more and more of a tool he could be, and the more Jason had to defend him.

Things had recently shifted between Jason and me, and I'd kept putting off the inevitable. Change was hard. This weekend I planned to spend some quality time with Delta to try to shore up our friendship and at the same time make some decisions about Jason and me. Of course, that wasn't going to happen now.

"Come on," I said aloud, slapping my hand against the steering wheel, my impatience beginning to boil over. After my last class, I wasted some time by running into town to get a coffee, but once I was back in the school parking lot, I busied myself by listening to tunes and playing some stupid game on my phone since Delta was refusing to answer any of my texts.

School had let out fifteen minutes ago, and I was still waiting.

Patience was so not me.

Taggart. Frickin. McGill.

Bane.

Both of the back-seat doors flew open, startling me. A light-blue backpack landed on the rear right-side seat and the door slammed shut. Someone climbed into the seat behind me and closed the door. Then the front passenger side door opened and Becca plopped down into the seat, smiling like a Cheshire cat.

"Hey, Sis. Sorry for the wait."

Looking at my sister was like staring into a mirror, except for the clothes and the smile. Even though Becca was eleven months younger than me, she could easily be confused as my twin. She was the same height and weight as me, same auburn hair worn the same way, same hazel eyes and snub nose we'd inherited from our mother.

Ignoring my sister, I swiveled around in my seat and looked into the back. The boy sitting behind me stared back through long shaggy hair. If I was being completely honest, Taggart could be considered… in a scruffy Ian Somerhalder of *The Vampire Diaries* sort of way… cute. He gave off that type of vibe, rough around the edges with shoulder length brown hair that probably never saw a comb, frequently wearing the same disheveled clothes to school for days in a row, with his shoulders always slouched and his head down. Looking closer I saw his dimpled chin and dark eyes were outlined by a white cord attached to a pair of earbuds in his ears, dangling down the front of his shirt and disappearing into his pocket. The expression on his face was blank, unreadable.

"Oh, hell NO!" I exclaimed, facing my sister.

"Come on, Cassie," Becca said, her smile changing into one of concern. "He doesn't have any other way home."

"And whose fault is that?"

"I'll get out," came a barely audible voice from the back seat, followed by the opening of the door.

"Taggart, don't," Becca commanded, which seemed to freeze the boy in his tracks. Turning back to me she pleaded, "Cassie, how will he get home?"

"He can walk for all I care, or maybe he can get one of the Wilsons to come get him."

"Cassie, you know neither of the Wilsons can drive anymore, and it's a five-mile walk from here. Please, have a heart."

I placed both of my hands on the steering wheel and stared out the front window, the anger rising off me like heat from the blacktop.

Becca reached out her hand and laid it on my arm. "Cassie, he's my friend."

I wanted to scream at the top of my lungs…*WHY? Why are you his friend? After everything he's done and the reputation he's earned, why are you letting yourself be dragged down with him? Why? Why? Why!*

But I didn't. No matter how I frustrated my sister's relationship with Taggart made me feel, I could never stay upset with her for long. So instead, I sighed and said, "Close the door."

When I heard the door close behind me, I pushed in the clutch and started the car.

"Seatbelt," I said robotically.

My Subaru Baja roared to life. I loved my car. The moment I'd set eyes on the beach-friendly beauty I knew I had to have her, even though it was $3,000 dollars above the budget my father had given me. But when I made my mind up about something… that was it.

I turned the Subaru out of the parking lot and headed south down Fairview Lane. Though it was in the lower nineties, well within giving thought to turning on the A/C, both Becca and I had our windows rolled down to allow the wind to whip our hair. I glanced into the rear-view mirror and although I couldn't see Taggart's face, I could see the tips of his hair as it was caught by the fast moving current of air.

Fairview Lane ended when it ran into the intersection at Bryant-Lynn Expressway, so I turned right and headed for home. As I accelerated past my normal 5-6 miles over the speed limit, Becca swiveled around in her seat and began talking to Taggart.

"I heard Mr. Mallard had a meltdown with Jimmy Franklin this afternoon," she said.

Mr. Mallard was the school's American History teacher – and Jimmy Franklin, well, let's just say academics wasn't one of his strong points.

All I could hear from the backseat was a grunt.

"How bad was it, really?" Becca asked.

"I wasn't paying attention," Taggart answered reluctantly.

"Oh, come on. I heard Mallard's face turned red."

"I wouldn't know."

That's the way the rest of the conversation went, Becca needling Taggart for details that he wasn't interested in coughing up. Typical.

A short distance out of town, the scenery changed as the number of houses decreased, the size of the lots increased from feet to acres, and the trees returned. A half mile ahead, the gate was down and lights were flashing at the railroad crossing for the Amtrak train that ran along the coast from Washington DC to Boca Raton, Florida. I shifted the Subaru into neutral and allowed the car to coast all the way up to the white painted lines, then stopped. There were no other cars waiting on our side of the tracks, but two were already waiting on the other side.

The patch of road in front of the security gate was flat, so I left the car in neutral and removed my feet from the pedals, taking the opportunity to stretch and relax. I looked over at my sister, who was staring back at me with the same Cheshire cat smile she had before.

"You look like you've got a Mexican jumping bean rammed up your butt. What gives?" I asked.

"I got in."

It took me a few moments to register what she meant, then it came flooding back to me in a rush.

"Perlman?"

As wide as Becca's smile was before, it now threatened to break the boundaries of her face.

"Perlman."

"Oh my god -- Becca!"

Itzhak Perlman was a violin virtuoso who'd been welcoming gifted students of the violin, viola, cello, and bass into an exclusive musical community since 1994. They chose approximately 40 musicians from around the world each year, ages 12-18, to attend a seven-week summer program on a beautiful waterfront campus on Shelter Island, New York. Becca, who had a very special talent on the violin, had been applying to the workshop since she was 12.

"I know, right," Becca said.

"That is so awesome. When did you find out?"

"Mom texted me during school. Turns out, she's been opening the letters for years and sealing them back for me to open later. She totally has no self-control."

"Can't say that I blame her, given the mind-meld the two of you have about music. Seven weeks in New York. I'm so jealous."

A blaring horn from the approaching train interrupted our conversation.

"You know what this means, right?" Becca asked.

"What?"

"A hardcore weekend of shopping. I don't have anything to wear for New York."

"You don't have to dress-up for those thick-skinned, self-absorbed transplants. Your music says enough," came Taggart's soft voice from the back of the car.

Becca looked toward Taggart, who I could see in my rear-view mirror looking out the side window. She mimicked his pouty face. "Someone isn't as happy about this as the rest of us."

"No surprise there," I said under my breath.

Becca was about to say something else when her eyes suddenly grew big and she started fumbling for the seat belt release.

"CASSIE!"

The impact came from the rear, violently forcing me back into my seat and propelling the car forward, crashing through the crossing gate before eventually coming to rest. At first I was dazed, then anger surged through me. *Who had rammed us?* There hadn't even been screeching brakes, giving us at least a little warning. When I had time to look around, the blood froze in my veins.

We were sitting on the train tracks.

A blaring train whistle pulled my attention to the impossible sight of my sister Becca, holding a hand against her forehead and looking bewildered, framed against a train bearing down on us.

Two

This isn't my bedroom.

Where am I?

The room was dark, except for a sliver of light that came from somewhere at my side. The light illuminated a guardrail on the bed where I was laying.

I smelled antiseptic, like the room was filled with hand-sanitizer. It was everywhere. *Is this a hospital room?*

My eyes didn't want to focus, and I was really, really thirsty.

I could barely make out a figure sitting in the corner, but not who. Drawn shades on the window next to the blurry figure, with no sunshine trying to get in. *Was it nighttime?*

Something was wrapped around the lower half of my right arm and my left foot throbbed.

Why am I here --? I wondered. *Did something terrible happen?* I couldn't remember. The more I tried to focus my thoughts, the sleepier I became.

Becca. I was supposed to pick up my sister, wasn't I?

Thinking about it was too much effort…I felt weighted down from exhaustion.

I let sleep take me again.

Three

TRAIN!

I bolted upright in the bed at the thought, which was a mistake because my stomach lurched. I doubled over and rolled onto my side, fighting the urge to vomit. I felt someone at my side, rubbing my back and brushing the hair out of my face.

It was Mom… or rather a tortured version of her. Her eyes, usually sparkling with life, were red and puffy from crying, underscored by dark circles from lack of sleep. Rarely caught without makeup, her face was gaunt and barren, hair falling limply around her flushed skin.

Please let this be a look of concern. Please let it be worry…and not something else.

"Where's Becca?" I managed to rasp.

My mother turned away, her bottom lip quivering. The subtle change spoke volumes. She shifted slightly and behind her, I saw my dad. My heart sank. He, too, looked like someone who had been through a 72-hour police interrogation. The wrinkled t-shirt he wore matched the lines on his face.

"Honey, don't worry about your sister right now," Dad said. "You need to focus on yourself. You've been through a lot."

I pushed my mother away and sat up, my body fighting a wave of dizziness. I wasn't sure if it was the anger that flashed through me or the fear of what I might hear, but I couldn't help myself.

"No," I cried. "Don't do that. Why are you keeping the truth from me?"

Tears forming in my eyes obscured the room.

The hospital room door opened and a young blonde wearing light blue scrubs and holding a clipboard started into the room. Obviously sensing the family drama taking place, she stopped in her tracks.

"Where is my sister?" I yelled at her. "Is she on this floor?"

The nurse didn't answer me, instead she looked at my mother with a lost expression.

"Can you please give us a few minutes?" Dad asked softly.

The young nurse attempted a smile but looked relieved instead. "Certainly. I'll come back by later," she said making a quick escape.

"I want you to tell me right now. How is Becca? Why are both of you here and nobody is with her?"

There was a pause. My mom turned to look at Dad and the two of them seemed to carry out a telepathic conversation. When Mom turned back to me, her face had hardened.

"She's gone, Cassie. The doctors say she died instantly."

Even though I heard my mother's words, I refused to accept their meaning. I shook my head and glanced at dad, hoping for some sort of reprieve. A sadness was in his eyes that had never been there before and seeing it made my body go numb. Everything and everyone in the room fell away as my thoughts turned inward and found only darkness.

My focus returned when I felt something on my face. Mom had gently placed her hands against my cheeks. Looking up at her I watched as her steeled expression slowly melted away and revealed the agonizing pain she had been hiding from me. I realized I had stopped breathing and when I opened my mouth the gloom dropped over me like a blanket of thorns and the tears came full force.

Maybe my parents were right. Maybe it was better that I didn't know.

Four

Laying there in bed, I felt the walls closing in on me. I had been crying for almost the entire day. When I wasn't sobbing, mom was.

Jason and Delta had tried to visit, but I wasn't ready to see either of them… or anyone else for that matter. One of them, or maybe both, had left me a bouquet of flowers and a white teddy bear. I wondered if that was a fair trade for a sister.

The only break in the pattern was when the doctor paid us a visit and filled me in on my condition. My right arm sustained a compound open fracture—which in patient-speak meant it was broken in two places and one of the bones punctured the skin—requiring plates, and pins to put it back together. My right foot looked like a flesh-colored over-inflated balloon, but the x-rays confirmed nothing was broken. The bruises over most of my body looked like a tattoo artist's idea of a sick joke. My neck ached every time I turned, the result of a mild case of whiplash, but it wasn't bad enough to warrant a neck brace or anything. The doctor let me know that I should expect to experience headaches for a couple of days.

I listened to it all in some sort of fugue state, nodding when I thought I should, attempting to smile when the doctor was trying to show me compassion. None of it really registered. It was like I was watching a foreign film, but someone had forgotten to turn on the subtitles.

"You're very lucky," the doctor finished with, but his body language told me he regretted the words before they finished leaving his mouth. He recovered quickly by adding, "You can go home later today, after the result of one last test comes back. I'll go ahead and get the process started so the nurse can untether you from the I.V."

I wasn't looking forward to going home though, or anything else for that matter.

***

Later, one of the nurses told me my parents had been refusing to go home or take a break until I woke up following the surgery to repair my arm, which had to wait because the doctor didn't want to put me under general anesthesia right away because of the blunt head trauma. It had been two days straight for them. After I woke, my dad went home to take a shower and put on clean clothes. When he returned, Mom did the same. Both of them looked and smelled fresher, but it was only window dressing. It was like spreading newly opened frosting on a two-week-old cake. Maybe it was just me. I imagined that the clothes they had been wearing – the ones infested with the stench of fear, worry, and stress, were either in the trash can or a bag destined for Goodwill.

Goodwill. Surely there had to be something ironic in that.

Mom brought me fresh clothes, my favorite t-shirt and a fuzzy pair of sweats, which I changed into without bothering to shower first, getting help with the IV in my arm from the nurse. I thought the clothes I'd been wearing before the accident must have ended up as a bloody mess in the corner of the emergency room floor, scooped into a plastic bag by some orderly, but Dad found them hanging in the closet. Got to give props to the hospital for efficiency. I asked him to take them away, which he did without a word.

My parents and I mostly sat there in silence waiting for my release. Dad had to step out into the hallway often to answer non-stop phone calls. Mom, the one who normally had the phone to her ear, occupied the cheap recliner next to the window, staring into space. I hadn't heard her phone ring once. She must have turned it off.

Though Mom would never admit it, Becca had been her favorite. Our mother had a background in music as a pianist for a couple minor jazz bands, and when I quit band after the first year, it crushed her. "But honey, you show so much promise," she had said.

"I can't stand it. I'm all fumbly fingers. It makes me feel stupid."

"That's natural. Everyone goes through that when first starting out."

"But I'm not enjoying it. Shouldn't I be enjoying it? I'm not... not even a little bit."

She kept after me for a while longer, but I could tell she had already given up on me. Things were a lot quieter around the house for weeks after that.

Becca and her skill with a violin made up for my disappointment in spades. The two of them were peas in a musical pod. I didn't mind. I was happy Mom had someone to pass along her considerable knowledge to.

Had. Past tense. And Becca had finally gotten into the Perlman program, something the two of them had been chasing after for years.

Tears filled my eyes again.

After a while the pseudo-trance I'd inhabited since hearing the news began to fall away. What I felt replacing it was considerably more potent. I could feel myself becoming restless, irritable. Finally, I couldn't stand it any longer.

"What happened?" I blurted out, wiping my eyes.

Both of my parents looked at me. Mom's face was blank and Dad's forehead furrowed.

"Who ran into my car?"

"I don't think we need to be talking about that right now. This can wait until we're home and settled, then we'll—"

"Dad… it's all I can think of. Please, I need to know. I'm going crazy not knowing."

My dad took a deep breath. "Your mother—none of us for that matter'—need to be re-living what—"

"I'm fine Paul," mom said, her gaze returning to a spot on the wall she had been fixated on for quite a while. "Go ahead and tell her."

Dad waited a few moments before he got up and walked to the side of my bed.

"You remember Tim Ledbetter, lives down the street from us? Owns that store on the square and always goes wild with the Christmas decorations every year. He ran into you and forced your car onto the train tracks. The police said the only reason you were spared was because the car came to a stop on an angle… and when the train collided with your car… it wasn't a direct hit. The force of the impact was partially dispersed."

"But Becca --"

"Was seated right where the impact was most severe."

The image of Becca superimposed against the silhouette of the rushing train popped into my head, forcing me to close my eyes tight.

I did remember Mr. Ledbetter. He and his family were one of New Haven's few Black families, which was a bit unusual for South Georgia. He owned a sporting goods store. His son was our age… a cool guy with a weird nickname who went to my school. The few times I had run into Mr. Ledbetter, he seemed nice.

"But what happened? He didn't even hit his brakes."

"The police theorize that Tim might have had a heart attack. I'm afraid we won't know until after the autopsy... or ever. He died in the accident as well."

Everyone is dead but me. At first I was numb, disoriented, but then I began to feel something else. Cheated. My compulsion to find someone, anyone, to direct my slow-burning rage at was over before it even began. Becca was ripped away from us, but the person responsible was dead as well. And even worse, he wasn't a bad person.

"With any luck, there won't be a third fatality," my mom murmured.

"What do you mean?" I asked.

"Taggart has been in a medically induced coma ever since the accident."

The back of my neck flushed with heat like it always did when I became upset. I hadn't even remembered Taggart was in the car with us. Dad must have taken my silence as a request for more information.

"Apparently, he wasn't wearing his seatbelt and got tossed around pretty bad when the train hit. He had some swelling on his brain, but the doctors say his signs are all positive and they should be waking him up soon. You never know with brain injuries though."

The rage in me—momentarily subdued—erupted again.

"Taggart lived... and my sister is dead. Tell me you didn't just say that."

Mom disengaged from her fascination with the wall and turned to look at me. The expression on her face could only be described as shock.

"Cassie! That is a horrible thing to say."

"I don't care! The only reason we were even at those railroad tracks was because of him. It's all his fault, and somehow he's the one who lives?"

"What do you mean the only reason you were there was because of him?" Dad asked.

Suddenly I was too embarrassed to offer an explanation. "Never mind."

"No, I want to know. Why did you say that?" Dad insisted, the raised pitch in his voice telling me that he expected an answer.

"Because if Becca didn't have to drive him around all the time, her transmission wouldn't have gone out when it did, and the three of us would never have been there at all."

Dad put his hands on his hips and frowned. "Cassie, I'm disappointed in you. That's twisted logic and you're misguided to look at things that way. Taggart is no more responsible for any of this than the train itself."

My dad turned away as if he was through with the conversation, then turned back to me.

"Taggart was your sister's friend, one of her few friends as a matter of fact. She would be disappointed to hear how you're talking about him."

That stung. Maybe deep down the truth behind my dad's words sparked what I said next, or it was me being defensive about the way my brain worked, but whatever the reason, I lashed back.

"And why is that you think? That Becca had so few friends? Have you ever considered that the reason is Taggart? You do realize that he set a New Haven record for the most visits to the principal's office. The kid has a serious problem with authority figures… or maybe it's authority in general… but whatever it is he's tested the limits of corporal punishment. Besides Becca, he has no other friends and the teachers despise him. He's an equal-opportunity jerk, belligerent and combative with everybody. He pulls cruel and destructive pranks. Maybe Becca thought of him as a lost puppy nobody wanted to play with when she started hanging out with him, but he's really a raging pit-bull that bites anyone who comes near. That kid is a prick and bad news. Everyone avoids him like the plague, everybody except Becca that is, which placed her dead center of plague central. Hell, a lot of my classmates avoid *me* because of Becca's friendship with Taggart. You haven't heard all the things that kid has done."

Mom mumbled something about unnecessary cursing, but dad stared at me a long time before responding.

"I may not know Taggart that well, and then again maybe I know him better than you think. Still, I knew your sister. I trusted her judgment. So, if she wanted to be friends with this boy when everybody else was turning their back on him, then there was a good reason. I guarantee you one thing though, that reason wasn't to put a kink in your social life."

I knew I had gone too far, and Dad's response made me regret my outburst even more. Sure, Taggart's mother abandoned him when he was young, leaving him at a bus stop, or something like that. And he ended up in the foster care system (who knew New Haven had one of those), bouncing around from family to family because no one could locate any of his family members. A real Lifetime movie kind of thing. Becca and I both were aware of all of this, in a vaugue sense that it is. Taggart didn't really hang out in our circle of friends, or any other circles for that matter, and neither of us had him in any of our classes. But the year Taggart graduated from junior high and became a high school freshman, two important events happened that changed everything… for him… and me. The first was when he moved in with an elderly couple who lived in the same neighborhood as our family. The second was when he asked Becca out on a date.

What was even more surprising was her answer. Yes! That was the day my relationship with Becca changed.

Dad regarded me for a few seconds, possibly debating whether or not to say something more, then he turned and marched out of the room, leaving Mom and me emersed in an uncomfortable silence.

"We're all upset," she finally said, taking the edge of the sheet on my bed and kneading it into a ball.

My dad had made a point, a good one. Tears rolled down my cheeks. Deep down I knew I had reached the part of an argument when you realize you've been wrong and all that is left is a half-hearted attempt to explain how you took the stance you did. I knew what I was about to say was pure rationalization, but I wasn't ready to give up my long-held belief that Taggart was a slow-acting poison.

"But, Mom. Taggart ratted on some boys accused of cheating on a test. You just don't do that. Then he embarrassed my best friend Delta to the point she had to check herself out of school for the rest of the day. He's also been hauled down to juvenile hall more times than you can count."

My mom grimaced and shook her head. "That's enough."

"One of these days we're going to be reading his name in the paper, like one of those Columbine kids, and we're going to --"

"Cassie, I said that's enough!" she snapped at me. "The boy's in a coma. Becca must have had her reasons for befriending him. You and I both know that New Haven is a small community, made up of upper-class retirees and a place where silver spoons are handed out by the gross. Noses here are perpetually pointed skyward. Spreading rumors and gossiping should be considered an Olympic sport here, and Taggart's story is definitely worthy of a gold medal, and even though I may not know the full story, like your father, I trusted your sister. Maybe you should have too."

Up until that point, I didn't think it was possible for me to feel any worse.

Boy, was I wrong.

Five

Watching the landscape drift by as our limo made its way from the gravesite, I could barely focus on the trees bending to the will of a southern squall headed our way. My distraction might have also been because of the pill I'd taken. My arm was hurting that morning, and I broke down and dug into the prescription I'd been trying to avoid. It did its job and dulled the pain, but it also made me loopy, and I hated that. Everything turned foggy. Stupid pill. Of course my lack of concentration could also have been from watching my sister get lowered into the ground and the knowledge that workers who never knew her would soon be filling that hole with dirt.

Some mid-grade pharmaceutical sure couldn't numb that.

My parents sat next to me in the back of the limo, sharply dressed, holding hands, and speaking in hushed tones I didn't bother to try to catch. I remembered the three of us standing over Becca after everyone had backed away, alone with our grief. Dad had been a rock all morning, like he always was, only breaking down once when he got up and spoke about Becca at the funeral. It was the first time I had seen him cry… and hopefully, my last. There was something about watching the man I idolized, a man who was my definition of everything pure and wholesome, reduced to the equivalent of a sobbing twelve-year-old boy that really shook me. I don't think I've ever hugged him any harder than I did when he returned to his seat.

My mom was another story. She did her best when I was around, but I was pretty sure she was taking some serious medication to get through it herself. I didn't blame her. The first couple of days after we returned from the hospital, she slept a lot. We all did. But Mom had pretty much been a robot while she, my Aunt Cathy, and Dad made the arrangements for the funeral and the gathering afterward. She showed moments of her old self at times, especially in the mornings when she was fresh from a drug-induced night of sleep, but in late-afternoons and early evenings, it was like a dark cloud engulfed her and nobody could get through. All Dad could do was be by her side and have that shoulder ready for her to cry on when the waves of depression hit. My Aunt Cathy, my mom's sister, was in New Haven when we returned from the hospital and she had been taking care of us all. Cathy drove down from Atlanta right away, but Uncle Don and the rest of the family arrived two days before the funeral and had been staying at the Holiday Inn Express.

Scheduling the funeral for that specific day… a Saturday… one week and a day from the accident had a purpose. It was originally going to be Friday, but someone said holding it on a Saturday would let the kids from school attend without disrupting a normal school day. I didn't bother to mention that the school would probably excuse anyone who wanted to attend and that most kids would rather the chance to get out of a half day of school instead of wasting a Saturday. Telling my parents that would only paint some of Becca's classmates in a negative light…which was right where some of them needed to be…but I bit my tongue.

"I'm glad the reporters took a day off," I heard my dad mumble. He was worried beforehand that they might be lurking around, mostly because they had been pretty relentless in trying to get a statement from us… well, mostly me, about the accident, but we weren't having any part of it. It turned out we worried for nothing because they stayed away. I guess even reporters have limits.

The number of people who showed up at the service surprised me. We all knew Becca didn't have many friends, at least not any she'd mentioned or who I saw her hanging with at school, and even though most of my friends would come out of respect, no one could have guessed the number of people who showed up. The main hall at the funeral parlor was packed. People stood along the walls in the back, and Dad told us on the ride to the cemetery that they had to open up two other halls to let the overflow guests sit and listen to the service piped over the sound system. I knew something was up when I saw the number of cars parked along the road when we pulled away in the limo heading to the gravesite.

Leave it to New Haven to make my sister's funeral the social event of the season.

Jason and Delta were there with me the whole time, and Jason looked genuinely disappointed when he wasn't invited to ride in the limo with us to the plot. I had finally let him come over to the house a couple of days before the funeral and not surprisingly, he was confused about why I didn't want to see him until then. I wasn't an idiot, I knew how tragedies like this could end up deepening a relationship and I just didn't want that to happen with us.

It took me a moment to realize we were already back at the house when we pulled in the driveway. Aunt Cathy tried to talk Mom into having the gathering at the church, but Mom insisted it be at the house. Since that was the only thing that animated her, nobody argued for very long. Never mind that our house was modestly sized and not very well laid out to host a bunch of people. Never mind that parking could be an issue and the congestion throughout the neighborhood was a concern. Never mind that most of the people coming had to drive over that same railroad crossing where Becca died.

Never mind.

So, we didn't.

As I stepped out of the limo, there were already a couple cars parked in front of the house. Mom slid out of the door behind me and walked briskly towards the entrance at the rear of the house that led directly into the kitchen. Dad hung by the driver's window to say something. I headed to the porch.

The weather had turned windy and cool and although they predicted rain, Mother Nature had decided to cut us a break. The front door stood wide open and welcoming; I strolled in and looked around. In addition to the furniture in our living room to the right, there were folding chairs wherever an open space allowed for one. I headed down the hall to the kitchen with the intention of offering to help, but changed my mind. I would only be in the way. At least that's what I told myself.

I headed upstairs instead.

At the top of the stairs, which felt like they had inexplicably doubled in length, I turned right away from my parents' bedroom and trudged down the hallway to my room, which was directly across the hall from Becca's. I opened the door and took a step inside.

Thud.

Was that a noise from inside Becca's room?

I stood there, waiting to hear if the noise repeated. Admittedly, I wasn't the sharpest tool in the shed right then, all drugged up and everything, so it should have been no surprise if I…

Thud.

There it was again. It sounded like a dresser drawer closing.

Surely none of the ladies from the church would be doing anything in Becca's room. Mom would freak. She had to ask Aunt Cathy to go in there and get the clothes they needed to bury Becca in, because she couldn't. *But who would be in there now?*

I marched straight over to the door and pushed it open.

The room was semi-dark, the blinds still drawn shut, but I saw a figure on the far side of the bed bent over Becca's nightstand. I recognized the dark blue cargo pants and matching long sleeve pullover.

Taggart McGill.

"What the hell are you doing?" I shouted. *Wasn't he supposed to still be in the hospital?*

Taggart stood up straight, surprise on his face, accentuated by the bruise across his right temple and the deep red coloration of his right eye.

"I… uh…"

"You have no right to be in this house, no right to be in my sister's room."

Taggart shoved his hands in his pockets and looked at the floor.

"She has something that belongs to me."

I had heard about people seeing red when they became angry, and I thought that was a great way to describe an emotion, but I never seriously considered that it was real. Until that moment. It was true. When you get pissed enough, you actually see red. Freakin' red.

"GET OUT… RIGHT NOW!"

Taggart looked up at me and opened his mouth as if to say something. Instead, he shook his head and started walking in my direction. He stopped in front of me, waiting for the way out of the room to become unblocked.

"You should have said something at the funeral," he said softly, his gaze fixed on the floor at his feet.

Speechless, unable to believe he'd actually had the gall to be at the funeral, I moved to the side to let him pass. I watched as he continued down the hall and listened to his footfalls as he disappeared down the stairs.

How could he? I stood there for a moment, struggling with the intensity of my feelings. I clenched my fists so tight the fingernails dug deep into my skin. I had listened to everything my parents said about trusting Becca's judgment and thought maybe I'd been too hard on the guy, that he deserved the benefit of the doubt. But now, with this, how could they expect me to trust him? Not only had he sullied my sister's room, what gave him the right to say that to me?

I looked at where I was standing and realized I hadn't been in my sister's room since she died. I reached over and flipped the light switch. Her bed was unmade, like always. Becca might have been a musical virtuoso, but she was also a highly skilled slob. A week's worth of dirty laundry stood piled just inside her closet door and two of her dresser drawers were open with undergarments spilling out of one and t-shirts the other. I couldn't help but smile when I remembered the constant bickering between her and Mom about her room, and how Dad refused to get drawn into the middle of it. Mom always told her that the way you treated your belongings was an indication of how organized in life you'd be. Becca would argue back that she knew exactly where everything was. The argument drove Mom nuts.

I threw myself on her bed, tears filling my eyes.

"Oh Becca," I said, pulling her pillow into my chest and curling my body around it.

I wasn't sure how long I laid there crying, but it couldn't have been that long. I heard cars pulling up in the street and noises of people starting to arrive downstairs. Knowing I was expected to join the gathering, I forced myself to sit up and rub the tears from my eyes.

I was about to head to my own room when a thought occurred to me. *What was Taggart searching for? What did Becca have of his that would be so important that he had to break into our house for it?* Okay, technically it wasn't breaking and entering because we were hosting an open house for Becca and the front door was wide open. But still, it took some pretty big balls to march in and start pilfering. Besides, the last I'd heard Taggart was still in the hospital. They'd only woken him from that induced coma-thing the day before and he was supposedly still under observation. Did he slip out of the hospital just so he could come here and look for whatever Becca had of his? If that was the case, then whatever he was after must have been something major.

I glanced around the room again, this time wondering where Becca might be hiding something. Our parents were good about giving us privacy, and neither Becca nor I had enough interest in the other one's life to snoop, so the necessity for a hiding place wasn't something that either of us would normally need. I gazed at her dressers, her desk where her laptop sat, the storage boxes, and piles of unused clothes in her closet, but none of them felt right. It was when I spotted her violin that an idea came to me.

Becca had two violins. One she kept at school for band rehearsals, which was cheaper, and another that was her pride and joy. It had some French name and was worth somewhere near $5,000. Mom had given it to her last Christmas, which ticked me off for months because all I got that year was a new iPad. But what I remembered most about it was Becca showing me that the carrying case it came in had a secret compartment in the back. My eyes immediately went to her violin sitting on its stand in the corner by her music stand, but there was no case nearby. I dropped to my knees by the bed, tossed up the disheveled sheets and blanket hanging off the side, then looked underneath.

There sat her carrying case.

Still on my knees, I pulled the case to me, opened the lid, and then worked the secret catch. The bottom half of the case opened to reveal a small lime-green journal.

For a moment, I was confused. Lime-green was Becca's favorite color. The journal was obviously hers, and it most likely contained notes about her music. So why would Taggart be searching for it? Maybe I was wrong about the hiding place?

I opened the journal to the first page and was punched in the gut seeing my sister's handwriting.

The Personal Journal of Rebecca Underwood For my eyes only

I stared…shocked. *Becca kept a journal? When did this happen?* Without thinking, I turned the page and found the date. It was from four years ago. I flipped through the pages until I found the last entry, which was more than three-quarters of the way through the journal. It was dated the day she died.

This journal was the real thing, which was weird because I never saw her writing in it, but then again, why would I? My mind flashed to what Taggart said, and then to a thought that had been festering in the back of my mind over the past week. It began as a passing worry, but slowly took hold and was now trying to take over. How could I stand up and speak for Becca -- when I felt so distant from her? It wasn't really anybody's fault. I think we just never had that type of bond. When she became friends with Taggart… well, that didn't make things any easier. But here in my hands I held proof that my little sister had something to say, quite a lot it turns out, and instead of saying it to me she poured her thoughts into a lifeless journal.

At first, I wasn't sure how I should feel about it. The longer I thought, the more depressed I became.

What I did know was that I missed my sister, terribly, and I would give anything to talk to her again. There I was holding her voice in my hands, or at least the next best thing.

It could be her uncensored opinions, her commentary about life in the Underwood household, her unbridled hopes and dreams, her ups, her downs, her unguarded life. Heck, I'd be thrilled with a collection of dirty limericks if she wrote them. It was as if I'd been handed a present… a way to cushion the transition from a normal life to one without my sister.

I flipped the journal back to the first page and was about to turn to the first entry when my eyes locked on four words.

For my eyes only

The tip of the first page was between my thumb and forefinger. I rubbed it between those two fingers. *Should I be doing this, or am I violating Becca's wishes by reading her most private thoughts?* But she was gone and all I wanted to do was be close to her again, so how could that be wrong? I mean, the secrecy of diaries was meant to protect the author from embarrassment. There's no chance of that now, so why not?

And yet I hadn't turned the page.

For my eyes only

Did death erase the purpose behind those words? When she wrote it, did I think she forgot to add the word EVER or that she understood her death would mean all bets are off? I was trying to think of what my sister would want if she saw me sitting here. I couldn't. I could read it and help myself feel better, or I could put it away and ensure her wishes remained intact.

But what if she'd want me to read it?

I let go of the journal and watched it bounce on the carpet next to the case. I pulled my hair away from my face and looked up at the ceiling. *Why is this so difficult? I should just read the damn thing. So why don't I? Because I'm being a freakin' idiot, that's why. Somehow I think I'm doing right by her, maybe for the first time. This is a test, and maybe I'm determined to pass it this time.* I had always let myself believe that Becca and I had both made choices. Hers was to befriend someone she knew would be social suicide, and mine was to turn a cold shoulder – not as punishment – but as self-preservation. We didn't know it at the time, but we were both being tested. One of us failed.

"Cassie, are you up there?" Dad called.

"Yeah," I yelled back.

"Our guests are starting to arrive," was his not so subtle hint that seclusion was no longer an option.

"Coming."

I picked up the book, shoved it back in the compartment, closed the backing, and slid the case underneath the bed.

Test passed.

Six

Mondays at school were hard enough without having recently lost your sister, but as much as I dreaded going back, I couldn't take being cooped up in our house any longer. The school and my parents agreed I could sit out another week if I wanted, to which I quickly answered, "no thanks." It was time to get on with things, even though I knew the first day back was going to be hard.

I WAY underestimated it.

My usual routine—before Becca's car went kaput and I became her ride to and from school—involved Jason picking me up in the morning. We would ride to school together, arriving about ten minutes before the first bell. At lunch our usual gang would head over to the Burger Barn to chew and chat. After school Jason would bring me home for a change of clothes and a snack, after which I'd head out in my own car to my part-time job at the vet clinic, where both Becca and I worked. I put in three days a week and every other weekend, whereas Becca only worked the weekends due to her recital schedule.

This morning I called Jason as soon as I woke up.

"Hey babe, you're up early," he said.

"Yeah, I kinda wanted to get a jump on things. Listen, I'm going to drive Becca's car to school today."

"Oh, okay. Is everything alright?"

The catch in his voice told me he wasn't sure what to make of this change in our routine. He was probably wondering if this was more erratic behavior because of Becca's death. The truth was, this was my first step towards an eventual breakup, which he would be less likely to understand.

"Everything's fine," I answered. "See you at school, okay?"

I hung up before he could ask any more questions.

The auto shop had repaired and returned Becca's car while I was in hospital… a full week ahead of schedule. I imagined the quick turnaround was a way for the shop to pay respect and offer condolences to my family. Becca's car was a hand-me-down car from my dad, a 2005 white Buick with a bunch of miles and now a fully rebuilt transmission. Dad offered to go through it and de-sensitize it for me, removing all of Becca's personal stuff, but I told him not to bother. I didn't want him to touch a thing, preferring to keep my sister around in a small way. I also didn't want to put him through that.

When I walked into the kitchen both Mom and Dad were there waiting, which was strange because Dad was usually up and long gone by the time Becca and I got ready for school. Both smiled when they saw me.

"There she is. Can I make you an egg, honey?" Mom asked.

"No thanks," I said walking over to the cupboard. "I'm running late. Just gonna grab a breakfast bar."

"Are you sure you want to do this today?" Dad set down his coffee.

"I'm sure I want you to stop asking me that," I replied, then softened it with a smile. "This is what I need, okay?"

Dad walked over and gave me a quick hug. "Then that's that."

I dropped the breakfast bar into my book bag and faced Mom.

Neither of us knew what to say. Instead we hugged, and when we pulled apart there were tears in both our eyes.

"See you this afternoon," I said and was out the door before the tears could turn into a full-blown meltdown.

Becca's scent engulfed me the moment I slid behind the wheel of the Buick. It was intermingled with the usual car shop odors, grease, and cigarettes. She was never one for bold, expensive fragrances, opting for subtler choices available almost anywhere. I imagined her sitting next to me, taking control of the radio and reaching up to touch her lucky strand of horsehair hanging from the rear-view mirror. It was from her first violin bow. Maybe if it had been my car that had broken down and we were driving hers instead, luck would have been on our side that day. I shook away that thought and fired up the engine.

I pulled into the school parking lot five minutes before first bell, parked Becca's car in my usual spot, and sat there. There was no way I was going through those doors until I had to. Dread rose in me like a spiked fever. I tried to imagine myself at the end of the day, on the other side of what was to come, and the feeling of relief waiting for me there. When the dashboard clock told me it was time to go, I took a deep breath hoping it would inflate my courage, finished off the last bite of the breakfast bar, grabbed my book bag, and opened the door.

On the short walk to the entrance, I spotted a familiar figure wearing a black hoody and jeans flying through the parking lot on a bike that was obviously too small for him. Taggart. A car honked at him as he cut in front of its path. *Typical Taggart jerk move.* He ditched the bike carelessly next to the other bikes properly locked in the school-provided stand, adjusted the backpack he was toting and started half-jogging towards the same entrance I was headed to. His eyes met mine. He stopped, slipped his thumbs through the backpack straps, and waited. I proceeded through the door and didn't bother to hold it open for him.

***

New Haven High School was doing its best to educate somewhere near 1,100 kids, and it felt like all of them gave me a hug during Becca's funeral. Those who didn't make it were waiting for me when I arrived at school. I couldn't walk anywhere without being stopped and accepting sympathy being expressed in one way or another. There were guys and girls hugging me that I had never met before. I'm sure they were doing so to make sure they weren't the only ones who hadn't. A few asked me about my arm or any other injuries I sustained in the accident, but thankfully no one dwelled on them for very long. Everyone must have sensed it was too soon to talk about the wreck itself. They couldn't have been more right.

I had to keep a tight lid on the grief clenching my heart as I passed by Becca's locker on the way to my own. Her locker had become a virtual tribute post, the breadth of the offerings taking up a good portion of the hall. There were loads of flowers, sheets of music, pictures, teddy bears, hand-drawn images, a tiny plastic violin, and much more.

I was helpless to stop a memory from popping into my head.

"Becca, Jason and I are going to the movies tonight. Wanna come with?"

"Nah, I need to get this new piece down before next week's recital. What are you going to see?"

"If I let you choose, will you come?"

"I really can't."

"You never have any fun."

"Who says I'm not having fun."

I walked away from her locker with tears brimming in my eyes.

Jason was waiting at my locker for me, smiling. Cards and small flowers adorned the edges of my locker as well, but nowhere near the spectacle of Becca's.

"Hey, babe. How's your arm?"

I lifted my arm and looked at the soft cast. "It's fine. I only wear this as a fashion statement now."

Jason smiled. "Nice look. Did you see your sister's locker?"

"Yeah. Pretty awesome." I turned the knob on my locker. "I just --"

"Just what?"

"I don't want to sound petty." I tried, without success, to swap out a couple of books from my bag with those in my locker. Jason took over when he saw how much I was struggling using my damaged arm.

"I doubt that could happen. What is it?"

"I wish some of these people had paid more attention to her when she was alive." I slammed the metal door shut to punctuate the end of my statement.

At that moment, I spotted Taggart making his way past my locker, his head down. I was more interested in everyone else who was following his progress down the hall, mumbling amongst themselves. No one came up and hugged him or offered a word of encouragement. I knew how much time he and Becca had spent together, as did everyone else. He must have been torn up inside, almost as much as me, but there was no one there for him. For a brief moment, I felt sorry for him.

Then the image of him standing in my sister's room popped into my head, and that feeling was gone. *Why did his latest foster family have to live near our high school? Bane of my existence.*

"Let's be fair, Cassie, your sister ran away from attention. All of this would make her uncomfortable."

"Maybe, maybe not," I replied, quickly moving back up the hall before he could lean in for our customary morning kiss. "Listen, we need to have a talk after I get off work this afternoon."

Jason's smile dimmed. "Okay. About what?"

"I'll see you at lunch," I replied, ignoring his question.

I made my way down the south hallway as fast as the well-wishers would let me, finally arriving at my biology class and taking my seat.

Our biology teacher was a spitting image of Mick Fleetwood from Fleetwood Mac…tall, lanky, with stringy white hair. I only knew this because Mom showed me a picture of Mick after she met Mr. Wilkins during a parent/teacher conference. He was quirky, often walking through the hallways with a cane, though he didn't have a limp. He had an easy-going way of speaking to us that didn't come across like he was trying to be your friend. All of this made him one of my favorite teachers.

"Cassie, I wanted to offer you my deepest condolences again, and tell you that Vice Principal Stevens has asked that you go by his office when you arrive."

I smiled and left right away. Vice Principal Stevens was one of numerous adults from school, Mr. Wilkins included, who had come to Becca's funeral. I got to know him a little while serving as an office volunteer last year, but I wouldn't say we were buddy-buddy. Mr. Stevens was well liked and respected, but not afraid to hand out discipline when warranted. I vaguely remember him offering condolences at the service, so I wasn't sure what he could want with me.

I arrived at the main office and waited at the front desk for Miss Worthy to hang up from a phone call. Miss Worthy was one of several administrative assistants at our school, but she stood out in my mind because she reminded me of a rumpled version of Sandra Bullock - sharp features and good looks, without the glamor, glitz, and the wardrobe. Miss Worthy was someone else I became familiar with during my stint in the office, and I liked her a lot. She always took the time to ask how I was doing and seemed seriously interested. Someone had once told me a rumor about her having an affair with Vice Principal Stevens, but I never believed it.

"Mr. Stevens asked to see me," I said when she put down the phone.

She ushered me straight in – but not before placing her hand on my shoulder and telling me how sorry she was.

When I entered Vice Principal Stevens' office, he was facing away from the door looking at a pair of monitors that displayed feeds from the numerous security cameras installed around the campus. He must have heard me enter because he turned around and smiled.

"Good morning, Cassie. Take a seat. How is it going so far?"

"Oh…you know, I'm looking forward to flying under the radar again. Still a lot of hugs and *I'm sorries*," I said taking in his typical dark shirt and sports jacket. To me, he always looked more like a middle-aged used car salesman than a high school administrator.

"I'm sure. I'm sure. I wanted to call you in and let you know a couple things. First, and this is most important, if things start to overwhelm you at any point this week, don't be afraid to check yourself out. We'll make sure you'll have an ample amount of time to catch up on the school work. Okay?"

"Yes sir, but I doubt that will be necessary. I think I'll be okay."

"That's good to know, but it's always best to have options. Secondly, I take it you saw the tribute in front of your sister's locker?"

I nodded and smiled. I hoped they weren't planning some sort of memorial assembly for Becca. If that happened, I might have to take them up on missing school.

"We left it there until you had a chance to see it, but I wanted to inform you we'll be boxing it all up after school today and sending it home with you. I hope you understand. It's become a bit of a safety hazard."

"Wouldn't want anybody to trip on something and sue the high school…or my parents."

The smile disappeared from the Vice Principal's face.

"I'm sorry," I said. "I'm still a little ragged. I understand the need to take it down."

A more hesitant smile returned. "Good. I also want you to know that my office door is open should you ever find a need to talk… about anything."

"I appreciate that, Mr. Stevens," I replied, leaning forward in my seat. "Is that all?"

"Yes, you can return to class now," he said, rising from his chair. "Have a good day."

The rest of the morning wasn't so bad. Biology was normal, and there was a test scheduled in psychology leaving everyone more concerned about how they would do and no time to worry about me.

It was third period, study hall, when my warning bells started going off.

I walked into the room to find Delta sitting next to Stooch, both facing away from the door and me, talking to Cheryl Petra and Michael Vasser. Cheryl and Michael were a couple, as were Stooch and Delta, together with Jason and me. Stooch was doing all the talking.

"…hasn't been to his locker yet. Don't worry, it'll work. This is gonna be classic."

"I don't know about this, Kev," Delta said.

"What's to know? This is for Cassie."

"What's for me?" I asked, slipping into the seat next to Delta.

All four of them looked as if I had walked in on a group make-out session.

"Oh hi, Cass," Stooch recovered quickly. Jason's best friend was like a generic version of Jason. He was a little shorter, a little pudgier, a little less cute, and a lot less dutiful when it came to the rules. The only thing bigger was his nose, which dominated his face. "Welcome back."

"Thanks, what's for me?"

Stooch smiled and reached over and squeezed Delta's hand. "It's a surprise."

Delta had a tendency towards wearing too much make-up, overusing her mascara until she resembled an anemic raccoon, but no matter how much I pointed this out she refused to change. Clothes, perfume, music, movies, food, whatever I recommended, she habitually went the other way. But today she was dressed conservatively in tan slacks and a light blue sweater, quite a departure for her. Sometimes I wondered if she was a Lady Gaga wannabe, possessing an overpowering desire to be different, without the amazing singing voice. Delta usually managed to stand out in a crowd, but unfortunately, I could never convince her that standing out wasn't always the same as being different. None of that mattered, though. To me she was always just plain Delta... until she started going out with Stooch.

Neither Delta nor Cheryl would look me in the eye, and Michael, who I'd never had a high opinion of after he hung a confederate flag from the back of his pickup truck, was smirking. I didn't mind the flag so much, but it was the fact that it didn't appear until after we had a huge debate about its significance in our history class.

"I'm not a big fan of surprises Kevin. So why don't you just tell me what it is."

"No can do."

I looked at Delta instead. "Delta, please tell me what these guys are up to. You know they're not big on restraint."

Delta looked at Cheryl, who maintained a blank look, then to Stooch.

"Kev, I don't think she's going to like it," Delta said softly. "It's too soon."

Stooch's smile had turned into an empty shell. "She'll thank me later."

"Does Jason know about whatever it is you're talking about?" I asked.

Stooch made a gesture with his fingers like he was turning a key in a lock on his lips and then threw the key over his shoulder.

This was getting me nowhere. Time to take a different approach.

"Michael, tell me what's going on or I'll tell Cheryl what your nickname was in third grade."

The smirk on Michael's face disappeared. Cheryl looked at Michael and tilted her head. Cheryl had only moved to New Haven a couple years ago and there was still plenty of dirt about Michael she wasn't aware of yet.

"You wouldn't," Michael said, the color draining from his already pale face.

"It has something to do with a certain body part and—"

"Stooch put something in Taggart's locker!" Michael blurted out.

I got up from my seat, walked over to Stooch, and looked down on him. "What did you do?"

The smirk that used to inhabit Michael's face now made an appearance on Stooch's.

"What do you care?"

I stood there staring down at Stooch, asking myself the same question. This was Taggart McGill, the so-called bane of my existence. The person, who, despite what my parents said, was at least partially responsible for my sister's death. The boy who broke into my house to steal something from her. Why would I ever care what happened to him?

"Is there a problem, Miss Underwood?" asked Mrs. Louis. It was the first time she had looked up from the stack of papers she was grading. Before I knew why I was doing it, I strolled up to the front of the class.

"Mrs. Louis, I need to be excused for a minute."

"The period just started, honey. You should have gone to the bathroom between classes."

Obviously our vice-principals message of support for me hadn't been passed down to the masses yet.

"I don't need to go to the bathroom." I quickly debated with myself over telling Mrs. Louis about the prank but decided against it. I wasn't ready to become a rat yet. "I need to get something out of my car before my next class."

"I'm sorry, but you'll have to wait until the end of the period."

"Tell me you're not going to warn that prick," Stooch said loudly from the back of the class.

"Language, Mr. Roberts," Mrs. Louis warned.

"Shut up, Kevin," I yelled back. "Please, Mrs. Louis. It's really important."

Mrs. Louis looked up from her papers and regarded me with skepticism. "I'll let you go ten minutes early, best I can do."

Frustrated and unwilling to return to my seat, I walked back and forth along the side of the wall like a caged feral cat we would sometimes see down at the vet clinic. Pacing was my natural coping mechanism for impatience, or when I was extremely nervous. Mrs. Louis looked up from her papers at me every few minutes. I expected her to ask me to return to my seat, but she never did. I kept up my restless activity until the clock read 11:45... fifteen minutes until the end of the period. That was when Mrs. Louis patience caved. "Okay, Miss Underwood, you may go."

I didn't bother with my books. Instead, I bolted out the door and down the hall to the right. I didn't know where Taggart's locker was located, never really cared, so I needed to get that information first. I made it to the office in just a couple of minutes, opened the door and waited behind a woman talking to Miss Worthy. I glanced at the clock... 11:49... then realized that my sore foot wasn't very happy with all the running. It was throbbing and on fire, so I sat down in a chair directly inside the door to take the weight off the foot.

When the clock hit 11:58 and the same parent was still discussing the attendance policy with Miss Worthy, I couldn't take it anymore. I rose from the chair and stepped up to the front desk alongside the woman.

"I'm really sorry to interrupt, but this is a borderline emergency, Miss Worthy."

When Miss Worthy recognized me, her demeanor changed. She went from being irritated for the interruption, to actual concern. "What is it, honey?"

"I need to know where Taggart McGill's locker is located."

Miss Worthy frowned and shifted sideways until she was standing in front of me. "You know we can't give out that information, Cassie."

"Like I said, it's kind of an emergency."

"And why is that?"

"Let's just say somebody is planning to pull a prank on him, and I'm trying to prevent it."

Miss Worthy stared at me for a moment, then reached down to a lower shelf out of my sight and returned a clear plastic binder. As she started flipping through the pages I glanced at the clock again.

11:59

"His locker is T52. That's right across from the chemistry lab."

"Thank you," I exclaimed as I ran out of the door.

I reached T52 just as the end of period bell went off. I was fairly certain Taggart had the same lunch as I did, which meant he would probably be coming by his locker before heading to the cafeteria. I parked myself in front of his locker and waited.

I didn't have to wait long. Taggart came up the hall from the left, his head down as usual. When he looked up in front of his locker and saw me, he froze.

"What do you want?" he asked. His right eye, which had been extremely red a couple days ago, had receded to looking slightly irritated through the hair hanging down in his face.

"I'm pretty sure there's something in your locker. Somebody is trying to pull a prank on you."

"They are, are they?" Taggart asked.

"Yes."

"How did they get inside my locker?"

"I don't know," I said. Now I was wondering if there was anything inside the locker. Maybe Stooch was just pulling everyone's legs.

"What's inside?"

"I'm not sure."

"You don't know much, do you? So why are you here?"

I paused before I answered, unsure what to say. I decided to tell the truth. "I don't know that either."

"You don't know why you're here?" Taggart repeated.

"I guess… I don't want it to happen."

"Why?"

"I just don't, okay."

"That's not much of a reason."

The two of us stood there, looking into one another's eyes. He was waiting for an answer, so I said the first thing that popped into my mind.

"Becca wouldn't want this."

Taggart studied me carefully, then he did something I couldn't ever recall seeing before. He grinned.

"Yes, she would," he said and reached out with both his hands, moved me out from in front of his locker, then stepped up and spun in his combination.

When the last number locked in, Taggart pulled up the handle and looked at me.

"Let's see what they got," he said and pulled open the locker.

The blasting noise that emanated from inside the locker was deafening, but it wasn't the volume that made me gasp, my heart stop, and my eyes fill up with tears. Both my hands flew to my mouth to stave off the scream I knew was coming, watching as Taggart stumbled backward – white as a sheet.

He quickly leaped forward, grabbed what looked like an MP3 player taped to the inside of the locker door, ripped it off and threw it to the ground – smashing it to pieces.

The sound of the blaring train whistle still echoed in the hallway.

Seven

It didn't take me long to find Stooch, peering around a corner at the end of the crowded hall. I knew he would be nearby, watching the results of his handiwork. The other kids in the hallway—still in shock and frozen in place—parted like the red sea as I made my way towards him. As I got closer, the smile on Stooch's lips faded, no doubt from seeing the red in my eyes and the rage on my face.

Stooch was a starting defensive back on New Haven's football team, four inches taller and at least fifty pounds heavier than me, but I plowed into him with no regard to any of that. I grabbed the neckline of his teal polo shirt, to which he responded by raising his hands over his head in a pseudo-surrender gesture. That didn't stop me. I pushed him back with all my might until he collided loudly with lockers on the far side of the hall. Out of the corner of my eye, I could see Michael, Cheryl, and Delta, all of them shocked by my actions.

"What were you thinking!" I screamed up at Stooch, my voice cracking. "In what world would anyone think that would be funny?"

Stooch was keeping his hands in the air even though I had his shirt bunched up under his chin. His expression had changed to something between fake curiosity and mock concern.

"Chill, Cassie," he said, his eyes scanning the crowd gathering around us. "I didn't have anything to do with that, and besides, it probably wasn't meant for you."

I was vaguely aware that my broken arm was throbbing, but I could care less. I was fuming, not only from the blatant cruelty behind the stunt, or the fact that somebody I frequently hung out with did it, but mostly because the guys and girls gathering around us had to know Stooch was lying. But nobody would turn him in for it… including me.

What a sick-ass joke. Why would he do that? That was the sort of stunt I would expect from Taggart---oh, my, God! This is exactly the type of thing I'd have automatically blamed Taggart for. Could the jerk be innocent of other things too? Had I been wrong the whole damn time?

My mini-revelation sucked the wind out of my sails and caused me to relax my grip.

I let go of Stooch's shirt and stepped back, looking at him but not seeing him. How many other times had I laid other pranks, hoaxes, harsh tricks, at Taggart's feet that were actually someone else's doing? But if that were true, why didn't Becca stand up for him when I would rail about him? Instead, Becca never said anything. If he was being unjustly accused, why would she remain silent?

"What's going on?"

I turned my head to see Jason standing next to me, a confused look on his face. Behind him the hallway was jammed with kids watching what I was doing, with more than a few mouths hanging open. I looked back at Stooch and pointed a finger at his head.

"You're a dick," I said, then headed off to reclaim the book bag I'd left in study hall. As I passed Delta, I thought I noticed tears in her eyes. Honestly, I couldn't have cared less.

All I wanted to do was get away from the circus I'd helped create.

Jason caught up to me as I entered Mrs. Louis empty classroom.

"Cassie, what was all that about?"

Ignoring him, I found my bag where I'd left it, reached inside to grab the bottle of prescription pills I happened to not inform the office about, then dry-swallowed one. The pain in my arm had progressed from throbbing ache to serious discomfort.

"Did you know?" I asked as I slung my bag over my shoulder and walked past him towards the door.

"Know what?" he responded, taking me by my upper arm. "You won't even tell me what happened."

I might have had concerns about Jason's choice of friends, now more than ever, but he had never lied to me and I trusted the innocence in his eyes.

"Your best friend is sick, seriously demented. You should think about that."

"What did he do?"

I considered telling him about the mp3 player but decided against it. "I don't want to talk about it right now. I just want to be alone."

"You're not coming to the barn for lunch?"

"No. Alone means alone. I'll see you tonight after work."

I walked out of the room, ignoring Jason's pleas to talk, and ran straight into Delta standing right outside the door. Her arms clutched her notebook to her chest in a death hold, and lines of recently dried tears streaked her face like war paint.

"I swear Cassie, I had no idea what Stooch recorded—" she started, tears filling her eyes again.

At that moment I wanted nothing more than to find an empty room, hug Delta until my shoulders hurt, and weep with her until my tear ducts ran dry. Instead I said, "Not now,

Delta," and walked away as quickly as I could toward the cafeteria.

In the lunchroom, I bypassed the dual serving lines, ignored the calls of friends and stares of classmates, and then exited the side doors that led to an outdoor patio. Immediately outside was a circular seating bench, off to the left were a couple picnic tables tucked underneath an overhang on the far wall. At the farthest table sat Taggart, alone, where he and Becca had eaten lunch together for three years.

I slipped into the seat across from Taggart, who had a half-eaten sandwich in one hand and a book in the other. He put down the sandwich and wiped his mouth with the sleeve of his hoody.

We stared at each other for a couple moments.

"What are you reading?" I asked.

Taggart looked around the courtyard before responding.

"Aren't you afraid you'll start to glow?" he asked.

"What do you mean?"

"I mean, I'm radioactive, aren't I? The longer you sit here talking to me the more likely you'll get contaminated," he said with a straight face. But it was more than a deadpan stare. It was a poker face worthy of Las Vegas.

"Like Becca did, you mean."

His eyes turned hard and he closed his book. "Your sister was immune."

Our eyes remained locked, but inside I was jumping out of my skin.

"You're wrong, you know," I said.

I felt like I was five years old again on the playground, holding a staring contest. Damned if I would blink first. Taggart's blank expression told me I was probably going to lose this one.

"You should have been the one speaking at Becca's funeral, not me," I said.

Taggart blinked. Bingo!

Taggart's gaze dropped. He shifted uncomfortably in his seat. I thought about asking him if he was looking for Becca's journal in her room, and why, but decided against it. Better to take things slow.

"I asked you a question before," I pressed.

Taggart glanced down at the closed book. "Theories of Astrophysics."

"We don't have an astrophysics class. You're reading that for pleasure?"

"It interests me."

Again, we probed each other with our stares.

"Didn't my sister ever tell you that the way you dress is a bit clichéd? I mean, look at you. The isolated loner, the social outcast, in a dark hoodie? Really?"

I wasn't sure what changed, maybe something in his posture, but he seemed to soften.

"It might be cliché, but it's practical."

"How so?"

Taggart pulled a pair of white earbuds from inside the sweatshirt and plugged them into his ears, then pulled up his hood, which completely covered his face, blocking me—and everything else—out.

I leaned over the edge of the table, pulled back his hood and yanked out his buds. He didn't resist.

"Point taken."

"Obviously not."

I had to grin at that, but I wasn't deterred. "When we were in junior high, somebody slipped a tampon in the front flap of my best friend's purse. When she opened it, the tampon fell on the floor for everybody to see. She was at lunch when it happened with a lot of people around. She was so embarrassed her mom had to check her out of school early. She still flushes when she remembers it."

"So?"

"So… they found tampons in your jacket that same day."

"So?"

"So… did you do that to her?"

"You told everyone that I did."

I paused for a moment before answering. "Because they found tampons on you."

Taggart opened his book again and began reading.

I watched a few of our classmates come and go from the cafeteria door, all of them making sure to glance in our direction. I was probably upsetting the social network of the school by sitting here with Taggart, the same network I unconsciously adhered to via my own choices, but I didn't care. I needed answers.

I reached over and closed the book, but Taggart kept his eyes down.

"What did you mean when you said Becca would be okay with that prank?"

Taggart now appeared uncomfortable, shifting in his seat and fidgeting. He moved the book around on the table.

"Please, I need to know. You seemed to know her better than anybody, so why would you say that?"

"She wouldn't have wanted that prank. Not that one," he said, still refusing to look up.

"I get that… but what did you mean?"

When he finally looked up, it was as if he was in pain. His shoulders hunched, his breathing was heavier, and he was wringing his hands together. I was about to ask what was wrong when all of the hardness abruptly disappeared from his face and he looked normal again.

"Becca believed that pranks, tricks, insults, the berating of the weak, all of that only had power if the ones being targeted, the victims, gave into them. What you think of yourself is all that really matters. Getting angry at the ones who belittle others to make themselves feel more powerful serves no purpose and only fuels their inner-demons. She understood embracing a prank takes away its negative influence."

Listening to Taggart say those words, I could hear the sentiment coming out of Becca's mouth, but not in such an articulate way.

"Excuse me."

I was so focused on Taggart, I'd not seen the two other boys walk up. The smaller of the two, the one wearing over-the-ear headphones and a faded t-shirt proclaiming him a Browncoat, stood slightly behind the other boy, who I recognized immediately.

Taggart must have recognized the taller boy as well, for he stiffened in his seat.

The taller boy was somewhere near five foot ten inches tall, thin with bony shoulders, unusually bushy eyebrows, and a pointy chin. He wore a pair of dark glasses, low on his nose, which allowed him to look over the top.

And he was Black.

"I'm Chewy…Chewy Ledbetter."

The son of the man who caused the accident that killed my sister, stood there in front of us rocking back and forth from one foot to the other, unable to be still. Both Taggart and I sat there, not sure what we were supposed to say.

"I'm sorry I missed Becca's funeral, but my mom thought it would be a bad idea for me to go… under the circumstances."

"That's okay," I said weakly. Taggart opened his backpack and slid his book inside. Apparently, his interest in the conversation was gone.

"Have the reporters been bothering you much?" Chewy asked.

"They've pretty much left us alone for the funeral and since."

"I wish that were true for us. My mom can't go anywhere without at least one or two following her." His constant swaying back and forth was starting to get on my nerves.

In a way, I felt a kinship with Chewy. I mean we both lost someone we loved dearly. The only difference was that the person he lost was responsible for taking away the person I lost. None of that was his fault, though. "How is your mom doing?" I asked.

"Not good. You probably didn't know this, but she was diagnosed with breast cancer a couple of months ago."

"Oh no."

"Yeah. Her first chemotherapy session was supposed to be this week, but all that is on hold now, I guess."

I didn't know what to say to that, so I said nothing.

"I really liked Becca," Chewy said, doing me a big favor by changing the subject. "She totally rocked the violin."

I remembered that Chewy and Becca were in orchestra together, although I couldn't remember what instrument he played. All I could do was nod my head.

"This is Tunes," Chewy said, hitching a thumb over his left shoulder. "He's in band too."

"Hey," I said to Tunes, who nodded his head and smiled in return.

"I was wondering if I could ask you a favor," Chewy said.

"What is it?" I asked.

"Not you," Chewy responded, "Taggart."

I looked at Taggart, who stopped what he was doing and raised his eyebrows.

"I hear you've spent so much time at the police station that you know everyone there by their first names."

Taggart's eyes darkened.

"I was wondering if you might arrange it so I can talk to one of the detectives."

When Taggart didn't respond, my curiosity got the better of me. "Why would you want to do that?"

Chewy stopped rocking and put his hands on the table. "So I can talk to them about the accident," the boy answered. "I need to make them understand my father was murdered."

Eight

I wasn't sure which would have shocked me more, seeing purple butterflies fly out of Chewy's mouth or hearing the words he had just uttered.

"Did you say murder?" I asked, disbelief dripping off every word.

"Yes," Chewy said. His pinched face told me he was dead serious.

"Maybe you should sit down." I slid across the bench to make room for him.

Chewy slipped into the spot, not bothering to remove his backpack. Amazingly, once he was seated his swaying started up again, although much subtler. He acted as if he was on board a boat on the water, moving with the ebb and flow of the tide. His friend, Tunes, hadn't moved, so I slid over more.

"There's room for both of you."

"He doesn't sit," Chewy said nonchalantly.

"What do you mean he doesn't sit? Ever?" I asked.

"Only when he has to in class, but otherwise, no."

I took a closer look at Tunes. He was a couple inches shorter than Chewy, and younger, probably a freshman, with a pinch of Hispanic somewhere in his bloodline. He wore his straight black hair cut in a bowl shape, and his left eyebrow was split in two by a slice from what looked like an old scar.

"Does he speak?" I continued.

"He prefers not to."

I nodded my head, amused. I pointed at his earphones. "Can he hear us?"

"You'd have to ask him, but he probably won't answer you. Tunes is really laid back. It surprises me his bowels even move."

I smiled and looked over at Taggart who was zipping up his backpack and making ready to leave.

"Aren't you even going to listen to what he has to say?" I asked, my blood heating up.

"Not interested," he said, refusing to look at any of us.

"Please, you're my last hope. I can't get anyone else to listen to me," Chewy said.

Taggart stepped away from the bench and slung his backpack over his shoulder, ignoring Chewy's plea.

I was really irritated at this point and my broken arm was throbbing more than ever. This was exactly why I hated the guy in the first place, and so typical of him. So, what was I doing there? Why had I bothered to make an effort to understand the guy my sister was so damned protective of? Okay, maybe it was because I had a deep need to better understand who my sister was, but surely there was a better way. Anyway, watching him crap on someone who was obviously crying out for help wasn't me.

I couldn't help myself. "Taggart!" I yelled.

To my surprise that stopped him. He looked at me and what I saw in his eyes wasn't what I expected. It wasn't anger, or frustration, but something else completely. It was confusion. That didn't last for long before it changed into irritation as he dropped his backpack like it was a bag of trash and retook his seat.

When Taggart didn't say anything right away, staring at the folded hands in front of him, I realized I would have to moderate the conversation.

"Okay, Chewy, why do you think your father was murdered and how do you think Taggart can help?"

"The police are saying that my dad must have had a heart attack or something on the way home and that's why his car plowed into the back of yours."

"That is what I heard as well," I said.

"But my dad was in EXCELLENT health. I mean he ran two or three miles a day, he watched what he ate, he paid attention to that stuff. He and Mom had their annual checkup last month. Mom didn't do so good, but Dad got a clean bill of health. No issues. Period."

"That doesn't mean that something else didn't cause him to lose control."

"My dad wasn't a drinker… I mean sure he'd have the occasional beer at a party or something… but he wasn't an alchy or a druggie. He didn't even like taking aspirin when he'd get a headache. Anyway, they didn't find any alcohol or drugs in his system."

"Okay, but still." I looked at Taggart hoping to get some kind of support, but he was more interested in the dirt under his nails than what we were saying.

"But still what?"

I wasn't sure where to go from there. Chewy obviously wasn't ready to face the reality of his father's death… or more accurately, the unfairness of it. Still, I didn't want to be the one who crushed him with the truth.

"It could have been an undiagnosed heart condition or something like that. People drop dead for no reason all the time."

"My dad ran a marathon last year, but before he started training for it he had a complete physical that looked for things like that because he'd heard the same thing. His doctor told him his heart was as strong as a horse. I'm not buying the 'just cause' excuse."

"Did they perform an autopsy?"

Chewy's rocking was becoming noticeable again.

"Yes, but my mom doesn't think I need to see the results. Thinks it's unnatural for a kid to read an autopsy report. The next of kin can request a copy, but you have to be eighteen first. And I can't get anyone at the police to talk to me. That's why I need Taggart."

"Okay, but Chewy, why would anyone want to kill your father? Just because you can't explain why he died, doesn't mean there was, what do they call it? Foul play."

For the first time, the poor guy looked unsure of himself. Maybe this was the way to open his eyes.

"Did he have a lot of outstanding debts, a gambling problem, or some other part of his life that you think he might have kept secret from you and your mom?"

Chewy dropped his head slightly and shook it. His body was still again. "No, my dad was as boring as they come. Wasn't he, Tunes?"

Tunes was still standing by the table, staring down at his feet and apparently lost in his musical retreat. Still, he nodded his reply to Chewy's question.

"His hobby was building model airplanes in his spare time," Chewy added.

"Chewy, this is New Haven. Do you remember the last time we had a murder here? I can't think of one."

"Five years ago. A woman ran over her husband with her SUV because he was sleeping with their nanny. I looked it up." He looked more dejected than ever.

"There you go. No one would want to murder the owner of a sporting goods store in New Haven."

Taggart's head snapped up.

"Your father owned a sporting goods store?" Taggart asked.

Chewy and I both looked at Taggart, surprised that he was now part of the conversation, then Chewy nodded his head.

"Which one?" Taggart asked, more insistent now.

"Champion Sports."

Taggart took that in and stared off into space.

"Why would that even matter?" Chewy asked.

Taggart rose quickly and grabbed his backpack. "I'll help you, but I can't do it today. Meet me after school tomorrow. Can you drive?"

"I don't have my license yet," Chewy replied.

"I can drive," I volunteered, although I wasn't sure why.

"Don't be late," he said and then rushed off into the cafeteria.

***

The rest of the day was mostly more of the same, a continuous line of people offering condolences. After I left Chewy and Tunes, I skipped the rest of lunch and hung out in an isolated corner of the library. I managed to avoid Jason, which wasn't easy since we'd been attached at the hip for years. Delta made a couple more attempts to approach me, but each time I shut her down and walked away. I wasn't ready to go there yet.

After my last period, I half-ran to Becca's car, my nerves shattered. Once inside I slumped over the wheel and wept silently, the kind with no tears. How could the school, someplace where I rarely ran into Becca, bring back so many memories of her? Was this what it was going to be like? Oh god, I hoped not. I tried to tell myself things were going to get better, but I wasn't very convincing. I started the car and pulled out of the parking lot.

My spirits rose somewhat as I drove towards the Honey Rose Animal Hospital, where my part-time job awaited me. I had brought along a change of clothes so I could head straight there from school and bypass going home. That allowed me to delay the painful task of convincing Mom my day at school was *fine*.

I pulled into the side lot for employees, parked my car and fortified myself for another round of pity, sympathy, comforting thoughts and general commiserations. I looked at the soft cast on my arm and wished there was a way to make the constant reminder of the accident disappear, if only for a little while. I really did appreciate the sentiment, but after a while it started sucking away my energy and made me feel numb. I was long past that stage.

The Honey Rose Animal Clinic had only been open four or five years and I'd worked there practically since it opened. Becca joined as soon as she became old enough. The brand-new facility wasn't big, but it was just minutes from our house, the flexible work hours made it perfect for after school and weekend work, and the money was decent.

And there were also the animals.

Becca and I both loved working with all of the creatures the clinic saw, and early on I'd decided that veterinary medicine would be my major when I went away to college. Becca mostly handled the receptionist and scheduling duties, occasionally helped out by walking the dogs, but I learned everything I could. Dr. Weathers, the man who ran the clinic, was the same age as my dad and he took a liking to me right away. It wasn't long before I was helping with procedures normally requiring certification - blood draws, dental cleanings, placing IV catheters, anesthesia monitoring, and communicating directly with clients.

Becca had her passion, music. Mine was animals.

I walked through the front door to find the reception area surprisingly empty. Most days when I arrived, there was at least one client there picking up or dropping off. Mary, one of Dr. Weathers two full-time employees, was behind the counter. When she spotted me, she jumped up and came over to embrace me. The plumpness of her body was comforting.

"We weren't expecting you in here today, doll. How are you doing?"

"I'm fine," I answered. "I couldn't sit at home any longer, so I thought I'd come in."

Mary held me by the shoulders at arm's length. "You didn't have to do that, but you won't hear me complaining. I heard about the prank someone pulled on that boy at your school, with the train whistle, which is so deplorable."

"How did you hear about that?"

"Tara came in earlier to pick up her check. She told me."

Tara, a junior at my school, worked the days I didn't. "Yeah, we have some real jerks at our school."

"They're all over, doll. It's been slow out here, but Dr. Weathers could probably use a hand. Brutus is back."

Brutus was a seventy-five-pound Alaskan malamute with a sweet disposition and a habit of swallowing things he wasn't supposed to. He was only fourteen months old but had already become a regular.

As I started walking toward the back I pointed to the hamburger at Mary's desk.

"What have I told you about that?" I asked with a half-smile.

"I didn't get fries this time," she responded quickly.

I pushed my way through the swinging door, and as I did Dr. Weathers was leading Brutus through the door to the hotel, where we housed all the animals. Brutus's tail, which was already active, went into hyper-drive when he saw me.

"What are you doing here?" Dr. Weathers asked as he continued leading Brutus into the x-ray room. Underneath his white lab coat he wore his usual shirt and tie, which I had always found strange given who his patients were, and he had taken his glasses off and slipped them into his outside pocket.

"Did you break your glasses again?" I asked.

"No, just a precaution. You know how Brutus can be rambunctious sometimes. You didn't answer my question."

I thought about listing out all the reasons, but decided to go with the most direct… the most honest.

"I needed to be here."

For the next couple of hours I lost myself in work, doing my best to forget about my dead sister and the crazy notion of a suspected murder in New Haven.

Nine

All I could think of driving home was Chewy and, more specifically, Taggart's sudden change of attitude and willingness to help. That, more than anything, is what prompted me to offer to drive them.

Why was Taggart so eager to help? Did he want to be the one to disprove Chewy's ridiculous theory and therefore crush the person who took away his one and only friend? Was he that cruel? Surely he didn't believe any of what Chewy was spouting? For my part I was still trying to figure out the relationship my sister had with Taggart, and this seemed to be a convenient excuse to further that? Whatever it was, I was committed now.

First, I had to do something I had been dreading for a while. I had to break up with my boyfriend. As hard as the day had already been, I briefly considered putting it off—again—but today was always going to be a mess, so it was actually the perfect time.

I told Jason we needed to talk after work and sure enough, when I pulled into my driveway, there he was, his truck parked by the curb with him leaning against the hood.

He still wore the clothes from school, his normal boot-cut jeans, plaid shirt with rolled sleeves, and cowboy boots that were overdue for wherever old boots go to die. His short brown hair was still wet, like usual, from the shower he had taken following practice. He smiled when I climbed out of Becca's car, one of those smiles that made me question what I was about to do, but I swallowed hard and forced myself to return a smile I knew was a watered-down version of the one he was used to.

He pushed off his truck and walked toward me, but I motioned for him to stop.

"Let's sit in your truck," I said.

I could tell right then by the way Jason looked at me, the confused frown and pinched lips, that he was aware something was up, and it was something serious. We rarely sat in his truck because he knew how I felt about it. When I could talk him into it, we would usually drive my car. I didn't have anything against trucks, but it was what he had done to it and what it represented that bothered me. I would say a large percentage of the guys our age owned trucks. It was just something that was expected in New Haven, I guess. But Jason, and a few others who could afford it, took it to an extreme. Those fog lamps, the lifts, everything about that damn truck screamed "redneck." Jason wasn't. It was another of his little inconsistencies that drove me nuts.

He opened the door for me, then after I was in, he jogged around and clambered behind the steering wheel.

"This isn't going to be good, is it?" he said after a few seconds of silence.

I wanted to say it depended on your perspective, but instead I said, "Probably not."

"Does this have anything to do with what happened this morning and Stooch's bonehead stunt? You know he didn't mean anything by it."

"This doesn't have anything to do with that, well… in a way I guess it kind of does. I've wanted to have this conversation for a while now and just haven't found the right time."

"I know you've been different ever since… you know… the accident, but your mom said it would pass."

"You've talked to my mom?"

"I was worried about you, Cass."

That was probably true, but I wondered if it was just as likely he was worried about losing his arm candy during football season. I quickly scolded myself. Jason had never treated me that way and I didn't need to twist the circumstances to justify my actions now.

"This has been coming since long before the accident, Jason." I tried to swallow, but my mouth had gone dry. The back of my neck felt like it was on fire. "I've never had to do this before and I don't know any other way, so I'm just going to just say it. I want to break up."

Jason blinked rapidly, multiple times in succession.

"Why? What did I do?"

"It's not anything you did."

Jason pulled the collar down on his shirt. It was something I noticed he did a lot when he was playing football, particularly when he was nervous or excited.

"Then I don't understand, why?" he asked.

"I don't think we're a good fit anymore."

"A good fit? What does that even mean?"

Tears began to form, but I took a deep breath and fought hard to keep my emotions in check. I swore to myself I wouldn't let this get overly dramatic, and blubbering like a six-year old would be the exact opposite of how I wanted this to go.

"I like you a lot, Jason. More than you might think, especially now, but over the last year or so I've realized we've grown apart and it's time to do something about it."

Jason just stared back at me, the muscles on the left side of his face rippled as he gritted his teeth. When he spoke again it was in a lower tone.

"We seemed to fit just fine at the beach a couple weeks ago when you had your legs wrapped around me."

I rocked backward, surprised by his response. My mouth was dry before, but now it felt as if someone had poured a bucket of hot sand in it. I knew it would be up to me to keep things under control.

"Please don't do that, Jason."

"Do what?"

"Be hurtful. I'm being open and honest with you, like an adult, and you come back at me with that hateful remark," I said, ignoring the fact that I'd overheard my parents say things to each other in the heat of an argument that were equally hurtful. Acting like an adult didn't carry the weight it used to.

"Fine, then tell me, honestly, why we don't work anymore?"

I'd heard a quote once from one of my dad's favorite authors, George R.R. Martin. He said, *Most men would rather deny a hard truth than face it.* I should have put more stock in that before saying what I did.

"Jason, I care for you…but I don't respect you."

My words hung in the air like toxic fumes. I worried that Jason would blow-out a molar given how furiously his jaw was flexing.

"How so?"

"For one, the people you hang around with. Kevin being the prime example."

"They are your friends too, Cass."

What he said was true. Of the dozen or so whom we regularly hung out with, two or three were close friends, Delta being one of them. Another five or six I was friendly with but realized I'd probably never see again after graduation. It was the rest of the group that worried me. Skipping class, smoking, and casual sex was one thing, but trashing everything from mailboxes to city landmarks, drinking until you passed out, drugs, and full-on sex parties was beyond what I was comfortable with. All of that and the way Jason allowed himself to be talked into participating (after he dropped me off, of course) was what really worried me.

"Some of them are… yes… but most of them I wouldn't be around if it weren't for you. And I wonder why you put up with them. Jason, I know you, we've been together for a long time, and I know deep down that you're not like them."

"You think I'm better than them?"

"Not better… just different. Take what Stooch did today. That prank was sick, hurtful, and downright wrong, but a second ago you were trying to defend him. And it wasn't just this prank. I've never liked Stooch. He has a mean-streak below the surface that worries me. What worries me more is that you don't see it, or you do and you choose to ignore it, with Stooch and Michael, and others."

"So that's it then, you suddenly don't like my friends."

"No, that's not all."

"Oh, great. What else then?"

"You seem to be coasting through life. You are obviously smart, but you don't apply yourself."

"Now you sound like my mother."

"I listen to mine; maybe you should try listening to yours. God knows I've tried to get you to take your grades serious, but nothing seems to work. I know your family has money and your future is probably already laid out for you, but that shouldn't be an excuse to blow school off. The only thing you seem to really care about is sports."

"And you. I care about you."

I sighed deeply. I wanted to reach out and put my hand on his arm, but then he'd see how bad it was shaking.

"I know you care for me, and believe it or not I care for you as well, but in the long run I don't see a future for us."

Jason shifted in his seat.

"Then why now? Why couldn't you wait until school was over? You're probably going to some west coast college, and I'll still be somewhere close to New Haven. We could have at least enjoyed our senior year together. Why mess up things now? You can't tell me this doesn't have something to do with what happened to Becca."

"I know it may seem that way, but it doesn't. I just don't care for some of the people you've been hanging out with lately, and I don't like how you act when you're around them."

"Cass, it's not like I chose this. It wasn't like picking teams on the playground, 'you go here and you go there'. It's just friends of friends and you fall into a pattern. Sure, I'm not proud of a few things I've been part of, and yes, Stooch messed up today, but we've been friends since kindergarten. Shit, I know this is only high school and everything gets real once we graduate, so is it so bad that we have a little fun now?"

Like I'd said, Jason was no dummy.

"I think circumstances shouldn't determine who you are. Shouldn't it be the other way around… who you are will define your circumstances?"

"Now you sound like my mom after she watched some stupid self-improvement video."

I could tell this wasn't getting us anywhere. It would be better to just separate and let Jason digest this.

"You know," Jason said, not looking at me but staring at his steering wheel. "Somebody saw you talking to Taggart McGill during lunch."

God, it was true. People really will grasp at anything to avoid the truth sometimes.

"Yeah, and Chewy Ledbetter was there as well. Think maybe he'll be my next boyfriend?"

Jason didn't respond, his eyes remaining locked on the wheel.

"I'm going inside now." I opened the truck door. "I'm sorry things worked out this way, but I really do hope we can still be friends, Jason."

"Are you sure I'm the right element to be friends with?"

I paused before I exited. "What is that supposed to mean?"

"Nothing," he replied, suddenly interested in the stitching of the seat between us.

"No… really… I want to know what you mean."

He looked back up at me, his jaw set. "Just seems to me that you've suddenly decided you're too good for us local yokels. You may still be here in New Haven, but your mind is already away at college. I almost wish this was because of Becca, because at least then I wouldn't feel like I'd just been shitted on."

My lower lip began to quiver, so I sucked it in, unwilling to give Jason the satisfaction of knowing he had landed another blow. Yes, I was hurt, but angry as well. Angry that I wasn't strong enough to ignore the bait.

"Goodbye, Jason."

I climbed down out of the truck and made a beeline for the front door. As I was closing the door behind me, I heard Jason's truck fire up and roar off.

"Honey, is everything alright?"

I opened my eyes to see my mother standing in the hallway from the kitchen, a dishrag in her hands and a frown on her face.

"I'm fine," I said. "It was a really long day."

I headed up the stairs without waiting for a reply. I did want to talk to her, eventually, but my mom wasn't the person I needed right now. I was afraid she would turn into Jason's ally and take his side, which was something I couldn't handle.

I ran up to my room and when I burst through the door, someone was waiting there for me. Delta was sitting on my bed, but she stood up as soon as I entered.

"Your mom said I could wait here," she said.

I dropped everything and moved towards her. The tears were flowing before we embraced.

Ten

Delta crossed her legs. "I sure didn't see that coming,"

The two of us sat on my bed, as we had done a bazillion times in the past, totally ignoring the desk chair and window seat nearby.

"That's one of the reasons I tried to get you to reconsider going with Stooch. I knew I would eventually break up with Jason, but I wasn't ready yet so I kept it to myself. But the primary reason I had a problem with it was always—"

"—Stooch. I know, and I appreciate what you tried to tell me, but I guess I was blind to the side I didn't want to see. I mean, Kev can be really sweet, you know. Like he'd drive all the way across town just because I said I craved a DQ shake."

It had been a while since Delta and I really had sat down for a serious conversation, or any kind of conversation for that matter. I'd almost forgotten her habit of finishing other people's sentences. If you didn't know her it could be annoying, as a few of our teachers had demonstrated over the years by doling out time in detention. To me, it's Delta being Delta.

"I know what you mean. But there were times—"

"—that he could be totally psycho or something. Why are boys like that?" Delta said.

"It's not only boys. We talked about this in our Psychology class. It's like this, you know those balloons we buy at the fair every year, the ones—"

"The balloon within a balloon?"

"That's the one. Well, we are all like those balloons, an inner part that is the real us and an outer layer that we allow everyone else to see. Most of the time we can get a good read on people because their outer layer is mostly transparent, allowing us to see what's inside. But there are people who possess an outer layer that is less transparent, and sometimes even mirrored, so you only see—"

"—what they want you to see," Delta finished.

"Exactly." I reached behind me and grabbed one of my pillows, handing it to Delta, then took one for myself. Ever since we were kids, whenever the two of us would get into these deep conversations, we had to be hugging a pillow while we talked. I'm not sure why, but it became a thing. "Stooch is like that. I think that if people got a peek at his inner-balloon, they'd be shocked."

"What about Jason, how transparent is he?"

"That's part of the problem. I think the transparency is not always constant. It can change over time. I've known Jason for a long time, and I think his outer layer is becoming cloudy, but I knew him when it was completely transparent, and I understand the type of person he really is. He can be so much more, but he's content with his place in the world. That bothers me more and more, so I—"

"—broke it off."

"Yeah."

"Well, I'm ready to pop Stooch's balloon after what he did today."

"That's another part of my balloon theory. When you stick a pin in these balloons… or a person's outer personality… they don't pop, but rather slowly bleed out air until the outer layer is completely gone. For those people with a transparent layer, it's no big deal, but those folks with the mirrors—"

"It be like yanking the mask off that dude from the Scream movies."

"Well, not quite, but you're on the right track."

"So, the two of us are a pair of single chicks again. I guess it doesn't suck that bad. At least we have each other."

"Yeah, but—" the tears started to flow again. "—it hurts more than I thought it would. I really do care for Jason."

Delta handed me another Kleenex, took one for herself, and we both blew our noses.

"I don't think I cared for Stooch that much. I mean it's only been a couple months, but it was sure nice getting treated like royalty sometimes."

During football season, the high school team—and their respective girlfriends—would benefit from the outpouring of gratitude from local businesses, especially when they were winning like we were that year. I had to admit, it felt pretty amazing.

"You'll live," I offered.

"Yeah, I guess. What are you going to do about Homecoming?"

An icy chill ran through me. I had forgotten all about Homecoming. The game was—my mind raced to recalibrate the calendar—this coming Friday. And I was on the Homecoming Court! Crap! Naturally I wouldn't go, but Jason was my escort, and my timing couldn't have been worse. I was going to be known as the girl who dumped her boyfriend the week of Homecoming.

"I can't think about that right now. I have too many other things to worry about. The truth is me and Jason have been together so long I'm not sure how—"

"—to be single again. Don't worry, we'll figure it out together, girl."

I reached out and put both my hands on her leg. "I'm so glad you came by."

"Me too. So, what are you going to do about the whole Chewy and Taggart thing?"

I flopped back against where my pillows used to be, sending several used tissues flying up and off the bed, my arms splayed out to my side.

"Oh! Why did you have to bring that up? I was just starting to feel good again."

I ended up dumping everything I'd been going through on Delta in what felt like one massively long sentence. That included admitting that I may have been a crappy sister to Becca. I told Delta about my desire to better understand who Becca was, and that meant I needed to get to know Taggart McGill.

"You remember what Taggart did to me in junior high, don't you?"

I sat back up quickly. "Of course I do, but let me ask you something. I remember you telling everyone that Taggart did that to you, but how did you know it was him?"

"He sat behind me in fourth period, right before lunch."

"Did you see him messing with—"

"—my purse? No. But they found those others in his jacket."

"But how did they know to look in his jacket for them?"

"I think they fell out when he was taking his jacket off for in gym class and one of the teachers saw them. Why? What does any of that matter?"

"I guess I'm not so sure he did it now."

"Well, I am. Listen, Cassie, Taggart has been pulling that crap for years, and I can't for the life of me understand what your sister was doing hanging around with him, but that dude is trouble. If you want my advice, walk away from him and this obsession Chewy has. There's nothing good that can come from it."

I nodded my head because some part of me agreed with everything she was saying. But still.

"I hear you, I really do, it's just that—"

"Just what?" Delta asked, crossing her arms and tilting her head slightly to one side.

"I can't settle things in my head. All this time since Becca and Taggart started hanging out, I ignored it. No, that's not true. At first, I was really angry with her. I was upset that she was contaminating our lives with him. But she didn't want to hear anything I had to say, so that's when I basically shut her out and went my own way.

"Now Becca's gone and I'm realizing… maybe I was wrong. With the exception of her being friends with Taggart, I think I knew her pretty well and I should have tried harder to understand what it was she had with him. There's something we're not seeing, something only Becca saw in him, and until I figure out what it is it's going to tear me up."

I hadn't realized it, but the tears were streaming down my cheeks again.

"Why do we do that Delta? Why do we take the ones we love the most for granted? Why do we get so caught up in our own lives that we're unable to look past petty resentments? And when we finally do wake up, it's too late."

Delta was crying with me too at this point.

"My sister is gone, Delta. She's gone… and I can't—"

I collapsed into her lap and she wrapped her arms around me. I knew she wouldn't be able to finish that sentence for me.

***

When I pulled into the school parking lot the next morning, something was off. I coasted down the row of cars and saw several of my classmates standing near my assigned slot. When I pulled closer, I saw what was so interesting. Someone had gathered up all the trash barrels from around the school, probably half a dozen, and placed them all in my spot. Delta's parking space was only three down from mine and hers received the same treatment, but she drove a mini-cooper and managed to squeeze in anyway.

I stopped the car in front of my spot, stared at the barrels for a couple of seconds, my knuckles turning white as I strangled the steering wheel. I seriously contemplated backing up to get a good running start, then stepping on the gas pedal and plowing into them. Who could blame me? Then I remembered what Taggart told me about pranks, specifically Becca's philosophy, and I smiled. I continued down the row and parked in my sister's unused spot.

I wanted to believe that Jason had nothing to do with this. Nevertheless, I had hurt him yesterday. I didn't mean to, but when somebody is that hurt, they are capable of just about anything. The fact that Delta's spot had been targeted as well seemed to point the finger more towards Stooch than Jason. I could totally get behind that idea. That's when I chuckled, realizing I was making the same mistake again. If this were a couple of weeks ago I'd be blaming Taggart McGill for this and cussing him. *Could I really have been so wrong about him?*

That reminded me of the first thing on my morning agenda. If I was to find out what I could about Taggart before transporting him and Chewy to the police station this afternoon, it would mean skipping first period and taking somebody up on an offer.

As I made my way into the building, I spotted the bicycle Taggart was riding yesterday laying on its side next to all the others that were properly stored on the stands. I shook my head and shoved through the glass doors. I headed straight for the office, ignoring the flurry of morning activity around me. For once, Miss Worthy was by herself in the reception area, so I asked if Mr. Stevens was available. She held onto my gaze for a couple of seconds, then disappeared into the vice principal's office. She returned a minute later and told me to go right in.

When I marched in, Mr. Stevens was standing behind his desk and slipping on his sports coat.

"What can I do for you Cassie?"

"The first thing is that I want to let the school know I won't be participating in anything related to Homecoming this year. I hope everyone understands."

"Of course. I believe they have already made contingency plans."

"Good. Also, I was wondering if I could take you up on your offer to talk, if that's okay?"

"Don't you have Biology this period?"

"I do, but this can't wait."

"I see. Well, of course, of course, have a seat."

I sat in the same chair I had used yesterday and set my book bag beside it. Mr. Stevens continued standing behind his desk.

"What is it that's so urgent?" Mr. Stevens asked.

"I really need you to tell me everything you can about Taggart McGill."

Mr. Stevens furrowed his eyebrows, causing a deep crease to form between his eyes.

"Taggart McGill?" he asked.

"Yes Sir."

"Your big emergency is that you need to know about Taggart McGill?"

"I didn't say it was an emergency. I said it couldn't wait, and it can't."

Mr. Stevens slipped into his chair. "Even if I could discuss him with you, which I can't, why couldn't that wait until you had a free period?"

"Because my only free time is third period and lunch. You're never in your office during third period. I know because I've tried before, and at lunch I have an errand to run. I need to know more about Taggart before the end of school."

"What happens then?"

"I can't really say."

Mr. Stevens paused, taking time to study me closer.

"Cassie, what's going on?"

So far he'd followed the script pretty much as I imagined. I knew he couldn't say much about Taggart. Teachers and school administrators could get into all sorts of trouble for spilling those beans, but if I could get him to leak at least a few tidbits, I would consider this a win. To do that, I couldn't come at him head-on. It had to seem like his idea. That's basic adult communication 101.

I lowered my eyes. "You know that Taggart and Becca were friends, right?"

"They were dating, weren't they?"

I shook my head, keeping it lowered at the same time. "No, they only had one date, and technically they called it off mid-way through the date and decided being friends was better. They were just very close."

"I see."

"Taggart and I, on the other hand, have never really hit it off and I'm trying to get a better handle on him so I can try and be a friend to him like my sister was."

"And you thought you could get some information from me that would help your cause?"

"He does spend a lot of time in your office."

Mr. Stevens grinned. "That may be the understatement of the year."

Now was the time to roll the dice. I rose from my chair. "I'm sorry for wasting your time, Mr. Stevens. This was stupid. I thought that since you knew me you might --"

"Cassie, sit down."

Cha-Ching.

"Maybe I can tell you a few things without technically violating his trust."

The smile I gave him was wide, and genuine, but probably not for the reason Mr. Stevens thought. I wasn't a hundred percent sure my shameful manipulation had worked, or rather, Mr. Stevens was simply going along with it because he felt sorry for me. It didn't really matter. I was about to get what I'd come here for.

The vice principal sat back in his chair. I considered sweetening the pot by promising him I wouldn't tell a soul, but decided against it. Though I had no intention of spilling, he was smart enough not to trust the word of a high school student.

"Let me start off by saying that Taggart is an intelligent young man. I can't tell you his score, but he is in the upper one percent in the country on his ACT's. He's the first student at our school to accomplish that."

"You're joking. The teachers never call on him in class. I assumed it was because he never knew the answers."

"The teachers never call on him because he refuses to answer their questions. This was something the New Haven school system learned early on with Taggart. However, his grades are such that we've learned to adapt. As bright as he is, he's also very misunderstood, and the main reason is because of Taggart himself. The opinions of others, including his teachers, mean very little to him, so he makes no effort to correct misperceptions. Although I can't go into specifics, I will say that a good many of the things Taggart is accused of via the rumor-mill are untrue."

"How can that be so? I know of at least a half dozen pranks he's pulled that I'm certain he did."

"Do you? Really? I'm not saying he's totally innocent of everything, but there are a lot of shenanigans attributed to him that he had no part of. He's sort of become the de facto fall guy around this school. Let me ask you this, do you know who the biggest scapegoat of all time is?"

"No, sir."

"The Devil. Wars, pestilence, drought, famine, natural disasters, you name it. Satan gets the blame. In Christianity, evil is synonymous with the Devil. Over the centuries, the Devil became history's favorite whipping boy. Mark Twain once said, and I'm paraphrasing, '*We never hear the Devil's side. We have none but the evidence of the prosecution, and yet we have rendered the verdict. That is un-American*'."

"Huh."

"Taggart offers no defense, to anything, so anything and everything gets laid on his doorstep. He couldn't care less. I would wager that the only person he did want to know the truth was your sister."

"But you seem to know."

"Not because of anything Taggart did to defend himself. I have the benefit, most of the time, of seeing all the facts without his help. After a while, a pattern takes shape and you figure the rest out yourself."

"If this is true, then why don't you do anything about it? Why don't you set the record straight?"

"Because one, it's not our job here to control the content of the students' rumor-mill, and two, Taggart would have a fit if he even knew I was telling you this. As cruel as it sounds, he doesn't care, so neither do we."

"Excuse me for saying this, Mr. Stevens, but that kinda sucks."

"You wanted to know something about Taggart, so there you go. Good luck getting him to care about anything you have to say."

Eleven

The remainder of the morning was a blur. I was still reeling from what Mr. Stevens had told me. Not only had he confirmed that much of the reputation attributed to Taggart was a myth, but the person who I thought was as dense as a lead pipe, was actually a Brainiac.

I'm sure I looked like a zombie as I trudged from class to class. I certainly had the attention span of a one. Focusing on my schoolwork wasn't happening. I didn't see Jason once, which wasn't a surprise, but a lot of my friends came up to me in the halls and before classes expressing their surprise about our break up. Apparently it was already common knowledge, which shouldn't have been a shock given the display left in my parking spot. Still, it unnerved me to hear others talk about us as a couple in the past tense. Maybe I was being overly sensitive, but some of my "so-called" friends seemed more upset about the death of our relationship than the death of my sister.

In study hall, Delta had moved from our normal seats to a spot near the front of the room, far away from Stooch, Michael, and Cheryl at the back. She spent half of the period planning how we were going to get back at Stooch for the trash barrel stunt—even though we didn't have any proof it was him—and the other half trying to get me to tell her what Mr. Stevens had said. I desperately wanted to tell her what I found out, but the temptation had to wait. I loved Delta to death, but she was a bit of a blabbermouth. As soon as I told her it would be all over school. Sure, nobody would believe it… I wasn't even sure I believed it… but everyone, including Taggart, would know I spoke to Mr. Stevens about him and that couldn't happen. I was already walking on thin ice, so I wasn't about to start using a pogo stick.

As soon as the bell rung for lunch, I made a beeline for my car and out of the parking lot in record time. I have to admit that I was so nervous I may have exceeded the speed limit by more than my normal five mph.

I pulled into the driveway and parked, and then sat there staring at the house. It was one of the oldest in the neighborhood, wood-framed as opposed to brick, roughly half the size of most of the other homes in the newer parts of Grayson Acres. There was only one car in the open-ended garage, suspended off the ground by car jacks with all four tires missing. I knew the owner wasn't home. At least I hoped so.

Did I really want to do this? It wasn't too late to turn back and forget about the whole thing. I mean, nobody would know, even about my conversation with Mr. Stevens. I could simply go on pretending things were the same as they always were. Couldn't I? Why put myself through something so stressful?

I focused on the horsehair hanging from the mirror, and suddenly I knew the answer to all my questions. I stroked the hair from Becca's bow and climbed out of the car.

I rang the doorbell.

When I was about to ring the bell a second time, I heard a noise on the other side of the door as if somebody was struggling to get it open. Then the door abruptly opened wide, and Mr. Wilson was standing in front of me.

It had probably been ten years since I'd last seen Mr. Wilson. He used to be a New Haven policeman, retired now, but he was one of the officers who took the robbery report when my dad's riding lawnmower was stolen from our storage shed. At the time I was eight, and I remember being in awe of having a real policeman in our house. The years since hadn't been kind to Mr. Wilson and standing in front of him now I saw that for myself. Forced to take an early retirement and go on disability because of a bad back, it looked as if the inactivity had sucked most of the life from him. When I last saw him, he was a little overweight, but not so bad you'd start making donut jokes. His younger version had a clean-cut appearance, short-cropped hair, and tanned skin that looked as if he came by it naturally instead of underneath superheated lamps.

The man on the other side of the glass door was a shadow of his former self, and it made me sad to see him this way. He was bone thin and inches shorter because of the way he stooped over, as if he was carrying a hundred-pound invisible man on his shoulders. Instead of taking steps, his feet slid across the floor. He sported a full beard of white hair with nothing on the top of his head, and his pasty skin resembled the moldy wallpaper in our basement bathroom. One of his hands was on the open door; the other used a walking cane to keep him balanced.

I flashed him a smile. "Hi, Mr. Wilson. I don't know if you remember me, I'm Becca Underwood's sister."

Mr. Wilson pushed open the storm door.

"Cassie?"

"Yes, sir."

"Who is it, Fred?" came a woman's voice from inside the house.

"Cassie Underwood, Becca's sister," Mr. Wilson called back without bothering to turn.

"Oh. Well… what does she want?"

"What do you want?" he repeated.

"I would like to ask you a few questions if it's not too much of an inconvenience."

"She wants to ask us some questions," Mr. Wilson relayed, his focus still on me.

"About what," was the reply from inside.

"About what?"

"Taggart and his relationship with my sister," I answered.

"Taggart," was all that Mr. Wilson passed along.

"Taggart's at school," Mrs. Wilson hollered back.

"Has he done something?" Mr. Wilson asked, breaking the cycle.

I couldn't help but smile as I shook my head because this was becoming downright comical. Mr. Wilson smiled back at me.

"Please come in," he said, maneuvering out of the way so I could pass.

Directly inside the door I came face to face with a wall of medals, citations, certificates, pictures, and other mementos that commemorated Mr. Wilson's long public service in the New Haven Police Department. I stood there staring at it, ashamed of how little I knew about Mr. Wilson and what he had been doing for the city.

"This is impressive," was all I could think to say.

"A lot of memories, good and bad," he mumbled. "Grace is in the kitchen, to the right and down the hall."

As I made my way towards the kitchen I couldn't help but notice how intricately decorated their house was. Every nook and cranny held some sort of homemade craftwork.

When I entered the kitchen, Mrs. Wilson was seated at a small table in the corner, a step-walker positioned nearby, and a plate in front of her that contained a sandwich and half a pickle. I had never met Mrs. Wilson, though I understood that she was retired as well from her position as a nurse supervisor at the hospital. She seemed ten years younger than Mr. Wilson, and sitting there she looked like she was in good health, but Becca had told me that she too had back issues that she refused to have surgery to correct.

"Cassie, it's so nice to see you," Mrs. Wilson said, reaching over and pulling out the chair to her right from under the table. "Come sit with us."

"We were just sitting down to lunch," Mr. Wilson said as he made his way slowly to the counter. "Can I make you a sandwich?"

"Oh, no thank you. I didn't mean to interrupt your lunch. I can come back at another time if you want."

"Don't be silly," Mrs. Wilson said, picking up her sandwich and taking a bite. "If you don't mind us talking with our mouths full, then we'd enjoy the company."

I sat down in the chair Mrs. Wilson had offered.

"Fred and I were at Becca's funeral, but the deacon at our church who drove us messed up the time, so we got there late and had to sit in the overflow room. It was a very nice service," Mrs. Wilson said. "I'm sorry we couldn't make it to the procession line and say our condolences in person. Did you get our card?"

I had no idea if we received their card or not, Mom and Aunt Nancy handled all of that, but still I said, "Yes, it was very nice. Thank you so much."

"I told her not to send one," Mr. Wilson commented, taking a bite of his sandwich. "No way a $2.15 Hallmark card convey what it needs to."

"It cost me almost $7, Fred. Oh my… is that morbid, dear?"

I decided I liked Mrs. Wilson. "No ma'am, not at all. I was wondering though, was Taggart there? Was he at the funeral?"

"Damned kid," Mr. Wilson exclaimed.

Mrs. Wilson frowned and put down her sandwich.

"I believe he was, although we didn't actually see him. He was supposed to be in the hospital, still under observation, but he pulled out all his tubes and wires and disappeared. The doctors were quite upset with him… and us. We should have known nothing was going to keep him away."

Mr. Wilson placed a plate on the table and carefully slid into the chair on my right.

"You said you wanted to ask us some questions about Taggart," Mr. Wilson said.

"Yes sir."

"Do you mind if I ask why?"

Though I'd had plenty of time to think about the answer to this question, I hesitated before answering.

"I'm not proud of this, but I originally blamed Taggart for what happened to my sister."

Mrs. Wilson looked at her husband, then back at me.

"I never understood their friendship, and I think that's because I didn't have enough faith in my sister. I didn't know Taggart. I thought I knew him, but I'm finding out that I really didn't. And my sister, who I thought I knew, it turns out that Taggart knew her better."

Mrs. Wilson picked up her pickle and took a bite. "I seriously doubt that dear, but I wouldn't beat yourself up. Most people hold things tight, like a pickpocket who has scored big and has to walk home through a neighborhood filled with other pickpockets. Taggart is more secretive than most and a little of that must have rubbed off on your sister."

"I'm just trying to understand them both better, but Taggart isn't being very cooperative."

"You've tried to talk to him?"

"Yes ma'am. But he didn't say much."

"That's not a surprise," Mr. Wilson responded. His sandwich was gone already, and a tiny sliver of mayonnaise dotted his beard. I made a motion to a spot on my chin and Mr. Wilson took the cue and wiped his face with the back of his sleeve. "Thank you. If we were eating ribs you might have to hose me down."

I laughed at that, enjoying how relaxed the two of them were around me. My anxiety about being in their… and Taggart's… home was beginning to fade.

"The boy can be very tight-lipped," Mr. Wilson continued. "But I must say ever since the accident he has been less… self-centered."

Mrs. Wilson nodded her head in agreement.

"I was hoping you could tell me more. I need to find a way to get him to open up to me."

Mrs. Wilson seemed to be contemplating her half-sandwich. "I sympathize with you, Cassie, I really do, but it don't feel right talking about Taggart behind his back. It's taken us years to get him to trust us. I'm afraid talking to you could ruin that."

Mrs. Wilson's manner, her aloofness, the way she wouldn't look me in the eye, told me I wasn't going to get anywhere with her. That mind was made up. It was looking as if my trip had turned into a colossal waste of time.

Mr. Wilson rose from the table slowly with his now empty plate and started walking towards the sink.

"Grace."

Mrs. Wilson looked up from her plate with an expression I recognized instantaneously. My mom gave the same one to my dad when he voiced an opinion contrary to hers.

"He will shut down again, Fred. You know he will," she said, her voice adopting a tone that was sterner, but nothing like my own mother would use if she were in the same situation. "Now take your pill before you forget."

Mr. Wilson put his plate in the sink then opened a pill bottle he picked up from the counter and popped one into his mouth.

"Peanut allergy," the man said after taking a sip of water from the faucet. "Supposed to be a new treatment to make me less sensitive."

"I have a cousin who's allergic to bee stings," I offered. I didn't know what else to say and saying nothing seemed insensitive.

Mr. Wilson leaned heavily on the counter behind him.

"I know it's a risk, Grace, but here me out," he said, then he directed his attention to me. "Cassie, I need you to answer me honestly. Does Taggart have any other friends?"

A month ago I would have responded with 'are you kidding,' but now I hesitated. Not because I didn't know the answer, but because I wanted to think of a way to cushion it.

"No, sir. I have never seen Taggart with anybody other than Becca."

Mr. Wilson nodded his head. "We suspected as much."

Mrs. Wilson appeared confused now. "No one?"

"No, ma'am."

"Grace, that means he is all alone now and sitting here at our table is a girl who… I believe… is trying to be his friend. How can we not help her? We are not betraying Taggart by talking to her. We would be doing what parents are supposed to do and work in his best interest, even if he doesn't see it that way. His doctor even told us that."

"Doctor?" I said.

Mrs. Wilson looked at her husband, indecision written all over her face. Then she looked down at her sandwich, picked it up and took a large bite.

"I guess that's the first thing you need to learn about Taggart," she said through a mouthful of bread, lettuce, and meat. "He sees a psychiatrist from time to time."

"Oh," was all I could think to say.

"Start at the beginning, it will make more sense to her," Mr. Wilson said as he started making his way back to the table.

"You're the one who mentioned the doctor," she quipped.

"Taggart has had a rough upbringing," Mr. Wilson said, ignoring his wife's remark. "His mother passed when he was young, and the circumstances in which she died left some emotional scars."

Wait…what? "His mother died?"

"Yes."

"I always thought he was abandoned. I mean, I think somebody told me that."

"I'm afraid not."

"Becca never said anything either." I thought things were spinning after talking to Mr. Stevens earlier, now I was positively disoriented.

"It was quite traumatic for him. The doctor is pretty sure some of his issues began before then, however. You see, there was evidence his mother abused drugs, heavily, but she seemed to have cleaned herself up and was on the straight and narrow when she died."

"How did she die?" I asked.

"Brain aneurysm. It happened when the two of them were in a gas station bathroom and Taggart was locked inside with the body, in total darkness, for hours before anyone found him."

"Oh my god."

"You can see why he'd be troubled by it."

"That's why he won't use the bathrooms at the school. Those metal stalls remind him of where she died."

"I can tell you're a bright one. Back then, I was one of the first ones on the scene and let me say this, the boy was a mess."

"So, nobody could find any of his family? His dad?"

"None. One witness, an older woman I think, recalled that the two of them were on their way to Ft. Lauderdale to visit the boy's grandmother, but no match was found and nobody there reported a missing person. The bus originated in Atlanta, but no missing persons matching their description came up there either. The father apparently wasn't in the picture any longer—at least that's what the witness said."

"They had no choice but to place him with DHS," Mrs. Wilson continued, taking over for her husband. "But that only made matters worse. Don't get me wrong, the families that took Taggart in were good people and they tried their best with him, but he was… oh… let's say… difficult."

"You knew him then?"

Mr. Wilson took the baton again. "No. After that day when we found him, I didn't see him until four years ago. Most of what we know came from his DHS file, and his psychiatrist."

"When did he start seeing the psychiatrist?"

"When he was twelve, I believe. One of his previous foster families was concerned about his reluctance to engage socially, so they sought help. It seemed to help, a little, so we've kept a relationship with the therapist."

"How many foster families has he lived with?"

"The poor boy jumped around more than a two-year-old in a bouncy house. There were quite a few. The remarkable thing is he has excelled in school despite everything, almost as if he uses knowledge—or rather facts—as a safe haven from the uncertainty in his life."

"He's been here with you four years?"

"That's true."

"So you've obviously done something different the others couldn't do."

The two of them looked at each other and smiled.

"To tell you the truth—" Mr. Wilson paused and shook his head. "I'm sorry, I hate it when people say that and there I go saying it myself. I always tell the truth, so to use that phrase implies that I somehow wouldn't. What I really mean to say is, I'm going to be more frank than I might normally be. The reason I think we've made it work with Taggart is because, at first, we needed him more than he needed us."

"I'm sorry, I don't understand."

"Look at us. Neither of us can drive and we are almost invalids."

"We're not that bad, Fred."

"When we first took in Taggart he could see how much we needed his help with even the simple things, and somehow he could relate to that. It hasn't always been smooth sailing and there was plenty of teeth gnashing, but he's becoming a well-rounded human being. Your sister had a lot to do with that."

I smiled. "Can I ask why you took him in?"

"Our own son had moved out a couple years earlier; we had the space and we're used to the responsibility. A fellow church member brought him to our attention, thinking it would be a good combination, and they were right. We had been foster parents previously, a long time ago, so all we had to do was renew our status."

You could say I ran out of questions, but the truth was I couldn't remember any of the ones I had thought of beforehand. I was in a freefall. Thrown for a loop by what I had just learned. I was starting to understand why Becca had become friends with Taggart, and why she had kept it from us all.

"So, Cassie, I shouldn't have to tell you to be extremely careful with how you use this information. Taggart is very private and shut-off to the world. Your sister was the lone exception. I don't know how his classmates see him, but I can't imagine it's too favorable, knowing how he can be. He has a kind heart, but I fear nobody sees it. Both my wife and I are hoping you can step in and fill that void your sister left. He really needs that. It won't be easy, but believe me when I say that Taggart is worth it."

Twelve

When I got back to the school somebody had removed the trash barrels from my parking spot. I pulled in and killed the engine, but I didn't move. In fact, I remained there in my car for the who knows how long. I couldn't face tackling algebra right now. It was the first time… EVER… I had purposely skipped a class, but I needed to collect my thoughts and process what I'd learned that morning. In a way, it felt as if I had stepped into an alternate reality.

The boy who I blamed for so much, who I had dubbed the bane of my existence, wasn't who I thought he was. I shook my head when I thought about how frustrated I was with my sister because of her friendship with Taggart and how I thought it would ruin my up-and-coming social status. Geez, I really had been so wrong about everything, and worse still, so shallow. What a moron.

I guess my brain decided to defend itself because my thoughts went in the other direction. I decided it was still all Taggart's fault. If he hadn't been so secretive, convincing my sister to keep his secrets as well, I would never have felt the way I did. I told myself that if I knew who Taggart really was, I would have been more understanding. My relationship with Becca wouldn't have been so strained.

Or would it? A question weaseled its way into my carefully pieced together scenario, one whose answer came attached with a significant amount of self-doubt. No matter how hard I tried to push the question aside, it kept begging for an answer.

Did I use my sister's blossoming friendship with Taggart to avoid talking to her about my head-first dive into the popularity pool? Had I distanced myself from Becca, not because of who she was friends with, but because I was inwardly ashamed of who I was turning into, and I didn't want to deal with her recriminations.

That possibility slapped me in the face like a cold, wet towel. An actual light bulb went on in my head as I considered the truthfulness of those questions. If it were true, I was such a hypocrite. I'd been telling myself that my loss of respect for Jason had been building for a while, but maybe the truth was I never truly respected him. Maybe I'd turned a blind eye to his faults so I could become semi-popular, and all this time my manufactured inner-anger was directed towards someone who, it turns out, was completely harmless.

Boy… self-realization was a bitch!

Right before the last bell, I got out of my car and made my way to the gathering area right outside of the school. When the bell sounded, a flood of people came streaming out of the school doors, a few of them stopping long enough to confirm the demise of Jason and me as a couple.

I didn't have to wait long before Chewy appeared by my side, his friend, Tunes, in tow with his ever-present headphones. As he did yesterday, Chewy continued to rock side to side when he stopped in front of me.

"Where's Taggart?" Chewy asked.

"I haven't seen him yet," I answered.

"He isn't backing out, is he?"

"You heard me when I said I haven't seen him yet, right?"

"Because that would be totally lame."

I didn't bother to respond. He wasn't listening to me anyway.

Tunes raised his arm and pointed to the far door where Taggart was all but sprinting in our direction. He was wearing the same clothes he had on yesterday. The bruise on his forehead from the accident was barely visible now.

"Let's go," he said as he passed us heading for the parking lot, pointing at Tunes as he did. "But not him."

Chewy had taken a few steps and then stopped.

"Tunes goes where I go."

Taggart stopped walking, but didn't turn around. "You wanted my help, and I say no friends."

Tunes looked like someone had just stolen his headphones and Chewy's jaw was set, so I decided to intercede. "What does it matter if one more comes?"

Taggart turned around. "We don't need him."

Chewy didn't hesitate. "Then never mind. I'll find another way."

Taggart looked at the three of us like we were a math problem he had to solve, then finally said, "Okay, fine, he can come, but he stays in the car."

As Taggart turned back towards the parking lot, I called out to him. "What about your bike?"

When he looked back at me pointing to the bike laying on the grass where he had left it that morning, there was definitely irritation.

"It's not my bike."

"I saw you riding it."

"Still not my bike."

"Whose is it?" I asked.

He shrugged his shoulders.

"I think that's Billy Harrington's bike," Chewy said.

"Where did you get it from?" I asked

"It was on the curb in front of some house in our neighborhood."

"Billy Harrington's house," Chewy said.

"So you stole it?"

"I needed to get to school and whoever it belonged to deserved to have it taken for leaving it near the street."

Mr. Wilson's warning about this not going to be easy popped into my head.

"Go get it. We'll put it in my trunk and return it afterward."

"You're kidding, right?"

"None of us are going anywhere until you put that in my trunk."

I was totally expecting Taggart to forget about the whole thing and go storming off, but instead we all watched as he marched straight over to the bike, picked it up with one hand, then returned and stood in front of us.

"Should I go round up the band next? Maybe we can have a parade down to the station?"

I suppressed the smile and maneuvered through the crowd of people and cars back to my car. I popped the Buick's trunk, and after watching Taggart place the bike inside, climbed behind the wheel.

For some reason Taggart took the rear seat on the passenger side first, so Chewy sat next to me in the front, gently swaying as usual. Tunes jumped in behind me. It took several minutes to fight the congestion onto the main road, then we were heading downtown.

We rode in silence for the first five minutes, until Chewy said, "I loved my dad."

I glanced at Chewy, who was looking back at me, then stole a glance at Taggart in the backseat. His face was blank.

"Of course you did," I replied, not certain if it was the right thing.

"No, you don't understand. I REALLY loved my dad. I bet if you asked all the kids at school if they loved their dad's, half would probably say 'sure,' the other half would say 'he's okay.' My dad was my best friend, just ahead of Tunes."

I wasn't sure where this was going or really what to say.

"My dad and I would build model planes together all the time. Really intricate ones. We also used to make these awesome music videos."

"What kind of music videos?" I asked.

"It was more a combination of air guitar and karaoke, actually. We'd pick a song we both liked and film ourselves singing it and pretending like we were performing live. It was a lot of fun."

"What would you do with them?"

"Nothing. It was only for us," Chewy said, his voice starting to trail off now. "We just liked doing it."

I peeked back at Taggart once more, but his expression was still unchanged.

Conversation ended for the remainder of the way to the New Haven Police Department, only a ten-minute drive from the high school. The station house stood a short distance from the courthouse, located on the city square, which was important because of the limited parking around the police station. People usually parked at the square and walked over. As I navigated down the one-way street I couldn't help but notice the colorful banners displaying our schools banner hanging from the street lamps. Many of the storefront also had posters promoting the football team in their windows. New Haven might have its faults, but they sure loved their football.

I parked on the square and switched off the engine.

"You need to stay here while we're inside," Taggart said to Tunes in the backseat. "And there's no negotiating this time."

Tunes nodded once.

Chewy and Taggart both opened their doors and climbed out, then Taggart stuck his head back in the door.

"You need to come too," he said to me.

"I thought I was just the chauffeur in this little adventure."

"I… I need you to come too," he repeated, but he wouldn't look me in the eyes.

I turned the key switch so I could roll down the windows, turned it off, then got out of the car.

"Don't let anyone steal my car, Tunes," I said as I headed off to join Chewy and Taggart.

I had never been to our local police station and wasn't sure what to expect. As we approached, I was impressed with the fresh coat of paint and how meticulous the shrubbery lining the front of the building was maintained. I shouldn't have been surprised because all of the public areas in New Haven were well looked after. Undesirables such as thugs and gang-bangers were a foreign concept in this town. I imagined that the worse thing our local police force had to contend with were post-game teenage parties that got out of hand or maybe a domestic dispute or two. It made me think as we pushed our way through the entrance doors, just how ludicrous our visit today was.

Inside the building, there was a small waiting area with a row of a dozen folding metal chairs to the right of the entrance. A pony wall with glass to the ceiling ran across the front of the waiting room, with a door at the far-right end. On the other side of the glass wall I could see several desks, most of them unoccupied, and offices beyond those. Behind the wall directly across from the entrance was a woman sitting behind a reception desk typing on a keyboard. Taggart stepped up to the glass partition in front of the desk and spoke to the woman. I couldn't hear what the two of them were saying, but shortly afterward she made a phone call and Taggart joined us, sitting down in one of the folding chairs.

Chewy and I sat next to him. Chewy's swaying seemed more exaggerated now.

"How many times have you been arrested?" Chewy asked in a hushed tone.

"None," Taggart answered, his eyes focused straight ahead.

I knew Taggart had to be lying because I had personally seen him in the back of a police car twice, but of course that didn't jibe with what Mr. Stevens had told me this morning and confirmed by Mr. and Mrs. Wilson. What was I missing? Or was everybody else missing something?

We waited for approximately twenty minutes until a uniformed officer, probably in his mid-twenties, with sandy hair and a matching mustache, walked through the door. As he approached, Chewy became very still.

"Hey, Taggart," the officer said, unsmiling.

"Hey, Matt," Taggart replied, standing. I guess he really did know these guys by their first names.

"Is this Trevor?"

I had never heard Chewy's real name before, but I guessed it suited him. Chewy stood up, so I followed suit. When I did, I got a closer look at Officer Matt's name tag. It read MATT WILSON.

"Yes sir, I'm Trevor, though most people call me Chewy."

"Who's this?" Officer Matt asked, gesturing in my direction.

I was still staring at the officer's name badge as more pieces of the Taggart puzzle fell into place. All those times my friends blabbed about Taggart being arrested—including the two times I'd witnessed it—was nothing more than him getting a lift from a family member. Mister and Mrs. Wilson's son—the police officer. The depths of my stupidity seemed to be endless.

"She's with me," Taggart answered, which made me feel awkward, but I guess that meant something because Officer

Wilson nodded once before turning around and heading back from where he came. All of us followed him.

We walked down a short hallway and turned into what appeared to be a conference room. There was a long rectangular table in the center of the bare room with eight chairs around it. Sitting at the far end of the table was a thin man with a balding head wearing a grey suit. On the table in front of the man lay a manila folder.

"Have a seat," Officer Wilson commanded as he walked around the table and took the seat to the left of the grey-suited man.

The grey-suited man opened the folder in front of him and looked at Chewy.

"Trevor, my name is Sgt. Brown, and I am one of the detectives here in New Haven. Officer Wilson informed me of your concerns and desire for some answers, and although we don't normally do this… we are making an exception because of Officer Wilson's specific request."

Which I knew had really come from Taggart, but still, I wondered why the police were being so accommodating. There had to be something else going on here.

"I'm aware your mother is against passing this information to you, but I'm confident you'll keep this meeting between us once you've heard what is in this report. Are we clear on that point?"

"Yes, sir," Chewy muttered softly.

"Good. Then what I have before me are the results of the autopsy performed on your father, and what it says is that your father died of a burst aneurysm in the brain, resulting in loss of control, which led to the automobile accident he was ultimately involved in. There were no unusual circumstances or special conditions that precipitated his illness, so his death was attributed to natural causes."

Chewy looked as if he had been promised a seven-course meal and had been handed a Big Mac instead.

"May I take a look at that?" Taggart asked, which prompted Sgt. Brown to glance at Officer Wilson. Officer Wilson, Taggart's foster-brother, nodded his approval. The detective didn't appear to be all that happy about Taggart's request, but he closed the file and slid it across to him.

"But my father was completely healthy. There were no signs—"

"A brain aneurysm is easily missed by even the most thorough of exams. His coworkers stated that he was experiencing a severe headache that day, which is consistent with the tell-tale signs of an aneurysm, and he left work early because of it."

It was excruciating watching the truth choke all the hope from Chewy. He looked at Taggart, probably hoping that someone would be on his side and offer an argument, but Taggart was absorbed with the file.

"But—"

"Son, there's no evidence of foul play here whatsoever. I'm sorry."

Chewy's face went expressionless for a moment, then he plastered on the best fake smile he could muster, stood up and stuck out his hand. "Thank you for taking the time to answer my questions."

Sgt. Brown shook his hand and for some reason shook mine as well. Taggart didn't offer his, still studying the document he had been handed.

"I guess that's it then," Officer Wilson said, staring directly at Taggart.

Taggart closed the folder and exited the room, leaving the four of us in his wake, staring at each other.

"Thank you for doing this," I said to Officer Wilson, then Chewy and I hustled to catch up with Taggart.

We caught up with him outside the building and the three of us walked back to the car in silence. When I opened the door Tunes popped up from where he was laying down in the back seat. After everyone had piled in, I started the engine.

"Where does Tunes live, Chewy? I'll take everyone home."

"He lives in Grayson Acres too, on Meadowlark Street."

We drove all the way back to our neighborhood before anybody said anything.

Taggart broke the silence.

"You should post your videos."

"What?" Chewy asked.

"The videos you and your father made. You should post them on YouTube or TikTok."

Nobody said anything, but it was an amazing thought and it surprised me. Not so much the idea itself, but rather who thought of it.

But it was what he said next that really shocked me.

"Did your father have a proper burial, or was he cremated?" Taggart asked as I pulled into the Wilson's driveway.

Chewy turned around in his seat and looked at Taggart.

"He was cremated, why?"

"I wanted to get a look at his body."

Now it was my turn to twist around in my seat. "What the hell are you doing Taggart? You heard the detective. No sign of foul play... WHATSOEVER! What are you thinking?"

"I'm thinking that Chewy's father was definitely murdered."

Thirteen

I was glad that we were already sitting in the Wilson's driveway because otherwise Taggart's remark would have caused me to jam on the brakes. I didn't think it possible to be any more shocked than when Chewy first told us he believed his father was murdered.

Boy, was I wrong.

I didn't say anything right away because I was reading Taggart's face, looking for signs that he was joking or lying, but his expression was bland as always. The scowl on Tunes face sitting next to him reflected a healthy bit of skepticism also.

"I knew it!" Chewy exclaimed.

I ignored Chewy's outburst and kept my attention on Taggart. What was he up to? Going along with Chewy's request to help him adjust to his father's death was one thing—if that was his intention—but egging on the poor kid bordered on outright cruelty.

"Were you not in the same room with us when the detective explained the autopsy results? How could you possibly say that?" I asked.

"The police made up their mind from the start. There's no way they were going to rule this a homicide," Taggart said.

"So what was the point of even going there?"

"I wanted to get a look at the autopsy report and the only way that would happen is if the victims grieving son threatened to make waves in the newspaper unless they showed it to him."

"I never said I was going to the newspaper," Chewy commented.

"I said it for you. I had to ensure they took us seriously."

So that was why the police were so accommodating. I knew something was up.

"And you saw something in the autopsy report that trained professionals overlooked, something that convinced you Mr. Ledbetter was murdered?" I asked.

Taggart nodded.

"What was it? What did you see?" Chewy asked.

"During an autopsy it is common practice to make note of any marks or wounds on the body, regardless of how insignificant."

Chewy's eyes lit up. "And there was a wound?"

"Not a wound exactly."

"Then what, exactly?" I asked.

"There was a note about a mosquito bite on Mr. Ledbetter's lower calf."

"A mosquito bite?" I said, doing my best to contain my disbelief.

"Yes."

I was completely turned around in my seat now and fighting the urge to crawl over the back. "You determined that a man who has no enemies, no criminal history, no ties to anything illegal at all, was murdered because there was a mosquito bite on his leg?"

"That wasn't the only factor."

"Oh… what else was there? Evidence of a hangnail?"

Taggart crossed his arms. "I don't think you're taking me seriously."

"Ya think?! What was the other factor?"

"I can't share that yet."

"You can't share that yet?" My level of frustration was growing by the minute. "And you wonder why I'm not taking you seriously."

"I believe him," Chewy chimed in.

I jerked my head to look at Chewy and opened my mouth to say something, then stopped. I was about to lose it on the one person who deserved it least. Instead, I took a deep breath and got myself under control.

"Of course you do, Chewy. Listen, I'd want to believe that my sister died because of some diabolical plot and not some random medical condition as well, but it's a fantasy. One that for some reason Taggart is trying to convince you of."

"It happened," Taggart said.

I felt like a fire hydrant whose cap was holding on by a thread, threatening to spew water sky high. I wondered if one of the reasons Taggart was seeing a shrink was acute paranoia.

"How are you so sure?"

"Because it's happened before."

"What?"

"There have been other deaths with similar circumstances as this."

I couldn't believe what I was hearing. How could I ever allow myself to get caught up with such a delusional psycho? I searched the driveway around the car.

"Where are the cameras?" I asked.

"What cameras?"

"The hidden camera's that must be everywhere. There has to be, because we're being punk'd, right?"

"Punk'd?"

"Pranked. This has to be one of your pranks."

Taggart spoke directly to Chewy. "This is not a prank. Your father WAS murdered."

"THAT'S ENOUGH!" I yelled, unable to hold it in any longer. I reached under the dashboard and pressed the button that allowed the trunk lid to pop open. "Take your stolen bike and get out."

Taggart opened his mouth to say something else, but I cut him off.

"Get out, now. And stay away from Chewy or else I'll tell the Wilsons and their son what you've been doing."

That shut him up, but it was the way he reacted that gave me pause. Instead of becoming angry or frustrated because I had ruined whatever he was up to, his head and shoulders dropped and he seemed to sink in his seat, defeated.

Taggart got out of the car without another word, grabbed the bike out of the trunk, and walked slowly away.

"But what if he was right, Cassie?" Chewy asked softly.

I watched as Taggart entered the open garage and put the bike down. "Trust me, Chewy, I don't know what he was up to, but you heard the detective same as I did. It was your dad's time and that's it."

Still, I was confused by Taggart's reaction to my scolding. *Could he actually believe the nonsense he was spouting?*

I put the car in reverse and backed out of the Wilsons' driveway. I dropped Chewy off in front of his house, almost pulling away before I hearing Tunes opening the backseat door. I had forgotten he was even back there.

By the time I got home and shut the door to my bedroom, my head was swirling. Confused thoughts churned inside my head like a barrel of snakes. Taggart's childhood was a mess, no doubt, and he was most certainly different from anyone else I'd ever been around, but if I believed what Mr. Stevens told me, he wasn't the person I thought he was either. According to the vice principal, Taggart was innocent of most, if not all, of the mischief attributed to him throughout the years. The Wilsons were also very convincing. And I had to admit, during the little time I had been around him these last couple days, I couldn't see him as someone capable of such a mean-spirited hoax. So why was he doing this to Chewy? The simplest answer was that misunderstood or not, Taggart was enrolled in Bonkers University, majoring in Conspiracy Theory. Beyond that, the least probable answer was he was telling the truth about Mr. Ledbetter being murdered. That just didn't make sense. Cold-blooded murder here in New Haven? That was simply nuts.

I plopped down on my bed and before I could get comfortable, my phone chirped. The caller ID told me it was Delta, so I hit speakerphone.

"Hey, Delta."

"Yo, girl. Where'd you go today?"

I thought about how much I should tell Delta concerning the day's activities. "I had some errands to run. Still trying to figure out what to do about the Chewy Ledbetter thing."

"Did you go with them to the police this afternoon?"

"Yeah, I did. I thought everything was settled, but apparently not."

"I told you, stay away from that mess. I know you think you were a crappy sister and getting closer to Taggart McGill might help you answer some questions, but I'm telling you… that boy has something up his sleeve, you wait and see."

"You may be right, but I found out things about him today that really surprised me."

"What kind of things?"

"Let's just say a lot of what we've heard about him isn't true."

"Says who?"

"People I trust who have no reason to lie. I'm more confused than ever."

"I'm sorry to hear that. You know if you need my help with anything you just have to call, right?"

"Yeah, I know. Thanks, Delta. Right now I have to think."

"Well, I hope you figure it out. See you at school tomorrow?"

"I'll be there. Bye."

"Bye."

I ended the call, dropped the phone on the floor, then pulled one of my pillows over my face. I let myself imagine what would happen if I told Delta that Taggart believed a murderer was running around New Haven. Man, would the school have a field day with that one. How long would it take before that rumor warped into a version where Taggart admitted being a murderer? That led me back to the same question I'd been asking myself the whole time: *Why was Taggart playing this game with Chewy?* I struggled to believe that even the version of Taggart I thought I knew before today was capable of this.

I yanked the pillow off my face and threw it across the room, watching it bounce harmlessly off my closet door. I had learned a lot about Taggart today, so much of it a complete shock, but I still needed to know more. I thought about maybe going to see Taggart's shrink and asking him, or her, but I knew that would be useless. A shrink wouldn't be able to tell me anything because of the whole confidentiality thing. I was able to play on Mr. Stevens feelings because he was sorry for me, but that wouldn't work on a complete stranger.

Becca had trusted him, that much I was certain of. Shouldn't that be enough? But trusting Taggart the way my sister did meant I would have to believe Taggart's theory of a killer in our small town. Surely, Becca would have recognized the boy had delusional tendencies. Right? If only she were here to talk with me. To tell me what she knew about Taggart.

Then the thought hit me. Maybe she was.

Her journal. The one I'd left alone. Becca could tell me who the real Taggart was. Everything I needed to know would no doubt be found there. But what about my promise to uphold her wishes?

For my eyes only.

Wasn't reading it still a violation of her trust? But wouldn't Becca want me to use her words to help her best friend. I mean, this wasn't about my own selfish need for answers and understanding anymore. Yes, I missed my sister. Becca could never, ever talk to me again. I knew if I read the diary, it would be like hearing NEW words from her, as if she were still alive. But this wasn't me grasping for a justification to read the journal, guilt-free. I needed real guidance, and who better to give it?

I walked across the hall, quietly letting myself into Becca's room and closing the door behind me. Nothing had changed inside, and my guess was it would be a while before anything did. Mom was still too raw, and Dad, well, he acted like nothing had happened. It turned out denial was a great coping mechanism.

I found the violin case under the bed where I left it, reclaimed the journal from its hiding place, and headed back to my room.

When I stepped into the hallway my mother surprised me. I must have startled her also because she jerked when she saw me and closed her eyes tight, as if she was fighting through a brain freeze after swallowing a large bite of ice cream. When she opened her eyes again her gaze went to the journal in my hand. I searched her face for recognition, or curiosity, about what I was holding or why I had it, but there was nothing.

"Dinner's ready," was all she said, turning around and making her way back downstairs.

I tossed the journal on my bed and followed her.

The two of us ate in complete silence. She didn't even bother to find out how my day went. I couldn't blame her and welcomed the silence. I thought about flipping the tables and asking about her day, but I already knew the answer. It was another day without Becca, and that was all that mattered.

I moved my food around the plate for a while, then excused myself and told her I was tired and would probably go to bed early, which wasn't true. I really only wanted to get back to my room… and the journal. I briefly wondered if she resented the fact that she had to take medication to sleep at night while I slept like a baby, but I doubt she was thinking that way.

Once I was back in my room, I closed the door, kicked off my shoes, sat cross-legged on my bed, and stared at the journal.

Time for one last gut check. Do this, or not? Once I read the first page there was no going back, because I knew I wouldn't be able to stop myself. Becca would want this. She would want me to help her friend, right?

The last words Taggart said before I threw him out of my car repeated over and over in my head. *"This is not a prank. Your father WAS murdered."*

I opened the journal.

The first line of the opening entry read:

I love Taggart McGill.

Fourteen

March 20th

<u>I love Taggart McGill</u>.

I should probably explain that, though I'm not sure why. This is only for me anyway. Nobody is ever supposed to read it. I guess it will be cool to read it again when I'm old and have kids of my own. But the real reason I'm writing this down is because a friend suggested I do it to help crystalize my thoughts… so I guess it makes sense. Sort of. This feels weird.

Let's start at the beginning.

Last night I had a date with a boy. It wasn't my first date, but it was definitely the most unusual. His name is Taggart McGill, and it wasn't exactly a date. It started off that way, but it turned into something else and that's why I'm writing this.

You know what, that wasn't actually the beginning. I should back up a little more.

I was born December 5th 1998. Ha ha… just joking.

My name is Rebecca Underwood… everyone calls me Becca and I like it that way. My older sister (by just 11 months) is Cassie, some people call her Cass, but she prefers Cassie. We live with our parents here in New Haven, Georgia and have all my life. We used to have a cat named Whisper, but our neighbor ran over her last year. He was really sorry… and so was I.

A week ago Taggart stopped me when I was walking home from Tammy's house (a friend who lives nearby). Taggart lives just down the street from us with the Wilsons. He doesn't have any parents himself because he was abandoned (or at least I thought so — more on that later) when he was really young. He's lived with a lot of people in New Haven and now the Wilsons are giving it a try.

I didn't know much about Taggart before I went out with him. I've seen him around school and everything, but he's a year older than me. He's a freshman and I'm still in junior high. Oh yeah, he's REALLY cute. God, I would absolutely die if he ever read this. It's hard to tell he's cute though because of the way he dresses and his long hair hangs down in his face a lot. I can totally see him as the lead singer for one of the bands I like (Drag The River or Double Clutch), but trust me, he be cute!

The thing is, what I did know about Taggart wasn't very nice. He was always by himself, never with any friends, and I heard he was always getting into trouble with his teachers. When we found out he was moving in down the street I overheard Cassie talking to some of her friends and she didn't sound too happy about it.

Me… I guess I didn't really care one way or another.

That is until he asked me out. Like I said before, he stopped me when I was walking home. I heard someone call out my name from behind me, my full name… Rebecca, and when I turned around it was Taggart. Every time I had seen him before, he was always wearing dark colored hoodies or long sleeve shirts with jeans full of holes. But on that day, he was wearing a pair of brand new cargo pants and a light blue t-shirt. His hair was also nicely brushed away from his face. He looked… noticeable if that makes sense.

Anyway, he came straight out and asked WOULD YOU LIKE TO GO OUT WITH ME? It was a question, but the way he said it almost sounded robotic, as if he had rehearsed it in front of a mirror a hundred times beforehand. If I hadn't been so shocked, I might have laughed.

I have to admit (and if you can't be honest in your own journal when can you), my first reaction was to say NO. I was afraid of what my friends would say, what Cassie would say. But then I thought about how he had obviously changed his clothes and brushed his hair for this, and the courage it took to ask a complete stranger on a date, and it made me wonder. Why me? Of all the girls in our two schools, why did he pick me to ask out? And there was the fact he was so darn cute!

So it was curiosity more than anything else that made me say YES. He smiled – have I mentioned what a great smile he has? His whole face changes… for the better… and his dimpled chin really stands out – then he suggested a date and time, to which I agreed, and then he ran away like he'd just set the timer on a bomb. What had I gotten myself into?

Our date was last night. I didn't tell my parents because I knew they wouldn't let me go out with a 15-year-old with only a learner's permit, much less a boy with a reputation. I told them I was going to Tammy's house to study. It was the first time I'd outright lied to them (other than a few minor fibs) and it made me feel dirty, but I wasn't going to back out on the date and this was the only way it would happen. Cassie knew what was going on, because I tell her everything… mostly… but she wasn't too happy about it.

Taggart picked me up on the corner (he was wearing the same clothes he had on when he asked me out) and we headed off for the Burger Barn. Right away I could tell he was uncomfortable. He answered all of my questions with just a couple words, and wouldn't say anything unless I started things off. If he had any friends I'd have thought the date was a dare and he really didn't want to be there at all.

We had just begun eating our burgers (I actually ordered chicken strips) when he suddenly put his down and told me he was sorry. I asked him what he was apologizing for and he told me he had never been on a date before (like that was a big surprise) and he didn't know what he was doing. I told him that was okay, but then he said that he had never even had a real "conversation" with someone his own age before. That kind of shocked me. I mean how does someone grow up and not talk to the other kids? So I asked him that, and his reply was a bit strange… but maybe not. <u>He said he didn't need anything from anybody</u>. He described teenagers as being superficial and cliché, and getting to know them was a waste of time.

This is probably a good spot to point out that Taggart didn't talk like a normal teenager. At least not any I've been around. He sounded more like an adult… with his use of big, complicated words… but underneath that, he acted like a small child in lots of ways. Even I have learned that there were no absolutes in the world, but he seemed to look at things as either black or white. Anyway, I'm getting ahead of myself. Sorry.

So I asked him if he thought so little of us (yes — to use one of my dad's favorite lines -- my panties were definitely in a twist), then why did he ask me out on the date. This is what he said… and this is his word for word answer… BECAUSE I WANTED YOU TO BE MY FRIEND.

I know… right?! My heart melted right there and then. Of course I asked the natural follow up question: Why do you want to be friends with me? But he didn't have a good answer for that, at least not one he was willing to share with me, so I didn't push it. But I did ask him something else.

That must mean you need something from me, right?

That's when he smiled again and OH MY GOD… I didn't care what he said after that. I made up my mind I wasn't going anywhere. But what he did say sealed the deal. He said… I've recently decided I do need someone my own age to know me, and it's only fair that I reciprocate.

Okay, so maybe it wasn't the most romantic of lines and I doubt Nicholas Sparks (one of Mom's favorite authors) would be using that one anytime soon, but still, I was intrigued. I pointed out to him that a date wasn't the only way to do that, which seemed to embarrass him. So I told him as of right then our date was officially over… and our friendship was just beginning.

The first thing I told him was… as part of our new friendship… he didn't have to dress any different for me and I actually thought he looked dorky in those clothes. That earned me another smile.

He told me that I couldn't tell anybody about what we discussed when we were together. Privacy is VERY VERY important to him, *and he wouldn't be able to talk to me if he thought I would repeat any of it to another soul. I promised him, even though I knew it would probably be the hardest thing I would ever do… not telling Cassie about this… because we share most everything, but I did. I told Taggart how hard it was going to be for me… to keep everything inside… and that's when he suggested I start a journal. He said he keeps one and it helps "crystalize" his thoughts (yes… that was his word not mine).*

We finished eating our meal and instead of going to the movie he drove us to an isolated spot on the beach I had never been to before… and I thought I had explored everywhere in New Haven. He spread a blanket he kept in the trunk of his car on the sand and we sat down together and talked.

And talked and talked and talked and talked and talked and talked and talked and talked.

It was as if someone popped the top on a can of Coke that had been shaken. Taggart's thoughts spewed out everywhere, and I sat there listening to it all… mesmerized. When time came for me to be back home, I didn't want it to end, so I had him drive me back and wait down the street. I checked in like normal, said goodnight to everybody, then turned around and snuck out my bedroom window. Before that happened Cassie hounded me to tell her how things went. I told her I was tired and I'd fill her in in the morning. She didn't really like that, but Taggart was waiting for me. I jumped back in his car and we returned to our spot (which it has now been dubbed) and talked some more.

And talked and talked and talked and talked and talked and talked and talked and talked.

When the sun started coming up… which was the most beautiful sunrise I'd ever seen… we packed up and Taggart drove me home. Before I left I gave him a hug… and to be honest… it was so awkward I wonder if he had ever been hugged before… or if he had let himself be hugged.

I climbed back in my bedroom window just over an hour ago. I sat on my bed for a while, then I remembered I had bought this notebook with the intention of jotting down original music (yeah — that never happened), so I pulled it out and I've been writing ever since.

I've learned so much about Taggart McGill in one night. Some of it is downright horrifying, other parts broke my heart. He bared his soul to me and it took my breath away. The fact that someone like him, with such a sharp mind and a confused heart, could be walking down the same halls as the rest of us and nobody has a clue of what the true person is like, just blows my mind. I've decided that he's the best kept secret in New Haven… and now he's my secret.

I REALLY want to tell the whole school what I've learned, to set the record straight and burn off the fog of negativity that surrounds him. But I can't, and I won't. Not even with Cassie. I'll feed her as few details as I can about last night, but that's it. Taggart has opened my eyes and not violating his trust is more important than what other people might think of him, or me.

I love Taggart McGill, but not in a romantic way (but maybe someday).

He is my friend.

More importantly… I am his first.

I hear Cassie moving across the hall, so it's time to put this aside. More to come later.

Fifteen

I awoke, disoriented, to music blaring from my alarm clock. I was still wearing my clothes from the night before and I was on top of my covers, not in my bed. Something stiff poked me in the side when I rolled over, it was Becca's journal. I realized I had cried myself to sleep. I touched my face and felt the salt from tears that had dried there.

I remembered thinking I wasn't going to be able to go any further after reading the first entry. Her words… her wit… her feelings… her expectations for the future, it all brought the pain crashing down like an avalanche. I cried the hardest then. I could have stopped reading and known what I needed to know about Taggart, but just as I predicted, I was down the rabbit hole and there was no turning back. Over the course of those few hours, I ran the gauntlet of feelings, spending equal time giggling… then sobbing. I made it all the way up to her very last entry, written the morning she died, but I couldn't go any further. The emotional whiplash and exhaustion were too much for me and I couldn't bring myself to read those final words.

Every entry Becca made in her journal started with the same four words… *I Love Taggart McGill*. Now I knew why. I also understood why Taggart was in Becca's room searching for the journal. For a person like him, to have a journal like this found and its contents public knowledge was beyond terrifying. If I had any hope of developing a friendship between us, he couldn't know that I'd read the journal— which would be next to impossible since I already wanted to give him the biggest 'I'm sorry' hug ever.

I dragged myself out of bed, buried Becca's journal deep in my underwear drawer, and then jumped into the shower to get ready for school. While hot water just short of scorching battered the back of my head, my mind wandered to what I learned during the night. Most of what I discovered confirmed what Mr. Stevens and the Wilsons had relayed to me, but what surprised me even more were the things I learned about Becca herself. The biggest shocker… she was sure she was going to make it into the Pearlman conservatory (*Pearlman…Schmerlman*), and she dreaded it. She really disliked how Mom had turned her love of music into a competition. Of course, she would never say that to Mom, keenly aware of how that would crush her, but it ate at her and I think she would have soured on playing music at all if it hadn't been for Taggart encouraging her.

There were lots of other revelations.

She was considering becoming a vegan.

She almost got a tattoo of a violin on the small of her back, but she backed down at the last minute.

She didn't like going to church. She found it to be fake and not unlike a poorly run cult.

She didn't think much of my boyfriend, Jason, labeling him *empty calories*, but she never said as much to me.

She wondered if I had slept next to the pod, a reference to one of her favorite horror movies, *Invasion of the Body Snatchers*. She was right, I had.

For some reason she was fixated on whether or not our parents were going to get divorced.

She was really disappointed that I got the car I did, and she ended up with a hand-me-down, but for the most part she was comfortable playing the role of the 'second child'. She felt guilty sometimes about the attention Mom showered on her because of music, but she knew I was cool with it and that helped a lot.

It tore her up that she couldn't tell me the truth whenever I would question her relationship with Taggart and the things I accused him of doing. She wished I could be more open-minded and tolerant. I cried more than a few tears over that one.

As I read the entries Becca made over the span of multiple years I noticed the subtle change in the way she expressed herself and questioned how much of that was her growing up and maturing and how much was due to Taggart's influence. What was it Taggart had said about how Becca felt about pranks? *They only had power if the ones they are targeting gave it to them. What you think of yourself is all that really matters. Getting angry serves no purpose and only fuels their inner-demons.* Was that really Becca… or was it Taggart? I quickly tossed out that thought. There was no denying that Taggart was a powerful force in Becca's life. I witnessed that firsthand. But she was not some sort of disciple. Taggart only needed… wanted… one friend, but Becca still tried to be friendly to everyone. She might have been spurned because of her ties to an outcast, but she didn't shun others. Becca was her own person.

I hurriedly finished getting ready for school, although I had no intentions of going. Despite getting next to no sleep last night and being an emotional wreck, I was becoming more and more energized. My purpose for reading Becca's journal was to answer the multitude of questions about Taggart McGill, least of which was his trustworthiness. I now had my answer and that could mean only one thing.

There was a good chance a murderer was loose in New Haven and that person was ultimately responsible for my sister's death.

I debated taking this to my parents, but quickly decided it was too soon. All Taggart had was a suspicious mosquito bite and vague references to it happening before, definitely not enough to involve anyone else. There had to be something more that he wasn't telling us.

I shoved my phone into my bag and rushed out of my room. At the bottom of the stairs I yelled to Mom, whom I heard futzing around in the kitchen, that I wasn't interested in breakfast and had to get to school early.

"Oh, okay honey. Have a good day."

As I pulled on the front door I almost ran into Jason, standing there with his arm raised poised to knock on the door.

"Whoa, what's the hurry?" Jason asked. He was dressed in jeans and a plaid shirt, except instead of his old boots, he had donned a pair of black Nike trainers. I couldn't remember ever seeing Jason NOT wearing his cowboy boots. He would wear them even when we went to the beach. I was never sure which was more true, he was afraid of the water, or he loved those boots.

"What are you doing here?" I asked, deliberately dodging his question because I was in a hurry and I didn't want to explain things to him.

Jason shifted around and fidgeted with the strap his keys were attached to.

"I wanted to catch you before you headed to school and make sure you knew I had nothing to do with the trash barrel thing yesterday."

"You could have just called or sent a text."

"I know, but I wanted to tell you in person. I looked for you during lunch yesterday, but I couldn't find you."

"I know it wasn't you, Jason, but I bet you know who did it."

"Stooch swears to God it wasn't him. He knew you and Delta would blame him."

"Oh Jason, open your eyes. Never mind. Are we done, because I've really got to go."

"I… uh… I wanted to ask you something." He was pulling at his collar.

"What is it?"

"Am I still escorting you for Homecoming? You know the parade is tomorrow."

Internally I kicked myself. This was a conversation I should have had already, but things have been, well, I've been distracted. I shrank in front of him.

"I'm really sorry, I should have said something before now. I've already told the school that I'm dropping out of the Homecoming Court."

"Then what should I do with the corsage I bought you?"

I shrank another couple inches.

"I'll pay you back for it."

"I don't want you to pay me back, and I really don't want you to push me away."

"Jason—"

"Please, Cass, can't I get a second chance? I swear I can change."

I put my hand on his shoulder. "Maybe you can, Jason. But you need to do it on your own. Now I really need to go, okay?"

The dip of his head and the crestfallen look on his face as he turned away normally would have broken my heart, but not today. I'd put myself through so much emotional stuff in the past twenty-four hours that I was numb to it, so I dashed to my car and sped off.

I didn't have far to go because the Wilsons' house was a mere block over and two streets up. I parked next to the curb and as I walked briskly to the front door, I noticed the bike that Taggart had been riding the past couple days was lying in a yard, near the curb, a couple of houses down. I smiled as I knocked on the door. Taggart may have learned his lesson, but the owner certainly hadn't.

Mr. Wilson answered the door.

"Hi, Mr. Wilson. Has Taggart left for school yet?"

"Yes, he has. He's been gone fifteen minutes or more."

"Thank you," I replied and ran back to my car.

Taggart was probably walking to school, having abandoned the bike, and with a fifteen-minute head start, he was probably still on Bryant-Lynn Expressway, unless he took a few shortcuts through private properties, which was totally possible. But that wasn't the case. I caught up to him halfway between his house and school.

Approaching him from behind Taggart looked like a drifter, wandering aimlessly between random destinations, kinda like John Rambo at the beginning of my dad's favorite movie – *First Blood*. His hood was up, backpack on his shoulders, and he strolled along as if he didn't have a care in the world.

I pulled onto the easement in front of him, shifted the car into park and looked into my rearview mirror. He came to a complete halt, staring at the rear of my car, then slowly started walking again and approached the passenger's side. I rolled down the window, expecting him to stick his head in, but he continued walking leisurely past my car as if I wasn't there.

"HELLO," I called out, but Taggart pretended not to hear me. I was pretty hard on him yesterday, so this might not be so easy.

I jumped out of the car and jogged to catch up to him, falling in step when I did.

"Need a lift?" I asked.

Taggart's earbuds were in place, but I knew he could hear me even though he gave no indication I was there. I'd never experienced a cold shoulder this frigid before, but I was undeterred. I couldn't allow myself to be.

"Listen, I'm sorry about yesterday."

No reaction. I doubled my steps to pull ahead of him, trying to catch his eyes, but he was staring down at the ground.

"I wasn't very nice, and I hate myself for it."

Taggart kicked an empty can in his path, sending it flying down the embankment.

"Please let me make it up to you. Let me give you a ride."

Taggart slowed down, then stopped completely. He still hadn't looked at me.

"You're offering me a lift?" he finally said.

"Is that so surprising?"

"Yes."

"Well, I am."

Taggart looked up the road in the direction of our school, contemplating a decision, then without a word turned around and walked back to my car. Again, I hurried to catch up. Taggart tossed his backpack into the rear seat and we both climbed in.

Instead of driving off I swiveled around and faced him directly. His attention was on the strand of horsehair hanging from the rearview mirror.

"It feels strange being in her car without her," he said, his eyes still on the bowstring.

I didn't respond right away, allowing us both to savor a happy memory. Then it was time to ask a strategic question.

"The other day in my sister's room… what were you looking for?"

Taggart's gaze moved from the rearview mirror to somewhere down the road. "It's not important."

Exactly the answer I was expecting. "If you tell me what it is, I'll look for it and see you get it back."

"It doesn't matter anymore. Can we get moving now?"

He was obviously eager to change the subject, which I had no problem doing because I had accomplished what I wanted. "Fine, but I should probably tell you I'm not going to school."

Taggart looked confused. "You're not?"

"No."

"Then where are you… and apparently I, going?"

"Back to the police station."

Taggart's eyebrows dipped and he tilted his head to one side. "And why would we do that?"

"Because I was hasty yesterday and shouldn't have passed judgment on your theory without hearing all the details first. But I think the police should hear them also."

Taggart looked at me intently. "What changed your mind?"

This is where I had to be careful. If he sensed I found the journal and read it, he would withdraw like a turtle into its shell. But asking him what he was after in her room should have given him the impression I was ignorant of its existence, and therefore not suspect anything.

"I thought a lot about what Becca would do if she was here. She would give you the benefit of the doubt. She always did. So that's what I'm doing," I said. I felt at ease saying it because it wasn't technically a lie.

Taggart seemed to accept my explanation, because he relaxed his shoulders.

"We can't go to the police."

"Why not?"

"Two reasons. The first is that it would be an exercise in futility. What I have is very thin, and they'll laugh us out of the station."

"Okay. And the second reason?"

Taggart looked off into the horizon, refusing to answer me.

"Please. Tell me what you know, so I can make up my own mind."

He looked back at me, then sighed deeply.

"Do you know how rare it is to die of a brain aneurysm?"

"No. Pretty rare, I guess."

"Roughly thirty thousand people suffer a ruptured aneurysm annually in the US, and approximately forty percent of those die from it. That's twelve thousand people a year. If you were to extrapolate that number to the states based upon their relative populations, it would work out to be three hundred and sixty here in Georgia per year, or one per every twenty-eight thousand residents. The population of New Haven is a hair under that. Statistically, we should experience one death due to a ruptured aneurysm per year. That would mean that over the past ten years we could expect to see ten deaths attributed to this malady. Do you know how many we have experienced in that time frame?"

I shook my head, because not only didn't I know the answer to his question, I wasn't entirely sure I had kept up with his facts and numbers.

"Twenty-one."

My mouth dropped open. I might not have understood everything he said, but I knew that double normal was a lot.

"Of course that may be a bit biased because I had to factor in the number of deaths attributed to unexplained causes and filter out the average heart disease deaths. Also, it totally discounts any correlational influence of geographic factors different parts of the US may have, but I would say it's definitely within one or two."

"One or two what?"

"Bodies."

"You think someone is triggering people to have aneurysms and making it look like natural causes?"

"I told you it was thin, but to me it's obvious."

I thought I had prepared myself to go with anything Taggart might say, but this was incredible, if it were true.

"How long have you known about this?"

"Since Monday, when Chewy told us he thought his dad was murdered."

"You worked all that out in one day?"

"Actually, that night."

"Are you some kind of genius or something? Do you have one of those—what are they called—photographic memories?"

"Eidetic memory, and the answer is no."

"Then, how do you know all that stuff?"

"Someone doesn't need to possess a bizarre memory tool to be classified as highly intelligent. I'll admit to being what some consider gifted, but most of what I told you could be sourced on the internet."

"Half of the material on the internet is fake, surely you know that?"

"That's an exaggeration, but certainly you need to know where to look."

"So, what made you believe Chewy in the first place?"

Once again, Taggart looked away without an answer.

I put my hand on the shift column. "We have to tell the police about this."

Taggart reached over and put his hand on top of my own, preventing me from shifting into drive. "We can't," he repeated calmly.

"And why not," I snapped back, allowing my frustration to seep out again.

"Because someone from the department might be responsible."

Sixteen

Taggart's warning caused me to recoil and pull my hand away from his. What he said had taken me by surprise, but I managed to recover quickly.

"What about the Wilsons' son, Matt? Surely you can trust him?"

"Yes, but he's only a patrolman. He helped me by calling in a favor so we could see the autopsy report, but he won't be much use beyond that."

"But somebody has to do something, right?"

"What would you have them do, put an APB out on statistics? You said it yourself, why would anyone want to kill Mr. Ledbetter? Where is the motive? There's just not enough to bother the police with, and if by chance our murderer is a member of law enforcement, we've then alerted them to our suspicions."

"So what do we do?"

"Right now, we get to school before we're late."

I wasn't happy with the lack of a plan, but I couldn't think of a better course of action. I shifted the car into drive and pulled back onto the road.

We had only gone a couple miles when I had a thought.

"What about the others? The other ones who died mysteriously? Maybe there was a motive to kill one or two of them and this is like those movies where the killer hides the true motive by taking out a bunch of others."

Taggart's expression when I glanced in his direction made me regret opening my mouth.

"Over the span of multiple years?" he replied, using equal amounts of skepticism and sarcasm in his tone.

"Okay, maybe that was stupid. I'm just trying to help."

"It's best to wait to involve others until we have more," he said.

"We? What's this *We* Kemosahbee? I was just trying to convince you to take this to the police. I know I said I wanted to help, but I'm no detective… and neither are you."

"Maybe so, but I possess something the police do not. Something very valuable."

"And what is that?" I asked.

"Belief."

"About that, you still haven't told me why. What was it that convinced you to help Chewy in the first place? I was there, and it was like a light bulb went on in your head. What are you not telling me?"

Stealing a look in his direction, I could tell he had no intention of answering. He turned away from me, facing the scenery as it passed by. I was quickly learning that Taggart was the Fort Knox of secrets. Becca held the key to that vault, but he still kept a few mysteries from her. I guess that was only natural. I mean, who is ever one hundred percent open with anyone? We all keep secrets. From what he'd told Becca and she subsequently wrote in her journal, he even withheld information from his own psychiatrist. But what was he hiding now? More important, could it come back and bite me in the ass?

"I need to speak with Chewy again," Taggart said, still looking out his side of the car. "I have more questions for him."

"Okay, we can all have lunch together. What then?"

We were approaching the school, but Taggart remained silent. By the time we pulled into my parking space, Taggart still hadn't answered. I threw the car into park and was surprised when I looked over at him.

He had scrunched up his face like he'd sucked on a lemon, closing one eye shut and tilting his head to the side. His face went completely blank for a second and then I thought he was going to cry. My heart ached for him. Becca made it clear in her journal that the simple sharing of information that the rest of the world took for granted was extremely difficult for Taggart. The stuff that was more personal, protected, was pure torture. It always took a toll when he shared. I witnessed him this way before when he told me about Becca's philosophy about pranks, but I didn't know what it was at the time. I did now, and that told me that whatever he was about to say was painful for him.

When his emotional spasm subsided, he looked at his hands—took a deep breath—and said, "I'm not sure what we do next, but I have a request."

I killed the engine.

"We're in the favor asking stage already?" I said, deciding to keep things light. "Wow. Give a guy one lift and he thinks he owns you."

"I said request."

"Tomayto, tomahto. Fine, but you're not going to ask me to Homecoming are you, because I've already had to rain on someone's parade about that today."

Taggart looked at me like I had just quoted him the lyrics to a Taylor Swift song.

"Never mind. What's the favor?"

"I need you to quit your job at the Animal Hospital, at least for a little while."

My ears burned. Why was this guy always doing that to me? One minute I thought we were getting along, maybe actually becoming friends and the next he'd say something that made my blood boil.

I took a deep breath before I replied.

"Why on earth would you ask me to do that?"

"It's a precaution, but a very necessary one."

"A precaution? Precaution against what?"

"Bad intentions."

"Because you think someone at the clinic is this murderer?"

"Possibly, yes."

"Taggart… from everything you've told me, anyone could be this murderer. Why someone at the clinic more than anyone else?"

He stared at me.

"If you want me to do this, then you have to give me a reason. You need to talk to me, Taggart."

Taggart looked back down at his hands.

"The owner of the Animal Hospital moved to town twelve years ago and it was shortly after that the unexplained deaths began."

I was aware that Dr. Weathers worked for another clinic in New Haven before opening his own vet hospital, but I had no idea when he moved to town or whether Taggart was lying.

"I know what I'm asking is hard, especially since you're interested in veterinary medicine as a career, but I don't ask it lightly. If we push this and we're not careful, we can expect retaliation. And if that happens… I won't know where to look. I just—"

"Okay."

Taggart straightened up in his seat and whipped his head around to face me. "What?"

"I'll do it. I asked you for a reason and you gave me one. I don't believe Dr. Weathers has anything to do with this, but I can tell him I came back too soon, and he'll understand. Fair enough?"

"Yes."

I cocked my head to the side. "Is that all I get?"

"I don't comprehend."

"Usually when someone grants another person a favor, and a really big one I might add, they would expect to hear a *thank you* in return. I'm just saying."

"Thank you," Taggart said, accompanied by what might have been a smile, but it disappeared so quickly it was difficult to tell.

I smiled back. There was no way I would believe Dr. Weathers was involved in this crazy story, but Taggart had opened up to me and I needed to reward him for that so we could build trust. It was a small price to pay.

"That must have stung," I said, which earned me a real smile in return. Becca was right… his whole face did change when he smiled.

"We'll meet again at lunch?" he said.

"I'll grab Chewy and meet you at the same table we were at before."

We both exited my car and headed to the school. I watched as the swarm of students in the hallway swallowed up Taggart.

Walking through the hallways between classes, I noticed all of the Homecoming decorations that I had obviously missed the two days prior and realized what a head case I had been. Was I still a head case now? Probably, though to a lesser degree. It seemed as if I've been inside my head for so long… ever since wakening up at the hospital… that the past two weeks were a blur to me. Life had continued on, but I hadn't taken much notice. I wasn't feeling apologetic, however. Sorry folks… experiencing a life event here… leave a message and I'll get back to you later.

Arriving at study hall before anyone else, I took the same seat Delta had moved us to yesterday. I had just put away my books when Mr. Wilkins startled me by maneuvering his lanky body into the next chair. It felt odd seeing a teacher in another teachers' classroom, especially sitting in a student's desk.

"How are we doing, young lady?"

"I'm doing fine Mr. Wilkins. Things are getting better each day."

"Good. Good. Keep in mind, there will be good days and bad days. When I lost my wife, I had a terrible time adjusting at first. Eventually things even out. I understand you missed some classes yesterday afternoon."

Gotta love that teacher grapevine.

"Yes, sir. It turned out to be one of those bad days you mentioned."

"Who's having a bad day?" Delta asked when she appeared next to Mr. Wilkins. I internally winced when I saw how much make-up she had on. I loved her to death, but sometimes she could put that to a test.

"No one. You two keep it that way, understand?" Mr. Wilkins said as he extracted himself awkwardly from the chair.

Once Mr. Wilkins was gone, Delta took over the seat and was on me.

"So, what's the what?"

I wanted to blurt out that Taggart McGill was definitely not who put the tampons in her purse to embarrass her. I also wanted to set the record straight about all the other things Taggart had on his rap sheet. But if I caved in and explained everything to her, no matter how many pinky swears I made her take, it would eventually leak out and Taggart would know I had talked to the Wilsons, or even worse, read the journal. No one would ever know the true story about when he was accused of narking on kids who cheated on a make-up English exam. Those kids actually paid him to provide the answers—from memory—and later they broke into his locker and stole back their money. Becca told the teacher, much to Taggart's displeasure. Nor would anyone know the true story about Taggart and Tim Robertson's fight when they were juniors and Tim was expelled but Taggart wasn't. Taggart's good grades weren't the reason he was spared. It turned out Tim had dragged Becca into the boy's bathroom, which everyone knew Taggart avoided at all cost. Taggart went in to rescue my sister, but Tim was so chicken-shit he pulled a knife. Taggart was able to get Tim in a bear hug and Becca ran and got a teacher.

I could spend the entire period telling Delta about all the misperceptions and the untruths about Taggart I'd read in Becca's journal, but I wouldn't.

"Not much," I answered. Given our last conversation, I knew she wouldn't be satisfied with that answer. It was time for operation redirection. "What are you doing for homecoming?"

We spent the period discussing her Friday night plans. She already had another date to the game, no big surprise there. When Stooch and the others sat down in the back, neither Delta nor I paid them any attention. *Don't give them the power*, I heard Becca say in my mind.

When the bell rang for lunch, I grabbed my book bag.

"Are you going to the Barn for lunch?" Delta asked.

I shook my head. "I'm going to have lunch with Taggart."

"Are you still on that ride?"

"Call me tonight," I said, ignoring her question, choosing instead to act as if I was late for an appointment.

I found Chewy, and his constant companion Tunes, coming out of the band room. Tunes saw me first, tapping Chewy on the shoulder and pointing in my direction.

"Hey guys, heading to lunch?" I asked.

Chewy looked at me like I had two heads.

"Yeah… why?"

"Because Taggart and I would like to ask you some more questions, if you don't mind."

"I thought you told me to stay away from Taggart? That he was up to something?"

"Well, it turns out I was mistaken. Sorry about that. Let's go, he's at that same table as Monday."

"Wait a minute. So now you're saying you believe him… that my father was murdered?"

I looked around to see if anybody in the crowded hallway had heard Chewy's question, but everyone seemed oblivious to us. I stepped in closer and lowered my voice.

"Keep it down, loudmouth. Can we just go out to the patio? Taggart will answer your questions."

"Okay," Chewy said.

The two boys fell in behind me as I weaved my way through the crowd to the patio doors. Outside Taggart was sitting at his usual table. Chewy and I took the seats across from him, and Tunes stood off to the side.

"Hey, dude. I hear you have some questions for me?" Chewy started, rocking as always.

"I do. How well do you know your father's store?"

"First things first," Chewy replied, then turned to look at me. "I want to know why you changed your mind. How do I know both of you aren't yanking my junk?"

Taggart made a face. "Yanking your junk?"

"You know what I mean."

"Ewwww, Chewy." I looked to Taggart and jerked my head in Chewy's direction. "Tell him what you told me about the statistics."

He did. He told him everything, in more detail than he used for me. The twelve thousand people dying each year from brain aneurysms, three hundred and sixty here in Georgia, and that New Haven should statistically experience one a year. That we had experienced twice our projected number over the last ten years. Hearing it all again, I was as shocked and more convinced that something was definitely wrong in our small town.

"So, you're saying my dad was murdered by a serial killer. Right here in New Haven?" Chewy solemnly said when Taggart finished.

"It appears so. I ask you again, how familiar are you with your dad's store?"

"Pretty well, I guess. I mean, I was in there all the time with him."

"Did he go out for lunch, or did he eat in?"

"I told you he was a heath nut. He brought his lunch with him every day, and he ate in his office."

"Does the store have security cameras?"

"Yes, two… no three. He added one a while ago."

"Where are they located?"

"One that points at the main entrance, one that points at the registers, and one in the storage room."

Listening to Taggart interrogate Chewy was like a high school version of Law & Order. The whole thing felt surreal. As they did the day before, kids who walked by our table didn't try to hide their stares. A former member of the Homecoming Court was sitting with the class outcast and a couple of band nerds. We were turning the social-universe on its ear, but I couldn't care less. In for a penny, in for a pound. And I was curious, which caused me to ask what I thought was an obvious question.

"What's the camera in the storage room for?"

"That's the one he added last month. He had problems with workers stealing from him, so he added one back there to catch them in the act," Chewy answered, obviously eager to explain.

"Do you know how often the recordings reset?" Taggart started again, glaring at me while he talked. I think I was being admonished for the interruption.

"Sure. The two out front will keep a week, but the one in the storage room will hold a month?"

"Damn it," Taggart exclaimed, punctuating it by slapping his open hand on the table.

"Is that bad?" I asked.

"It means if the person who did this to Mr. Ledbetter did so in the store, we no longer know who was there that day because the tapes have already been recorded over."

"Did what exactly? Used a poisonous mosquito to bite Chewy's dad and give him an aneurysm?"

"I said that the autopsy report documented a mosquito bite on Mr. Ledbetter's calf, I didn't say it *was* one. I believe it was in fact a puncture wound that looked like a bite, and yes, a substance was administered that resulted in the fatal brain bleed."

"What kind of substance?" Chewy said.

"I'm still researching that. There are numerous drugs that can induce aneurysms, but they all have other side-effects that are not present here."

"But, wouldn't he have felt that if somebody gave him a shot?" I asked.

"Depends on the needle gauge. If a micro-needle was used, he probably wouldn't have felt anything. However, the pain reduction will have to be balanced against the limitations of injection depth and volume. It's all a factor of reduced needle dimension, so he was most likely distracted in some way to keep him from noticing when it happened."

"That's something else we could have seen if we had the recordings," I added.

"What about the receipts?" Chewy blurted out. "The cash register receipts. We still have those."

"We can look at those, yes, but I really don't think the person we're after would be foolish enough to make a purchase with a credit card."

"I can tell you who was there."

Shocked, we all turned to the person who had just spoken: Tunes.

"He speaks," I said.

"Please explain," Taggart said, unconcerned with anything else.

"Yeah, Tunes, what gives?" Chewy added.

"The MAC address. You know, media access control address."

"Go on."

"Mr. Ledbetter had free Wi-Fi at his store. Any cell phone that attempts to connect to the network is automatically assigned a DHCP IP address, which is kept in a table on the server. That table will have the associated MAC address for the phone, along with the date and time it connected."

"So anybody who went into the store that day will have their MAC address on file?" Taggart asked.

"Yes. We can't use it to track the phone or determine who owns it, but if you give me a specific MAC address I can tell you if it was in the store that day."

"So… Tunes speaks and he's a nerd," I said.

"I prefer the term geek," he corrected, smiling.

"My apologies. And what if this person doesn't own a cell phone?"

Tunes reverted back to his silent-state and hunched his shoulders.

"Who wouldn't own a cell phone?" Chewy asked, slightly more agitated. "Do you have the list of names, the twenty-one who died? Maybe we can see who they were and find a pattern?"

"I've already done that. Nothing was apparent."

"We should all look at it," I suggested. "More eyes the better, right? You could have missed something."

Taggart frowned. "Doubtful."

"But possible. We can meet at your house after school."

"No," Taggart snapped. When he saw how everyone was looking at him, he softened his tone. "Not my house."

"Then we can meet at my house," I offered, once again inserting myself smack-dab in the middle of everything.

"Okay."

"We'll have to do it after dinner. Let's say 6:30?" I looked directly at Taggart when I said it.

Taggart nodded his head, but his scowl told me he was none too happy about it.

"This is great. You bring the list, and I'll bring the snacks," Chewy said.

"Don't get your hopes up, Chewy," I offered. "I doubt we can find something Taggart didn't."

Chewy smiled at me, but it was forced. I suddenly understood exactly how he felt. Taking action, doing something… anything, filled a void.

When Becca was yanked out of my life it brought down the walls on me. It left me shattered. I wondered if I could ever feel completely whole again. I was still struggling even now, but I realized that Taggart was the spackle for my reconstructed walls. He filled a void. But was that all he was to me… spackle?

The rim of Chewy's eyes had turned a shade of red I'd seen many times over the last couple weeks; my parent's eyes, in the eyes of countless friends and relatives, and in the mirror. He was fighting to hold back the tears. "Why would anyone do this?"

"I don't know," Taggart answered, even though Chewy's question wasn't directed to anyone in particular.

Maybe it was in the way he answered, I don't know. I couldn't put my finger on it, but I got the impression Taggart wasn't telling the truth.

Seventeen

Our small group, as odd as it was, stayed together for the rest of lunch, thinking of all sorts of insane theories about who our murderer was and why he/she/it (yes, even aliens were mentioned) was offing the residents of New Haven. Taggart remained mostly silent.

Before we parted, I offered Taggart a ride home after school, which he hesitantly accepted. Later that afternoon, as I watched him make his way to my car, I got the distinct impression he was uncomfortable.

"Where to?" I asked.

Taggart appeared confused. "Uh… home, I guess."

"Nope. Try again."

He was obviously flustered, which was my intention. I was no dummy. I knew that the only way I would feel on equal footing with him—and his giant intellect—was if I kept him off-balance.

"I need to get home," he said as he slipped on his seat belt.

"Why?"

"I… I have homework."

"Really? That's the best you can come up with? You probably treat homework the way the rest of us use dental floss."

"I floss."

No doubt, his teeth were almost perfect.

"I want the two of us to go somewhere and talk. And not about surveillance tapes or murderers. Can we do that, please?"

"Why?"

"Why what?"

Taggart paused, taking a deep breath through his flaring nostrils. "Why do you suddenly want to talk? You've never liked me, and the only reason you're here now is because you feel obligated to help Chewy."

His words hung in the air, their intensity and honesty taking me by surprise.

"Did Becca tell you I didn't like you?"

Taggart averted his eyes. "She said you didn't understand me."

That was pure Becca, never saying anything belittling about anyone, always finding a way to spin it in a positive way.

"Are you kidding? Listen, nobody understands you, except for Becca, and now I'm trying to do something about that. Would you rather I leave you alone?"

My words floated between us. They were more forceful than I'd intended, but this was never going to work if I always had to wear kid gloves.

"Where would you have us go?" Taggart finally asked.

I breathed an internal sigh of relief. "Thus my question when you got in the car. I want you to choose."

"Why?"

I sighed again, this time an actual intake and exhale of air, letting him know I was getting impatient with his questions.

"I want to learn more about you, and since you're not the most talkative person, I have to use other means. Where you choose to take us will tell me something about you."

The beginnings of a smile appeared at the corner of his mouth.

"What would you learn if I asked you to go to the Puck?"

The Puck was a local hangout for people our age that offered all sorts of non-electronic games, like pool tables and foosball, as well as a wide variety of arcade games.

"I'd know that you didn't really want to talk because you can't hear yourself think in there."

"And if I wanted you to take me to the city dump?"

"I'd know you had a sense of humor."

The beginnings of a smile had now turned into a grin. Then it disappeared.

"And if I asked you to go to the conservatory?"

The conservatory was located ninety minutes away in the nearby town of Crystal Springs. It was where Becca traveled three days a week for her music lessons.

"Why would you want to go there?"

"I miss her music."

I knew exactly what he was talking about. For the longest time I'd wondered why everything felt so different at the house, so empty, besides the obvious reason. Then it struck me, it was Becca's music. Whether she was working with Mom or playing for fun, the soothing music of her violin was ever-present. I couldn't believe there was once a time when I wanted to take that violin and smash it to pieces.

"I know what you mean, but you're stalling. Pick somewhere."

Taggart shifted in his seat, put his hands together as if he was going to pray, but instead tapped the tips of his forefingers against his mouth. I was about to suggest someplace like the beach, secretly hoping he would take me to his and Becca's secret location, but then he nodded his head once and dug into his pocket. He pulled out what looked like a small white pill. He held it in front of his face for a moment, just looking at it, and then popped it into his mouth.

"What was that?" I asked.

"A coping mechanism."

"You use pills as a coping mechanism?" This was something new. Becca had never mentioned anything about pills in her journal.

"This is the first time."

"What do you need a coping mechanism for?"

Now it was Taggart's turn for a deep sigh. "You want to interact, so we're going to interact. Head towards downtown."

I started up the car and drove, in my head running through the possible places we could be going in the middle of town. There was a small park, but it wasn't much. The word to describe it was quaint. There were some shops, antique stores, a dilapidated movie theater the town had been trying to renovate forever, and of course the city courthouse. A block over was a vacant lot where the farmers market would setup on Saturdays. The police station was a short walk from there, but then why wouldn't he just say "police station" instead of downtown?

I was also wondering what the deal with the pill was. What was it? Where did it come from? Maybe it was something as minor as an aspirin. That was a coping mechanism, right, curing a headache? But he'd said it was his first time and how likely was it this was his first headache? And who took one aspirin anyway?

When we approached the courthouse circle, Taggart had me take a right and go down a side street a couple blocks. He pointed to a row of a dozen parking spots, all but one of them unoccupied, and directed me to park at the end on the left. Directly in front of us was an older building, well maintained, with two signs hanging on the brick wall. The bottom one was hand-carved and informed the reader they were in New Haven, population of 25,157.

The sign above, the larger of the two, read TRAILWAYS BUSLINE.

A chill went down my spine. I knew exactly where I was, but unsure of what to expect. Taggart had never taken Becca here, or at least she never wrote about it, but they had talked about it several times.

I turned to Taggart who was staring straight-ahead, sweat beading on his forehead. His breathing seemed measured, controlled, but otherwise normal.

"My mom and I arrived on a bus right here. I was four years old. The bus originated in Atlanta and was destined for Ft. Lauderdale, where we were supposedly going to see my grandmother. I don't remember any of that. In fact, I remember very little of my life before that day. The things I do remember are very silly and trivial; playing with a favorite toy, teaching myself to tie my own shoe, eating my first pancake. What I don't remember is anything important. Nothing about my father. I can't recall anything substantive of my life before New Haven. I have this mental block. My mind has formed a protective barrier around this certain memory and it won't allow me to move past it to access anything else… except a precious few. I understand why. Something happened on the day I arrived that was so horrible, so damaging to my psyche that my mind's only recourse was to bury it deep. Somewhere it couldn't hurt me. I didn't have any say in the matter. Still don't."

Taggart paused, his eyes still locked on the building in front of us.

"You see that gas station behind us?"

I looked into my rearview mirror and saw the Quick-Serve. I twisted around in my seat to get a better look out of the rear window, and that was when I remembered.

"That's Jason's. I mean it's his dad's. He owns a bunch of them around town, but I think this was his first."

My eyes locked onto the bathrooms on the right side of the building.

"I was found in the bathroom of that gas station with my mother. I was told no one knew how long I had been in there, but it had to be a long time. My mom had some kind of attack and died, leaving me in there all alone with her body. In the dark. They found a pre-paid cell phone on the toilet they think she was using to illuminate the room, but it lost its charge. I was four and apparently I couldn't get the door unlocked, or maybe I didn't even try, but whichever it was when they found me I was curled in a corner shivering like an abandoned puppy."

I began to notice that the way he was talking to me seemed more natural, less stilted and cold. I don't know if this was because he was reverting to a child's perspective of the experience or influence from the pill, but it unnerved me.

Taggart turned toward me, his lower lip drawn between his teeth. I knew better than to say anything, and even if I'd wanted to, I wasn't sure I could right then.

"That doesn't sound all that bad, does it? Being locked in a room with a dead body? In pitch-blackness? I mean, as far as terrible things go, I'd think that would be low on the list. Don't you think so? What's strange is how I can imagine it, but I can't remember it."

Tears flowed down my cheeks. I knew this story already, having heard it from the Wilsons and then reading it in Becca's journal, but hearing it come from his own lips was tearing me apart.

"She was your mother, Taggart, and you were only four."

"Yeah, I guess that makes it different. Do you want to know another thing that's weird, something else I have no memory of? Crying. I can't remember ever doing it, not once. I'm sure I did, I mean what infant wouldn't be able to cry. But here's the thing, even today, I still haven't. I didn't shed tears at Becca's funeral. That's not normal, right? Everyone should be able to cry."

He was still looking at me, but I didn't know how to answer his question, or if I should even try.

"I'm telling you all this, Cassie, for your own good. You seem determined to pick up where your sister left off, to honor her memory in a way, but you should understand what that means. I'm not normal. I had to take a pill prescribed by a psychiatrist just so I could tell you all this. Not only do I prefer solitude, but being around other people makes me extremely anxious. Most of the time I feel like I'm being smothered. At best I can be dismissive and uncaring, and when I'm at my worst, argumentative and unruly."

Wiping the wetness from my face, I felt like I could finally say something useful.

"You've been reading too many performance reviews from your teachers."

"They've not been wrong most of the time."

"But you didn't need the pill when you were talking with Becca? You seemed comfortable when you were around her."

"I… that… it was different with her."

"How?"

"It just was."

He was becoming agitated, cleaning dust off the dashboard where there wasn't any, so I let it drop. It was time to change the subject.

"So, how are you feeling now?"

Taggart's smile was ear to ear. A true Cheshire cat smile and it made me smile to look at it. I did find it alarming how fast his mood changed.

"I'm feeling great. Really relaxed, actually. I imagine this is what being intoxicated feels like."

"Then why don't you take your pill more often? Wouldn't that help?"

"Probably, but it has side-effects. The doctor said the drug would calm my nerves and boost my willingness to be open, but it would also dull everything else and I can feel that happening. I'm having to concentrate just to think, it's slowing my cognitive ability, and for me, that is almost as bad as the anxiety. You have no idea how hard I have to focus in order to sound semi-intelligent right now. The pill is making me feel stupid, and actually, I prefer the isolation."

"Oh."

"Except with you. I took the pill because --"

I was pretty sure he didn't mean to let that last part slip out because he immediately turned away and started playing with a loose thread on his hoody. It was too late though. Ever since I first started to delve into the mystery that called himself Taggart McGill, especially after I read my sister's journal, I found myself feeling something I never thought possible. Jealousy. What the two of them had was special, and I envied that. I was being selfish, but I began to wonder if maybe someday Taggart and I might develop the same bond. Now I knew that wasn't possible. Taggart required chemicals to be able to reach that same level of comfort with me that he and Becca achieved naturally, unforced. That made me more than a little sad, because I was beginning to really like this guy. It wouldn't be fair to take my disappointment out on him though. It was time to be the bigger person.

"I'm *very* glad you took the pill, but I want you to know something. Even though I'm loving this version of you, you never have to take the pill again to talk with me, not if you don't want to."

"How can you say that, knowing how I can be sometimes?"

"Because, now I understand the person inside, the real Taggart McGill. I can deal with everything else if you don't like the pill. And we need you sharp if we're going to catch this killer."

Taggart smiled again. I was surprised how easy they came now.

"I do have a question though," I said.

"Yes?"

"I don't suppose you can get any more of those pills? I'd really love to slip one into the drinks of a couple kids at school."

Eighteen

Taggart and I sat in front of the bus station for what seemed like an eternity. In reality, it was only a couple of hours. We chatted, A LOT, about nothing. That is, we didn't talk about the past. Nothing about Becca, or me, or Taggart's jaded history, or anything about the possible murderer stalking New Haven. We didn't mention anything about us. Nope. We had a real conversation about life in general and the future. It was awesome. Both of us were completely drained from the emotions of the past two weeks, so we gravitated towards subjects with no drama. I talked about which colleges I had been considering going to, wanting to become a veterinarian, where I would want to live and work, and who some of my idols were; my parents, my biology teacher Mr. Wilkins, one of my aunts who put herself through college. Taggart wasn't sure if he wanted to go to college, but rather spend the time traveling the world on a motorcycle to discover where he would fit. He wouldn't admit to having any idols, but he did say he found Bruce Springsteen's lyrics compelling. The longer we talked the more he'd slip between big picture topics such as his frustration with the leadership of our country or wondering how society had eroded into such a blame-oriented "bitchfest". Then he'd jump to trivial subjects like the overuse of speed bumps throughout the city. He didn't take anything at face value and was amazed at how many people did.

While we talked, I felt like an adult. Not the way you feel when talking to actual adults about adult things—that was more like a lecture, or a bizarre form of reverse osmosis. For me, talking to most adults was always about them trying to implant some sort of life lesson into my subconscious. Being treated as an equal whose opinion is taken seriously was rare. For Taggart, the pill was giving him an opportunity to express himself to another human being in a way he hadn't experienced before, not even with Becca, and I was the lucky recipient. Listening to the way his mind worked was hypnotic, and I recalled what I had read in my sister's journal. She had said that Taggart didn't talk like other boys, sounding more like an adult with his use of big words, but it was more than the words. He seemed more mature, wiser, sage even. But I could also see him struggling. At times, he would take long pauses, concentrating on something in the air only he could see, he was trying to remember something just out of his mind's reach, and if it wouldn't come to him, he'd smile and change the subject. It upset me to know how much that bothered him, but I didn't let that stop me from enjoying myself.

Our detour down the denial trail could last only so long, and I was the one who yanked us back on course.

"Can I ask you something, and you don't have to answer if it makes you uncomfortable?"

Taggart regarded me carefully, before nodding his head.

"I understand your need for privacy, I really do, but there have been so many rumors about you. Things you have supposedly done, that I now realize must all be pure fiction, or at least twisted versions of reality. You said earlier that I never liked you, and I'm embarrassed to admit you weren't wrong. I can't apologize enough for that. But Taggart, I didn't know you. How could I? How could anyone?"

"Is that an excuse for propagating misinformation?"

"I'm sorry?"

"The stories about me, the *twisted versions of reality* as you call them, you passed them along as truth also. Didn't you?"

I hung my head, ashamed and embarrassed, sorry now that I opened this particular can of beans.

"Cassie, I don't think less of you because of it. You were caught in a social dynamic beyond your ability to understand and therefore beyond your capability to resist."

My head snapped up. "Bullshit. I'm not some sort of lemming you know."

"That's not what I meant," he replied, his voice lower now. "You were operating with imperfect information."

"And that's my real question. Why didn't you ever stand up for yourself? Or why didn't you at least let Becca stand up for you? Why let us go on thinking those things?"

The weak smile Taggart gave me was the same one Mom used to give me when I asked her things she knew I wouldn't be able to understand the answer to.

"I struggle with contact with others, you know this, but it's more than that. It's hard to explain."

"I really wish you would try."

Taggart's nostrils flared as he drew in a deep breath.

"I view the world as a petri dish brimming with horrible pestilence, not actual viruses, but emotional contagions. Isolating myself in a vacuum, a bubble so-to-speak, one which is thoroughly clean and free of these contagions, is the only way I knew to protect myself from all that. I didn't— and still don't—have any interest in what anyone is saying about me. It remains outside of the bubble and doesn't factor into my life. Engaging in things such as dispelling rumors or correcting misreported facts not only doesn't interest me, it violates my vacuum. Besides, it's downright infuriating. Do you realize how much time you and your friends devote to that practice? I might not choose to engage, but I can't help but listen. Our generation has perfected the skill of character assassination under the guise of playful humor. We've evolved from driving a single dagger in the back to using hundreds of tiny pricks, innocently delivered via text messaging or other social media, but the effect is just as devastating. That kind of bombardment, over time, can overwhelm even the sturdiest of adults. But this is happening to teenagers. I believe the damage done has become the most undiagnosed mental crisis amongst people our age. And can you blame anyone for not seeing it? It's all around us. The most popular late-night comedians make outrageous social commentary and attack anyone who appears on the public's radar, absolving themselves with three simple words: *I'm just kidding.* That's actually the biggest joke of all."

Taggart paused. I thought he was having difficulties again, but then he smiled and continued. I remembered a line from Becca's first journal entry, about Taggart talking like a shaken can of Coke with a popped lid. I knew exactly what she meant now, and it was awesome.

"To be fair, during a recent spacewalk on the International Space Station by Russian astronauts, they discovered living organisms clinging to the outside. The astronauts identified the organisms as sea plankton that likely originated from Earth, but the team couldn't find a concrete explanation as to how these organisms made it there—or how they managed to survive. Thus an innocuous piece of road scum, one that undoubtedly hitched a ride numerous times, made it all the way up to the International Space Station and dispelled the notion that nothing can grow in a vacuum. So I guess I shouldn't be surprised that my viewpoint could be just as flawed. I attempted to insulate myself in an emotion-free void, but I failed to recognize the one element that kept that from happening. Me. I ended up being the contaminant in my own habitat."

My mind was spinning. Clearly, the tactic of keeping Taggart off-balance to level the playing field regarding his giant intellect was failing miserably, but somehow that didn't bother me. I enjoyed the feeling of being challenged. It gave me a rush, and I wanted more.

My phone chirped in my bag, interrupting us. I looked at the caller ID and felt a rush of humiliation.

"Hey, honey," my mom said when I answered the call. "Are you going to be much longer at work?"

"I'm headed home now." Although I'd contacted the vet clinic earlier and told Mary I wasn't coming in today, I hadn't told my mom yet and she was obviously assuming I was still there working late. I didn't see it necessary to dispel that belief.

"Well, dinner is ready and waiting."

"Uh… Mom… .is it okay if I bring a friend to dinner?"

"Delta? You know she's always welcome."

"No, I'm talking about someone else. Taggart McGill." I watched Taggart's face as I said this to gauge his reaction. Though Taggart had been over to help Becca study numerous times, he had never eaten with my family—to my great relief. I was sure that was his preference, completely backed by Becca. But I was determined to do things differently and luckily I saw only subtle surprise in Taggart's expression when I popped the question, not abject fear.

There was a long silence, so long in fact that I wondered if the call had been dropped, but then Mom spoke.

"Absolutely honey. He's most welcome."

"Great. We'll be there in a minute."

I hung up and extended my cell phone towards Taggart.

"Do you want to call the Wilsons and tell them you won't be home for dinner?"

Taggart looked at the phone in my hand, then at me, confused.

"You need to let them know," I said, pushing the phone at him again. "They'll be worried otherwise."

Taggart shrugged his shoulders and took my phone. The call he made consisted of five words—*I'm eating at Cassie Underwood's*—and I'm sure it wouldn't have taken place without my prompting, or the pill, or maybe a combination of both. In fact, I was a little surprised he agreed to the invitation in the first place. May as well squeeze as much out of this pill as I could.

As promised, we reached my house in minutes. When Taggart and I approached the front door to my house, I hesitated. Taggart kept walking a few steps before he noticed I had stopped and then did the same.

"What's wrong?" he asked.

Now standing in front of the house I was second-guessing myself. I was sure Taggart would do all right because of the pill, although I hadn't thought to ask when I could expect it to start wearing off. I hadn't really considered the effect it would have on Mom. Was she strong enough to deal with this? Was I pushing things? What if she broke down or something? That would certainly make Taggart feel responsible and that wasn't what I wanted.

"I'm worried about my mom," I said, answering Taggart's question. "This has really been hard on her, and I'm concerned this might be a mistake."

"Do you want me to go? I don't mind."

"No. But if things go south you might have to make a hasty departure."

"Can do."

When we walked in the front door, my mom was standing there waiting. She must have been peeking through the blinds, waiting for us to pull up. She hadn't looked this good since the day of the funeral. She'd combed her hair, put on a modest amount of makeup, wore a pair of slacks and polo shirt instead of her recent default of sweatpants and t-shirt. A bracelet Becca had given her for last birthday, one with a tiny violin dangling from it, was on her wrist again.

Taggart and Mom stared at one another. My mom had on her greeting smile, but its edges dipped and a tremor took hold.

Suddenly, Taggart stepped forward and disappeared into my mother's open arms. I watched as she hugged him so tightly to her chest that I thought he was going to burst. The pill was obviously allowing him to do this, and I was now more grateful than ever that he had taken it. Mom started weeping silently, her shoulders shaking as she did. That was when emotion bubbled up from somewhere within me and I felt my insides collapse, tears filling my own eyes. My hands flew to my mouth to prevent a whimper from escaping and I quickly stepped into the living room. It took a couple of seconds, but when I regained control, I entered the kitchen.

I recalled Mom telling me when she'd called that dinner was ready, but as I looked around, I noticed corn heating on the stove, garlic bread browning in the toaster oven, and a half-eaten Lasagna warming in the oven. I peeked into the trashcan and smiled, finding a pair of TV dinners sitting on top.

A couple minutes later, Mom and Taggart wandered into the kitchen, arms linked together. Mom chatted about something related to school and Taggart nodded his head continuously.

"Where's Dad?" I asked.

"He decided to go to church today," she said letting go of Taggart and busying herself with the plates. "I told him I wasn't ready yet."

Dinner between the three of us was a little bit awkward, but went off better than I'd expected. Mom led the charge with the conversation, which was the most I'd heard her talk since the accident. Taggart held up his end by answering the tedious questions she floated his way.

I glanced at the clock on the wall and wiped my mouth.

"It's almost six-thirty. They're going to be here soon," I said.

"Are you expecting more company, Cassie?"

"A couple of our classmates from school. We're in a study group together."

My mom's eyebrows furrowed momentarily, but she didn't say anything. The doorbell rang and I rose from my chair.

"Don't worry about the dishes, honey. I got this. You go host your study group."

Taggart thanked Mom for the dinner, to which she responded with an unforced smile, then he followed me to the front door. Chewy and Tunes were standing there waiting.

Nineteen

"Hey guys," I stepped out of the way to allow them into the house.

"I smell lasagna," Chewy remarked as he entered, his nose pointing to the ceiling.

Under normal circumstances, I might have offered Chewy a plate, but I felt it was better to usher him downstairs and away from my mother. One, because I wanted to avoid another emotional encounter right now, and two, I really didn't want her asking questions about what we were up to. Chewy might do something stupid, like tell the truth.

"Let's go downstairs to the basement."

We took the stairs, flicking the switch to the overhead lights at the bottom. Our basement was supposed to be Dad's "man cave," but Becca and I had co-opted it a long time ago. House rules prevented us from having boys in our bedrooms, so I would bring Jason down here from time to time. Becca used it to have Taggart over more than I ever did with Jason.

Taggart went immediately to the bar and sat on a stool. Chewy and Tunes took over opposite ends of the couch, which left me standing in the middle of the room.

"This is nice," Chewy said. "My dad never finished our basement. I guess now it will never happen."

"How is your mom?" I asked, remembering her breast cancer.

"She's a mess. Grandma is here helping, but the medical insurance dad had is apparently low rent and the life insurance was only enough to cover the cost of the funeral and pay off a few bills. We're not sure how we're going to be able to afford the treatment she needs. But let's not waste time, where's the list?"

Taggart tapped the side of his head with his finger.

"Are we supposed to mind-meld or something? Do you have a piece of paper we can write on?" Chewy asked, looking at me.

I grabbed a legal pad and pen from the desk in the corner, then sat down between Chewy and Tunes.

"Let's have them."

Taggart rattled off the names, pausing to help me get the spelling right:

Robert Price
Don Morgan
Melinda McClellan
Robert East
Alice Bell
William Lutz
Peggy Stiles
John Marks
Frances Hendrix
Todd Wyatt
Barbara Collins
Benny Fowler
Francis Potter

Gene Lee
Eddie Teague
Bill Franks
Jerry Tyler
James Chow
Christian Salvador
Derrick Stout
Tim Ledbetter

"Remind me again what this list represents?" I asked.

Taggart dragged his barstool closer to the couch.

"This is the list of New Haven residents who have perished over the past ten years whose deaths were attributed to unexplained causes, or specifically a brain aneurysm."

"And there should have been—?"

"Approximately ten."

Both Chewy and Tunes slid closer to my side so they could look at the list.

"I know some of these names," Tunes said.

"I do too. So what do we do now?" I asked.

"Well," Chewy started, standing up, "we see if any of them have anything in common. If there's someone murdering people in New Haven, then there has to be a pattern. Right? Some motive that links the victims. We need to find out everything we can about the people on the list and see if anything pops out."

"And how do we do that, Sherlock?" I asked.

"Actually, I prefer to be compared to Monk," Chewy said.

Chewy glanced at Taggart, who was being surprisingly silent, seeing as this was his theory in the first place. When Taggart didn't respond, Chewy looked back to me.

"Well… we divide up the list and do research. There are twenty-one names and four of us, so that's five apiece. We already know some of these, including my dad, so it shouldn't take that long," Chewy said.

"What kind of information are we looking for?"

"Things like what they did for a living would be a good start. Were they active in community events? Political affiliations. Where did they live? Maybe this is a geographical pattern?"

"And where do you think we're going to find all this?"

"Obituaries and social media," Taggart finally chimed in. "Start there, and then talk to the relatives. It won't take long to get a general idea about a person."

"Why are you reading obituaries?" came a voice from across the room, drawing our attention.

Delta was standing there on the bottom step, grimacing like she had taken a wrong turn into a men's bathroom.

Busted.

I handed Chewy the legal pad and walked straight to Delta, who still looked confused. I took her by the hand and led her over to the opposite end of the pool table, away from prying ears.

"Your Mom said you were with a study group. What's going on?"

"It is a study group, of sorts, only not one that involves school." School had been the least of my worries the last couple of days.

"This has something to do with Chewy believing his father was murdered?"

I hesitated. I could try to spin a fib about how this was a school assignment—Delta wasn't in my AP courses – but she would see right through that. I had to take the risk, so I nodded my head. "What I didn't tell you is that we think it's true."

"That his father was murdered?"

"Yes. Taggart has some compelling evidence to support the possibility, and we're going to check it out. That's all."

"Taggart? How can you believe anything he says? Come on, Cassie."

I looked over at Taggart, aware that I had to be careful with what I said or I would lose his trust. "Delta, he's not what you think. He's not what anyone thinks. Most of what you know about him is wrong."

Delta looked at Taggart, seemingly unconvinced. I pulled on her arm until she faced me and I looked deep into her eyes.

"Delta, I'm asking you, as my best friend, to believe me. The other day you promised to help me any way you could. I'm calling in that promise. You have to trust me on this, and above all else, you CANNOT breathe a word to anyone."

Delta's face softened into a smile that resembled a grimace more than anything else.

"You're doing this? All of you? What about the police?"

"The police are not going to believe us until we find something substantial. As soon as we do, they'll be our first call."

"Then I want to help."

I wrapped my arms around her neck and hugged. When I let go I put on my best serious face and looked her in the eyes again.

"I'm serious, Delta. Not a—"

"Don't worry. Nobody would believe me if I told them."

We re-joined the trio of guys. Chewy and Tunes were looking over the list and Taggart was sitting nonchalantly in his chair.

"There's five of us now," I proclaimed, making sure to flash Taggart a stern look.

"Hi, I'm Chewy and this is Tunes."

Tunes nodded his head and smiled.

"I'm Delta. I'm really sorry about your dad."

"Thanks."

"Your dad works with my dad," Tunes added, surprisingly.

"That's cool… I guess. So what's the plan here?" Delta said.

Chewy took the initiative and devoted the next five minutes to explaining his original suspicions, Taggart's theory involving skewed statistics, and everything else.

Delta took the list from Chewy, studying it carefully while the rest of us watched.

"Do you have to go to the bathroom?" Delta asked out of nowhere, looking at Chewy.

"Delta!"

"What? My little brother wiggles like that all the time when he holds it too long. It bugs the crap out of me."

"It's okay, Cassie," Chewy said calmly. "I don't mind. It's just something I do. Have since I was really young."

Chewy may not have minded, but I was embarrassed enough for all of us.

"Oh," Delta's replied, but her expression remained unchanged. "So it's a condition or something?"

Chewy nodded his head. "I can't control it unless I take medication. It has a fancy name that I can't pronounce. We just call it *body rocks*."

"Okay, cool. If I understand this right, about half of the people on this list really did die from natural causes, but wouldn't you expect that? I mean New Haven is primarily a retirement community, so our mean average age is higher than normal and therefore I would expect the percentage of our deaths by natural causes to be up."

"I've already adjusted for that," Taggart replied. "But I do believe that very fact is a reason why this hasn't been noticed by the coroner. Granted, I still think this isn't something that couldn't be detected unless you were specifically looking for it, as I was, but because New Haven does produce a positively skewed number it makes it easier to be overlooked. If you wanted to drown someone and make it look like an accident, would it be easier in someplace like Miami…or Tempe Arizona.”

“Good point. But it's going to make it difficult to pin down a pattern when you have so many random variables mixed into your population.”

Delta may be blunt, the biggest gossip-hound at school, a reality TV fanatic, and incapable of applying makeup with any kind of restraint, but the girl knew her math.

Taggart straightened in his chair. His demeanor had me wondering if his white pill had begun to wear off. It had been a good six hours since he took it.

“That's true, but all we need to do is identify a pattern within a subset and then extrapolate that finding in all the other data to prove its validity.”

“Why ten years?”

Taggart was taken off-guard. “What?”

“Why a sample size of ten years? Was that chosen at random or was there a reason for it?”

Taggart moved to the edge of his chair.

“I began with the current year and analyzed annual data first. I moved backward until the numbers fell back to within norms, and that was at eleven years.”

“So this killer, if he really exists, could have been doing this for longer than ten years if the number of his victims stayed within one, maybe even two, standard deviations.”

Taggart's expression didn't change, but it was the tone of his reply that told me he wasn't happy about being second-guessed. “Yes, that's true.”

“None of that changes what we need to do, right?” Chewy chimed in. “We each need to take some names and find out everything we can about them. Then we'll compare notes and see if there is common ground.”

“Yes,” Taggart answered quickly, probably glad to have the subject changed.

"Well, we can do some of that now," Tunes chimed in, which drew a look of surprise from Chewy. I wasn't the only one noticing Tunes increased participation.

"What do you mean?" I asked.

"Chewy's right here. He's the son of one of the victims and he can tell us everything he knows about his dad. Won't that help us recognize things in common with the other victims when we start looking at them?"

"What do you think, Taggart?"

Taggart nodded his head. "It's sound logic."

"How about it Chewy?"

Chewy shrugged his shoulders and re-took his seat on the couch beside Tunes. Delta and I took a seat on the carpet in front of him, crossing our legs.

"Where should I start?"

"Was your dad born and raised in New Haven?" I asked.

"No. I think he moved here when he was in junior high. He went to UGA after high school, and then worked in Atlanta for several years after he graduated, before moving back here. That's when he opened his first store. My mom was born and raised here, and it was a couple of years after they got married that he relocated the sporting goods store to where it is now."

"What organizations was he a member of?" Taggart asked.

"The Optimist Club and the Chamber of Commerce are the only two I know of. He'd been an Optimist four or five years, but I'm not sure about the Chamber of Commerce."

"Has he had any legal issues with past employees?"

"Dad really didn't talk about that stuff around me, but I'm pretty sure he went to court a couple years ago and that had something to do with an employee. I don't know the specifics though."

"That should be easy to find out. How about other disputes? Shoplifters? Anything in general that maybe never got official?" I asked.

For some reason Taggart was beginning to look bothered. Was this line of questioning too boring for him?

"He's always telling us stories about catching shoplifters and some of the people who applied for jobs there, but he never used names."

"What was your father's political affiliation?" Taggart asked abruptly.

"Huh?"

"Democrat, Republican, Independent, Communist?"

"You think my father was a communist?" Chewy asked.

"I don't know what your father was, thus my question."

"I don't know."

"Well, who did he vote for in the last election?"

"I'm not even sure he voted at all," Chewy replied with a raised voice, clearly irritated. "This isn't getting us anywhere. My dad wasn't a closet anarchist, he didn't have a case of road rage and piss someone off, or bankrupt some poor soul who refused to pay a bill. He didn't do a damn thing to deserve to die."

"Chewy could be right," Delta said calmly. "Whoever is doing this could be picking his victims at random. We'd never find a link if that's true."

We all sat there alone with our own thoughts. If they were anything like mine, they weren't very positive.

"What next?" Delta asked.

"We stick to the plan. We divvy up the list and we meet back here tomorrow to start comparing notes," I said. As I started writing names on five different pieces of paper, I couldn't help but feel the futility of the entire endeavor.

Twenty

On Thursday we all met again at my house after school. It took Mom by surprise to see Chewy on the front step when she answered the door. I was worried she would figure out it wasn't a study group meeting in our basement, but to her credit she didn't ask any questions. She simply gave Chewy the hug he deserved, told him how sorry she was about his father, then let him and Tunes follow me down into the basement. That night was about as productive as the first. What tiny amount of information we had collected produced zero leads, leaving all of us frustrated.

Taggart hadn't been at his usual table during lunch at school and he barely said a dozen words during our meeting. He also purposefully found ways to avoid being anywhere near me. It made me worry that he regretted our talk the previous night. Was he embarrassed by the things he revealed while under the influence of the anti-anxiety pill? I hoped not. I wanted to pull him away from the others and say how much I looked forward to getting to know him better, pill or no pill, but every time I came near, he repelled away from me like a magnet with an opposite charge. I finally decided not to push it and let him come to me when he was ready—if that time ever came. It made me sad to think that might never happen.

At the end of the night we all parted with a resolve to see this out to the end, even if that was a dead-end.

Friday night, as I again escorted Chewy and Tunes down into my basement, it was Chewy who pointed out the obvious.

"Taggart's not here?" he asked.

"Nope," I answered, not bothering to elaborate by telling him I was wondering the same thing and that I was more than a little bit worried. "I guess he's running late."

Chewy flopped down onto the couch. "Taggart doesn't run late. You could set your watch by that guy. I really think the dude's some sort of android."

"Is Delta coming?" Tunes said.

"No. Tonight is Homecoming." I made my way back to the card table where the information we'd been gathering was piling up. "We may be on a mission to catch a murderer, but nothing trumps social karma as far as Delta is concerned. Don't worry, she already gave me the stuff she learned so far."

"Does she have a date?" Tunes asked, doing his best to sound disinterested.

"Yes," I answered, but then decided to throw him a bone. "It's just somebody she agreed to go with so she wouldn't have to go alone. She doesn't really like him."

This seemed to give Tunes some satisfaction, which made me chuckle. Tunes and Delta? Stranger things have happened, I guess.

"I gathered a lot more information today," I offered as an icebreaker. "I spent the entire afternoon at the library going through old obituaries. It's been years since I've gone there on a Friday."

"Should we wait for Taggart before getting started?" Chewy asked.

"I've been watching him catalogue our findings, so I could probably do it if you don't want to wait," Tunes remarked, taking a seat at the table next to me.

"Good. Let's not wait then.," I replied, pulling out the legal pad we'd been using to document our findings. Maybe the work would help keep my mind off Taggart's whereabouts. It surprised me how much I even cared.

We'd been going at it for almost an hour when my phone rang. It was Delta's number.

"Is the game that boring?" I asked sarcastically.

"Cassie, I think you need to get down here right away," Delta shouted over the sounds of an excited crowd in the background. There was something in her voice that told me this wasn't the overly dramatic version of Delta. Something was wrong.

"What's going on Delta?" My tone caused the boys to raise their heads and look at me.

"Just get down here now," she answered, and the line went dead.

"What's up?" Tunes asked.

I stared at the phone.

"There's something wrong at the football game. I need to go over there."

"I'm coming with you," Chewy said, springing up from the couch.

"Me too," Tunes was quick to add.

The New Haven football stadium was closer to the junior high than the high school, centrally located closer to the center of town, which allowed it to service all of our local teams. Compared to the other schools in our conference, our field was a mecca for football fans. It had been renovated not once, but three times that I could remember, and it put some junior college fields to shame. When you have money to burn, the philosophy *if you build it they will come* can be put to the test whenever you wanted. In this case it worked, because right after the latest upgrade to the stadium our high school team began a run of wins that hadn't ended yet. The stadium was packed every Friday night.

When my car crested the hill that looked down over the stadium, we saw an ambulance in the middle of playing field with football players and coaches from both teams down on one knee. I didn't bother to hunt for a parking spot, instead pulling off the road and stopping in front of the maintenance building. By the time we made the main entrance, the ticket takers had wandered off and were watching the ambulance pull out of the service gate. I walked between the stands and the concessions building then started looking around, spotting Delta by the fence watching the ambulance drive away. I called to her and rushed over. She turned around to face me, mascara-stained tears running down her cheeks.

"Delta, what's going on? Who was in that ambulance?"

"Stooch," she replied, a sob catching in her throat. "They're saying he wasn't breathing."

I took her in my arms, watching the ambulance disappear around the corner, unable to process what was happening. Sure, Delta had broken up with Stooch and the guy was an A-1 jerk, but she still had feelings for him. I turned slowly, taking in the scene of unease everywhere I looked. Spectators milled around, unfocused, still in shock and looking for answers to a tragedy that had been played out in front of their eyes. Vice-Principal Stevens was talking to my biology teacher, Mr. Wilkins, along with many others from the faculty. I spotted Mary from the clinic talking to Dr. Weathers, who I knew had a son playing on the JV team. My boss was probably re-thinking the decision to let his son play football right now.

Turning my attention back to the field I noticed a figure out of the corner of my eye that initially my brain failed to register. I mean, him at a football game, it didn't compute.

But there he was. It wasn't a mistake. Only twenty feet down the railing from me talking to an adult I didn't recognize.

Taggart.

"What is he doing here?" I said to no one in particular.

Chewy must have heard me because he followed my gaze to where Taggart was standing.

I let go of Delta but still held onto her hand, turning my full attention to Taggart. He appeared to be having a serious conversation with a rather large man, salt and pepper hair, wearing a tweed sports coat.

Just as I was about to head over to them, Taggart abruptly spun around and walked at a fast pace towards the exit gates. The stranger watched him leave, then headed off towards the concession stands.

"Who do you think that was?" Chewy asked.
"I have no idea," I replied, still in a state of shock. "But whoever he was, Taggart sure was chatty with him."

Twenty-One

The next day, Saturday afternoon, we decided to meet in the back room of the Puck, much to Taggart's dismay. Three days in a row at my house was pushing it. I already suspected my parents were working up the nerve to ask questions about what we were up to, and besides, it was a way to get back at Taggart for not telling me what he was doing at the football game. I chose one of the card rooms at the Puck because it was a no-adult zone, and I knew the atmosphere would drive Taggart nuts.

The Puck was one of New Haven's oldest businesses. When I was still going out with Jason, he and his posse went through a phase where they spent plenty of time there, hogging the pool tables or foosball tables. I knew my way around, and it was somewhere we wouldn't be noticed.

The card rooms—or private party rooms as they were officially called—had to be reserved ahead of time and could be used for anything, but you usually found them occupied by a Texas Hold'em match or a serious d20 party, a modern version of Dungeon & Dragons. Sometimes marathon games could last the entire weekend. Since the Puck rarely got busy before the sun went down, we decided to meet at one o'clock and take our chances.

Chewy, Tunes, and I marched in together, the two of them hitching a ride with me. Taggart and Delta said they would meet us there. Right away I remembered how dimly lit the interior of the Puck was, regardless of the time of day. Arcade games lined the outer walls giving it a NASA mission control feel, which was quickly erased by the synthetic bleeps, loops, and other rapidly-oscillating tones emitted by the classic games like Pac Man, Centipedes, Space Invaders, and others. The atmosphere always made me feel like I'd traveled back in time to the eighties. It was an epileptics worse nightmare, and I'm betting Taggart's as well.

As expected, there were only a few die-hard gamers at the Puck that time of the day, so we found an empty room in the far corner. I turned on the light, which was considerably better than the main hall, and inside we found a pair of circular card tables, each with four folding chairs. There was also an old divan that had seen better days, pushed up against the far wall. I pulled out a chair and sat down, watching as Chewy and Tunes took opposite ends of the couch.

"Are you sure Delta is coming?" Tunes asked.

"She said she'd be here."

"How is she doing?"

After leaving the football field the previous night, I'd driven everyone home, except Delta and Tunes. Tunes had insisted on accompanying Delta and me to the hospital. We waited for word about Stooch's condition along with dozens of our friends, classmates, and parents. It wasn't too long before a doctor came out and talked to Stooch's parents, and when we saw his mother buckle and fall into her husband's arms, we knew the worst was true.

Kevin "Stooch" Steuer had died.

The three of us were in shock as we walked back to my car. On the horizon, the glow of the lights from the football field told me the game was still going on—and that made me think of Jason. He was there on the field, ripping off runs for huge chunks of yardage or throwing bullets to a speedy group of receivers, blissfully ignorant that some devastating news would soon find him. My heart ached for him, but I needed to be with Delta. I would call him later when the time was right.

First, I had to call Taggart and find out what he was up to at the game. When he answered all I could do is ask was where he had been that night. He spouted some lame excuse about doing work for the Wilson's, which I knew was a lie, but I decided to not push the issue then. I asked if he had heard about Stooch, and he said his foster-brother gave him the news, so I told him about our plans to meet at the Puck.

"Cassie!" Tunes said loudly, snapping me out of my trance.

"I'm sorry, what?"

"How is Delta doing?" Tunes repeated.

"She's shook up, but okay. I spent the night with her last night, and we talked a lot. She and Kevin hadn't been dating long, but it still hurts, you know?"

Tunes nodded, but I wasn't sure he really understood.

The three of us sat in silence, each of us in private grief counseling sessions. I'd heard from friends that after Becca had died, the school had brought in grief counselors for students. It didn't matter how well a person knew Becca, or if they were social with her at all. Apparently, studies had shown sudden death in a close community, especially a school setting, could be upsetting regardless of the connection. I imagined the counselors would be making a return trip to our school next week.

Delta stepped through the door and Tunes sat up straight on the couch. She was wearing an untucked Duck Dynasty t-shirt, plain jeans, and boat shoes. She was also totally make-up free, which was unheard of outside the walls of her house.

Delta looked around the room. "Good, I'm not the last one."

"We're still waiting on Taggart," Tunes said, confirming the obvious. *Somebody should really talk to him about trying to be a little more subtle about his crush on Delta,* I thought to myself. With this group, that would probably be me.

"I'm sorry about—" Chewy said from the couch.

"Thank you," Delta replied, taking a seat next to me at the card table.

I reached out and put a hand on her knee.

"How you doing, girl?" I asked softly.

"Okay, I guess. Just weird. I got online this morning. I know you told me not to, but I couldn't help myself. Half the kids at school are sorry for me because they think Stooch and I were still dating, and the other half are pissed because they don't think I have the right to be sad because I dumped him. Of course they're not saying that to my face, just making snide comments on other people's pages."

I thought about what Taggart had said, about one dagger turning into hundreds of tiny pricks.

"Don't get sucked into any of that, Delta. You have to be—"

She wasn't listening. Her hands had gone to her face and her shoulders moved in rhythm to her silent sobbing. I wrapped my arms around her until she finally ran out of tears. Chewy and Tunes smartly kept their attention focused elsewhere.

"I know I have to be the bigger person," Delta said, pausing to blow her nose with a Kleenex from her pocket. "It just pisses me off so much. Did you talk to Jason?"

I recalled the phone conversation I had with my ex-boyfriend earlier that morning. I could tell by Jason's voice that he was hurting, and while he was grateful I called to tell him how sorry I was, Stooch's death wasn't the only thing he was upset about.

"Yeah, I talked to him."

"Is he doing okay?

"—ish."

"I was thinking last night—during all that time I wasn't sleeping—I know I might be out of line, but maybe breaking up with Jason isn't such a good idea. Especially when you consider everything with Becca."

I was shocked. "What?"

"I mean, think about it. You put a wall up between you and her because of her friendship with Taggart. You regret that now, right?"

"Sure I do."

"And that wall was mostly because of how she hung out with someone you thought was a lowlife, and how that made YOU look. But aren't you doing the same thing again with Jason? Judging him based on who he hangs out with? Maybe you'll regret that one day as well?"

Delta's words infuriated me, but she was hurting and still trying to be a good friend. I took a deep breath before I answered.

"It's true, I screwed up with Becca. I should have trusted her judgment and not have accepted stories and rumors about Taggart as hard truth. I was a kid, and I was stupid. It makes me wonder what I really know about anyone at school, and what others are saying about me. You know what I mean? It's really sad how much of our opinions are formed by half-truths and gossip.

"I'll regret what I did to Becca for the rest of my life, but it's not the same with Jason. First off, the people Jason hangs with is not his only problem, but they are a big part. Secondly, I've personally witnessed those so-called friends breaking the law and doing other things I hate, so there is no—"

"—misunderstanding this time. I get it. I was just making sure."

"Thank you."

"I don't mean to break up the Dr. Phil hour, but do you know what happened to Stooch?" Chewy asked. I was grateful for the change in subject. "Did you see how he got hurt?"

Delta shook her head.

"I didn't actually see the play. No one really watches the game, you know, at least no one our age. But I talked to Mr. Wilkins right after it happened. The game had only started, in fact we had just kicked off and Stooch was on the coverage team. He tackled the other player, which Mr. Wilkins says he usually does because he's such a ball hawk. That's what Mr. Wilkins called him. Anyway, Mr. Wilkins said it looked like a normal tackle, nothing out of the ordinary, but Stooch looked a little woozy after getting up. When the team lined up for defense the referee stopped the game because it looked like Stooch had a nosebleed or something, and then he collapsed right there on the field."

Delta pulled the tissue out of her pocket again, but all she did was hold it in her hand. Her eyes had turned misty, but there were no actual tears.

"The coaches and trainers ran out there and right away you could tell it was something bad. It was the way they acted. Someone called for the ambulance, and that's when everything got really quiet and still."

"His poor parents," I said.

"They weren't even there yet," Delta replied with a look of mock shock. "Cathy Bellringer said they usually don't get there until mid-way through the first quarter. I guess they're not really football people. They passed the ambulance on the way to the field and had no idea what was going on until they received the call."

"Oh, geez," Chewy commented.

"Delta, I need you to tell me everything that happened before the game began," Taggart's voice came from behind us.

I turned around and there he was, leaning against the doorframe. He wore a black long sleeve t-shirt underneath a jean jacket with cut-off sleeves and pants that I was sure unintentionally matched with the jacket. Perspiration dotted his forehead and his hair was slicked back, signs that he had been sweating for a while.

"What do you mean?" Delta asked.

"I've never been to a game, so I don't know what the ritual is."

That's the second lie he's told. My instinct was to confront him with the truth and find out exactly what he was up to, but for some reason, I held my tongue.

"What do you mean you've never—" Chewy began.

"Why do you need to know that?" I cut-off Chewy, shooting him a hard look and a subtle shake of the head. "What's that got to do with anything?"

"Yeah," Tunes chimed in. "I thought we were here to go over the list?"

"Delta?" Taggart simply said, ignoring both me and Tunes.

I stood up and placed myself directly in front of Taggart so the only thing he could see was me and the others wouldn't be able to see his face.

"What are you doing?" I whispered. "Delta doesn't need to re-live it."

Taggart's face softened ever so slightly. "This is important."

I looked deep into his eyes and wanted to believe he was telling the truth, but I wasn't sure.

"I can answer your question," I said as I moved away from him and leaned against the card table. "The players are supposed to arrive at the high school two and a half hours before game time. They get suited up and go through their initial warm-ups, then they get loaded onto a bus that takes them over to the junior high. From there, they go through the Titan walk down to the field and run through the banner the cheerleaders have painted. After that the game starts."

"What's the Titan walk?"

"You do know our team mascot is a Titan, don't you?" Chewy asked.

"I do now. But what is a—"

"The Titan walk is where everyone forms kind of a tunnel that the players walk through as they head from the bus down to the field," Delta answered, cutting me off and taking control of the conversation. "Somebody stole the idea from another school out west and it became something we always do."

"Who's in this—"

"Tunnel? Everyone. Kids from school, parents, teachers, everyone."

"And do people in this *tunnel* interact with the players?"

"Sure. They give high-fives. Why is this so important?" I asked.

Chewy suddenly sat forward on the couch. "Whoa… whoa… whoa. You're not suggesting what I think you're suggesting, are you?"

Taggart pushed himself off the doorframe, took a quick glance outside the room before closing the door, then turned one of the folding chairs around and straddled it.

"Kevin Steuer's body is being held at Cowell Funeral Home, pending disposition. We need to get a look at it."

The faint siren call of lonely arcade games outside the room was the only sound for seconds.

Delta spoke up first, and as usual, she was straight to the point.

"Are you defective? Why would you even say that?"

I realized what Chewy was speculating, though I couldn't believe it. "You think he died of a brain aneurysm, don't you?"

Taggart nodded.

Now Chewy rose from his spot on the couch. "Geez dude, conspiracy much?"

Taggart didn't react to Chewy, keeping his attention focused on me.

Chewy walked over and stood directly in front of Taggart. "I know it's tragic and all, but football is a dangerous sport and kids do die playing it. There's no reason to believe our serial killer has suddenly gone YA. I mean, what could Stooch have in common with any of the others on our list?"

"He was a football player. I'm sure he bought stuff from your dad's store," Tunes answered.

"Come on, so did half the people in New Haven. That's no connection."

Taggart looked up at Chewy, and then his gaze found Tunes and Delta one at a time before returning to me. "You are right, of course, but the only way we'll know for sure is if we look at the body."

"The police will do a proper autopsy," Chewy pointed out.

Taggart leveled his gaze at Chewy. "The police won't know what to look for, just like your father."

"So, we'll make sure they know what to look for," I said.

Taggart shook his head. "There might not even be an autopsy, which is why we have to do something tonight."

"What do you mean there won't be an autopsy? Sure there will," Delta said.

Taggart shook his head again. "This morning I spoke to the Wilsons' son Matt, the police officer. He says it is not a certainty. The County Medical Examiner is supposed to make that call, but apparently the Steuer's are against it. They have religious objections. They're Jewish and object to the practice."

"Don't you think they'd want to know what killed their son?" Chewy asked.

"I'm sure they don't believe anything criminal took place. They must balance the information gained about why he passed away, which incidentally won't change a thing, against the things that have to be done to his body to obtain that knowledge."

"So we convince them," Delta said.

"Convince who? The police? The Steuers? Persuade the loving parents to go against Jewish law and desecrate their son's body for the sole purpose of a theory that most of you aren't 100% convinced of?"

The silence that followed underscored the fact that no one, me included, attempted to refute Taggart's last point.

"So what's your plan? Because there's no way they're going to let a bunch of high school kids take a gander at a body," Chewy pointed out.

"As I said, they are holding the body at Cowell Funeral Home until a decision can be made. I propose that we go and look for ourselves because if they decide against an autopsy, a Jewish burial is supposed to happen within 24 hours of death. I'm sure they'll make a consideration for people to travel, but we need to move fast. We also need to get hold of the football jersey he wore."

"Why? Man… that's just creepy," Delta said.

"And examining a dead body isn't?" Chewy pointed out, which drew a 'screw you' look from Delta.

"It's all creepy," I interjected before Delta could respond, my lame attempt to keep things on track. "But Taggart, why DO we need the jersey?"

"Steuer had a nosebleed and some of his blood might have made its way onto that jersey. We can have that blood tested to determine if there was a toxin in his system."

It made sense, and although I wasn't completely sold on Taggart's suspicion that Stooch was another victim, I could see the value in making sure the jersey wasn't destroyed until we ruled it out.

"Okay, but how do we get it?"

"His clothes are probably still at the hospital, awaiting release to his parents. We'll need to check there first."

"If the jersey is there, how do you suppose we get it? They're not going to give it to anybody but family."

Chewy's negativity was starting to get on my nerves, but it gave me an idea. "Technically, the jersey belongs to the school. I mean they hand them out before games and collect them afterward. Maybe someone could go to the hospital—"

"—and pretend to be part of the team and ask for it," Delta added, picking up on my thought. "We could say the school wants to use it as part of a memorial for Stooch."

I snapped my fingers and pointed at Delta. "That's good. But who's going to be the one to ask?"

"Maybe you can ask Jason to do it?" Delta suggested.

"I don't think he's up to doing me any favors right now, and besides, what reason would we give him?"

Silence was my answer. The five of us were inside our own heads, searching for an idea.

"I can do it," Tunes announced sharply, almost as if he was trying to convince himself.

"No offense, Tunes," I said, "but you look like a football player as much as I do."

Tunes smiled and shook his head. "I can say I'm the team manager."

"And I can go with him as a cheerleader," Delta added. "I shouldn't have any problem coming up with a few tears to sway them."

I could totally see Delta as a cheerleader, in fact she was one for the Pee Wee leagues when she was twelve. She'd tried to get me to do it with her, but I wasn't interested in devoting so much time to something that didn't seem to have a real objective. Delta only did it for one year, and she never told me why she quit.

"It might work, but you'll have to leave your headphones at home, Tunes. Can't risk them not taking you seriously."

We all watched Tunes slowly removed his headphones from around his neck and set them down beside him on the couch.

"I can do that."

"Great. That only leaves Stooch's body," Chewy said.

A cold chill ran down my back. It wasn't only the fact that examining a body up close really grossed me out, but Cowell's was the funeral home where Becca's service was held.

"So what, we just walk into a funeral home and ask to see him? Like window shopping?" Chewy asked.

"No. We wait until there's no one around," Taggart spoke up.

"And how do we do that?" I asked, fairly sure I knew the answer already.

"We break in tonight."

Twenty-Two

Chewy, Tunes, and Delta were waiting for Taggart and me underneath the dim light of the streetlamp at the end of the block by my house. When I caught them in my headlamps, they looked like an odd group of dysfunctional hoodlums. All three of them wore jeans and hoodies, but Delta's hoodie was bright pink, Chewy's was two sizes too small, and Tunes still had his headphones on his ears… outside the hood.

I pulled up and the three of them hurriedly piled into my backseat.

"Could you be any more noticeable, Delta?" I asked as I gunned the accelerator.

"I can't help it. I don't own anything dark, and Chewy said to wear hoodies."

"I didn't know you could see yours from the moon," Chewy remarked.

"Well, at least I don't look like McGilla Gorrilla in mine."

"I forgot mine was in the wash, so I had to grab my little brother's."

"Really? You thought a slightly wrinkled hoody wasn't good enough to commit burglary?"

"Stop it!" Taggart snapped. "It doesn't matter. Did you get the jersey?"

"Piece of—" Tunes started.

"—cake," Delta finished.

"It's back at my house," Chewy said.

"They apologized to us. They had to cut it off him," Delta added solemnly. "We told them it was okay, we would sew it back together."

As I continued through town, I was amazed at how still everything was. It turned out that New Haven in the middle of the night was a little eerie. There were no cars, no people, the storefronts were dark, and the city was absent of any signs of life. I didn't know about anyone else, but moving around at this ghostly hour only heightened my sense of wrongdoing. There was mischief, and then there was misdemeanor. What we were up to definitely fell into the second category—regardless of how well intentioned our actions might be.

Following Taggart's instructions, I drove by the Cowell Funeral Home, slowly, and then doubled back and parked in an alleyway between the pharmacy and general store across the street. The funeral home was located on the western edge of town, bookended by condominiums on one side and a large Methodist church on the other. Its rear butted up against an established subdivision, a high wooden fence serving as a barrier between the two. We sat across from it now, separated by a normally busy four-lane road, but at three o'clock in the morning, the traffic was non-existent.

The funeral home looked more like a health club to me. Four brick columns in front of the all-glass entryway centered on an expansive building with metal siding, just didn't say mortuary to me. I tried to recall what the inside looked like, but I must have been in an emotional haze the day of Becca's funeral because I barely remember any details.

"Tell me we're not actually going through with this," Delta said softly from the back.

I almost chuckled. Despite no one being in sight, she was still whispering.

"What do you have to worry about?" Chewy said, mimicking her muted tone. "You're only the lookout."

When we were back at the Puck, Delta protested when I suggested she stay behind tonight. She told everyone she didn't want to be left out, but there was no way she was going inside and looking at Stooch's corpse. That was when it was decided she would be our sentry, and Tunes naturally volunteered to keep her company. At first, it was only Taggart and Chewy who would venture inside the mortuary, but at the last minute I decided I needed to go with them. If Taggart claimed to find evidence of an injection, and Chewy didn't agree, there had to be someone to break the tie. Like it or not, I was the only available option.

"So, how are we going to do this?" I turned and asked Taggart, using my normal voice.

"I scouted Cowell's this afternoon. It's a top-notch facility, but they skimp in some areas. For instance, they have alarm sensors on all their doors but didn't go the extra step and install them on the windows. While I was checking the place out, I unlocked one that was out of the way and no one would notice. I have a general layout of where everything is, so it shouldn't take us long to locate Steuer's body and examine it."

"How did you get a layout of the building?" Delta asked, still whispering.

"They have a website."

"Oh."

"Do you have the gloves?" Taggart asked.

Never having burgled before, I wasn't sure what the best type of gloves to wear. Then I remembered the ones we used at the vet clinic looked very similar to those I saw TV detectives wearing, so I volunteered to bring a pair for all of us.

"Check," I replied, trying to sound ready and confident, but my stomach was doing backflips. "I went to the clinic under the pretense of checking on Brutus, since he seemed to be spending more time at the clinic than he used to."

I passed around the latex gloves then struggled with my own. It took a little adjusting, but I finally got one over the tip of the soft-cast at the end of my broken arm.

"These are nice," Chewy said.

Taggart looked back at Delta. "Any cars pull into the funeral homes parking lot, any at all, call Cassie right away."

I didn't bother to look, but I was pretty sure Delta was nodding her head.

"Let's go," Taggart said and opened his door.

When I was twelve years old and Becca was eleven, we snuck out of the house on Halloween night after everyone had gone to bed. Several of us neighborhood kids had made a pact to sneak into an abandoned house in the oldest section of our subdivision. The creepy old house had a reputation for being haunted, but no one really believed that. It was simply an excuse to break the rules and have an adventure. Adventure or not, I was terrified silly that night.

Tonight, as I got out of the car, I felt ten times worse. At twelve it was butterflies in the stomach, now it was dragons clawing at my intestines.

The three of us bolted across the road and disappeared into the shadows on the right side of the building. From there, Chewy and I followed Taggart as he crept along a wall until he reached a window located adjacent to a corner where the building became wider. He worked on the window with gloved hands, rocking it back and forth until it slid upwards. He climbed through the opening and reached his hand out to me. I grabbed hold with my good arm and Taggart carefully pulled me up.

Inside Taggart switched on a small LED flashlight, keeping it pointed at the floor. It barely gave off enough light to show where we were. The sprawling room was almost empty except for a pair of love seats and single chairs tucked into the corners. I recognized it as one of their many viewing rooms, though I didn't know if it was the one we used for Becca. As soon as Chewy was inside, Taggart headed through the door towards the rear of the building.

We took a couple turns and after we passed through an open doorway. I lost track of where we were, but Taggart obviously knew where he was going. After we went through our first closed door, we ran into a collection of caskets, all styles and makes. Chills ran up my spine and my feet were feeling heavier. Still, we kept moving past them through another closed door. Inside the next room, Taggart paused to use his flashlight to locate the light switch, surprising me by flipping it on, which surrounded us in brilliant luminescence.

Once my eyes adjusted to the light, I was looking at a windowless room. The space very much resembled a doctor's examination room, although much larger and with fewer amenities. Taggart continued past what looked like a checkup table with a large white plastic box suspended over it with several hooks and cords hanging from it, to another door made completely of metal. He opened that door and again switched on the light, turning toward us after he did.

"He's in here."

That was when my apprehension went into hyper-drive. I'd never seen a dead body in person. Becca's funeral was closed casket, for obvious reasons, and the only other funeral I had been to was my grandmother's. I was ten at the time. It freaked me out so much that my parents made me sit with my older cousin in the rear, as far away from the casket as you could get and still be in the room. They were afraid I would make a scene and ruin the service. Rightly so.

I started following Taggart through the door when I noticed Chewy hadn't moved. He was shaking his head, face all scrunched up as if he had sucked on a lemon and eyes squinted over the top of his glasses. His hands were stuffed deep inside the front pocket of his hoodie.

"I can't," he said.

I put my hand on his shoulder. "Chewy, we need you."

"I thought I could… but I can't," he repeated, shifting his weight between each foot now.

I knew I had to get him in that room somehow and there wasn't a whole lot of time for debate. I took my hand off his shoulder and held it out in front of him.

"Chewy, I'm doing this for my sister, so you need to do this for your dad. We'll do it together, okay?"

The effect on him was immediate. His face went slack, he stopped rocking, pushed his glasses up on his nose, then took hold of my hand.

"Okay. Together."

Hand in hand, the two of us walked through the door. The temperature immediately dropped. Inside the room resembled a meat locker, or at least the pictures of meat lockers I'd seen. The walls were all metal; in fact, everything inside the room was metal. And cold! My teeth had already started chattering and goosebumps rippled up my arms.

The sound of the door clicking shut behind us brought me dangerously close to hyperventilating.

I had imagined seeing a series of drawers where the bodies would be stored, waiting for us to check one by one, but instead mounted on the wall to our immediate left were two sets of three slabs. There was yet another set on the wall straight ahead. On the top slab of all the sets rested its own body, each covered by a white sheet.

I tried to swallow, but my throat was too dry. A shiver that bordered on a full-out spasm moved through my body, whether that was because I was cold or beginning to freak out, was anyone's guess. I tightened my grip on Chewy's hand and continued moving.

Taggart hadn't hesitated, moving straight to the body on the right and peering beneath the lifted sheet. Chewy and I remained glued where we were. Taggart returned the sheet as quickly as he'd lifted it and moved to the body on the left. His back blocked our view, but he raised the next sheet, then pulled it all the way down to the waist. When he started examining the upper part of the torso, I knew he had found what we were after. Chewy made slight a move forward as if he wanted to help, but didn't go any further.

"What are you looking for?" I asked.

"He was probably injected while going through the Titan walk, so the site will most likely be on one of his arms."

Taggart had lifted one of the arms and was manipulating it to look at it closer. He reached into his pocket, pulled out a small magnifying glass, and continued scanning the length of the arm. When he didn't find anything he switched to the other arm and continued his meticulous search. Suddenly he stiffened, then pressed his face closer, his interest obviously aroused.

"I found it."

Chewy and I looked at one another, my shock reflected back at me in his expression. Despite myself, my feet carried me over to the table. Chewy had let go of my hand and was moving as well.

"Look," Taggart said as I peeked around him, but it was Kevin's milky white face that drew my attention. It was so... vacant... flaccid... slack. He didn't appear to be sleeping, which was how a lot of people described a dead person looking. Instead, he just looked... dead.

Chewy stuck his head in from the other side and focused on the spot Taggart was magnifying.

"It does look like a mosquito bite," Chewy said.

I managed to shake off my fixation with the body's face and looked where Chewy was attempting to take a picture with his phone. The spot was directly above the wrist on the inside of the arm. Through the magnifying glass the skin was slightly raised and in its center was something resembling a tiny birthmark. I remembered enough of my biology and watching CSI with Jason, to know that if Kevin was still alive today, the area would be red from inflammation.

"The last time I got a flu shot it sure didn't look like that," I said, still not convinced.

"That was given to you under controlled conditions with you holding perfectly still. This drug, whatever it is, was administered with the subject in motion, so irritation can be expected."

The sound of a creaking door from somewhere else in the building scared me stiff, instantly causing me to forget how cold I was. I looked at Taggart and Chewy, who must have heard the same thing because they were both statues. After a couple of seconds, Taggart moved silently to the door and put his ear to it.

"Voices," he whispered.

Oh crap, oh crap, oh crap. I was going to be caught breaking and entering. My life would be over. What was I thinking? How had they talked me into this?

"Put the sheet back over the body and follow me," Taggart instructed softly and calmly.

Chewy did as instructed, then both of us moved next to Taggart.

"Sounds like they are in the front of the building. We're going out the back. No flashlights."

Chewy and I nodded. Taggart flipped off the lights, plunging us into complete darkness, then opened the door. The lights in the examination room were still on, which made it easy for Chewy and me to creep behind Taggart to the right and to a different door than the one we came in through. Once there, he turned off the lights and opened the door.

A bellowing Wookie began radiating continuously from Chewy's pants, causing me to jump several inches off the ground.

"Crap," Chewy half-whispered, half-shouted, digging furiously for the cell phone in his front pocket.

"There's someone in the back," said a muffled voice.

"RUN!"

Taggart's flashlight came on, and I followed him and the bouncing light down a narrow hallway, making a sharp turn to the left. Chewy's heavy breathing was close behind me. The three of us burst out of a metal fire-door into the night, half expecting to run straight into a group of New Haven's finest with handcuffs waiting for us. Instead, I stared at a six-foot wooden fence that ran the length of a small parking lot. We had exited the back of the building and were facing the barrier that separated the business from the neighborhood behind it.

The sound of clapping hard sole shoes on a Formica floor behind us jolted us into action.

"Hurry," Taggart called as he sprinted for the fence. Chewy and I followed him, ignoring the fact it appeared we were heading into a dead-end.

Taggart reached the fence first, turned and put his back against it, then placed his open hands on his right leg. I didn't hesitate or worry about my arm, the adrenaline flowing like a river through my veins. In one motion, I put my foot in his hands and launched myself for the top of the fence, using my good arm to grab hold. Taggart lifted my weight easily and I was up and over the fence effortlessly. I landed on soft grass and instantly started praying that a pit bull with teeth as large and sharp as steak knives wouldn't come tearing after me. My prayer must have been answered because the only thing in the backyard was a small swing set and a grill.

Chewy dropped awkwardly beside me, stumbling a couple steps before catching himself.

"You there… STOP!" I heard.

I looked to the top of the fence waiting for Taggart to appear, but there was nothing.

"I SAID STOP!"

Something hit the fence with a great deal of force. A pair of hands grabbed the top, then Taggart came rolling over and dropped to the ground between me and Chewy.

"Keep going," he instructed, not bothering to check how we were.

We followed him through an unlocked wooden gate, along the side of a house and into the front yard, adding trespassing to my list of violations for the night. The three of us emerged onto the street and looked in both directions trying to decide which way to head when a car rounded the corner at the end of the block and gunned its way towards us.

"Run," Chewy cried, taking off in the other direction.

"Wait," said Taggart, who was not moving.

As the car drew closer, I recognized it as my own, or rather Becca's. It came to a stop beside us, with Delta behind the wheel.

"Get in," she urged from the open window. We didn't waste any time obeying her, and once we were all in the backseat she stepped on the gas.

"I'm sorry. We saw the police pull up and tried to warn you sooner, but my calls kept going straight to voicemail. We finally got through to Chewy though."

"The reception was probably crappy inside that cold room," Chewy offered.

Tunes turned around from the front passenger seat and looked at the three of us in the back. "Did you have time to find Stooch?"

"We did," Chewy answered, still trying to catch his breath.

"And?"

"I think we have a murderer loose in New Haven," I answered solemnly.

Twenty-Three

Someone murdered Stooch.

Someone has been murdering people in New Haven for ten years or more.

Someone murdered Chewy's father, and that meant the same person by extension murdered my sister.

Lying in bed early Sunday morning, doing my best to ignore my aching arm from the night's calisthenics, the reality of those facts kept sleep away. After our group made its escape undetected, navigating through every backroad we could think of to avoid the police cruisers that were no doubt on the lookout, I dropped everyone off and coasted into my own driveway with the lights off. I successfully crept back into the house without raising an alarm, popped a pain pill, crawled into bed, and had been tossing and turning ever since. All kinds of thoughts were bouncing around inside my head, and I didn't like the direction any of them were heading. Something else was bothering me.

When Chewy first dumped his *my father was murdered* story in our lap, I thought I had become involved with a grieving son unable to accept the reasonless end to the father he loved. We talked to the police, and that should have been it. Chewy seemed to accept their explanation, begrudgingly, but to me he appeared ready to move on. Then Taggart seized hold of it. He wasn't willing to accept the answers from the police and with more digging, suddenly Chewy's claims had become a possibility. But why? Why was Taggart, almost from the day Chewy told us his theory, so certain that it could be real? The statistics were definitely concerning, and actually seeing an injection mark on Stooch's body was eye-opening, but for Taggart, it just seemed to prove something he already knew.

Then there was his lying about being at the football game and meeting that man.

That worried me.

Taggart was exactly like that old Winston Churchill quote: a riddle, wrapped in a mystery, inside an enigma. I had only known him, really known him, for less than a week, and I had barely scratched the surface of his complexities. What I'd learned from my sister's journal, though very helpful, still didn't provide the key to unlock his cavernous vault. It wasn't a matter of feeling like he was holding something back, because he withheld everything, from everyone. It was rather a sense that he was keeping something from *me* specifically. Some crucial bit of information that had something to do with these murders that he couldn't—or wouldn't—share. Now it's turned into outright lies. But why? And more important, should I be scared?

I didn't want to think so. I knew now that the front Taggart showed the world wasn't a front. It was part of who he was. But it wasn't all that he was, which is what so many of us had mistakenly assumed. Beneath layers of distrust and isolation, was a boy who was kind and sweet. Or was he?

Was I only seeing what I wanted to see? Did Becca?

The truth was Taggart didn't care enough about anyone else to hurt them, much less kill them. That didn't mean he couldn't be an unwitting accomplice, that's what bothered me the most. If even a fraction of that was true, that meant he could be partially responsible for Becca's death.

I rolled over and stared at the clock. 6:45. Maybe a hot shower and some walnut pancakes would help quell the storm raging inside my head? I'd have to find another way to catch up on my Z's.

An hour later, I was stuffing the last bite in my mouth when I heard steps coming down the stairs.

"Morning, honey," Mom said as she opened the refrigerator and pulled out the orange juice.

"Morning," I replied after I swallowed.

"What do you have planned today?"

"I have to meet up with our study group sometime, but I'm not sure when yet."

"And Delta is part of your group now?"

"Uh huh."

Mom grabbed a glass out of the cupboard, poured her orange juice, then set it all on the table in front of her and placed her hands on her hips. I was very familiar with this stance. It meant a grilling was headed my way.

"Cassie, what's going on?"

I put on my best clueless face. We had been down this road a time or two. "What do you mean?"

"You and Delta have been friends for as long as I can remember. She has NEVER been part of one of your study groups. Then there's Taggart, who, I understand, hardly needs to study, and the Ledbetter boy and his friend, who are freshman. What could the five of you possibly be studying?"

I was prepared for this. My mom was no dummy and this question was coming eventually. I replaced my clueless look with one I used most often when I needed to convey sincerity.

"It's not really a study group."

"I thought not. What is it then?"

I lowered my eyes and looked at the floor.

"I guess you could call it a support group."

"A support group?"

"For people who have lost someone close to them."

I didn't look up, but I knew my answer had the desired effect.

"Oh."

"I called it a study group because I didn't want you to be worried or feel like you needed to chaperone us. We hang out and share memories, that kind of stuff. It's silly, I know, but it's helped me. The others too."

I wanted so much to tell her that someone murdered Becca and we were hot on the trail of the killer. Okay, maybe it was a lukewarm trail. But I knew in doing that there were so many things that could happen… none of them good. Instead, I chose to bend the truth a little. At least for the time being.

"I understand honey. Completely."

I finally looked up at her standing there, eyes red, giving me a forced smile.

"Thanks, Mom," I said, smiling back.

I placed my dirty dishes in the sink and as I headed down the hall, I heard her calling to me.

"Yeah?" I answered from the bottom of the stairs, unable to see her in the kitchen.

"I was wondering if I might join one of your meetings sometime. Not as a chaperone, but as a participant? Would that be okay?"

I smiled to myself before answering. "I'll talk to the rest of the group, but I think that would be fine. I'll let you know."

"Thank you," was her disembodied reply.

When I reached the top of the stairs, I heard my cell phone ringing on my bedside table. I darted down the hall and grabbed it, putting it to my ear without checking the caller ID.

"Hello?"

"Is this Cassie?"

"What's up, Chewy?" I said, recognizing his mellow voice.

"Can you come over?"

"To your house?"

"Yeah. My mom and little brother are at church. I'm here with Tunes, and we have something really important to show you."

"Did you call Taggart?"

There was a noticeable pause before he answered. "No. I don't think he should be here for this."

That didn't sound good. "Why not?"

"Just come," he said, and the line went dead.

I was already dressed in a pair of black sweatpants and a long-sleeve t-shirt with the logo of the New Haven Band emblazoned across the back. It was one of the many Mom purchased for me to support Becca's pastimes. I grabbed my fleece pullover and shoulder bag on my way out.

There was a chill in the air when I stepped outside. A brisk two block walk over to Chewy's house was the perfect antidote to a night of no sleep. From the outside, the Ledbetter's house appeared to have the same basic layout as ours, as did most of the homes in this section of New Haven. Before I had a chance to press the doorbell, the door opened.

Chewy looked like I did before the hot shower and pancakes… disheveled, a red tint in his eyes from lack of sleep, and mismatched clothes that had no business being on his body at the same time. He waved me in then turned and flew up the stairs.

"We're upstairs," I heard him say as I walked through the door.

When I followed his trail into a second-floor bedroom, I was met with the greatest collection of Star Wars memorabilia I had ever seen. A life-size Chewbacca standing in the corner dominated the room.

"Wow."

Chewy was sitting next to Tunes, both staring at a laptop on Tunes' lap. When they heard my reaction, they both looked up in unison.

"Oh… yeah… this is my collection. Pretty impressive, huh?"

I stepped into the middle of the room and did a complete 360. Every nook and cranny contained some element from the Star Wars universe.

"So, I guess you're not a Captain Kirk fan?"

"That's my brother," Chewy said, looking back down at the laptop's screen. "He's the Star Trek buff. You should see his room."

I tore my eyes from the excess around me and looked at the two of them sitting there.

"So what was so important?"

Chewy looked at Tunes. "Tell her."

"You tell her."

"You found it, so you need to tell her."

"But you called her and this is your house, so you need to tell her."

"I can't explain it like you can."

"Sure you can, just --"

I clapped my hands together. "Guys! Please, just tell me what's going on."

Chewy looked at Tunes and tilted his head to one side.

"Fine. Remember when I said we could use the MAC address table from the security system at Mr. Ledbetter's store to tell whose cell phone had come into the store the day he died?"

"Yes."

"Well, after we told you that, we went to the store and downloaded a copy of the table to my laptop, but we didn't do anything with it because after you talked to the police, we just kind of dropped it. After last night and Chewy seeing the spot on Stooch's arm, we decided to start playing around with it."

"This morning?"

"Last night after we got back. We haven't been to sleep."

Glad to know I wasn't the only one losing sleep over this.

"But I thought we could only use that if we had a specific phone we wanted to check?" I asked.

"That's true, but I wanted to test my theory so I used Chewy's phone to see if it would work," replied Tunes.

"And did it?"

"Yes."

"Well, that's good. But I didn't need to rush over here for you to tell me that."

Tunes looked at Chewy and then down at the laptop.

"That wasn't the only thing he found," Chewy said.

My impatience rising, I took a deep breath.

"What else did you find, Tunes?"

"Not only did Chewy's MAC address show up on the database, but so did another."

"I'm confused."

"During the process of accessing Chewy's MAC address, I had to dump all the addresses of any phone he connected with as well. His phone stores the MAC address of every phone that calls him, texts, or send him pictures."

"She sent me a picture of her acceptance letter into Perlman," Chewy mumbled.

"What are you talking about?"

"Your sister, Becca, her phone was at my dad's store the day before the accident."

Twenty-Four

I chose to ignore the doorbell and started pounding on the door. After a couple seconds of no response, I went at it again.

"Maybe he went to church?" Chewy said behind me.

"He doesn't go to church," I replied through clenched teeth.

"How do you know?"

"Have you met him?"

"Okay, but I'm pretty sure the Wilsons do," Tunes pointed out.

"He doesn't," I repeated, even though I had no reason to say that other than what little I knew about him.

There was still no movement from inside the house. I decided to change tactics, pushing on the doorbell like it was the fire button on an Xbox controller and I had to defend the earth from alien invasion.

It worked like a charm because the door flew open and Taggart stood there in a black t-shirt with a white outline of the thinking man on the chest. He looked at the three of us with an equal mix of irritation, surprise, and embarrassment.

"Can we come in?" I asked sternly, trying to make it sound more like an order than a question.

"No."

I shuffled my feet. "Well, we need to talk."

Taggart stared at me, undoubtedly trying to decide how to deal with us. His hair was messier than normal, as if he had just climbed out of bed, but the red in his eyes and the dark half-moons beneath them looked anything but rested. If I wasn't so upset, I might have even kidded him about it.

Finally, Taggart jerked his head in the direction of a swinging chair at the end of the porch, so I walked over and took a seat. There was plenty of room for someone else to sit next to me, but neither Chewy, Tunes, nor Taggart made a motion to claim it. Chewy and Tunes both leaned against the porch railing, and Taggart stood there with his arms crossed.

I waited a few moments for Taggart to ask us what we wanted, but when I realized he had no intention of doing so, I plunged in.

"You've been hiding something from all of us since the beginning and now you've lied to us. We want to know what's going on."

His answer was immediate and sounded rehearsed. "I don't know what you're talking about."

"Really? You weren't honest to us about being at the football game when Stooch died because we all saw you there. To tell you the truth… wait. I always tell the truth, what I mean is, to be frank, that hurts me. You've gone out of your way, and I understand how far you've gone, to form this connection with us, especially me, but when it really counts you won't deliver the goods. How can we trust you if you lie to us? How is that supposed to make us feel? How do you think I feel?"

"You've talked to my foster parents?" Taggart asked, frowning.

That caught me off guard. "What?"

"You've talked to my foster parents," he repeated, this time as more of a statement than a question.

How could he know? I briefly thought about denying it, but it was clear he knew something. Why else would he say that? Besides, I couldn't sit here and berate him about lying when I turned around and did the same.

"They told you?" I asked hesitantly.

"No."

"Then how did you know?"

"Mr. Wilson says the same thing about telling the truth and being frank. It's not a common distinction, so you must have heard it from him."

"He's a nice man. They both are good people."

Taggart turned his head to look at Chewy and Tunes. "Were you all here?"

"No," I answered for them, even though they were both shaking their heads. "It was just me. Becca and I didn't talk much about you, really at all, so after the accident I felt like I needed to find out more about you. I'm sorry, but I didn't know where else to go."

"So, you've been keeping things from me that you felt wasn't pertinent. What else haven't you told me?"

I thought of Becca's journal and my conversation with Vice Principal Stevens. My bond with Taggart had improved so much over the past week, in fact, his relationship with all of us had, but now I feared revealing those tidbits would set things back. I couldn't let that happen, not now. Besides, it was clear where he was heading with this, and I wasn't going to bite. My irritation with him, which had briefly taken a back seat to guilt, was beginning to return.

"Don't try and turn this around. We want to know what you've been keeping from us."

"Not being forthcoming isn't lying."

"That's debatable, but the difference here is I didn't lie when confronted about it. I want to know what you know."

Taggart's gaze focused on my feet. "I... I don't—"

"Why were you at that football game? Who were you talking to?"

Taggart remained quiet.

"TELL ME."

"My therapist," he finally answered in a voice so soft I barely made it out.

That took me by surprise. "Your therapist? Surely you weren't having a session right there at the game."

Taggart shook his head.

"So why were you there?"

Taggart returned to his silent mode, his eyes still locked downward.

"Okay, different question. What was my sister doing in Mr. Ledbetter's store the day before the accident?"

His head snapped up. I could tell by the look in his eyes that I'd hit pay dirt.

"She wasn't."

"No? Then she was close enough for her cellphone to connect to the store's Wi-Fi. Maybe from the parking lot?"

Taggart was silent, but I knew I was on the right track.

"She drove you there, didn't she?"

It was barely noticeable, but his shoulders sagged and his head dipped up and down.

"What were you doing at my dad's store?" Chewy asked, bouncing off the railing and moving to stand next to Taggart. He was body rocking so hard he reminded me of a prizefighter.

Taggart's response was barely audible. "I went to apply for a job."

Chewy looked at me and I at him. Tunes came around and stood next to Taggart on the side opposite Chewy.

"You applied for a job? That's all?"

"Yes."

"But why would you need to keep that a secret?"

Taggart reached one of his hands around to his back pocket and pulled out a folded piece of paper, then handed it to me.

"I'm sorry."

I unfolded the piece of paper and looked at it. On it was the list of names Taggart had put together of possible aneurysm murders, with four of them circled.

Robert Price
Don Morgan
Melinda McClellan
Robert East
Alice Bell
William Lutz
Peggy Stiles
John Marks
Frances Hendrix
Todd Wyatt
Barbara Collins
Benny Fowler
Francis Potter
Gene Lee
Eddie Teague
Bill Franks
Jerry Tyler
James Chow
Christian Salvador
Derrick Stout
Tim Ledbetter

I showed the list to Chewy and Tunes.

"I don't get it," I said.

Taggart drew in a deep breath and closed his eyes.

"Robert East and his wife were the second foster parents I was sent to during my time here in New Haven. He wasn't a particularly pleasant person and had a very loose interpretation of what constituted reasonable punishment. His wife was a spineless puppet and did whatever her husband said. The man died while he was eating a cheeseburger at the Burger Barn for lunch one day and I ended up being placed with a new family.

"When I was ten, my foster parents at the time thought it would be a good idea for me to learn how to play soccer. Why not? All of the other kids were doing it and they decided I needed a way to fit in. So they enrolled me in the city soccer league. I was placed on a team with Todd Wyatt as my coach. Wyatt was one of those dads who only signed up to coach so he could make sure his son played all the good positions. He didn't know the first thing about soccer and he was clueless about how to coach, but he had a whistle and certainly knew how to scream. Naturally, when things didn't go as planned he took it out on his players, and the more decibels the better. Once I accidentally scored a goal for the other team, or maybe I did it on purpose, I forget. Anyway, he rewarded me with an especially vehement display of coaching expertise that day. He was a real estate agent and he died while he was showing a house a week later.

"James Chow was a teacher at New Haven junior high where he instructed seventh-grade science. By all accounts, he was a respected teacher, dutiful husband, and a loving father. He attended Trinity Baptist church where he also taught bible school on Sunday mornings. He liked to golf on weekends and he died on the 6th hole at his country club."

"You already know about Chewy's father and Kevin Steuer. All of those are just the ones where I could identify a definite link, but there could be others."

Taggart had kept his eyes shut while he delivered his monologue, but now he opened them and looked me directly in the eyes. In them, I saw a deep sadness.

"You were right to blame me for your sister's death," he said. "She's dead… all those people I just spoke of are dead… because they knew me."

I was stunned. In shock. My mind was going a million miles a minute, backwards.

"You're the connection?"

He nodded his head slowly. "They've all done something to hurt or harm me in some way."

We must have all been numb, except Taggart of course, because no one was talking. Taggart was silent for another reason, and now I knew why. I understood why he had been that way all along.

"When did you know?" I asked.

"I thought it was strange after Mr. Chow, but really I didn't become suspicious until Chewy told me his dad owned that store. My research about the abnormally high death rates and reading about the apparent bite on Mr. Ledbetter's body in his autopsy made me 80% certain. It wasn't until Stooch died, and we saw the puncture wound for ourselves, that I was 100%."

"So, why didn't you tell us?"

There was a long pause before Taggart answered. "I wasn't completely sure until last night. Before that, even with all the statistics and the mark on Chewy's dad, I still hoped, maybe, that the research we were doing to find a link would reveal another possibility."

I got it. The guilt he must have been dealing with would lead anyone to grasp at straws, even imaginary ones.

"Wait. What you mentioned Mr. Chow. What did he do to you?" Tunes asked.

Taggart turned his head to look at him. "I get good grades in school."

"Yeah, we know. Cassie told us you're supposed to be a Brainiac."

"I've never made anything less than an A. Except once. Care to guess who gave me a B?"

"Oh shit."

"One of the questions on a quiz he gave our class was based on inaccurate information. I answered it as it needed to be answered, but he insisted that I should have answered as it was stated in the textbook. It was a simple five-question quiz, but I got a B. He chose not to use that question on any later tests and the textbook was subsequently upgraded to a new version with the corrected information."

"You think somebody murdered Mr. Chow because he gave you a B?" I asked, not really expecting an answer.

"Clearly, whoever is doing this, is insane," Taggart replied.

Tunes shook his head. "Maybe it's just a coincidence. Maybe they're all just coincidences?"

"Five people, all dying the same mysterious way, all with connections to me? Even taking into consideration this is a small town, that's just not unlikely, it's impossible."

"Someone killed my dad because he didn't give you a job?" Chewy asked. I reached out and put my hand on his shoulder.

"I believe so," Taggart said to Chewy, and then he looked at me. "Which means Becca ultimately died because of me also. Obviously, there was no way anyone could have anticipated that Mr. Ledbetter would try to get home after he was injected and our paths would cross at that exact moment on the train tracks, but she died because of me, nonetheless. Whoever is doing this, almost killed me."

"But you just filled out the application the day before. How did you know he wasn't going to hire you? How would anyone know?" I asked.

"I didn't fill out an application. He told me not to bother."

Chewy furrowed his eyebrows. "But why?"

"Because he had no intention of hiring me."

"What?" Chewy exclaimed.

"He said he had heard stories about me and couldn't take the risk."

"And of course, being who you are, you didn't try to plead your case and set him straight," I said, doing my best to fill in the blanks.

"No, I didn't."

"But still, how would anyone know about that? My dad wouldn't have said anything to anyone. Did you tell anyone?"

Taggart nodded his head. "Four people. Becca, of course. The Wilsons, because they were the ones who encouraged me to apply. It's possible they mentioned it at church, because that's where they found out about the job in the first place."

"And who's the other person?" I asked.

"My therapist."

My mind went back to the night Stooch died. "When we saw you at the football stadium, you were doing what?"

"Surveillance. I confronted him after Stooch collapsed to find out why he was there."

"He's a suspect?"

Taggart nodded his head. "But I never told him about Stooch's prank with the train whistle in my locker, which I deduce is what put the target on his back."

"Everyone knew about that. Heck, even the people at my work knew about that."

"But why," Chewy interjected. "Why would anyone be doing this? Why would anyone want to be your psycho guardian angel?"

"I've been deliberating on that considerably, and I have a theory," Taggart stated.

"Go on. We're all ears," I said.

"I think there is a name missing from that list," Taggart said, gesturing at the paper in my hand. "And it's one that might be the key to everything."

"You mean other than Stooch?" Chewy asked.

"Yes."

"Who?" I asked, impatiently.

"Samantha McGill… my mother."

"You think your mother was killed by this same person?"

"Wait… I thought you were abandoned here," Chewy said.

"It's more than that," Taggart continued, ignoring Chewy. "I believe she was New Haven's first victim."

Suddenly it felt very cold outside. "Why do I have the feeling that's not all of it?"

"I believe my mother was running away from somebody. That person followed us here from Atlanta, killed her, then has remained in New Haven to keep a watchful eye on me."

"And?" I asked, although I was pretty sure I already knew the answer.

"That person is my father."

We all stood there in stunned silence.

"You think your dad is living in New Haven, pretending to be someone else?" Chewy said, placing his hands on top of his head. "That's messed up."

My mind was racing. A thought popped into my head. One that I'm pretty sure Taggart had already contemplated, but somehow, I knew it needed to be me to say it out loud.

"Then we need to go to Atlanta."

"Atlanta, why there? Taggart just said the creep is right here in New Haven," Chewy stated.

"If it is Taggart's father doing this, and I trust Taggart's instincts, then we can't just give every guy in New Haven a DNA test to uncover him. We need to find out more about the man, and our best chance to do that is in Atlanta."

"But it's a huge city. You're talking about finding a needle in a haystack."

Taggart looked at Chewy. "Do you know how you find a needle in a haystack?"

"You set the haystack on fire," Tunes offered, which made me chuckle.

"That is one way, but I think the people of Atlanta might object to that method. There is a more efficient way."

"Which is?" I asked.

"We use a magnet."

Twenty-Five

I adjusted my windshield wipers again, trying to find that perfect setting to clear the drizzly rain we'd been driving through for the last thirty minutes. Satisfied I'd found the right speed, for the time being, I leaned back and glanced over at Taggart. He was in the passenger seat, asleep, or pretending to be, his head propped against the side window with his hoodie pulled up over his head. Cruising up I-95 at six in the morning, ditching school, heading towards Atlanta on a Thursday sure wasn't how I envisioned things turning out when we first met.

Taggart had floored us that morning when he told us that not only was he at the center of the murders, but his father, someone he had absolutely no recollection of, was probably behind it all and living amongst us. It was unreal. I tried to imagine what it would be like to have someone lurking in the shadows of my world, watching from a distance as I grew up, issuing death sentences to anyone who did me wrong.

I shuddered at the thought.

Taggart hinted that he used to think everything went wrong in his life after his mother died, but I don't think he was so sure now. Although he couldn't remember much of anything before that day, I'm sure he contemplated who his dad was and where he was? What was he doing? That's what I would do. He mentioned the possibility that the nightmare of his life began long before New Haven. Maybe the blocked memories of his early childhood weren't caused by what happened in that gas station bathroom, but instead by something earlier, something leading up to that day that was even more horrifying.

At the sound of somebody stirring in the backseat, I looked in the rearview mirror. Delta and Chewy were both slumped against their respective doors, but I had the best view of Chewy. His chin was tucked into his chest, causing his glasses to slip down near the tip of his nose. I admired Chewy for the way he handled Taggart's admission, but at the same time, it reminded me of how disappointed I was in myself. Back in the hospital room right after the accident, I'd reacted terribly when I discovered Becca was dead and Taggart had survived. The anger, the blame I was so anxious to hang around his neck. Knowing that the accident was collateral damage from a deliberate act tied to Taggart, I realized now he was merely a pawn in someone else's chess game and holding him responsible was wrong. Chewy figured that out all by himself in a matter of minutes, but I had to get reamed out by my parents and do some serious soul searching before I woke up to that fact. I gained a lot of respect for Chewy that morning.

Taggart and I were both sure the answers about his dad's identity were waiting for him in Atlanta. It was where he and his mother had departed from before the bus deposited them both in New Haven. Back then Social Services were unable to determine who Taggart's father was, unable to even find a birth certificate for the child. But surely

Samantha McGill had left her mark on the city in some way and going there was the only way to get people to open up. Never mind it was a humongous city and looking for clues about his family would be like flipping through a *Where's Waldo* book. But deciding to accompany him was a no-brainer. Even Delta jumped on-board after we filled her in. I received a serious tongue-lashing for not calling her when it all went down.

We all wanted to leave right away, but for some reason Taggart said he couldn't go until Thursday. It didn't mean we couldn't be doing things before we left though. First, Taggart needed the football jersey from Chewy to have it tested, but he wouldn't let us know how he was going to do that. The cat may have been let out of the bag in terms of his big secret, but that didn't mean he'd stopped keeping things from us. Still, we trusted him enough to not sweat the details.

Knowing that Taggart was the murderer's common denominator, we next needed to construct a list of suspects to go with our list of victims. People on that list fell into two categories: those who knew and interacted with Taggart on some level, regardless of how minor, and people who moved to New Haven after he and his mother arrived. It took us a couple days to compile both lists, and they were extensive, but the number of suspects on both lists wasn't. There were only six names, and a few of them were startling.

Jeff Ford (one of Taggart's former foster parents), Vice Principal Stevens, Sgt. John Brown (the police detective who showed us Mr. Ledbetter's autopsy results), Mr. Wilkins (our biology teacher)—and the one that in my mind was circled in bright red highlighter—Kent Gleason (Taggart's psychiatrist). Taggart added an additional name, one which did, and didn't, surprise me, but not because the name didn't appear on both lists. It was Dr. Weathers from the vet clinic. Taggart and he had never crossed paths directly, but as Taggart had pointed out to me earlier, Dr. Weathers moved to town just before the murders began and he did have a relationship with Becca—who was Taggart's only friend. Although I still didn't think he belonged on the list, I didn't put up much of an argument.

Wednesday we learned that the Steuer's had won their battle to bury their son without an autopsy. That would take place on Friday. The fact that Mr. Steuer was a high-powered lawyer obviously helped their cause. I was relieved that we would be back from Atlanta in time. Stooch wasn't one of my favorite people and could be a real douche-bag, but he meant a lot to Jason, and I wanted to be there.

The drive from New Haven to Atlanta, according to Google Maps, would take almost five hours, with decent traffic. Even if we left early in the morning on Thursday, we still wouldn't have enough time to see all the people and ask the questions we needed to in one day, so overnighting would be a necessity. I knew we could crash at my Aunt Cathy and Uncle Don's house, but first I had to come up with a convincing story that would explain why I needed to skip two days of school, be in Atlanta overnight with four friends— two of whom were freshman. It was Taggart who actually came up with the idea.

"Didn't you apply to Georgia Tech?" he asked me when we were brainstorming one day.

"Yes, how did you know that?"

"Becca."

"I applied there also," Delta chimed in.

"Okay, we tell your parents the school is holding a fall pre-enrollment tour and an opportunity to meet with admission counselors on Thursday afternoon and the three of us want to attend. You'll need to stay the night because otherwise, you'd be driving back too late."

"That's good, except that they'll want to come—"

"So will my parents," Delta agreed.

"You have to convince them that you're really serious about Tech and for this first visit you really want to check it out on your own with your friends, without them looking over your shoulder. If you like what you see there will be another tour in the spring."

"I could probably make that work," I said.

"Me too, especially if you persuade your parents first," Delta said.

"What me and Tunes?" Chewy asked.

"As far as excuses for your parents, I'm still working on that, but Cassie can tell her aunt and uncle that they're a pair of prodigies looking to enroll early."

"I like the sound of that, prodigy," Chewy beamed.

"He left out the *child* part," Delta added.

Swaying my parents turned out to be a piece of cake. Georgia Tech was my dad's alma mater, and once they knew I was seriously interested in going there (not really – well, maybe), that I was going up there with Delta and Taggart, and I planned on staying with Aunt Cathy and Uncle Don, they were on-board. I guess years of playing by the rules and being honest (mostly) counted for something. Once I secured my permission, Delta quickly received hers. Chewy took advantage of his mom's worries about her health and the family's future by getting her to sign a fake permission slip that Taggart made up for an overnight class trip to some imaginary science camp.

Tunes, however, wasn't as lucky. His parents put a kibosh on the camp, telling him he would have to wait until he was a year or two older. Tunes was going to have to sit this trip out, and he was none-too-pleased. Delta softened the blow by informing him he would have the honor of taking her on an official date when we got back. He still wasn't happy about being left behind, but his mood certainly improved after that.

I was starting to zone out behind the wheel, so I reached over and punched Taggart in the arm.

"You have to talk to me," I said.

He pulled back his hood just enough so I could see his eyes through his floppy hair.

"Why?"

"So I don't fall asleep," I lied.

"Do you want me to drive?"

"No, I want you to talk to me."

He slowly sat up straight in his seat and pulled the hoody off his head and the earbuds from his ears.

"What do you want to talk about?" he asked, followed by a serious yawn.

"Anything. Nothing. I just want to talk. Why do you think Tunes wears those headphones all the time? Chewy says he's been wearing them since the first grade, but he doesn't know why."

"Attention deficit hyperactivity disorder," Taggart mumbled.

"Huh?"

"You've heard of ADHD?"

"Sure."

"The form of ADHD he has causes him to be distracted by sound, any sound. It can be very debilitating. He uses the headphones to block out distracting noises, which reduces anxiety and calms him. A kind of audio sedation. It's still not widely accepted, but the experimental technique introduces specific sound frequencies to each side of the brain, which speeds up the brainwaves, particularly in the left hemisphere, so hyperactivity is reduced. Also, by stimulating the right brain hemisphere, emotional reactions can be reduced, and improvements in attention and concentration are achieved, all without the use of drugs. He listens to binaural beat music, which is designed for headphones. There are those who claim that it's the equivalent to auditory snake oil, but it has obviously worked for Tunes."

"You're kidding," I said. "I thought it was some sort of music obsession or a fashion statement, like getting a tattoo or some kind of bizarre piercings."

"It may have evolved into something like that because I doubt he needs them now. He's been wearing them since 4th grade."

"How do you know this stuff?" I asked.

"I asked him."

I let my eyes leave the road to look over at him. "You talk to Tunes when I'm not around?"

"Yes."

I was taken off-guard by this and it left me feeling something odd. It was a combination of pride… and jealousy? Maybe even possessiveness. There was no denying I had developed feelings for Taggart, especially the exclusive bond we shared, but now I could see that he was slowly expanding his bubble and its boundaries. I guess I should have been pleased, both for him making that kind of progress, and for myself in helping him get there. Instead, all I could feel was a twinge of sorrow.

"Who else do you talk to?"

"I talk to everyone."

"Everyone?"

"Well, everyone in our group. One at a time of course."

Out of the corner of my eye I could see him fiddling with his earbuds. Thinking. "It's necessary," he finally said.

"It was necessary to know about why Tunes wears headphones?"

Taggart turned his head to look outside. "I was curious."

"Really? So what can you tell me about Chewy?"

"I know the karaoke video of him and his dad has reached fifty thousand views. He said it's gone viral. I also know he adopted his nickname Chewy from the character Chewbacca in Star Wars, but not because he was his favorite character. Instead, he chose Chewy because of their similar heritage."

"Excuse me?"

"Chewbacca's backstory was that his people, the Wookies, were a slave race used as both science experiments and miners. And like his people, Chewbacca was forced into slavery until he was freed by Han Solo and ended up swearing a life debt to him. As a young child Chewy was drawn to the fact that someone from a background such as that could rise up to become one of the most recognized heroes of all time."

"Wow, that's cool. How about Delta? What have you learned about—"

"Don't you dare be repeating anything I told you," Delta's voice suddenly came from the back.

"She quit being a cheerleader because the other girls made her feel like she was the ugliest one on the squad," Taggart answered anyway.

"TAGGART!"

A half-eaten package of powdered donuts came flying from the back and struck Taggart on the side of the head.

"You need to go back to being the quiet loner type."

"Delta, tell me you didn't believe—"

"No. Of course I didn't."

"Good. Because I could see you as second ugliest, third if you let me do your mascara."

The small pillow Delta had been using banged up against the back of my headrest.

"Since you're awake, you do know that Tunes has a serious crush on—"

"I know."

"So what are you going to do about it? I'm not sure it was the smartest thing, telling him he could ask you—"

"I know, I know. It was a spur of the moment thing. He was so crushed that he couldn't come with us. I know he's only a freshman, but he definitely has cute going for him, and now that I know about his ADHD—"

"You're not going to hold that against him are you?"

"No. Before, I just thought he was weird. I actually like him more now that I know about it."

"What's wrong with being a freshman or being weird?" Chewy spoke up, straightening his position on the seat.

"Nothing. It's just that I'll be leaving for college next year."

"What's that got to do with anything? It's not like you're getting engaged or anything. Besides, don't you remember, Tunes and I are prodigies. We'll be heading to college, too."

We all laughed at that, except Taggart. I did see a grin on his face though.

For a while, we let the sound of the road and the rhythmic pace of the windshield wipers fill the void in our conversation. Chewy broke the silence.

"Taggart, I have a question. You seem convinced that your therapist is our main suspect, right?"

"Yes."

"That would mean you think he could be your father also, right?"

"Again, correct"

"Then why are we driving to Atlanta?"

"Chewy, we already discussed this," I interjected.

"Yeah, we did, but that doesn't mean I understand it. We have loads of time, so let him explain it to me again."

"That's one possible theory, one that I strongly believe, but a theory none the less. We need to find something that will confirm it."

"He moved to New Haven less than a year after you got here and as your therapist, he's known every little detail of your life since you were how old?"

"Fourteen. But there are other therapists in New Haven. He couldn't have known my foster parents would bring me to him."

"Let's chalk that up to a lucky coincidence. Come on, he was the only person you told that my dad didn't give you the job and you saw him at the football game the night Stooch was killed. And he's not married and doesn't have any kids, so what was he doing there? That by itself is enough to make him look suspicious. How many middle-aged men do you know who are single in this town? What else do you want?"

"I told the Wilsons about the job. They could have told others."

"But that's unlikely because they know how much your privacy means to you," I explained, despite the fact that we had this discussion multiple times already.

"That is true."

"Does your therapist have a dimpled chin like you?" Delta asked.

Taggart shook his head. "No, but that doesn't mean anything. Cleft chins are hereditary but variable. While there is definitely a strong genetic influence, it is not a certainty. My mother had one but my father could have a perfectly smooth chin."

"Who cares?" Chewy asked. "We should be trying to steal this guy's cell phone to see if it shows up on the stores MAC address list, or get some of his DNA and have it tested against yours instead of wasting our time going to Atlanta."

"You're just upset that Tunes couldn't come along. Anyway, how are you going to get DNA tested?" I asked.

"Heck, you can send samples off to sites you find online and they'll tell you if you're related. It's not that hard."

"Those kinds of tests take as long as eight weeks," Taggart replied. "We could find out something this afternoon."

The car went quiet again, so I turned on the radio to kill the monotony of the drive. Still, the irony of both Taggart's and Chewy's situation ate at me. Chewy lost a father and Taggart was trying to find one. In both cases, the result would be… devastation.

Twenty-Six

Mid-morning the traffic on I-85 through downtown Atlanta was not something I was prepared for. Trying to change lanes and being honked at, going too slow and having someone stick their head out the window and yell at me was nerve-wracking, to say the least. It had me questioning whether I wanted to go to college anywhere near a big city. I had been to Atlanta with my parents before and seen my share of traffic snarls, but the experience was different when you were behind the wheel. It wasn't the blatant disregard for common courtesy or the 'every man for himself' mentality, but the sheer number of cars and how fast they were moving. I felt like I was running with the bulls in Spain. One moment I'd get used to the ebb and flow and work up the courage to attempt a routine lane change, the next I was zooming double-digits over the speed limit to prevent getting run over by a semi while trying to read the signs and anticipate my next move. Compounding matters was Delta as a back-seat driver, to which I finally responded with a snippy 'I got this.' I was stressed to the limit but doing my best to convey a *ho-hum* attitude to the others. I was not having a good time.

I followed Taggart's instructions and gladly pulled off I-85 onto West Peachtree Street. At the next intersection, I turned left onto North Avenue and a half mile later turned right onto Cherry Street, coming to a halt behind a line of red taillights.

"Where are we headed?" I asked as I waited for the cars ahead of me to creep forward.

"The Georgia Tech student center," Taggart replied.

"You do know that going to the college was only a cover story, right? We don't actually have to go there."

"Just trust me."

We crawled along until Taggart spotted a parking lot that didn't require a student parking sticker. After searching for an open space for several minutes, we found one that was a long walk from the entrance.

"We have to hurry," Taggart said as we all got out of the car.

"For what?" Chewy asked.

Taggart took off through the parking lot, Chewy close behind, weaving in and out of cars, walking at a feverish rate and leaving us shorter girls struggling to keep up.

"We need to be in front of the student center standing by the fountain at 11:15."

I looked at my phone. It was 11:05. "Why?"

"Maybe nothing, but maybe everything."

"Taggart, you're being cryptic again."

He didn't respond, instead he lengthened his strides and left us hurrying to catch up. We made it to a sidewalk that took us around the side of a large, four-story building. When we emerged on the other side, we came face-to-face with a sunken multi-level fountain. From its center rose an eighty-foot pointed structure resembling a twisted obelisk. The impressive artwork was made up of individual plates, each rotated slightly to produce the swirling pattern as height increased and it tapered off towards the top, capped by a pyramidal piece. The fountain stood in front of an amphitheater made up of staggered rows of seats on one side and an open walkway leading out into vast common area covered by thick rich grass. Everywhere you looked students lounged around the fountain, studying open books on their laps, or walking casually on their way to class or some other destination.

As we drew closer, Taggart focused on someone standing at the far side of the fountain. It was a man in a dark suit and sunglasses, his hands crossed in front, staring absently at the spraying water. The three of us followed Taggart as he headed straight for the man.

"Who's that?" I asked as I fell into step beside Taggart.

"Just follow my lead," he replied, which did little to improve the frazzled mood I had acquired from our voyage through traffic hell.

As Taggart approached the dark-suited man, I was thinking FBI or Secret Service. He had that look. About six feet tall, an athletic build that was obvious even with the suit, short-cropped hair, and a blank expression that would make professional poker players jealous. He was definitely from some branch of the government, except he didn't sport the traditional aviator sunglasses I imagined them all wearing. He wore Oakley's.

"I believe you are waiting for us," Taggart said to the agent.

Whoever this was, he didn't look at Taggart when he responded, choosing instead to continue admiring the fountain.

"I think not."

The two words that Taggart said next changed the agent's demeanor completely.

"Brain aneurysm."

The agent dropped his hands and turned to face Taggart, slowly taking his time to look at all four of us. He gestured at Taggart.

"You are to come with me."

"All of us are all going with you," Taggart responded back to the agent.

"We are?" Delta asked. She looked from Taggart to me. "I'm not going anywhere with Agent Smith or whoever he is."

The movement of the agent's head from side to side was so brief I barely caught it.

"Just you," the agent said, turning to walk in the other direction.

"They go where I go," Taggart called after him,

The man in the suit stopped walking and half-turned. "That's a problem, because I'm only taking you."

Taggart looked at Chewy, then replied. "Then never mind."

I smiled, remembering this exact scene, in reverse, playing out in front of our high school. Chewy smiled also.

The agent stared at us for a couple seconds, then reached into his pocket and pulled out a cell phone. While he made a call to someone, the four of us formed a circle.

"What's going on Taggart?" I started.

"The drug used for the murders must be a specialized neuro-toxin, so I did a little research. There are three or four drug companies in the Atlanta area with research facilities and resources capable of developing something of this nature. I took samples of the blood from the football jersey and FedEx'd it to each of them, anonymously, instructing the creator to meet with us here at this time. He is obviously a representative from one of those companies."

"That's smart, but what if no one had showed up?" Chewy asked.

"It would have reinforced my strategy of keeping you in the dark was the right thing to do and we would have proceeded on to the police station."

"He looks like FBI," I offered.

"I believe he is private security."

"Did you happen to think that they might want to make us disappear? You know, to cover up the fact their drug is being used to kill people?" Chewy asked.

"You watch too many movies, Chewy. Companies don't really do that," Delta said.

"Chewy is right," Taggart interjected. "That is a real possibility… which is why I made sure I didn't come alone."

All three of us stared at him.

"That was a joke," he said, but his face was flat as ever. "We are perfectly safe. A company wouldn't be held accountable for the actions of a deranged ex-employee, if that indeed is what my father is."

"This way," the agent called out to us, his cell phone back in his pocket.

We followed him through the open grounds to a large black Escalade, still running, parallel parked in a no-parking zone on the road. The agent opened the rear door and gestured for us to enter. Chewy and Delta went in first, taking the third seat, then Taggart disappeared inside, and next it was my turn. I hesitated. What was I doing? How had I allowed things to get this far? We were so far down a rabbit hole that I was seriously afraid of screwing up my whole future. Did Nancy Drew ever go to college, get a husband and raise a family? Look at what a mess Veronica Mars life turned out to be.

"Cassie, it's alright," Taggart said softly as he leaned out of the Escalade. "We're going to talk to some people, that's all."

I took a deep breath and climbed in.

Inside the SUV, the upholstery was all black leather. The windows were heavily tinted as well, the dim beams from the overhead dome the only source of light and making it virtually impossible to see outside. There was even a divider between the front of the car and the back, like a taxi, complete with a sliding window. Just as I slid in beside Taggart, he briefly stuck his head through the divider, and then sat back in his seat.

After the agent got behind the wheel, he closed the divider window, also heavily tinted, effectively cutting off our view of the surroundings and thrusting us into darkness. We were then quickly on our way, but where we were going was a complete mystery. We drove in silence for around thirty minutes, navigating mostly back roads and avoiding the interstates as best as I could tell. It was disorienting and my heart was racing so fast that I needed something to reassure me everything was still okay, so I reached over and took hold of Taggart's hand. I didn't look to see his reaction; I was just glad he didn't pull away. But then he gave my sweaty hand a gentle squeeze, and everything changed. It was like a healthy dose of Novocain surged up my arm, through my shoulders, numbing my entire body. My breathing slowed and I felt totally calm. With Taggart holding my hand, I felt fearless.

After a hasty turn, the Escalade dipped down a sharp incline and a minute later came to a complete halt. We sat there for what seemed like an eternity, the sound of the SUV's purring engine our only link to the outside world.

"What now?" Chewy asked, breaking the silence.

"I'm really not liking this Cassie," Delta whispered.

I was about to reassure her when the sliding window opened.

"Cell phones remain in the car," the agent commanded.

I heard the agent's door open, and a few seconds later the door next to Taggart swung open. Stepping onto the pavement, it was clear that we were now in some sort of underground parking lot, dimly lit, facing glass doors that opened into a small lobby containing a bank of elevators.

"Take the elevator to the seventh floor. Someone will meet you."

Before exiting the SUV Taggart stuck his head through the open sliding window again, looking at something in the front of the car, then climbed out and surveyed our surroundings. He then led us through the doors and pushed the button to call for the elevator. A few moments later, the doors opened and we entered.

At the seventh floor, the doors opened to a sharply dressed woman holding a cell phone between both her hands.

"Welcome. How was everyone's ride?" the woman in her mid-thirties, with a poor excuse for a smile on her face, asked. Before anyone had a chance to answer she said, "Won't you follow me." She began a brisk walk down a hallway to her left. We followed her a short distance into a rectangular conference room with glass walls looking into the hallway and windows covered with heavy blinds that lowered from the ceiling. In the center of the room was a large oak table with a dozen chairs around it that were so fancy they looked more like decorations than furniture. Mounted on the wall at the far end of the room was a massive digital display that had to be eighty or ninety inches. *Dad would be so jealous of that.*

It was then that it struck me. There was no noise. No sounds of employees hustling and bustling. No sounds of the city from outside. Nothing. Was the building empty? Were we outside the city now?

"Have a seat and make yourself comfortable," the woman said, standing to the side of the door so we could enter. "Dr. Feinstein will be with you momentarily. Can I get anyone something to drink?"

"Do you have any Red Bull?" Delta replied.

"I'm sorry, no. Bottled water or tea only."

"We are all fine, thank you," Taggart answered as he took a seat.

Delta shot Taggart a look, then took a seat in the chair closest to the door. When the woman disappeared, Chewy and Taggart took a seat next to Delta. I walked around to the other side of the table and looked out the window.

"Have you noticed there's no company logo anywhere, and no corporate name on anything?"

"Yes. I doubt it's accidental," Taggart responded.

"How about Dr. Feinstein?" Delta asked. "Did you recognize that name?"

"No, but the people we need to talk to wouldn't be listed on a public website anywhere."

As if he had been waiting for that exact moment, an older man dressed in a white lab coat with a matching white shirt and dark colored tie strolled into the room.

"Good morning," the man said in a high-pitched voice. "Or is it afternoon, I lose track. Has everyone been offered a beverage?"

"You don't have any Red Bull," Delta was quick to point out.

"I'm sorry," the man said, furrowing his brow and running his hand across the bald dome on top of his head. "Would you like me to send someone out for some?"

"No, she wouldn't," I said, shooting Delta a look that meant stop playing around.

"Oh, okay. Well, if you have a seat we can get on with the business of answering each other's questions."

I took the seat directly in front of me and realized I had misjudged the chairs. It felt like I was suspended above the ground on a pile of down feathers. The man walked around the table and sat beside me, facing the others.

"Let's start off with some introductions. My name is Dr. Feinstein, but please call me Abner. I am the lead researcher here."

"And where is *here*?"

"That's not really important right now. I prefer to focus on you. Who am I speaking to?"

"My name is Taggart McGill, and this is Chewy Ledbetter, Delta Remington, and Cassie Underwood."

"Chewy? That's an unusual name. Are you a Star Wars fan by chance?"

Chewy smiled. "Yes, sir."

"I am as well. Can't wait for the next one to come out." Abner smiled at Chewy, and I could feel the tension draining from the room. Dr. Feinstein had one of those smiles that seemed honest, disarming. He reminded me of my grandfather from Louisiana, my dad's dad. He showered us with a similar smile every time we visited.

Abner turned his attention to Taggart. "So, if I were to guess, I'd say you were the one who sent us the package?"

Taggart nodded.

"I have to admit, it came as quite a shock when we learned how young you were. You live here in Atlanta?"

"Actually, New Haven. A small community on the coast near the Florida border."

"I think I've heard of it, down by Cumberland Island, I believe. Great golf courses down that way. A very affluent community. Much of a drive?"

"Five hours," I answered. I was getting a little tired of the twenty questions and wished that Taggart would get to the point.

"And you all are high school students?"

"Yes. We are all seniors except Chewy, he's a freshman."

"But I'm a prodigy," Chewy remarked, which caused Delta to snort a laugh.

"Do your parents know you are here?"

All of us remained silent, unwilling to admit the truth. But of course, Taggart had other plans.

"There is someone back home who knows exactly where we are," Taggart said evenly.

"I see. Well, you must have some idea what the sample contained or you wouldn't have sent it to us. That raises two

234

problems: one for you, and one for me. Your problem is that you found it in the blood of someone who died unexpectedly. My problem is the fact that it exists anywhere else besides this facility."

"I would appreciate it if you could explain," Taggart said.

"Certainly, but I require some answers myself, if you'd be so kind."

"Absolutely, but I need you to answer one question first."

"Sure. What is it?"

Taggart leaned forward, placing his forearms on the table. "Is it possible to predict the secondary, tertiary, and quaternary structure of a polypeptide sequence based solely on the sequence and environmental information?"

Huh, I thought to myself. What was Taggart doing? Abner's friendly face seemed to undergo a subtle change, his features hardening.

"Excuse me?"

"It's a rather straight-forward bio-chemistry problem. Could you please answer it for us?"

"Son, I didn't bring you here to answer elementary chemistry questions."

"And I didn't come here to ask them, but I find it necessary. Could you just answer it and we can move on? Otherwise, I believe this meeting is over."

Now I understood Taggart's intentions, but Dr. Feinstein was obviously not happy with it. He began fidgeting in his chair beside me.

"Yes," Abner finally answered.

"Really? That's it? A one-word answer?" Taggart asked.

"You asked if it was possible and I answered. Now can we get on with this?"

"Not before you tell me the kind of polypeptide sequence that will be adopted given the circumstances previously mentioned."

"You asked your one question and I answered it. I'm not answering anymore."

"Then I have a request."

Abner sighed and his smile returned, though not as warm as it once was. "Have you changed your mind about the water, or is there something else?"

"No, I'd like for you to bring in the real Abner Feinstein."

Twenty-Seven

I was somewhere between my fifteenth or sixteenth lap around the conference room when Chewy lost his patience.

"Cassie, will you please sit down?" he snapped at me.

"Yes. You're even getting on my nerves," Delta tagged in.

I ignored them both and continued. I had been anxiously pacing since the fake Abner Feinstein got up from his chair and strode out of the room without saying a word. Until then, things were going so well, or I thought so. We had been waiting forty-five minutes now, the four of us alone in this conference room. With each passing second I felt my poise slip further away.

"Cassie, please," Delta pleaded again.

I stopped at the far end of the table, crossed my arms, and looked back at them.

"Have I ever mentioned that I'm not very good at the whole patience thing?"

"No surprise there," Chewy responded.

I shot Chewy a mock smile.

"How did you know?" I directed at Taggart, who had been sitting silently with his hands folded on the table in front of him since the imposter had walked out.

Taggart shrugged.

"I suspected right away when he wanted to chit-chat. His manner was too open, too social. He was trying to put us at ease to learn as much about us as he could."

"It was working, because I liked him," I said.

"That's the same reason it raised doubt in me. Lead researchers in facilities such as this are here because of their brains, not their social skills. They are totally committed to their work and I doubt would even know what Star Wars is. They're uncomfortable speaking to anyone outside of their field. If he tried to pass himself off as an administrator or someone from HR, I wouldn't have been so doubtful, but that's not what he claimed to be."

"But maybe he was the exception? Maybe he was a scientist who actually could talk to normal people?" Delta pointed out.

"Thus the reason for my test."

"All that proved was that you're good at pissing people off," Delta said.

"No surprise there," Chewy quipped.

"Then why are they playing games with us?" I asked.

"I believe I can answer that for you," came a voice from behind, startling me. I whipped around as the display on the wall came to life. On the screen was the video image of a man, shot from the waist up, dressed similarly to the fake Dr. Feinstein. But this doctor was younger, probably in his low to mid-forties, with a full head of brown hair combed so well that every strand knew its place.

And he wasn't alone. Other scientists appeared busy working in a lab in the background.

I felt movement on both sides of me and realized the others had come forward to stand beside me.

"First off, let me apologize for the deception," the man on the screen said. "The subterfuge was at the insistence of our head of security. He's not a very trusting man."

"Should we assume that you are the real Dr. Feinstein?" Taggart asked.

"No. There is no Dr. Feinstein. But let me answer your other question first. Right now, it's not exactly possible to predict the secondary, tertiary, and quaternary structure of a polypeptide sequence based solely on the sequence and environmental information for all lengths of sequences. In some respects, it's easier to predict DNA/RNA structure versus protein structure, but once you throw in the polynucleotide in a complex environment, things get more complicated. Accuracy is a big problem. We're not very good at getting things one hundred percent correct when we do this yet. However, we can get a few models that are likely and sometimes when compared to experimental evidence we get close to right."

We all looked at Taggart, who simply nodded.

"Oh… and I do know what Star Wars is," the face on the wall added. "I've just never seen the movies."

"What is your name, then?" Taggart asked.

"If you don't mind, I'd prefer to not answer that. Besides, it is not germane to the answers you seek."

"But that's not fair. You know our names," Chewy said.

"That's true, but in a few minutes we'll discuss why your names are relevant."

"Is there a reason we can't speak to you in person?" Delta asked.

Dr. Anonymous drew a hand through his hair to straighten it, which didn't need straightening, and gave us an awkward smile.

"Two reasons. First off, expediency. This lab is located on the far side of the facility, several stories underground, and it would take me some time to reach you. But probably most pertinent, your friend was correct in his assessment of me and my co-workers. Interpersonal activities are a struggle for me, but I do quite well in front of an inanimate camera and a speaker."

"So, you can't see us?" Chewy asked, scanning the wall around the screen for a camera.

"No, I cannot. It's not necessary and actually makes this easier for me."

"Your company manufactured the drug in the blood sample I sent?" Taggart asked.

Dr. Anonymous's expression turned sour.

"That particular toxin contained in your sample was an early prototype, MC606. It never made it out of the preclinical research phase and was subsequently red-flagged."

"Red-flagged?"

"Developmentally terminated."

"How long ago was it *terminated?*"

"Quite a long time ago. Fourteen years, I believe. I was only a technician at the time."

I glanced at Taggart, who was doing a good job of keeping a straight face given the fact he and his mother showed up in New Haven fourteen years ago.

"And what was MC606 being developed for?"

"I couldn't say."

"Couldn't or won't?"

Dr. Anonymous scowled.

"I believe we are getting off topic."

"Let me try a question that you can answer. Does your company hold any government contracts?" Taggart asked.

"Mr. McGill, let's not make this confrontational and strive to stay on point. That is in your best interest. I can end this meeting at any point and you will be returned to where we picked you up, but not before your cell phones have had their GPS locators wiped. After you leave here, it will be as if this conversation never took place. Do you understand?"

"You can't believe we're going to let you—" Chewy began saying until Taggart grabbed him by the arm and put a finger to his own mouth. Instead of continuing Chewy extended one of his own middle fingers at the screen.

"We're really not the bad guys," Dr. Anonymous said, adopting both a softer tone and look. "If we hadn't shown up where you directed us, you would have never had any reason to link our company to the problems you're experiencing. You can imagine our reaction when we discovered a group of high school students sent the sample to us. We could have remained silent, and if it were up to our lawyers we would have, yet here we are willing to help. However, we must be pragmatic in this matter, thus our caution."

"Fine. Then can you tell me anything specific about how the toxin works?"

"MC606 attacks the artery walls at the base of a healthy brain, primarily around forks or branches, weakening them until a rupture becomes inevitable. The timing of the effects ranges from almost immediately to hours afterward, depending on the dosage and brain chemistry of the subject. Less than a cc is enough to prove fatal. The toxin has a 100% mortality rate and the body expunges it from the bloodstream within hours. The sample you provided must have been collected shortly after the toxin had been administered."

"Why would you want to make such an awful drug?" I heard myself saying.

"I'm told it was being developed for incapacitation purposes only."

"Then why is your drug killing people in our city?"

Dr. Anonymous paused before continuing.

"Unfortunately, that's where the hard facts end and supposition takes over. Shortly after the toxin was red-flagged, a vial of MC606 went missing from our lab."

"Missing?" Delta asked.

"The company suspected corporate espionage, but nothing was ever proven. We, of course, were devastated."

"I can feel my heart breaking for you," Delta said sarcastically.

"I understand how you feel young lady. Please believe me when I say the people here hoped this day would never come. Can you imagine spending years of your life, passionate about a project you've stayed up nights struggling with, fighting to find funding for, only to have it spirited away one night at the bottom of a disgruntled employee's briefcase? But we aren't like some firearms manufacturer who learns that one of their weapons cut short an innocent person's life. We did not set out to create a weapon—"

Chewy coughed/barked something that sounded very much like *bullshit*.

Dr. Anonymous wasn't amused.

"As I was saying, we certainly didn't plan to let it loose. It was stolen."

"Surely you had suspects?"

"At the time of the disappearance, everyone who worked in that lab, myself included, was cleared of all suspicion. However, several months afterward one of our scientists abruptly left the company. Naturally, our security team followed up and investigated, but I was told the employee couldn't be located after that. He had simply dropped off the face of the earth."

Taggart took a half step closer to the screen.

"Can you tell us the name of that employee?"

The anonymous scientist looked impatient now. "That's not really my area, and I think I should turn this over to our head of security now. He will discuss this further with you."

Now it was my turn to move closer to the screen, even though I knew the scientist on the other side of the feed couldn't see me.

"Sir, please. Some of us have lost people we love because of your drug. Your company has already proven they don't trust us. And after the stunt with Dr. Feinstein, I'm not sure I trust them either. But I do trust you. I can see it in your eyes that this is tearing you up."

Dr. Anonymous dropped his chin to his chest. "I won't tell you how much sleep I've lost over this. The whole incident has left a black fog of doubt over the whole department."

"Did you know this person?"

"Not well. Most of our conversations were in passing."

"Then please, please help us."

Dr. Anonymous looked up into the camera again. We all watched, as he seemed to be contemplating a decision. Then with a quick glance over his shoulder, he began talking.

"I will call him Preston Jones, which isn't his real name of course. We needed to know all your names to see if one of you might be related, but apparently not."

"Was there a missing person's report filed on him or his family?"

"Not that I'm aware of. Technically he wasn't missing, we just couldn't locate him. He turned in his notice via email and all it said was that he was taking a position with another, undisclosed firm in a different state. His residence was empty and his neighbors had no idea where he and his family moved. They simply vanished in the middle of the night."

"Is there a picture of him somewhere?" I continued, deciding to take over the interrogation reins.

"I'm afraid not. At the time the only picture we had of our employees was on their ID card, and he did not turn his in when he left."

"Do you know if he had a family?"

"Yes, as I recall he was married, in fact at one time his wife was an employee of ours, as well. We'll call her Rachel Jones. She, unfortunately, was terminated."

"Terminated?" Delta asked, her eyes so wide she looked like one of the Powerpuff girls.

Dr. Anonymous smiled.

"Fired. There were performance issues, and then she failed a drug test."

I remembered the conversation with the Taggart's foster parents in which they described Taggart's mother having signs of drug abuse. How ironic, a junkie working for a drug company.

"Children?" Taggart asked.

"He never spoke of any. Again, we barely knew each other and from what I could tell, he wasn't the sort to pass out cigars."

"Can you describe him?"

"I'm sorry. I'm terrible with faces. All I can say is he was average. Average height, average weight, no features that stuck out to me."

"Did he have a dimpled chin?" Taggart asked.

"Not that I can recall. No."

"I have another question," I said, needing to voice something that had been bugging me.

"Certainly."

"Why haven't you asked why we are here or why we have that sample in the first place? Don't you want to know what's going on in New Haven?"

Dr. Anonymous pursed his lips. "Most of it is obvious or can be extrapolated from the sample itself. The arrival of the package told us that MC606 must have been used to kill and there was a person, or persons, fishing for answers because there is no way to trace it back to our company—unless it was Preston Jones who sent us the sample. I imagine you sent the same sample to most of the major drug companies in Atlanta?"

"Yes."

"Then there was only one question we needed to ask ourselves: Do we reveal what we know? I can tell you that was a spirited debate between the people in my department, our security people, and the legal department. Fortunately, morality won the debate, with a few concessions. The imaginary Dr. Feinstein was one of them. You now know what we know, but as far as any fallout MC606 may have created, we prefer to remain ignorant of those details."

"Can I ask why?"

Dr. Anonymous smiled weakly. "Although the chance of it is certainly remote, a few of us would still like to salvage some hope of sleeping at night."

Twenty-Eight

Back in Atlanta, the same agent who picked us up dropped us off in the same spot. Before leaving, he handed Taggart a large manila envelope. Inside was a pair of folders, one much thicker than the other, and another smaller envelope addressed to Taggart specifically. A quick check revealed that the folders contained the personnel files for Preston and Rachel Jones, although their real names were blacked out. Taggart refused to show any of us what was inside his envelope, which irritated me.

My Aunt Cathy and Uncle Don probably thought our meetings with the Georgia Tech advisors was a bust because of how solemn and uncommunicative we were after we showed up at their house in Gwinnett. The four of us barely touched the awesome dinner Cathy prepared, and then we hit the sack early because we were heading back to New Haven first thing the next morning, or at least that's what we told them. Instead, Taggart and Chewy took the first chance they got to sneak into the room Delta and I shared. We studied the two personnel files and compared notes until we could no longer keep our eyes open.

The first thing that we noticed about the files was that any mention of the company by name was obscured with a black marker. In fact, every name in the file was redacted. There was no way to tie the files back to their source.

Rachel Jones personnel file was the thin one. She came to work at the unknown company as Rachel (blacked out) in 1992 as an entry-level technician, which was surprising because her college GPA and pre-employment test scores were extremely impressive. Rachel was obviously intelligent, making the job she hired into seem beneath her abilities. The work history she listed on her application had large gaps in it, and her degree in chemical engineering was from an obscure online university. They must have been impressed with her scores and her interview because they hired her anyway. From what we could tell, she worked in several different labs within the company and moved around frequently. Otherwise, everything appeared normal. In 1993, she changed her name and her status to married. The following year, which happened to be the year Taggart was born, Rachel went on maternity leave for twelve weeks. Later that same year, she amended her insurance forms to add a dependent child. His name was Billy.

The next year was when notes began showing up in her file about excessive tardiness and occasional absenteeism. I thought that having a young one at home could be the reason, but nothing was ever mentioned about child-care. It wasn't long after that more notes appeared, but now the topics involved performance issues, erratic behavior, and outright insubordination. One note in particular caught my attention, and I was sure it did for Taggart as well because it contained only two words followed by six question marks. *Drug use??????* That was when a document was introduced that outlined a structured ninety-day plan to help correct Rachel's work performance issues. Two weeks after that document showed up, the final two pieces of the paper trail appeared—a failed drug screen test and termination form. Rachel had tested positive for barbiturates and been fired in 1996.

Preston Jones' personnel file may have been thicker because of investigative documents related to the drug theft, but on paper the man seemed to be as boring as an actuarial accountant. Preston started in 1985 right after graduating from Georgia Tech with a Ph.D. degree in biochemistry. Over the next eight years, numerous promotions showed up in his file in the form of status change requests that marked title changes and salary increases, but that was all. The documentation drew a picture of a man steadily earning more and more responsibility but did little to tell us about the man himself. In 1993, he amended his insurance form to add a new dependent and beneficiary (wife) – Rachel Jones, and in 1994 he updated it again to pencil in a dependent son – Billy Jones. In 1997, things went bonkers.

In January of that year, a lengthy internal memo appeared, attached to a report detailing the disappearance of a single vial of MC606 and the internal investigation that followed. It was written by the department head, name redacted, and it outlined how the vial disappeared from a locked cabinet sometime during the second week of January. Procedure stated that red-flagged inventory was only counted once a week. Several lapses in security measures were brought to light in the report, described in detail, all with recommendations for improvements. Every individual who came under suspicion was mentioned, fourteen in all who had logged into the lab that week, including Preston Jones, but no one stood out from the rest and ultimately no one was blamed for the theft. Copies of Preston's bank records, surveillance reports, and comprehensive background checks, were also in the employee file. As I read everything, I couldn't see a reason for suspecting Preston Jones. Like I said, boring. It turned out the memo attached to the report was a resignation letter, as a Dr. somebody (name was blacked out) assumed complete responsibility for the breach and soon left the company.

Six months after the MC606 went missing, the copy of an email was placed in the file. The simple communication said only this:

To: ▮▮▮▮▮▮ (assumed to be the new department head)
From: Preston ▮▮▮▮▮▮
Subject: Resignation

Effective immediately, I am resigning from ▮▮▮▮▮▮. I have been offered another position with a west coast company. It would be irrational of me to decline it.

Preston ▮▮▮▮▮▮

The people at the unnamed company weren't dummies. Papers in Preston's file showed that the company immediately went on the hunt. It proved useless. The Jones' residence was vacant, and there were no clues as to where they had gone. Neighbors who were interviewed described the family as mostly keeping to themselves and Preston was particularly standoffish. A moving van was seen loading up the contents of the home, but no one recalled seeing Preston or Rachel around to supervise. After an extensive search, the moving company was found, which led the investigators to a storage facility only miles from the Jones' home. They found it empty. The trail went cold there. The car registered to Preston turned up in a used car lot located in a suburb across town, but nobody could say how it ended up there. The family's bank accounts had been emptied and mail was forwarded to PO Box in Van Nuys, California, but according to the surveillance records, no one matching either of the Jones' description ever went by to collect it.

The papers showed that Preston had no family to speak of. He was an only child whose parents were both deceased, and his only living relative that could be found was an uncle on his father's side who hadn't seen or heard from Preston in over twenty years. Rachel Jones was more of a mystery. The company was unable to find any of her family, or to be more precise, any record of her birth at all. Although it did appear that Rachel Jones did everything that was listed on her application, the name she was using couldn't have been her birth name.

The company sent out inquiries to all of the drug companies on the west coast to see if anyone had recently hired a Preston Jones, but no one had ever heard of him. They expanded the inquiry to all of the major drug consortiums in the US, with the same results.

Preston Jones, and his family, had vanished.

We all agreed that he was now hiding in our little town. Something must have happened to cause Rachel Jones to take their son and go on the run. But what?

The four of us had poured over both files and learned a lot. Rachel Jones had to be Taggart's mother, but none of us knew why she ended up with a driver's license under the name of Samantha McGill. Maybe that was her real name, but that didn't explain why social services couldn't find any record of Taggart's birth. There were still plenty of questions. What events led to her taking her son and hopping on a bus heading to Florida? And why did Preston Jones steal the MC606 in the first place? Maybe he was involved in corporate espionage and intended to sell it, but that fell through? Did Samantha/Rachel discover what he had done and confront him? Maybe that was why she took Taggart/Billy and ran. But why the false ID? Did she feel she needed to revert back to her real name and change Billy's name to Taggart, all in an effort to hide from her husband? Where was she heading when she climbed on that bus?

And the biggest question of all: could one of the people I would soon be commiserating with at Stooch's funeral, maybe even hug and kiss on the cheek, be a cold-blooded murderer?

If any of these revelations shocked Taggart, he did a good job of covering it up. But I was certain he had to be spinning. I know I was. We all were.

Twenty-Nine

I stared at my reflection in the full-length mirror, assessing the outfit I'd chosen. The navy-blue dress was a couple years out of style, but I could still get into it and it fit the occasion. There was no way I was wearing the same outfit I wore to Becca's funeral, and what I had selected would do fine. Still, I chastised myself for not putting forth more of an effort. My hair was in sad shape and although I always went light on the makeup, my eyes clearly needed some help. The frown on my face wasn't helping matters.

There wasn't enough time to do anything about it now, especially my mood.

I felt like I had a depression hangover.

Knowing the truth now, how would I be able to act like everything was normal around everyone? Stooch's funeral was going to be a downer, for sure, but I wondered if it would turn out to be dangerous as well. I looked into the eyes of my mirror image and searched for some confidence. There was a cold-blooded murderer in our midst, a wolf in sheep's clothing hiding in plain sight, but I couldn't afford to let on what I knew. As Taggart pointed out more than once during our drive back, doing so could put a target on my back. Mine and everyone else's.

I wasn't crazy about going to Stooch's funeral in the first place, in fact there were plenty of times I tried to convince myself there was no reason to go, but here I was checking myself out in the mirror before subjecting myself to more misery and tension. Stooch may not have been one of my favorite people, but he didn't deserve what had happened to him and I couldn't help but feel some weird kinship because of the circumstances of his death. Besides, we'd shared a number of friends and in our world, not going would be the same as spitting on his grave. At least Taggart would be with me.

Taggart had resisted at first, but I told him that people on our suspect list would be there and it would be a good chance to see how they acted during the memorial. If we were going to figure out which one of them was Preston Jones, we needed to do something other than attempting to steal their cell phones to determine if they were at the sporting goods store when Mr. Ledbetter was injected. He ultimately agreed, begrudgingly.

It was time to go to a funeral, and quite possibly meet the person responsible for it. I grabbed my shoulder bag and headed out.

Right away, I determined there were just as many people at Stooch's service as there were at my sister's, but it was made more obvious by the fact that Temple Beth-El was so small and ill-equipped to handle the flood of mourners. Compared to surrounding cities, New Haven had a sizable Jewish community, but their numbers barely justified its own Synagogue, and the tiny building was swamped.

As soon as the five of us walked through the main door, we ran into the back of a crowd. People were standing everywhere. The sanctuary was packed, the atrium was overflowing, and I even spotted groups of mourners standing in the hallway that apparently led to classrooms.

Something I didn't anticipate was how my being there would affect everyone else. It was as if there were two services going on simultaneously. Many of my classmates who were there for Stooch and his family, had also been at my sister's funeral, and they offered me condolences… again. I guess the circumstances of the day reminded them of what I had recently been through, and they felt obligated to console me further. But I also came across a few adults who, for whatever reason, weren't able to be at my sister's interment. They needed to offer comforting words as well. In a way, it was like re-living Becca's funeral all over.

I also turned a few heads because of who I came with, but I didn't care. Tunes and Chewy were wearing matching suits, the color of their ties the only thing that set the two apart. I almost asked one of them to change into something else, an attempt to save them the embarrassment of being a topic of conversation amongst the fashion divas at school on Monday, but decided not to. It was probably the only suit either of them had. Tunes had naturally been wearing his headphones when I picked him up, but he didn't put up much of a fuss when I asked him to leave them in the car. Delta had picked a sundress that bordered on the disrespectful, both in length and its nearly luminescent color, but out of all her fancy dresses, it had been Stooch's favorite. She was determined to wear it.

Taggart surprised me the most. He had chosen to wear a black button-down shirt, sans tie, khaki pants, and black tennis shoes. After I persuaded him to tuck in his shirt and pull his hair back into a short ponytail, he really looked like a new person. Of course, that was quickly ruined when his face adopted its customary scowl upon arriving at the synagogue.

I took the lead and edged our way past the throng at the door, running straight into Vice Principal Stevens. He was standing in the outer atrium next to a potted plant on a short pedestal, talking to Miss Worthy. When he saw the five of us his face changed, but I couldn't decipher its meaning. Something like an electric shock shot through my entire body, paralyzing me for a second. Was it him? Was he Preston Jones? Was I standing less than three feet from a serial killer? Did he have a tiny needle hidden on him right now, waiting to strike?

I felt a soft nudge in the middle of my back, snapping me out of my mini-trance. I was pretty sure I had managed to keep a neutral look on my face, though it didn't matter. Taggart was looking at me, snapping his eyes back and forth between me and Mr. Stevens. It was time to go on the offensive.

"Hi Mr. Stevens. Hi Miss Worthy," I said as we approached. Chewy, Tunes, and Delta added their own greetings, but Taggart remained silent.

"Don't you boys look handsome," Miss Worthy gushed, reaching out and running her hand down Tunes' sleeve. "And I love that look on you, Cassie."

I thanked her, but also noted she didn't say anything about Delta's choice in wardrobe.

"Good morning gang," Mr. Stevens answered, adopting a quizzical expression as he looked at each of us. "I must say this is an odd grouping. I don't recall seeing the five of you together before."

"We kind of formed an informal support group. You know, something along the lines of Alcohol Anonymous, except we're more like Death Anonymous."

Both Mr. Stevens and Miss Worthy frowned at my poor, but decidedly purposeful, choice in humor. Looking at our vice principal I tried to detect anything in his features that resembled Taggart. Their eyes were the same color, hazel, and both of their ears were smallish and in tight against their head, but that was it. And his chin wasn't dimpled, not even a little.

"If I'm not mistaken, didn't you four miss school Thursday and Friday?" Mr. Stevens asked, pointing in turn at Chewy, Delta, Taggart, and then lastly myself. "Do you want to tell me where you all were?"

"Well, we'd better get moving before all the seats are gone," I said hurriedly and began ushering everyone past our vice principal, though Taggart wasn't being very cooperative. "See you on Monday."

Delta grabbed my arm as we made our way towards the sanctuary. "Did you hear that Worthy and Stevens were hooking up? Can't say that I blame him, I've seen his wife."

"Delta, haven't you learned anything yet?"

"What?"

"Spreading rumors, girl."

"What? That goes for adults too?"

I shook my head as all of us wove through pockets of people standing around making idle conversation, occasionally stopping to say "hi" to friends. A man I didn't recognize was standing directly outside the entrance, passing out what looked like programs. I took one as I passed by, and when I looked up there stood our biology teacher, Mr. Wilkins. He must have approached from the opposite end of the hall. This time I know the smile I gave him must have looked as forced as it felt.

"Hi, girls. Boys," he said. Our teacher was dressed smartly in a dark suit, with a white handkerchief folded neatly in the breast pocket. His customary walking stick was in his right hand.

I mumbled something, I'm not sure what, suddenly rooted where I stood. The line of people behind us, Taggart and the others included, were starting to back up.

"This is just awful, isn't it? Our little community has suffered so much pain and loss in such a short time."

We all nodded our reply, but I noticed that Taggart's attention was focused entirely on our teacher's walking stick. The black rod was about three feet tall with a round knob at the head that was tan in color. I remember Mr. Wilkins once telling us it was fashioned after a shillelagh, which was the national weapon of rural Ireland. It was called an Irish Blackthorn and although it appeared like it was made out of some kind of wood, it was actually constructed from polypropylene.

"We'd better find a seat," Mr. Wilkins said, looking over his shoulder. "We seem to be holding things up."

We couldn't find five seats together, so we ended up standing against the wall near the front of the room.

A few yards away from where we stood was Stooch's casket, surrounded by such a display of flowers and plants that I was certain the local shops must have been cleaned out. Unlike Stooch, the casket was a very unassuming.

I flashed back to the night in the funeral home and the feeling of standing inches from him. I recalled seeing his lifeless face, then it was suddenly replaced in my mind by his smirking expression just after his prank with the train recording. That only lasted a second before another memory took its place, one with him laughing so hard that drool dribbled from his mouth onto the ground after I said something I thought was modestly humorous. He found it riotous and couldn't stop laughing, which of course made all of us laugh as well.

A wave of sadness flowed through me.

I'm truly sorry this happened to you, Stooch.

I blinked away the memories, but then the sight of Stooch's parents and younger brother took their place. The Steuers were sitting together in the first row, alone, in full-blown zombie mode. I knew exactly how they felt. To me, it seemed like funerals were the highest form of cruelty. Dressing nicely, acting both outgoing and cordial, and putting on a false front for the large group of friends and family who seem to be attracted by your grief. And the entire time all you could think of was curling up in a dark room and riding-out the continuous waves of depression that seem to be crushing the breath from you.

On the other side of the room in an adjoining space stood a row of chairs positioned at a right angle to the pews. Occupying them were six men I didn't recognize. I spotted Jason sitting on a row perpendicular to the six men, along with what must have been the entire football team. My eyes met Jason's for a brief moment. He gave me a weak smile, before looking away.

"I'm surprised that Jason isn't a pallbearer," I whispered to Taggart.

"Only fellow Jews can be pallbearers," he replied in a normal voice.

At the start of the service, the rabbi tore black ribbons and handed them to the family members in the first row. Taggart whispered to me that they were to pin the ribbon on their clothes, symbolizing their loss.

As the service went on, I discreetly scanned the room, looking for Mr. Stevens, Mr. Wilkins, and any of our other suspects. I was surprised to find Sgt. Brown standing in the back of the room on the opposite side from us. Taggart had told us that the detective was married, but didn't have any kids, so why was he here? Could it be that he suspected foul play in Stooch's death, or was he responsible for it? Was he here not to pay respect but to watch the crowd and look for anything suspicious? Or maybe he was here to gloat? Whichever it was, if he was any good at his job, then the five of us should definitely show up on his radar.

I did find both Mr. Stevens and Mr. Wilkins in the crowd, for what good it did. Neither of them betrayed anything with their expressions or body language. I wasn't sure what I expected to see, but I felt a spark of anger when I imagined one of them secretly enjoying all this.

After the ceremony concluded and we were making our way back to my car, I felt a hand on my shoulder.

"Hello, Cassie."

I turned around to find Dr. Weathers standing there, his wife and step-son Jake, beside him.

"Hey, Dr. Weathers. Mrs. Weathers. Hi, Jake."

"We miss you at the clinic, but this is a terrible way to see you again. You were friends with Kevin, weren't you?"

"Yes, I was. He was the best friend of the boy I was going out with."

"I'm sorry to hear that. Football is such a dangerous sport," Dr. Weathers said. Jake dropped his head and looked away.

"I don't know—" Taggart said, having stepped up beside me. "—life is kind of tricky. A person can die from infection by just pricking their finger on a thorn. At least with football, you can see your opponent coming."

Dr. Weathers stared a Taggart, but didn't respond. That was when I almost gasped. Looking at the two of them standing there, face to face, I thought I saw a vague similarity. But that wasn't possible. No, that had to be my imagination. I was now starting to see a part of Taggart in every middle-aged man I met, desperately searching for his father. Sure, there was a slight indention on Dr. Weathers chin, but it was far from being a dimpled chin. I had worked side by side with this man for years. He wasn't a serial killer.

Was he?

Thirty

"You know it ticks me off when you do this," I said, unable to hold it in any longer. "Why won't you tell me where we're going?"

I passed the community center, driving north, waiting for Taggart to provide the next instruction like a bratty version of my phone's GPS. The skies had become overcast and the constant breeze was beginning to gust. At this time of year, the weather was very unpredictable, an enjoyable sun-filled morning was just as likely to end the day with a peaceful sunset or with an angry rush of wind and rain that blotted out the calming moon.

I knew how it felt. Having Taggart McGill as a friend could be just as dicey.

After the funeral, we had all returned to my house and started brainstorming our next move, intending to write our suggestions on a piece of paper. Not surprisingly, all we'd ended up with was one line at the top that read:

Go to the police.

We were in the middle of that debate when Taggart had suddenly shot out of his chair and looked at the clock, announcing to me, "I need you to drive me somewhere."

I was still in the dress I wore to the funeral, but Tunes and Chewy had shed their suit jackets and ties and Delta changed out of her dress into a pair of my sweatpants and long-sleeve t-shirt. Tunes had also donned his headphones again. Taggart still had his shirt tucked in and his hair pulled back, which both shocked me and gave me a warm, fuzzy feeling at the same time. Could he be remaining that way because he knew I liked that look on him? Did it really matter to him what I thought?

"You want to borrow my car?"

"No, I need you to drive me."

"Where to?" I asked.

"You'll see," was his cryptic answer.

I wanted to say "duh," but I knew it would be both pointless and useless. If Taggart wanted me to know, he would tell me, and anything I did to try to get him to do otherwise would be more effort than it was worth.

"Let me grab my keys. How long will we be gone?"

"Forty-five minutes. Maybe a little longer."

"You guys hang out here until we get back, okay? There are some drinks in the fridge and snacks behind the bar. Delta, I got you some Red Bull."

As we were leaving Chewy wasted no time getting out of his seat and headed straight to the small refrigerator next to the bar, while Delta and Tunes waved their goodbyes.

"Turn left at the red light," Taggart instructed, totally ignoring my question about where we were going.

Traffic was light this afternoon. There was only one car in front of me when I stopped at the light.

"It's because you don't think I'd come with you if you told me, isn't it?" I attempted answering my own question.

"Maybe," I heard him say.

I glanced over and saw the remnants of a grin on his face.

"You should know by now that the reason doesn't matter, except for the fact that you feel it necessary to keep it from me. I'll do what you ask, unconditionally, please don't keep me in the dark. Okay?"

"Okay."

We continued sitting there, waiting for the light to turn green, and still Taggart wasn't saying anything.

"So, where are we going?"

"We're going to see my therapist."

"What? Are you crazy!"

"He is a therapist, and I am seeing him, so—"

"But he could be your father. In fact, I think he's our leading suspect."

"I'm aware of that."

"Then, I'm turning around."

"No. Don't do that. What happened to unconditionally?"

I hated it when my own words were used against me. My dad was a master at it. It was like he was a catalog of Cassie-speak and could spew it back at me whenever the situation called for it. It was like his mutant-power.

"There are still limits. I wouldn't drive us off a cliff if you asked, and this is almost the same thing."

"This is no different than going to Stooch's funeral. I want to see how he reacts when I tell him we went to Atlanta."

I could see his point, but that still didn't mean I liked the idea. The light turned green and I turned left.

"His office building is five blocks up on the right."

I rarely came to this part of New Haven. It was mostly office buildings, many of them recently renovated, housing an assortment of doctors, lawyers, tax preparers, architects, and other miscellaneous businesses.

"You do realize that it will be next to impossible to tell anything, right?" I was thinking about my experience at the funeral and how I tended to see a little bit of Taggart in all our suspects now. "You might read things into what he says and the way he acts just because you want it to be true."

"I've been doing that most of my life."

"I'm sorry, I don't understand."

"When you're alone, without parents, every man you meet makes you wonder if it could be your father, or at least imagine what it would be like if he was your father. You picture yourself going home with him, sitting down and eating dinner with him, talking about your day and making plans together for the weekend. You see yourself playing video games together and letting him win occasionally so he won't get discouraged and leave. I'd meet someone new and I'd envision us going to ball games and he'd hold my hand as we climbed the stairs and search for our seats in the bleachers. Or he'd tuck me into bed at night and look under the bed to make sure the monsters I knew lived there had found some other child to torture for the night. I've had plenty of practice seeing things in people that never come true."

At that moment, I wanted to reach out and take hold of Taggart's hand, but to do that I'd have to turn and look at him, and I didn't want him to see the tears in my eyes. I waited for a couple seconds, to make sure my voice wouldn't catch in my throat before I said anything.

"Okay, I get it, but why am I coming?"

"Because you need to be there as a witness. It's essential that someone be present who can evaluate his reaction objectively."

"You think I'm objective? What about Mr. or Mrs. Wilson? Why not one of them? They at least know this man."

I could see Taggart shaking his head out of the corner of my eye.

"They've only met him once, and besides, they're not privy to any of this."

"You haven't told them?"

"Have you told your parents?"

"No, but I'm not the one with a father secretly watching my every move and killing anyone who so much as sneezes on me. They could be in danger."

Taggart didn't answer me, but I knew why. Anyone he encountered was in danger, and that included me. That had to be why he was taking this risk. He needed to find out who his father was, and do whatever it took to end this. All so we would be safe.

Taggart pointed out a two-story building on the right, so I pulled around to the rear and parked in the half-full lot. We made our way inside and took the stairs to the second floor, my anxiety level rising with every step. At the landing, I followed Taggart down the hall and entered an office at the end of the hall with **Dr. Kent P. Gleason, Psy.D., H.S.P.P.** etched on the glass door.

Inside the otherwise-empty reception area was a blonde-haired woman in her mid-thirties who sat behind a large desk, typing. The desk was a hardwood veneer, coated with high-tech lacquer and had a thick glass counter. I wasn't much into office décor, but it was impressive, which made the hideous painting of a collection of flowers in an oddly shaped vase on the wall behind the desk so peculiar. A pair of cloth chairs with a table between them was against the wall opposite the desk.

The woman looked up and smiled when we walked in.

"Hi, Taggart. You're a bit early today," the woman said. She had the whitest teeth I had ever seen and they contrasted sharply with her red lipstick.

Taggart kept his eyes on the floor when he responded. "Any chance we can get in early today?"

Maybe Dr. Gleason was out sick today and we'd have to come back later. A girl could hope.

"You're in luck," the receptionist said, which popped my bubble. "He didn't have an appointment before you today. Just a sec."

The woman, whose desk nameplate informed visitors she was Debbie Granger, picked up the phone and pushed a button. While she waited for someone to answer, all I could think was how she kept that red lipstick from finding its way onto those teeth.

"Taggart McGill is early," she finally said into the receiver. "Would you like me to show him in or have him wait?"

Debbie listened for a moment then nodded her head. "Very well," she said, then hung up and turned to us.

"He'll see you now, Taggart. Go on in."

When I started following Taggart toward the door to the right, Debbie called out to me.

"I'm sorry, you can't go in there with him. The doctor's sessions are private."

"We're making an exception today," Taggart responded and without waiting for an answer opened the door and entered. Naturally, I followed him.

"WAIT!" Debbie exclaimed.

My first impression of Kent Gleason up close was a bit of a disappointment. He was a slightly pudgy, middle-aged man with dark bushy eyebrows that contrasted sharply with his neatly trimmed salt and pepper hair. He wore khaki pants and a yellow sweater with a light blue button-down shirt underneath, the cuffs of the shirts sleeves folded back over the sweater. He looked like he'd be more at home hosting a cooking show on The Food Channel then roaming the streets of New Haven killing innocent citizens. Of all the suspects on our list, he looked the least serial killery.

As we walked in he was rising from behind an even more impressive desk than Debbie's, a concerned look on his face.

"I'm sorry, Doctor," Debbie said from behind me, obviously flustered. "She just walked past me."

"What's this all about, Taggart?" Dr. Gleason asked. His voice was deep and authoritative with a James Earl Jones quality to it.

"This is Cassie Underwood, Becca's sister, and I wanted her to sit in on today's session if that's okay with you?"

Dr. Gleason looked at me, his bushy eyebrows raised. I smiled back at him.

"Well, this is a surprise. I'm so sorry for your loss, young lady."

"Thank you," I replied. It always felt so weird thanking someone for feeling sorry for you.

"It's okay, Debbie," Dr. Gleason said to the receptionist still hovering behind me. "We'll be fine."

I watched Debbie pull the door shut, telling me with her eyes that if I had used paid parking, there was no way I was getting my parking ticket validated.

"Have a seat," the therapist offered, gesturing at the chairs next to the window. "I'd really wish you would have told me about your plan to bring Cassie during our last visit. I could have been more prepared."

I wanted to say, *Taggart doesn't tell you everything either?* Go figure.

But I didn't.

The office was modestly furnished and minimally decorated, though I wasn't sure what I was expecting as this was the first time I had been in a shrink's office. Apart from the desk and a credenza behind it, there was a pair of red-wing high-back chairs with exaggerated curves off to the side next to a large window with the drapes pulled shut, one pair facing the other, and an actual couch on the opposite side of the room. How I would have loved to be a fly on the wall during Taggart's time in here.

"It was my idea," I said. "I've been getting to know more about Taggart since Becca passed away and I thought, how better than visiting with his therapist."

Taggart and I took the seats opposite the chair Dr. Gleason settled into. The therapist crossed his legs and leaned forward, folding his arms on top of his legs.

"Frankly, I'm surprised he told you about me at all."

"Believe me, it wasn't easy. Getting him to talk is like trying to send a text with your pinkies. But I'm sure you know all about that, right?"

"Indeed. Well, this is a bit of a fuzzy area. Surely you realize that I'm not at liberty to talk about Taggart, even with him in the room. I can only confirm what he tells you directly. Really what I hope to achieve is to facilitate a conversation between the two of you."

"Yeah, that's not going to happen. We went to Atlanta on Thursday," Taggart spit out.

At first, Dr. Gleason didn't act as if he heard Taggart. Then he sat back in his chair and furrowed his eyebrows, so much so that if they were made out of Velcro he would have difficulty getting them apart.

"What were you doing in Atlanta?" he asked. His voice seemed to have lowered an octave or two.

"Looking for answers."

"About your mother?"

"Actually, my father."

For some reason Dr. Gleason looked at me, which made me feel extremely uncomfortable, then he swiftly returned his attention to Taggart.

"You recall our previous discussions about this course of action?"

"I recall everything."

"Then you remember me telling you that although making that trip and asking the questions you needed to ask might prove cathartic, it could also have a negative impact on your psyche and manifest itself into depression. Therefore, I should have accompanied you."

"You told me once, back when I first started coming here, that you had moved here from Atlanta."

"That's true."

"When I was there, I did some checking. I couldn't find any record of a Dr. Gleason anywhere."

"I was in a practice with the two other doctors then. My name wasn't on the business listing, so I'm not surprised by that. My home number was also unlisted, for obvious reasons, as it is here in New Haven. Why were you looking for my name?"

"I was curious."

"About me?"

"Yes."

The doctor seemed to be looking at Taggart now with a different purpose. What started out as friendly banter had taken a different turn. The wrinkles on his furrowed forehead told me it concerned him. He turned to me and smiled.

"Miss Underwood, I wonder if you might step outside to the waiting room for a couple of minutes. I need to talk to Taggart alone."

"She stays, or we both go," was Taggart's definitive response.

Dr. Gleason had apparently slipped into therapist mode because his face was now unreadable. When our conversation first began he was expressive, his features in sync with his emotions, but now he only stared at the two of us as if he had been tranquilized with a powerful emotion suppressor.

"Taggart, I'm sensing a level of hostility that concerns me. Do you want to tell me why that is?"

"Why were you at the football game last Friday night?"

Again Taggart's therapist looked at me. This time his emotionless face gave me the creeps.

"I told you that night I was there to watch the game. I understand the team is having a special year."

"You're not married, you don't have any kids, so how could that even interest you?"

"I like football, like most everyone else."

Examining the way the therapist was dressed, I seriously doubted that.

"You're lying," Taggart hissed, barely able to contain his emotions now.

Dr. Gleason sprang from his seat, which made me jump a little.

"This session is over. Something that happened in Atlanta has obviously bothered you and we need to have a conversation when we can be alone and get to the bottom of this antagonism. I'm sorry things seemed to get off on the wrong foot today, Miss Underwood, but maybe we can try this again sometime."

"Buckhead Park," Taggart said as he stood up. I followed suit.

"Excuse me?"

"I know who you really are and I know about MC606."

"You're not making any sense, Taggart."

"Meet me tonight at Buckhead Park."

"I have no idea what you're talking about, Taggart, and I'm not playing these games with you."

"Five p.m. Be there or I'll tell everyone what you've done."

Taggart grabbed my hand and pulled me along as he stormed out of the room.

Thirty-One

"He did what?"

We were back in the basement at my house and I watched Delta rise from her spot on the couch beside Tunes, looking none too happy. I didn't blame her, since I was still upset myself.

"He told his therapist that he knows who he really is, all about the toxin, and wants to meet him tonight at five p.m.," I repeated for her benefit, but also because hearing it aloud helped me come to terms with what he'd done. The emotions raging inside me were ricocheting back and forth between frantic and furious, but I was doing my best to show the others I was calm and in control. Nothing could have been further from the truth.

Taggart ignored everyone's stares and strolled over to the bar. He grabbed a pad of paper off the countertop and tore off several sheets.

"What the hell?" Delta asked. As always, her directness summed up my entire one-sided conversation with Taggart during our drive back in three words. He had been as uncommunicative as always, but I could see he was upset. All he would say was that he wanted to explain what he did, and what he planned, to all of us.

Chewy was standing next to the pool table with a cue in his hand. "That's where you went, to see your—"

"—father. We don't even know that he is your father for sure, do we?" Delta said.

"Did something happen there that—" Tunes started.

"Yeah, what happened? Why are we so sure it's him suddenly?" Delta finished.

We all watched as Taggart took a pen and wrote something on the piece of paper he had torn off. He finished writing, turned around, and held up the paper for us to see.

"I don't know that he is my father, Delta, but I intend to find out. Cassie and I delivered him a message, and now we're going to convey the same message to everyone on our suspect list," he said calmly.

"What does it say?" I asked, unable to read what he wrote from where I was standing.

"Same thing I told Dr. Gleason. That I know they're my father and I want to meet at the park tonight or I'll tell everyone about MC606."

My heart sank. I had an inkling things were getting out of control after leaving the Therapists office, but now I was certain of it.

"So you're setting a trap," Chewy stated, walking over to stand next to the couch.

"Exactly. Whoever shows up will be—"

"—your father, and our murderer," Delta completed the sentence.

Tunes rose from the couch. Now everyone was standing and/or pacing. It was obvious by the expression on the boys' faces they were gung-ho for this new plan. Of course they would be. They were young and didn't know any better. Even Delta seemed noncommittal. I had to say something to stop this.

"I don't like it." I pointed out. "If your father is indeed one of these six, he'll know this is a trap and won't show up. Then all you will have accomplished is tipping him off to the fact that we know about him."

The downward turn of Taggart's mouth and the sagging of his shoulder indicated I was taking the wind out of his sail. He wasn't angry, but disappointed.

"He'll be there," Taggart said. "He won't be able to resist. Besides, I think he's already tipped off. I'm sure someone followed us on our way back here."

"What? You're just saying this now?" I said.

"I'm not positive. But if it's true, then this man is obviously obsessed with me."

"That certainly makes him bat-shit crazy right there," Delta commented.

Taggart half-smiled, but I didn't find it funny at all.

"Which means he's not completely rational," Taggart said. "We haven't involved the police, and I think he'll know that, so he'll be confident and curious. Besides, just showing up at the park isn't proof of anything to anyone but us."

"But we are going to call the police, right?" I said. It was both a question and a statement.

"And let them know your plan, aren't you?" Delta finished, retaking her seat. Tunes sat next to her.

Taggart looked at me as if he was about to tell me the truth about Santa Claus.

"We have nothing to tell them. All we have are statistics and coincidences, but no proof. And have you forgotten that the detective is one of the people on our suspect list?"

"Okay, but what about the personnel file we got from the drug company? Isn't that proof?" I asked.

"Of what? That a man *MAY* have stolen a newly developed toxin and subsequently disappeared. The file is redacted so heavily you can't even tell where it came from.

How's that going to prove he's my father and that he followed me and my mother here to New Haven, murdered her, and has been secretly spying on me for fourteen years?"

I started pacing around the room. I knew I was grasping at straws, but I had to find a way to make Taggart change his mind. "But what about the blood sample from Stooch's jersey? They tested it and identified the drug."

"But we don't know who that drug company is and even if we knew, they would never admit to that for fear of lawsuits. They only told us because we're just kids and we took advantage of a scientist with a soft heart. They'll clam up and act like they've never seen us before if the police go knocking on their door. We don't even have the name of the scientist we spoke to."

"We can have them exhume Stooch's body."

"The drug will be long gone from his system, and the mark we found could have other explanations."

"There's got to be something else we can do?"

Taggart lifted the papers in his hands again. "This is it."

My aimless wandering back and forth reverted to circling the pool table. "But then what? Let's say he shows up. What do we do then?"

"**WE** do nothing. I'm doing this alone, and when my father shows up, I'll kill him."

I stopped dead in my tracks.

"Whoa there." Chewy said, beating me to the punch. "Did you say kill?"

"Yes."

I was the first to reach Taggart, but we all encircled him, everyone talking at once.

"Nobody said anything about killing him."

"Are you crazy? You'll be the one who'll go to prison."

"Why would you even say that? Tell me you're joking."

Taggart set the papers down on the bar, then walked a couple feet away to escape our verbal bombardment. When he turned around, his jaw was set.

"I've just told you we have no proof, and this man must pay for what he's done. This is my fault. I need to be the one who makes him atone for what he's done. I can't allow anyone else to die."

"Taggart, you can't," I pleaded. "This isn't you. You are not your father. You're not a killer."

"I can be," he replied flatly. "I know where Mr. Wilson keeps his old service revolver."

I clasped both of my hands on his cheeks, forcing him to look directly into my eyes.

"Listen to me very carefully, Taggart McGill. I can't believe I'm saying this, but I care for you, a lot. I understand what Becca saw in you that no one else could. However, if you kill this man, then I can no longer have anything to do with you. Doing this would be as awful as what he's done and turn you into the same sort of person. I don't want to see that happen. This is not your fault. This has been happening *TO YOU,* not because of you."

Taggart's gaze tried to dip downward, but I held his face firmly.

"And I'll tell you something else. Becca wouldn't want this either. Got it?"

Taggart looked back at me for several seconds before finally nodding his head, or as much as he could with his face clamped between my hands. I let go of him, but something in his eyes left me unsettled. Had I changed his mind? I needed more insurance, which meant I had to keep an eye on him. If I couldn't persuade him to forget about the idea with the park, then I'd have to accompany him to make sure he wouldn't try anything.

"So, it's decided, I'm helping you do this, and killing is off the table, right?"

"No killing," Taggart repeated.

"All we need to do is identify who this is, and then we can figure the rest out." I sounded more confident than I felt.

"I'm helping too. What's the plan?" Chewy asked, looking relieved.

"There's a gazebo in the center of Buckhead Park. I planned on meeting him there. There are plenty of vantage points in every direction if you and Cassie want to be lookouts."

I had been to Buckhead Park plenty of times when I was younger, but not recently. The park, nestled in the southwest part of town, was cradled between the newly constructed city pool on one side and a set of tennis courts on the other, with a walking path linking it all.

"You can see that gazebo from the pool parking lot, so I'll watch you from my car there," I offered.

"Me and Tunes can be at the courts pretending to play tennis, watching also," Delta chimed in.

"We can?" Tunes looked at her like she had proposed streaking.

"Sure, you want to help, don't you?"

"Yeah, but I don't know how to play tennis."

Delta smiled. "It's not gonna matter, sweetie."

"If I remember right, there's a thick patch of trees near the gazebo. I can hunker down in there and watch. We got your back, Taggart," Chewy added lastly.

"I have a weird thought," Delta said. "What if more than one person shows up? Somebody who's curious could drive out there. How will we know which one is your father?"

"Leave that to me," Taggart answered. "I'll be able to tell, and I'll get them alone."

"Then it's settled," I said, feeling a little better about things, kind of. "So, I guess all we need to do now is deliver these notes to our suspects and get ready. We should probably get to the park early, maybe 4:30?"

"That should be fine," Taggart answered.

I wondered. I really wondered.

***

I pulled into the city pool parking lot around 4:25. The parking lot was deserted because the pool was closed during this time of the year. I directed my car over to the section that bordered Buckhead Park and maneuvered into a spot directly facing it.

"Park over there along the fence instead," Taggart pointed out. "Your car will be less noticeable."

I did as he instructed, sliding in beside a six-foot wooden fence intended to prevent the unsupervised use of the pool, which was a joke because I had been here late at night multiple times with Jason and the gang. I threw the car into park, then killed the lights and engine.

"This is a good spot," I said to the others.

The gazebo Taggart had mentioned was only about fifty yards from where we were, with a direct line of sight and nothing in the way. The octagonal building boasted a wooden construction, a double roof, white paint and red shingles. Inside, the building was small, maybe large enough for a dozen people with nowhere to sit.

Straight in front of the car, I could see the walking trail that circled the entire park. My heart ached as I remembered how Becca and I would ride our bikes on it when we were little, then have lunch inside the gazebo with our parents. I could see a few people still wandering around the park despite the impending nightfall, but the gazebo was empty.

I directed my attention to the far side of the park where the tennis courts were, anticipating seeing the lights come to life. Twilight had come and gone and darkness was beginning to settle in, but there was nothing happening at the courts. We had dropped off Tunes and Delta on our way to the parking lot, so they've had plenty of time to figure out how to turn the lights on.

My cell phone chirped with Delta's ringtone.

"What's the matter?" I asked when I answered.

"It takes seventy-five cents to turn on the damn lights and neither one of us has any change," Delta said, her voice trembling with agitation.

"They don't have money for the lights," I repeated to Taggart and Chewy.

"How much do they need?" Chewy asked from the back seat.

"Seventy-five cents."

"I got that. I'll run it over to them and then get into my spot."

"Chewy is bringing it over," I said as Chewy exited the car and started jogging across the walking path.

"Tell him to hurry; it's getting spooky out here," Delta added.

"He's coming. No more calls unless you see something, okay?"

"10-4," Delta answered, and the line went dead.

Taggart and I waited in silence for what seemed like forever, until the court lights flickered, then lit up the night.

The courts were a greater distance from the gazebo than us, likely 100 yards, but they also had an unobstructed view. They were older courts, and the lights weren't the brightest, but what beams reached the gazebo created eerie shadows that someone could easily hide in.

I could barely make out Chewy as he headed to the patch of woods he had chosen as his vantage point. The woods lay on my left and the nearest spot to the gazebo, only about 30 yards away. The only area we didn't have covered was the section of the park to the north, where I could see a pavilion that was typically used for parties and picnics, as well as many pieces of playground equipment and the main parking lot.

"You don't have to do this, you know," I said, continuing to look out across the park. "We can find another way."

"Yes, I do," I heard him say.

"Why? Why you?"

"He's my father."

"That's not the reason. I know you, Taggart. That man means nothing to you. There's so little that you care about. I'm not even sure if you care who he kills next."

I regretted the words as soon as they left my mouth. I was upset… scared… and I really didn't want him to do this. After delivering the notes to our respective suspects, taking special care to make sure someone would discover them in time, Taggart had asked me to take him back to his house to change clothes. When he got back in my car, he was wearing his favorite hoody and I thought I noticed a bulge in his back along his pants line. Maybe I was imagining it?

"We've discussed my idiosyncrasies," Taggart said.

"You mean being weird?"

"If you call being a borderline sociopath weird, then yes, that. I've always accepted my therapist's postulation that my difficulty interacting with others and forming meaningful relationships was rooted in circumstances of my mother's death and then being raised by strangers. But now, knowing what I know about my father, I'm wondering if the reason is genetic… or, at the very minimum, a contributing factor. What if my weirdness is inherited? My acuity obviously originated from him. He was, after all, a skilled chemist at the forefront of his field."

My first instinct was to protect his feelings, but decided that honesty was something he valued more. "I guess it's possible."

"But if he committed these murders, then his psyche must have a deep flaw that can be inherited from those same genes. What if I inherited more than just his intellect?"

The doubt on Taggart's face was unexpected, and it made me worry. Not because I thought what he was saying might actually be true, but because I knew what it was like to question your own motivations and how uncertain that could make you feel.

"Taggart, you can't think that way. We barely know anything about your father. You don't know how he was raised or what shaped him into the man he is. So don't try to deduce something based on a maybe."

Taggart was silent for a second or two, and then, "For the record, I care."

"I know, I'm sorry, I don't even know why I said that." I turned to look at him in the dark, but he was looking straight ahead. "Please forgive me?"

Taggart's silence seemed to stretch forever.

"It's just, I can't take the chance that—" he began, and then went silent again.

"Take a chance of what?"

Taggart threw open the door and climbed out. "It's time for me to go."

"TAGGART," I called to him, louder than I intended.

He looked back at me from outside.

"Are you carrying a gun?" I asked.

"No," he answered quickly. Too quickly.

"Please don't do anything stupid. Okay? For me."

He closed the door without saying a word.

Thirty-Two

I wanted to scream as I watched as Taggart walked away towards the gazebo. Was he lying to me? Did he have a gun? If so, did he intend to kill his father? Maybe he was planning to use it to take him prisoner? I didn't know what to think. Could he murder someone in cold blood and make us accomplices? Should I call someone? The police? My parents? The Wilsons? My head was spinning, and it felt like I should do something.

But what if this was just my overactive imagination, and he didn't have a gun? Then I would have ruined his plan for nothing and lost his trust forever. Damn, this was impossible. I needed someone to tell me what to do.

Then another idea came to me. I didn't have to call anyone. Maybe I could do this myself. I would go out there and wait with Taggart for his father to show and stop him if he made any kind of move for a gun. That was it.

As I reached for the door handle, my cell phone chirped with Delta's ringtone. My eyes went to the tennis court. I could see a far-off Delta standing next to Tunes with her hand to her ear.

"You see something?" I said.

"Somebody just drove through the park entrance," Delta said.

I could see headlights appear over a crest, then pull into the first row of parking spaces. The lights remained on for several seconds, then switched off.

"Could you tell who it was?" I asked Delta.

"No, it was too far away and too dark."

The interior dome light of the mysterious car came on as the driver's side door opened and someone got out. It wasn't long before I could make out the outline of a man walking slowly, approaching the gazebo.

My phone chirped again as a second call came in.

"Watch them close," I instructed Delta, then pressed the button to accept the new call.

"Are you seeing this?" Chewy's whispery voice said.

"Yes. Can you see who it is?"

"I can't believe it."

"Who is it Chewy?" I said, feeling like I was literally going to jump out of my skin.

"It's Mr. Stevens. Mr. Friggin Stevens!"

An icy chill ran down my back as I recalled the conversation I'd had with our vice principal about Taggart. I didn't manipulate him into telling me that stuff about Taggart. He wanted me to know.

"Keep an eye on them."

"Wait, there's another car pulling into the lot." Chewy's breathing had quickened.

"Oh, crap."

"They're getting out of the car now. Oh jeez, it's the guy we saw with Taggart at the football game. His therapist."

Things were unfolding rapidly and I needed to act swiftly. "I'm going out there."

"Wait, what? Why?"

"Just watch us close," I said, hanging up and opening my car door.

I hurried past the front of my car and about to cross the walking path when a woman strolling with a leashed dog blocked my path.

"Cassie?"

I stopped and scrutinized the dog walker. She looked familiar, but I couldn't place her. She was dressed in a stylish half-zip running shirt, darkly colored, with matching bottoms. A headband covered her ears and around her neck hung a cloth lanyard with a pair of keys dangling from it, along with what looked like a small container of pepper spray. An energetic dachshund was pulling at the leash in her hand, eager to greet me.

I suddenly recognized Miss Worthy from school.

I glanced towards the gazebo. Mr. Stevens was a measly couple of yards from the structure, and Taggart's therapist was also making his way in that direction.

"Hey, Miss Worthy. I hardly recognized you dressed like that. I didn't know you owned a dog."

The dachshund jumped up on my legs, begging for attention. I hunched down to scratch it behind the ears as Miss Worthy halted, settling directly between me and what was occurring at the gazebo.

"Oh, he's not mine. I'm taking care of him while a friend is out of town."

I looked through Miss Worthy's legs and could see that Mr. Stevens was at the gazebo now, talking to Taggart.

"He's a friendly one," I said, rising.

"What are you doing out here all alone at night? It's not really safe for a girl as young and pretty as you."

"I know," I said, slowly inching to the side until she wasn't blocking my view to the meeting taking place. "But you're alone, too."

Was Taggart pulling at his hoody?

"Yes, but I have this," Miss Worthy replied, reaching down to the end of the lanyard and showing me her pepper spray. "I never leave home without it. Do you own one?"

No, Taggart wasn't going for a gun, but he did shift position. His back was now to me, blocking my view of Mr. Stevens. I couldn't see what he was doing. Miss Worthy was saying something to me again. Try something?

"What?" I asked.

"I said… try mine."

Before I could act, Miss Worthy thrust the dispenser at me and pressed the top, emitting a fine mist into my face. I was stunned. Before I could raise my hands, she had sprayed me a second time.

My brain finally caught up to what was happening. I stumbled backward, covering my face with my hands, expecting a flood of burning pain that being dosed with pepper spray brings on. Instead of pain, a wave of dizziness swept over me.

I lowered my hands and saw two Miss Worthy's. Then two became three.

Then everything went dark.

Thirty-Three

I recoiled from the overpowering smell, coughing reflexively. It was like a cat pissed right under my nose. The ammonia scent was everywhere.

"Wakey… wakey."

I stirred, almost like I was awakening from a deep sleep. My bearings were returning, but the grogginess wouldn't let go. I could tell that I was lying on my side and the floor was cold. My head hurt, but it was a dull ache. I could hear something that sounded like a fan blowing, and somebody was saying something, but I didn't understand what they were saying. When I opened my eyes, everything was blurry. I was having trouble sitting up because my hands and feet were bound by something that was biting into my skin. When I finally got myself upright, the pain in my head doubled. Something else, a scent I didn't recognize, had replaced the ammonia smell, but it was almost as unpleasant.

"There you are."

The voice was familiar, but couldn't place it yet.

"I was worried that I overdosed you."

I was trying to zero in on the last thing I remembered. We were at the park. Taggart was talking to Mr. Stevens in the gazebo. Was he in trouble? I needed to get to him, but there was something in my way. A hot dog? No, not a hot dog, an actual dog associated with a hot dog. But there was somebody else. Somebody who was walking the dog?

"Miss Worthy?" I croaked out.

I heard fingers snapping. "Right here, dear."

I concentrated on the sound, and my vision sharpened. Miss Worthy was squatting next to me, smiling, still in the running outfit I remembered her wearing at the park. Her headband was gone, as was the lanyard around her neck. In her hand, broken in the middle, was a small white ampule.

"Sorry about the ammonia carbonate, but we don't have much time and I needed to elevate your heart rate, blood pressure, and brain activity by activating the sympathetic nervous system."

Instead of replying, I took the time to look around. My soft cast was missing and black zip ties were binding my hands and feet. A pair of fluorescent lights hung overhead, but only one of them worked. Still, there was more than enough light for me to see that the room was small and the walls were covered with white tile. Next to the lights on the ceiling was some sort of vent, from which the fan noise originated. I panned down to see a two-sink vanity counter in front of me with a full-length mirror to the left. Mounted on the wall above the sinks, one for each, were little yellow air fresheners and soap dispensers. Looking over Miss Worthy's shoulder, I saw a paper towel dispenser mounted on the wall behind her. I could feel cold steel against my back and realized I was propped up against a stall.

This was in a public bathroom.

"I don't understand," I said, but only because I was terrified and… it was the truth.

"You're going to have to speak up, honey. The vent is connected to the light switch and I can't turn it off," Miss Worthy said as she rose and moved to the sink where a small black satchel was sitting. I watched her as she dropped the spent capsule into the bag and then turned around to face me.

"It—it was… you? You're… the… one?" I was using every fiber of strength I possessed not to cry, but despite my best effort, my voice still quivered.

"Surprise," Miss Worthy said, holding her hands out to the side with her fingers extended, doing an impression of jazz hands. "Not who you expected?"

"But Mr. Stevens was at the park. I saw him talking to Taggart."

"Yes, he was. You probably don't know this, because you kids are so wrapped up in your own little world, but Mr. Stevens and I have been seeing each other for quite a while now. But shhhhhh, don't tell his wife. I needed better access to the student files and Principal Williams is such a prude, so Tim was Plan B. He called me after receiving your clever little note, so I convinced him he needed to go out there and talk to Taggart. He never says no to me. I imagine they had quite an interesting chat."

I didn't know how long I was unconscious, but by now Taggart had to have figured out he had been tricked and that I was missing. He and the others must be looking for me. *Please let that be true.*

"Where am I?"

"The where isn't nearly as interesting as the why. How about we start there, shall we?"

I'd seen all the movies and done the math, so I had a pretty good idea how this was going to play out. In my head I imagined myself channeling Buffy Summers or the Veronica Mars, being snarky in the face of danger, but so far, I was failing miserably. I could feel my hands shaking. I balled them into fists to hide from her.

"Okay. Why… am I?"

"Cute, but I understand. You probably think I'm going to kill you. I have to, right? I've revealed myself and therefore have no other option but to eliminate you. So your snide response means you're either incredibly brave or you assume there's nothing else to lose, so let's not make things easy for the bitch. Am I right?"

I just stared at her.

"I thought so. Well, you know what they say about assuming. You're an open book to me, Cassie. I've been watching you for years. I probably know you better than you know yourself, because let's face it, you're only eighteen and despite your feelings to the contrary, you don't know jack. Nope, bravery isn't your strong suit, so I'm going with the theory that you believe there's nothing to lose. But that's your mistake, missy. I have no intention of harming a hair on your head. I just wanted to have some time alone with you to set the record straight. But something can certainly persuade me to change my mind, so would you like to amend your answer?"

I felt a small glimmer of hope grow within me. But was it false hope?

"You have to kill me. I know who you are and what you've done."

"Again, you're doing that assumption thing. You think I intend to stick around? No, sadly, it's time to move on. I've enjoyed my stint here in New Haven, but I've out-stayed my welcome and greener pastures await."

Maybe it wasn't false hope, but was I willing to bargain my life against this nut-job's future victims?

"Okay, then why? Why am I here?"

"It's simple. You are the reason why. Everything that has happened over the last couple of weeks is because of you. This is all your fault."

"You murdered three people because of me?"

"Technically, I only attribute two to you. Your sister was an accident, but I didn't lose any sleep over that because she probably needed to be erased, anyway. I was more traumatized by the fact that I almost lost Taggart. What were the odds that Ledbetter would last long enough to crash into your car when he did? I almost had a heart attack when I heard."

The anger rising in me pushed aside the fear. I knew the tears filling my eyes now were coming from an altogether different place inside me.

"My sister never did anything to you! She didn't deserve to die, no matter what your twisted mind thinks."

"She was a distraction. Taggart needed to focus on his future, and she was diverting him from that. But you are right, the blame rests solely on your shoulders."

"How can this be my fault? Before that day, I couldn't stand Taggart. I wanted nothing to do with him."

"That's accurate enough, but he loved you anyway."

That shut me up. Taggart loved me? What was this lunatic talking about?

"You've got things mixed up. Taggart didn't love me. He spent all of his time with my sister. If he's even capable of it, it was Becca he loved."

"You children, you think you have it all figured out when, in reality, you're clueless most of the time. Tell me, why do you think Taggart was spending so much time with your sister?"

"He liked her, of course."

"That's true… or it eventually turned out that way, but he asked your sister on a date and the two of them became best buds because he wanted to be around you. There was no pressure with her, and that was important because, as you've seen, Taggart has certain emotional issues."

I was reeling, replaying the last four years of my life in my head.

"How could you possibly know that?"

"Because Taggart told me."

She had to be lying. Taggart didn't talk to anybody.

"I can see in your face that you don't believe me, and you're right, he didn't tell me directly. He told his therapist, and I listened to them discuss it at length."

During my four years in high school, I'd barely said more than a few sentences to the woman leaning back against the counter in front of me now, but as I listened to her and heard her telling more lies, I was picking up on the fact that the woman liked to talk in partial truths.

"You listened to the two of them?"

"Not there in the room with them, of course. I recorded their sessions and listened to them afterward. Besides working at the high school, I also work nights for the cleaning service that takes care of the building where Dr. Gleason has his office. The night before Taggart's appointments, I'd place a digital recorder that could capture up to twenty-four hours of conversation on top of the credenza behind Gleason's desk, then I'd pick it up the next night. I planned on picking up the recording from this morning's session tonight, but there's no point in that now. That's how I knew that asshole Ledbetter rejected Taggart for that job. But aside from my regular Taggart updates, I also picked up some interesting gossip fodder. I bet you didn't know that New Haven's star linebacker was seeing Dr. Gleason for depression, did you?"

I gradually realized how easily this woman had wormed her way into Taggart's life.

"He's talked at length to the shrink about you. Gleason wasn't thrilled when Taggart told him what he was doing with your sister, but over time his opinion changed when he saw the 'so-called' positive influence she was having on him. Gleason's acceptance of the situation disappointed me, but I found it useful to monitor Taggart through him over the years."

"You took the job at the school just to be near him?"

"Oh, I've worked at all of his schools in one capacity or another. I've also attended the same churches his foster parents worship at. I've talked to the Wilsons every Sunday since he moved in with them. They're good people, except I've been told Mr. Wilson cusses a bit much. That's probably because of his background as a policeman. I'm a volunteer at social services as well, so I'm able to monitor how his placements are going."

"But why?

"Excuse me?

"Why? Why are you doing all this?"

The monster standing in front of me, calling herself Miss Worthy, crossed her arms over her chest and furrowed her eyebrows in a look of confusion.

"Isn't that what a mother's supposed to do?"

Thirty-Four

"Taggart's mother is dead," I replied before thinking.

"Hardly," Miss Worthy answered, gesturing with her hand like she was shooing away an annoying fly.

Whoever the hell this woman was, she had to be lying and telling half-truths, so the last thing I planned on doing was believe her. You didn't have to be Dr. Gleason to see how messed up she was. I could envision some sort of past where she'd endured severe emotional trauma and her coping mechanism was to form a dream world that included a child… and an abandoned one such as Taggart fit that bill flawlessly. But that also meant I needed to be careful about how I spoke to her. What I remembered from listening to Delta drone on endlessly about her reality TV shows, particularly her favorite, *My Psychiatrist and Me*, challenging a mentally unbalanced person's belief system could lead to violence, and that would be bad for me.

Thinking about Delta made me think about the others. Were they searching for me? Surely kidnapping rose to the level that warranted finally calling the police. But how would they find me?

I formulated my next question carefully.

"You said that you were leaving New Haven. What about Taggart?"

Miss Worthy opened her arms and looked around the room. "That's actually why we're here. I will give Taggart the opportunity to come with me, if he chooses, but he must pass a couple of tests first."

"What sort of tests, and what do they have to do with a public bathroom?"

"You really aren't that bright, are you? That's my issue with standardized tests in our schools. Sure, they can lead to the undervaluation of children simply because they're terrible at taking tests, but they can do the opposite as well. Take you, for example. You've always had great scores, but you have the common sense of a fence post, don't you?"

I bit my lip and kept my mouth shut.

"What's the matter? Truth got your tongue?"

I couldn't hold it back any longer. "I'm sorry, but I'm usually a little slow right after I've been drugged."

Miss Worthy seemed to consider my response, then smiled. That look on her face, which used to make me feel calm and secure, now sent chills down my spine.

"Taggart would say that this is where it all began. He has this phobia about public restrooms, and this one, well… let's just say it's like his kryptonite. His first test will be to overcome his aversion and move past that point in his life. I'm going to help him do that."

The bitch wanted Taggart to return to the spot where his nightmares were born. I remembered how anxious he was when we were sitting in a car across the street, under heavy medication, and now she wanted him in here with us. I remembered that he once went into a bathroom to help Becca, but coming in here would be asking so much more from him. I wasn't sure he could do it, even for me.

"If you're Taggart's mother, as you claim, then who was it who died in here with him?"

"My bitch of a sister," she said matter-of-factly.

What? "What?"

"It was her own fault, of course. Can you imagine, our parents thought I was the black sheep of the family until she came along. They may have thrown me out of the house when I was fifteen, but she ran away from that cesspool when she was seventeen. So how's that for vindication? She had her share of problems, but I won't bore you with the details. Let's just say she was in and out of rehab most of her life. We weren't really close, but she found me in Atlanta shortly after Preston and I were married, though I'm still not sure how. Anyway, she was looking for a handout, like always, to feed her habit. She must have been desperate too, because she usually avoided me like the plague. But things changed when she saw Taggart... well, his name was Billy back then. She really took a shining to her nephew. I guess I can see why. The damn child looked more like my sister than me... his own mother. It was that dimpled chin, just like our worthless excuse-for-a-mother had. That cinched it. Imagine my surprise when she cleaned up her act and got a steady job across town in Lawrenceville. Preston wanted to let her come over to spend time with the boy, even letting her babysit sometimes, and I couldn't say no without appearing heartless. I'll admit things were going along fine for a while, but I probably should have guessed something was up. The last couple of months, she kept dropping in unannounced. I don't think she believed me when Preston disappeared and I told her he was on a business trip. I came back one day from running errands and she and Billy were gone. Boy, was I pissed. There was no way in hell I could let her get away with that, though. Who did she think she was? She was so easy to track down. I knew where she was heading, where she always went when things hit rock bottom. She didn't have a car or the money to fly to Florida, so she had to take the bus. I caught up with her here in New Haven, right across the street, in fact. She had to pay for what she did, of course."

"You're… really Taggart's mother," I uttered, my head still spinning as the truth took hold.

"Have you not been listening to me? You really are a mess. For the life of me, I can't understand what Taggart sees in you."

"If that's true, then your sister wasn't the only one who had a drug problem. Weren't you fired because of a failed drug test?"

Miss Worthy tilted her head to the side, reappraising me. "Well, well. You were busy in Atlanta. Yes, I had some issues with post-partem depression combined with the fact that I had become bored with our situation, so I partook in some recreational pharmaceuticals. But I was never as dependent on them as my sister. In the end, I did her a favor."

"But you left Taggart in here… with her body… all that time?"

"The boy needed to be punished. I watched him with her. He wasn't resisting or fighting, not one little bit. No, ma'am, he had gone with her willingly. He needed to learn a lesson as well."

My mind rushed through everything I thought I knew, trying to fill in the blanks. I had cracked the equation for X, and now I was tasked with solving for Y. I had to figure out what pieces were still missing.

"The ID she had on her? McGill?"

"One of the fakes she must have held onto from her less than upstanding past. Technically, what she was doing was kidnapping, so obviously she felt the need to assume a different identity. Taggart was the name of a stuffed animal she had when we were little. When the police found her and Billy, or Taggart as he had become, all they had to go on was that ID, the story from the witnesses, and their resemblance to one another. Taggart had gone mute, so like the police normally do, they put two and two together and came up with five."

"What about Taggart's father?"

"Oh, him. He's long dead. I spread pieces of Preston all over Atlanta. If Taggart had his memories back, he'd tell you. He helped me."

She was lying again… she had to be.

"You're lying."

"Oh, not at all. Granted, it was unintentional. I'll always remember the look on Billy's face when he woke early from his nap and stumbled across me in the middle of wrapping his father's severed head in cellophane. He wasn't very cooperative at first and could only do so much—he was only four after all—but I made him do his part."

I'd wondered if Taggart's nightmare had begun long before arriving in New Haven. Turns out, I was right. What else had this dreadful woman put him through?

"Did you kill your husband because of the MC606?"

"Well, look at you. Maybe there's hope for you yet. I guess your trip with Taggart to Atlanta proved fruitful. It's curious, though, that they would have told you anything. Regardless, yes, Preston didn't appreciate what I was trying to do for him and, unfortunately, he overreacted. You see, MC606 was Preston's baby. When they red-flagged it, it devastated him. But he wouldn't stand up for it, or himself. I was just trying to get him to use some leverage to get things back on track."

"You stole the vial?"

"Of course. I wanted him to keep working on it independently, or at another company, if need be. I used Preston's ID and blind spots in their security I'd noticed during my time there and liberated a vial. It was really Preston's property. I mean, he created it, but I wasn't greedy. I only took the one."

"But Preston wasn't on board with your plan?"

"That's the understatement of the year. He went ballistic when I showed him. He started yelling and screaming at me. Terrible things. He ranted about how it was all a pattern of behavior or some such nonsense, bringing up past issues that I thought had been resolved. Finally, he started talking about turning himself in and telling the truth, so I had to do something."

"What did you do?"

Miss Worthy, or Rachel Jones, twisted around to face the counter and picked up a cell phone that must have been resting next to her bag. She then moved towards me, crouched down beside me, and extended her arm with the phone, pointing it back at the two of us.

"Smile," she said, and I heard the phone click. I wasn't smiling.

She returned to her spot by the counter, continued with the phone for a few seconds more, then put it back down and reached into a black satchel. From it, she pulled out a cylindrical object the size of a spool of thread. The tiny canister was black, with a thin ring of silver metal circling one end and something like a rubber cap at the other.

"They probably didn't tell you about this little darling, did they?"

"What is it?"

She rolled the device back and forth between her thumb and forefinger, staring at it.

"It's the future. You know what two things are keeping drug companies from making money hands over fist? Not that they're not already, but greed is a powerful emotion. The first is the drugs themselves and mass-producing them in such to make them affordable. Turning the formulas into pills adds significant costs to the process, thus reducing profits, but the cheapest delivery method leads to the second reason the drug companies are constrained. Needles. People are terrified of them. What this little device does is rapidly desensitize the skin by cooling it to 4.5 degrees Celsius in a millisecond. It does what an ice pack does, but faster and in a more focused way. It numbs the skin and makes an injection virtually undetectable."

"You used that on your husband? Stooch? Mr. Ledbetter?"

"Yes, I did."

"How many others?"

"Only those who were deserving."

I shook my head. "But why didn't you just take Taggart and go after you murdered your sister? Why stay here?"

"I considered it. In fact, I had even decided to do that, but someone beat me to the bathroom and found the boy. After that, it was too late. Of course, I could have taken him from any of the families they placed him with, but I came up with a different option. I returned to Atlanta and finished covering my tracks, and since I needed to disappear anyway, New Haven was an opportune choice. I settled in here where I could keep an eye on my boy. Since I was starting over again, I chose opportunities that would place me in reasonably close contact with him."

My arm was aching, and my back was stiffening. I jerked my head toward the deadly object in Miss Worthy's hand.

"Do you plan to use that on me?"

"Absolutely not… unless you force me to. But I will use it on my son if he doesn't pass the second test."

"You'd kill your own flesh and blood? After watching over him for all these years, killed *for* him no less, and you'd murder him just like that?"

"I have been extraordinarily patient, waiting for him to come into his own. I may have actually waited too long. But now that he is ready, my determination and efforts will have all been wasted if his mind has been tainted."

By this point, I had no trouble believing this woman would kill her own son. She was a human version of a hamster—cute and cuddly, but absolutely capable of chowing down on her own offspring.

"What's the second test?" I asked.

"You'll just have to wait until he gets here to find out."

"As soon as you tell him where we are, he'll have this place surrounded by police. You won't be able to go anywhere."

"He already knows where we are because I texted him with a selfie of us together. And he'll come alone because I told him you die if I detect even a whiff of pork."

My anxiety spiked after hearing Taggart might be on his way and unaware of what he was walking into. I had to do something. I had to prevent Taggart from being manipulated simply because there was a needle at my throat. But would he listen to me? She claimed Taggart loved me, and as crazy as that sounded and felt, how could I trust anything she said or believed? I didn't think he would do anything that would put me in danger, or purposely hurt me, but this was his mother we were talking about. There was a shit-load of pent-up emotions in him, like the inner-workings of a beehive. I needed to be ready when she kicked the nest.

Miss Worthy started digging in her satchel again, giving me the opportunity to assess my options. The only thing I spotted that might be used as a weapon was a small metal trashcan right inside the door, overflowing with discarded paper towels. I could make a break for the door, which was about ten paces away from me, if my feet weren't tied. I could always use the numbing weapon she showed me, sitting next to the satchel, but I would have to push her aside to grab it and then figure out how to make it work. Maybe I didn't have to know how to use it? Maybe just having it in my hands would be deterrent enough. Not being in this tight space would be a big plus. Provide more options. So how could I change those circumstances?

"Taggart doesn't have a phone or a car," I said.

"I left your phone for him where your car was parked. And Mr. Stevens will give him a lift. He's quite accommodating. Don't worry, he'll be here. Shouldn't be long now. That's the

thing about small towns. Everything's only ten minutes
away."

Thirty-Five

I don't know where Taggart was when he received the text from his mother, but the muted sound of a barking dog came soon after Miss Worthy had dragged me to my feet and slapped duct tape across my mouth.

"That will be Jiblet, the neighbor's dog I borrowed. I have him tied up outside. He's an irritating little furball, but a pretty good watch dog."

When she heard banging on the door, she positioned me next to her at the end of the counter, then snatched up the black cylinder and stuck it in her jacket pocket.

"You make one squeak, and this will end badly for you," Miss Worthy whispered into my ear. "Come in," she called out.

The door gradually opened outward, and Taggart stepped inside. He was the most beautiful sight I have ever seen.

The hood on his jacket was up, hiding most of his face, but he was holding his hands out to the side, showing us they were empty. As the door closed behind him, he stopped just inside the entrance and let his arms drop.

"Push that hood off your head. I want to see you," Miss Worthy said.

He did as he was told. When I saw his face, tears filled my eyes. He looked like a weightlifter attempting to break a world record. The muscles in his face quivered. He was desperately trying to contain his emotions, as if he were struggling under a crushing weight. The boy I'd come to see as stoic and distant was enduring a massive internal struggle, trying to maintain control. Seeing it broke my heart.

"That wasn't so bad, was it? Now get that hair out of your eyes… it's always bothered me you wear it that way."

Taggart brushed his hair to the side, his hand shaking like a leaf as he did.

"That's better. Such a handsome young man, don't you think so, Cassie?"

I don't know why, but I nodded my head. I thought I caught a brief smile at the corners of Taggart's eyes, but it disappeared quickly.

"You're the woman who gave birth to me?" Taggart said, his voice measured and controlled.

"Yes, I am."

"Who… who was—"

"The woman who brought you here? That was my sister… your aunt. She stole you from me. I'm your proper mother."

"You may be my birth parent, but you are not my mother."

If Taggart's biting remark bothered the woman standing next to me, she didn't show it.

"A distinction that I'd like to rectify, if you're willing."

As if… I thought to myself.

Taggart looked confused. "You think the two of us can just walk out of here and start a new life together, as mother and son?"

"Exactly."

"And Cassie goes free, unharmed?"

Miss Worthy tightened her grip on my upper arm.

"I'm afraid not. I can't allow this little love triangle to continue. You see, if we leave her behind and go together, you will always be haunted by what-ifs. That will never work. I can't afford to have you distracted. Only two people will walk out of this room alive tonight. You must choose between us, either me or her. If you choose me, then she'll need to be eliminated. If you choose her, then she gets to live, but you'll have to sacrifice yourself instead."

You said you wouldn't hurt me I wanted to blurt out, but with the tape on my mouth I could only grunt and moan at her.

Miss Worthy looked at me as if she understood what I was trying to communicate. "What I said is that I wouldn't harm a hair on your head. If Taggart chooses me, he'll be the one to fix his own mistake."

"Can I propose a third option?"

Miss Worthy sighed. "I'm not killing myself, Taggart."

Yeah… I vote for that option!

Taggart seemed to be gaining some ground with his inner-struggle, as his shoulders relaxed, and a tranquil expression spread across his face. He shrugged his shoulders. "You really believe I would leave with you?"

"I'll admit it's fifty-fifty, but let's take a minute to ponder it, shall we? We are a lot alike. You thrive on reason and rational choice, and you don't allow your emotions to drive your actions. Just like me. I've watched you for so long. I know you better than you know yourself. A mother always does. And I've continually tried to do what's best for you. I've removed roadblocks and punished those who've hurt you, like any mother would."

"And Becca? Was she a roadblock?"

"That was an unplanned and unavoidable accident. Surely you can see that. Don't let yourself get be burdened with emotional baggage, not when you've been doing such a wonderful job. Isn't going with me the logical choice?"

"And my father?"

"Your father intended to have me put behind bars for simply trying to further his career, so silencing him became both necessary and justifiable."

The muted silence that followed made me uneasy. Taggart was taking too much time to think things over.

"I'll go with you," he said finally, causing me to stop breathing. "Hand me the needle."

Out of the corner of my eye, I watched Miss Worthy take the black cylinder out of her pocket, but then she let it hang at her side.

"I'm sensing that you're contemplating a bit of deception," she said. Before I could react, she turned towards me and pushed the numbing tool up against my neck. "Maybe I should handle this for you, just to ensure you're not tempted to change your mind."

Taggart whipped his arm behind his back and came back with a gun, pointed in Miss Worthy's direction. It was a revolver, and I could clearly see a bullet in each chamber. Earlier tonight I hoped Taggart wasn't lying to me when he said he didn't have a gun, and now I was relieved that he had lied to me.

I had gone from not breathing at all to doing it so fast that the inside of my nose was burning.

"If Cassie dies, you die with her," he said.

"Then the two most important women in your life will be gone and you'll be left here all alone. Not a pretty picture." I couldn't see Miss Worthy's face, but I imagined there was a smirk on it.

"But I will still be here… and you'll be gone. I will get over you… both of you."

Please wink and show me you're joking. Please wink… please wink.

"You'll have plenty of time to do that… because you'll be in prison for murdering your own mother."

"I seriously doubt—given the circumstances of what you've done here in New Haven—that a jury would convict me for trying to save a girl's life. Besides, as long as I have access to books, even solitary confinement would be nirvana for me."

If I knew Taggart was serious about pulling the trigger, I'd consider elbowing Miss Worthy in the stomach and diving for the floor. But no matter how hard I tried, I still couldn't see him doing it. Yes, he had brought the gun and planned to use it somehow with Mr. Stevens, but that could have been to subdue him. Yet, his manner indicated something was different. I thought I had seen all the subtle nuances in Taggart's blank stares, but this one was different. My mother often read romance writers who would have depicted it as smoldering anger. Maybe I was mistaken. Maybe he could do it.

Still, it was too much of a risk to take, for both our sakes.

"Taggart, look at you. Surely, you can see how the time you spent with Becca has confused you, and now there's this thing with Cassie. You don't know this, but I've listened to the sessions with your therapist, and I understand more than you think. It's just an infatuation honey. When you weigh that against everything I've done for you… and will continue to do for you… I think you'll make the sound choice."

When she mentioned the therapy sessions, Taggart's eyes met mine, but his expression remained unchanged.

"Yes, she knows how you used Becca to get close to her. Whatever you imagined would develop between the two of you is exactly that, imaginary. She could never have feelings for someone like you. Someone who would do that. She belongs to the Jasons of this world… not you."

I tried to use my eyes to communicate how wrong she was, but he dipped his head. Maybe he was considering his options.

Taggart pointed the gun to the ceiling and raised his hands.

"You win, I'll go with you," he said, slowly placing the gun on the counter between him and us, then sliding his hands into the hand pouch of his hoodie.

NO!!!! I moaned, simultaneously screaming inside my head, *what are you doing? You have the upper hand. Why would you do that?*

"But as you've pointed out, I have to be the one to do it. That's the only way you'll ever trust me. Take the gun as insurance. No tricks… I swear."

Miss Worthy regarded the revolver on the counter. I felt her relax the grip on my arm and remove the injector from my throat.

"Trust is a precious commodity, and I look forward to investing some in you. Until that happens, could you please back away a few more paces?"

But Taggart didn't move. He just stood where he was, staring at his mother.

"Did you not hear me?"

That's when Taggart's eyes found mine… and I knew. I don't know how I knew, but I did. I had never been as certain about anything in my whole life, but I was about this. It was indisputable, like the spring following the winter, or Einstein's law of relativity. I was that sure.

Whatever happened next, Taggart wouldn't allow anything to happen to me.

Still, I was petrified. Not for me, but for Taggart.

"This is not helping your—"

Miss Worthy cut short her comment when she saw Taggart retreat. When his back pushed up against the door, his mother took a step towards the counter, switched the injector from her right hand to her left, and then reached for the gun.

"One hundred," Taggart said.

"What?" Miss Worthy replied, hesitating.

The lights went out.

The room plunged into darkness, completely disorienting me. I lost my balance and fell forward onto my hands and knees, sending a jolt of pain up my damaged arm. I could hear sounds of scuffling feet a few steps away and imagined Taggart and his mother fighting for control of the gun, each trying to gain the upper hand. I was helpless to do anything.

"NO!" Miss Worthy screamed in the dark.

I heard and felt something bang into the stall next to me, followed by another collision somewhere across the room, and a muffled gasp. Then there was a bright flash and the deafening roar of a gunshot. My heart stopped.

The room lights came blaring back on as suddenly as they'd gone out, briefly blinding me. When my vision cleared, the first thing I noticed was the silver gun on the floor by the door. Taggart was locked hand-in-hand with his mother, spinning around wildly, struggling to keep the black cylinder in his mother's right hand from touching his body.

I had to do something. I couldn't just stand by and hope that Taggart could overpower his mother, especially seeing the insane way she was fighting. The gun. If I could reach it, perhaps I could get Miss Worthy to back away from Taggart. I started moving along the wall, not letting my bound hands and feet, or the pain shooting up my arm, slow me down. Foot by foot I crept along, like an inchworm evading a pair of hungry birds fighting over the right to swallow me. I was six feet from the gun when Miss Worthy gained leverage on Taggart and shoved him backward, right into me. I tried to duck before both of their legs collided with my shoulders, but a knee caught me square on the side of my head. An explosion of stars accompanied a sharp pain radiating from my ear to my forehead.

It took a couple of seconds for my vision to clear. When it did, I forgot about the gun and turned my head to stare at the mother and son. Both had gone sprawling, landing in a pile behind me. Taggart was lying prone, but Miss Worthy was already up in a sitting position. What surprised me was how completely still they both were, staring at a red dot that was forming on Miss Worthy's left wrist. The black cylinder was on the ground between them.

Miss Worthy pulled her eyes away from her wrist and looked at Taggart. He looked back at her. The realization of what had happened… and what was going to happen… passed between them.

Suddenly, the bathroom door flew open and a rush of bodies charged in. It didn't surprise me to see Chewy and Tunes bouncing back and forth brandishing aluminum baseball bats, looking for a reason to use them. The person leading the charge did shock me. It was Jason. My ex-boyfriend glimpsed the revolver on the floor, snatched it up, and pointed it at Miss Worthy.

Chewy slowly pulled the duct tape covering my mouth. "What are you doing here, Jason?"

Jason glanced at me. "Your Scooby Gang called and said you were being held hostage at my dad's gas station by the person who killed Stooch and that they needed my help. It was either do this… or binge-watching *Game of Thrones*. What do you think… did I make the right call?"

"Definitely. *Thrones* is seriously over-rated."

"Good to know," he said, smiling.

"What are friends for?" I said, returning the smile. A sense of relief flooded over me. We made it… with everyone in one piece. I turned to look at Taggart, still smiling, when it happened.

Moving with lightning quickness, Miss Worthy snatched the black cylinder from the ground, reached out, and jabbed it into the back of my leg.

I didn't feel a thing.

"NOOOOO!" Taggart yelled, reacting a second too late and slapping the injector from his mother's hand, sending it flying across the room.

"Did she just do what I think she did?" Chewy asked.

"Do what?" Jason asked in a voice on the brink of shouting.

"She injected Cassie," Chewy said, answering his own question.

I know I should have been freaking out. I mean, I'd been injected with a drug that was going to kill me, but I was calm, and initially confused. Why would Miss Worthy do that with a gun trained on her? Didn't she think Jason would pull the trigger? That's when I realized. She was already dead. The MC606 toxin was coursing through her veins too, effectively signing her death warrant, so what did she have to lose? And now I was in the same boat, but it still didn't feel real. Wasn't something that would kill you supposed to hurt? I didn't even feel the needle penetrate my skin. Or maybe I was in shock? I had always heard that shock was a bad thing, but this didn't seem so bad.

"Get to your feet," Taggart instructed his mother, rising himself.

"Is it over?" came a disembodied voice from outside. When no one answered her, Delta poked her head in the door and surveyed what was going on. "The police are on their way."

"The damn bitch injected Cassie," Chewy barked.

"Will somebody please tell me what that means?" Jason asked, his voice rising even louder.

Delta's eyes had grown wide. "I'm getting the antidote," she said, then disappeared.

Both Chewy and Tunes said aloud, in unison, the same thing I was thinking to myself. "Antidote?"

Confused, I turned my attention to Taggart. He was now standing next to his mother, one hand gripped tightly on her upper arm, both of their butts up against the sink counter.

"That's what was in the other envelope the drug company gave me," he said evenly. "It was the only sample they had left."

"And you thought you'd keep that a secret?" I asked.

"Yeah dude, not cool," Chewy added, lowering his bat.

Miss Worthy looked at Taggart with an expression that came close to resembling pride. It turned my stomach.

"You must have made quite an impression on my former employers," Taggart's mother said, then turned her gaze on me. "Looks like he'll get to choose between the two of us after all."

"That's hardly a choice," Taggart said, then bent over.

That's when a lot of things happened rapidly, but to me it seemed to play out in terrifying slow motion.

Delta came running back into the room holding an envelope, Jason—who was obviously confused by what was happening around him—became distracted by Delta's reappearance and looked away from Miss Worthy for a split-second. Miss Worthy then shoved Taggart and reached underneath the counter. An instant seemed like an eternity, but when it had passed, Miss Worthy turned back towards Jason with a black semi-automatic pistol in her hand, duct tape still dangling from the barrel. She calmly pointed it at my stunned ex-boyfriend and pulled the trigger.

The blast wasn't as loud as the revolver, but crimson red still exploded from Jason's shirt near his collar, sending him flying backward into the wall. The revolver he'd been holding tumbled to the ground.

It had all happened so fast and so unexpected that no one had a chance to react. I watched Jason crumble face-first onto the floor, blood spreading quickly around a hole in the back of his shirt. My first thought was to claw Miss Worthy's eyes out.

"If anyone moves a muscle, the next one goes through Chewy's eye," Miss Worthy commanded.

Everyone did as she instructed, frozen in time, except for Taggart, who was straightening himself. If I wasn't still bound by the zip ties, I don't know if I'd be able to do the same.

Miss Worthy glanced at Taggart. "You, back away into the corner."

Taggart slowly did as he was told.

"Now Delta, if you kindly place that envelope on the counter beside me."

Delta didn't move. Instead, she looked at me with a tortured face. She was holding my life in her hands and a mad woman was asking her to surrender it. If she gave it up, she'd be killing me. If she held onto to it, Chewy… and probably others… would be shot. The blood pouring onto the floor from an unconscious Jason was a testament to that.

I may have been dying, but I wouldn't want to be in Delta's shoes either.

"Delta, I won't ask you again."

"The police will be here any minute," Delta squeaked, clutching the envelope against her chest.

"The more reason for you to hurry. I will shoot every one of you if I have to, but I will have that antidote. NOW MOVE!"

The yell shocked Delta out of her indecision and she hastily stepped around Tunes and placed the envelope on the counter, then backed away. The envelope was already open. From my vantage point, I could see something like a clear plastic tube, the size of a large pen, inside.

Miss Worthy switched the gun to her left hand, keeping it trained on Chewy, then blindly searched for the envelope with her right hand. When she found it, she turned it on its side and shook, spilling out the tube. One end of the tube was flat and colored blue, and the other was bright orange and pointed, coming to a blunt end. Grasping the plastic pen as if it were a knife, she used her thumb to pop off a blue safety tip.

Taggart took a step forward.

"Uh… uh… uh," Miss Worthy warned, while moving the pistol until it was pointed at my head. "I know what you're thinking, dear. You rush me… I kill Chewy, but you couldn't care less about him."

Chewy looked at Taggart with a look that was equal parts disbelief and anger.

"You'd overpower me, and then you can still save your darling Cassie. Well, that won't happen. If you take another step, you won't have to wait for the drug to do its job."

Taggart remained still and watched as his mother jammed the pen into her upper thigh.

Delta let out a sorrowful whimper.

Miss Worthy smiled at Delta while pressing down on the end of the pen with her thumb. When she was finished, she tossed the empty cartridge at Taggart. I watched as it bounced off his chest and fell to the floor.

The sirens echoing in the distance confirmed Delta was telling the truth, but it didn't matter as my fate was already sealed.

"Now, all of you are going to lead the way out of here and when we—" Miss Worthy began, but suddenly she hesitated, her eyebrows furrowed.

"Delta, go tell the police to call for an ambulance," Taggart said calmly, bending over again.

Delta stared at Taggart, uncomprehending, then looked at me. My attention stayed with Miss Worthy, who looked like she was in genuine distress. Sweat beaded on her forehead and her complexion had darkened. She was no longer paying attention to anyone in the room.

Both her hands, the pistol still gripped in one of them, snapped to the sides of her head. I heard a gasp escape her. She stumbled back against the counter but kept her balance. She turned her head towards Taggart. Something was in his hand. He looked at the woman in front of him... his mother... who was in obvious pain... in the same way someone might regard a stranger. I watched as he stepped around her, raised his hand to let me see a plastic pen similar to the one Miss Worthy had taken from Delta. He popped off the bright yellow safety tip and jammed the pen down into my thigh.

This time it hurt.

"Taggart," I heard Tunes say behind me.

Taggart's eyes went to Tunes before he swung around towards his mother. She was holding the pistol in both hands, attempting to point it at her son, but acted like it weighed a hundred pounds.

"You... have... to... be," the woman croaked, sounding like each word was taking great effort to get out. Then, in one final desperate push, "You have to be pun—"

Miss Worthy crumbled to the ground.

Thirty-Six

"Why are they keeping me here? I feel fine," I stated for what felt like the hundredth time, jerking on the bedding as I spoke.

We were in the emergency room of the same hospital I was taken to after the accident that claimed my sister's life. I was sitting on an examination table in a curtained off area with medical monitors to my left.

"And you probably are fine, but monitoring is not unwarranted," Taggart answered. He was standing over by a gap in the screen, his hands folded in front of him.

"But you gave me the antidote, crisis averted, right?"

"Yes, but the antidote didn't come with any sort of instructions or warnings about side-effects, so caution is needed. Although it is supposed to counteract the effects of the toxin, we don't know what other effects the drug might have on you. There's also the fact that the antidote is approximately 15 years old, so there's a concern about viability due to shelf life."

"You mean I could still die because it was too old?"

"No. I don't believe so. They wouldn't have provided it to me if they knew it couldn't be of any use. But still… we shouldn't take any chances. You took a pretty nasty bump to the head, and a sleep agent rendered you unconscious, so the paramedics wanted to bring you in to be safe. We're just taking advantage of that."

I don't know why, but I seemed more concerned about dying now than I did right after she injected me. Maybe it was my latent hypochondria making a guest appearance.

Before the police and the ambulances showed up at the gas station, Taggart had instructed all of us not to say anything to anybody about the toxin and the drug company. No one understood why, but we all agreed anyway. After that, it had been a mad rush to get Jason and me to the hospital, so I still hadn't wrapped my head around everything Taggart's mother had said in that bathroom.

"Why can't I at least check on Jason? It's not like I'm contagious or anything."

Taggart stepped closer to the bed. "He's still in surgery. They promised to give us an update as soon as he came out, but they were confident he was going to make a full recovery."

"Yeah… well… their definition of full recovery might not be the same as Jason's. She shot him in the right shoulder, his throwing shoulder, so unless he can still throw touchdown passes, he won't be a happy camper."

"I'm sure," Taggart said, his gaze dropping to the foot of the bed.

Another uncomfortable silence descended between us, one of many that had been occurring ever since arriving at the hospital. We had been avoiding it long enough, and I was certain Taggart wouldn't be bringing it up, so I took a running start at the elephant in the room.

"I still can't believe you told Delta about the antidote, but not me."

Taggart shifted his weight, keeping his eyes lowered.

"You think I should have told you?" Taggart asked.

"Duh! Do you have any idea—" I started, but the emotion reached up from my diaphragm and closed off my windpipe.

"I was—apprehensive."

I took a deep breath and regained my composure. "You were afraid? Of what?"

"That you would make me use it… if it was injected into someone," he said.

Now I was confused. "Well… yeah. And why is that so bad?"

"I needed to save it for a specific purpose."

"Oh, right, in case you were injected. Well, good call." I should have known it was easy enough being brave when you know there's a safety net waiting to catch you.

"No… not me."

"Then who?"

His answer came as silence. When it dawned on me what he meant, all I could think to say was, "Oh."

"I needed to make sure that if you were injected, I had a way to save you. I couldn't afford the risk of you or anyone else trying to talk me into administering it to someone else."

My embarrassment was total and complete. He had been saving the golden ticket for me all along, and I just accused him of doing it for selfish reasons. I wanted to crawl under the bed. I had to quickly change the subject, but fortunately, Chewy, Tunes, and Delta rushed in and did it for me.

"That detective won't be far behind us, so we'd better make this quick," Chewy said as he made a beeline for the first chair he saw.

"What the hell, Taggart?" Delta asked, her hands going straight to her hips when she stood next to me at the head of the bed. "Why did you have us lie to the police?"

"Technically, you didn't lie, you withheld pertinent facts," Taggart answered flatly. He looked just as relieved to be interrupted as I was.

"Don't play word games with me. Why did you want the poison and the drug company kept a secret?"

"I'm playing the long game. What if we told them? They'd never be able to tie Miss Worthy or the drug back to its source. The drug company has seen to that. What would be gained by divulging what we know? Nothing. Nothing but more questions, suppositions, unsupported claims, and parental discord when the true nature of our trip to Atlanta became known. On the other hand, our silence could prove beneficial to our futures, as having a powerful drug company who owes you a favor can do."

"But we don't even know who the drug company is. How could we have them in our pocket?" Delta pointed out.

"But we do know who they are," Taggart answered.

"How?" I asked. "They kept us in the dark. We couldn't see where we were going and there were no company markings anywhere."

"I noted the odometer reading of the SVU before we left Georgia Tech and then again when we arrived at our destination. I used those miles to match the locations I had previously researched. Only one came close… Selphaxsys."

"That's amazing," Chewy said.

"They could have driven us around in circles, throwing off the miles?" I observed.

"Doubtful. We were a bunch of kids, not Jason Bourne."

"I for one couldn't care less if we tell the cops what we know," Chewy said, his legs and bright red converse basketball shoes feet hanging off the side of the chair.

"That's fine for you Chewy, you know what really happened to your dad now, but what about the other victims' families?" I asked. "What about Stooch's parents? Don't you think they deserve to know how their son really died?"

Chewy shrugged his shoulders.

"I'm not sure it would make a difference," Tunes said.

"It could actually be more painful for people to know the truth," Taggart muttered, looking down at the floor.

That made me reassess my thinking. What was the right thing to do? Sure, we could tell them about Selphaxsys and the toxin, but then we would hurt the company that gave us the information we needed in the first place—and an antidote that saved my life—when they had no reason to. I thought this decision would be easy, but now I was having doubts.

"Tell them… don't tell them… I guess they could talk me into either," Delta said, one of her hands coming off her hips to push some of my hair behind my ear. "What I really want to know is why you made me think I had the real antidote? Why the deception?"

"And what was that she injected herself with, anyway?" Chewy added.

"It was one of Mr. Wilson's EpiPens. He's highly allergic to peanuts," Taggart answered, then turned to Delta. "I stripped off the original labels to make it look less commercial. The subterfuge was in case we found ourselves in that very scenario, where we faced a foe who would stop at nothing to get their hands on it. I needed them to believe it was the real thing, and your acting ability is suspect."

"But why tell anyone about it, then? Why not keep to yourself?" I asked.

Taggart nodded his head. "I could have, but we didn't know if the murderer knew the antidote existed or not. I needed to plan for all contingencies, so someone other than me needed to think it was real. That's where Delta came in."

"Where was it, really?" Chewy asked.

"Taped to the inside of my calf."

"Why didn't you just call the police when—" I started asking.

"—we found out you were missing?" Delta answered. "We wanted to, but Taggart stopped us."

Everyone looked at Taggart.

"I knew if the police were summoned they would never have let me become involved, and my relationship with that woman was the best plan we had."

"And giving her your gun… that was part of the plan?" I asked. "I almost had a heart attack when you did that."

"I didn't give it to her. I put it in a spot where she would have to detach herself from you to gain access to it."

"She could have dragged me with her."

"True, but she would have still needed to remove the injector from your body."

"But you couldn't have known the power would go off at that exact moment."

"Actually, I did. Jason was at the fuse box. He and I were both counting to one hundred. His instruction was to throw the switch when he reached 100. I just had to ensure you were separated from Miss Worthy by that time."

"You were counting to a hundred inside your head… the whole time… while you were talking to her?"

"Yes."

I was speechless.

"How are you feeling?" Delta asked, slipping her hand in mine.

"I'm fine, just a little tired," I answered, squeezing her hand.

"It would probably be better if Cassie was alone when the detective showed up," Taggart suggested. "Maybe you could go check on Jason?"

"We can do that," Chewy said, popping up from the chair. "I'm starved too. You think they have pizza in the cafeteria?"

"I doubt it," Delta said as she followed Chewy out of the curtain. "We'll be back shortly, Cass."

Tunes was the last one to go, beaming broadly as he pulled the curtain behind him.

And then the uncomfortable silence was back. It was becoming a little tiring, always being the one to start a conversation.

"How are you feeling?" I asked.

Taggart appeared surprised. "Me?"

"Yes, you. You just met your *real* mother—who was a major piece of work, I might add—watched her die, and found out your father is dead as well. That's a lot. So yeah, how are you *feeling?*"

The whisper of a smile appeared at the corner of his lips. "What does Spock say… *Logic is the beginning of wisdom, not the end.*"

"You are not some unemotional person like Spock. Your mother was way off-base there, you know that, right?"

Taggart gave me an unconvincing smile.

"Becca didn't think you were emotionless," I said, deciding it was time to lay all the cards on the table.

Taggart's smile disappeared.

"I need to ask you something, and I really need for you to tell me the truth. Okay?"

Taggart lowered his head, then gave a barely noticeable nod.

"Was it true what your mom—"

"Please don't call her that."

"Sorry. Is it true what Miss Worthy said… about why you and Becca became friends?"

Taggart reached out and clenched the sheets on the bed with his fists.

"I will not be mad," I continued. "I just need to hear it from you."

Taggart took a deep breath. "It's true. I wanted to get closer to you, and maybe by some miracle you might notice me. So yes, I became friends with your sister for that purpose."

I told Taggart I wouldn't get mad, and I wasn't… exactly… but it did bother me. Using my sister that way was wrong.

"I see," was all I could say.

"But two things happened instead."

"Go on."

"The first, my planned backfired because although you noticed me, you despised me. You went out of your way to avoid me, which unfortunately meant you avoided your sister as well."

A wave of guilt swept over me. I started this and I needed to finish it.

"And the second thing?"

"Your sister became the most important person in the world to me."

My heart swelled. "I can't blame you there. She was special."

More silence filled the room.

"Why me?" I asked.

"What?"

"Why was it so important for me to notice you?"

Taggart shrugged his shoulders.

"You can do better than that. I think you owe me a legitimate reason."

"Why does anyone like anyone else?"

"But you're not anyone, not by a longshot."

"Neither are you," he responded with a half-smile. "Becca either. You both were never fake. You acted the same around everybody, whether they were your friends or someone you just met. The two of you were kind, courteous, never conciliatory or berating. You never joined in when your friends picked on someone because they were bored. Whenever you entered a room, I couldn't take my eyes off you. It was all that… that is… until—"

"Until?"

Taggart must have decided he had said enough because he didn't look like he intended to finish the thought. That was okay. I had a pretty good idea what he meant.

"Until I started hanging out with Jason and his group."

Taggart still said nothing, but his non-response told me I was right.

"What about now?"

"Pardon?"

"What's your opinion of me now?"

Taggart had opened his mouth to reply when the curtain drew back and Detective Brown walked in. I expected him to be wearing a suit and tie like he did at the station. Instead, he sported a pair of plain brown slacks and a black polo shirt with the police insignia sewn on one arm.

"Your parents should be here shortly, Cassie, and your foster-parents are waiting for you in the lobby, Taggart. I know you've both been through a lot, and I'll get out of your hair as soon as I can. I just have a few questions if that's alright?"

"Sure," I answered.

"I got word before coming up here that we executed a search of Miss Worthy's address, and the entire apartment has been ransacked. Would either of you have any idea about that?"

I looked at Taggart, but he didn't seem surprised.

I shook my head.

"Maybe she did that herself?" Taggart answered.

"How do you mean?" the detective asked, his eyebrows furrowed.

"She said she was planning on leaving town tonight. Maybe she was in a hurry and didn't care about being tidy?"

"And why do you suppose she felt the need to leave tonight?"

"I couldn't say, and she didn't say."

The detective considered this for a moment, then turned his attention to me.

"Cassie, I know Miss Worthy claimed to be Taggart's biological mother, but why do you think she kidnapped you?"

I looked at Taggart. "She was under the impression that the two of us were in a relationship, and she didn't approve. She was planning on leaving town and wanted Taggart to come with her, so she was forcing him to choose between the two of us. I'm pretty sure she was about to shoot me if she hadn't suddenly collapsed."

"Are you?"

"Am I what?"

"In a relationship with Taggart?"

"NO," Taggart and I both answered simultaneously.

Detective Brown gave a quick smile at that before becoming serious again.

"You know, it was pretty reckless trying to handle things on your own and not calling us before you did. Jason Tidwell wouldn't be lying in surgery right now if you had."

I grimaced on the inside and held my breath, hoping against hope that Taggart wouldn't respond truthfully.

"Yes sir. I know that now, sir. It just that… it was my… mother."

I let out a long sigh. Maybe there's hope for him yet.

"Do you know what happened to her?" I asked, attempting to change the subject. "It was weird, the way she just fell out like that."

"No, we don't, but they'll do a full autopsy, and we'll find out. We'll also do a DNA test and confirm that she was your mother, Taggart. For tonight, consider yourselves lucky," the detective said, looking at me now. "All of you."

"Yes, sir."

"I might have more questions for you later. If so, we'll give you a call. Get some rest."

Detective Brown started to leave, but paused at the door and robbed me of that feeling of relief. He turned back around and put his hands in his pockets.

"I got the weirdest note earlier tonight. It said *I Know Who You Are, Meet Me Tonight at the Park*. I don't suppose either of you knows anything about that?"

Taggart and I looked at one another with our best impression of someone without a clue.

"No sir," we both answered.

"Hmmm. It's just an odd coincidence that Miss Worthy took you from that park, Cassie. What did you say you were doing there tonight?"

I hadn't said, but I would not draw this out any longer than I had to.

"My friends, Tunes and Delta, were playing tennis and the rest of us were there to watch. I had gone back to my car for my phone when I ran into Miss Worthy."

Detective Brown nodded slowly, looking back and forth between the two of us.

"Have a good night," he said, then disappeared.

Taggart went to the curtain, peered outside, then pulled it closed it again.

"Who do you think broke into Miss Worthy's apartment?" I asked.

"Selphaxsys."

"Really? How would they know?"

"Because they probably followed us from Atlanta. I'm sure they're the ones I saw tailing us here in town. They're tying up loose ends."

"What the detective said made me think. What happened at the park when Dr. Gleason and Mr. Stevens both showed up?"

"It didn't take very long to ascertain neither of them had anything to do with the murders. I left them rather abruptly when Delta called to say you weren't answering your phone."

"You owe both of them an apology."

Taggart nodded. "I'm not sure why, but if you think that's prudent. First thing tomorrow."

"Good idea."

I swung my feet off the bed so I was sitting upright off the side, then I patted the spot next to me with my hand.

"Sit next to me," I said.

Taggart blinked several times, then took a seat next to me, staring straight ahead.

"Where were we?" I asked innocently.

"I think maybe I should go so you can rest."

"Are you trying to get away from me?"

"Why would you think that?"

"I think you'd sit through a lecture about the social significance of Twitter rather than talk about your feelings with me."

"What's a twitter?"

"Exactly. How can you express your feelings if you can't even talk to me?"

I could see that I was making Taggart uncomfortable, but I didn't care.

"We talk."

"Not like you apparently do with your therapist."

Taggart paused.

"That was privileged communication between me and my therapist. Nobody was supposed to hear that."

"I didn't listen to the conversation. I just got the Cliff Notes version."

"She was quoting remarks I said a long time ago."

"Are you telling me none of it's true?"

"I… it's confusing."

"You cared for my sister, right?"

"More than I ever thought possible."

"I found her journal."

Taggart looked at me, fear in his eyes.

"And I read it… well, most of it… which is how I know she cared just as much for you. She began every entry with the words—*I Love Taggart McGill.*"

Taggart turned his head away from me. "Becca and I never felt that way towards one another."

"I know. Love can take a lot of different forms."

Taggart nodded his head, but continued to look away from me.

"You never answered my question."

"Which question was that?"

"What's your opinion of me now?" I asked.

Taggart looked me straight in the eyes for the first time.

"You like fast cars, but you rarely go more than five miles over the speed limit. You're tolerant of opinions that differ from your own, but not afraid of expressing a non-popular one. You're witty without being snarky. And most of all, you have a kind heart and when the coastal breeze plays with your hair, you get this tiny smile on your face that I doubt you even know you're doing."

I tried to swallow, but there was a humongous lump forming in my throat.

"I once called you the bane of my existence," I admitted.

Taggart smiled.

"As long as I can be part of your existence, you can call me anything you like."

Epilogue

Taggart paused before he pulled on the door leading into the police department.

"I'm not sure I'm ready for this," he said, looking at me as if he I was making him walk the plank.

"Then don't do it. Nobody is pressuring you."

"But you think I should?"

"Yes, but don't do it because I want you to. Do it because it feels right."

Taggart nodded, but when he reached for the door a voice calling his name came from the parking lot. We turned around to see Chewy, Tunes, and Delta running towards us. Chewy was leading the group, running even faster than the night we broke into the funeral home and displaying a smile almost as long as a six-inch sub. As he got closer, I noticed he wasn't slowing down. In fact, at the last minute, he leaped into Taggart's arms and wrapped his legs around him.

"Whoa, what's going on?" I asked, laughing at the spectacle Chewy was making of himself and the hilariously awkward expression Taggart had on his face.

Delta and Tunes came trotting up, both out of breath. I didn't notice it at first, but they were holding hands.

"I knew Taggart and you had this thing to do, but Chewy couldn't wait. He had to come," she said between gasps.

"Thank you… thank you… thank you… thank you," Chewy's muffled voice was heard coming from somewhere buried in Taggart's shoulder.

"What's he thanking Taggart for? What don't I know?"

"Chewy's mom got a call from her doctor a little while ago. It seems all her medical expenses, including the chemotherapy drugs she needs, are being paid by some anonymous benefactor. She won't owe a dime. It looks like she and Chewy won't have to move after all."

"I don't understand. Who would—"

"Selphaxsys," Chewy raised his head and announced. "It had to be. Taggart must have said something to them."

I watched as Chewy separated himself from Taggart and waited for him to say something, but all he got instead was a confused look.

"Did you do that?" I asked.

Taggart shook his head. "I don't know what he's talking about."

I watched him, acting and saying one thing, but I could tell the opposite was true. Taggart was lying. He had somehow arranged for the drug company to take care of Chewy's mom medical expenses. I guess that's what playing the long game meant. The enormity of what he had done filled my heart to the bursting point and my eyes with tears.

A line from my sister's journal popped into my head. *I Love Taggart McGill!*

Chewy mustn't have believed Taggart's lie either, because he hugged him again. This time, I think I caught the shadow of a smile on Taggart's lips.

"We've got to get inside," Taggart said softly.

Chewy let go of him and quickly turned his back to us, pulling his forearm across his face.

"You guys want to go get a shake when you're done? My treat," Delta suggested, smiling through misty eyes herself.

"This might take a while, so why don't we postpone it until after our support group meeting. And remember, I promised my mom she could be part of it tonight."

"Looking forward to it," Delta said.

"See you then," I said, then entered the police station through the door Taggart was holding open for me.

They must have been expecting us because we were quickly ushered into the same conference room we visited when Detective Brown had shown Chewy the autopsy report for his father. Officer Wilson—Taggart's foster brother—was waiting for us and he beckoned us to take a seat.

I could see that Taggart was tensing up again. I rubbed on his back and felt his stiff shoulders sag a bit.

"Relax, it's just a phone call, and it doesn't have to lead to anything if you don't want it to," I said, slipping into the chair next to him.

The police had tracked down Taggart's grandparents in Florida. At first, he had been adamant about not communicating with them, but then he relented. Everyone's insistence that he do something, even if it was just a phone call, had eventually yielded results.

"Are you ready?" Officer Wilson asked.

"Let's get it over with," Taggart answered.

In the center of the table was a phone shaped like three-pointed a star, without a handset, designed exclusively for conference calls via speakerphone. Officer Wilson looked at a small piece of paper and dialed a number. After a couple seconds, we could hear the phone ringing. It rang only two times before it was answered.

"Hello," came an elderly man's voice.

"Mr. Note… this is Officer Wilson from the New Haven police force. I believe you're expecting our call?"

"Oh yes. We've been waiting by the phone for half an hour."

"Well, I'm here with Taggart and a friend of his, Cassie Underwood. Taggart wasn't completely comfortable speaking to you alone this first time, so he asked the two of us to join him if that's okay."

"Oh…okay. That's fine."

"Say hello," I prompted him.

"Hello," Taggart responded, robotically, causing me to shoot him a look that said, *really?*

"Hello, Billy… or would you prefer to be called Taggart?" the voice answered.

"Taggart is what I know. I assume the police have filled you in about the circumstances here?"

"Yes… yes, they have. Quite alarming… and confusing, actually."

"I imagine so. Do you have any questions I could answer?"

"Just one actually."

"And what is that?"

"Why hasn't anybody mentioned anything about your sister?"

Acknowledgments

I've said it before, and I'll say it again—*It takes a village to raise a child*—or a book! The path to placing it in your hands is so full of twists, turns, diversions, abandonment, and revitalization that it could make its own an entertaining story. So many people supported me along the way, and they each deserve mention.

First up are the folks who took the time to read my early drafts of all my manuscripts and supply insight on how they thought I could improve. Critique Partners, Beta Readers, Friends, the list goes on. It has been their efforts through the years that have molded me into what you see today. Thank you, all! In alphabetical order – Angela Brown, Patricia Burroughs, Lindsay Carlson, Sonja Cassella, Alexia Chamberlyn, Kristi Chestnutt, Crystal Collier, Maddy D., Gerardo Delgadillo, Julie Dao, Patti Downing, Melissa Embry, Elise Fallson, Chris Fries, Anne Gallagher, Sierra Godfrey Fong, Aaron Green, Christy Hinz, Donna Hole, Solange Hommel, Hannah Kincade, Liz Larson, Lori Lopez, Laura Maisano, Linda Masterson, Alex Perry, Summer Poole, Flor Salcedo, Jessica Salyer, Lola Sharp, Tiana Smith, Portia Stewart, Tara Watson, and Nancy Williams.

Special recognition is reserved for these following individuals as their contributions significantly impacted the trajectory of my career. In one way or another, each of them boosted my morale or propped up my self-confidence when it needed it most. A most heart-felt thanks to Lisa Regan, Dianne Salerni, Barbara Poelle, Sarah Negovetich, and Tina P. Schwartz.

I must give **ultra-special recognition** to my editor for *PRICK*, the awesome Shelly Stinchcomb. She was not only my editor in this endeavor, but also the books compass and champion. Her support went way beyond the place where the paycheck ended, and I can safely say that she is one of the main reasons why this book is published. A heartfelt thank you, Shelly!

Last, but most assuredly not least, is my family. My kids—Cody, Jaime, Casey—and especially my best friend and wife, Kim. She has always been much more than my number one cheerleader. She is my sounding board and brainstorm partner. Thank you all for believing in me and allowing me to pursue this dream. It means the world to me. Love you!

Oh…wait…there's one more! You, my faithful reader. I can't forget about you. Thank you for taking a chance on Taggart and Cassie. You are why authors like me do what we do.

Much love!

A Letter From DL

I want to say thank you for choosing to spend your hard-earned income on PRICK. If you enjoyed reading it as much as I did writing it, please consider signing up for my newsletter at my website (listed below). It's the perfect way to keep up to date with news about all my latest releases. Your email address will never be shared, and you can unsubscribe at any time.

This book is self-published, meaning there is no corporate publisher to market it or help spread the word of its existence. It's only me. That's why it means so much if you could leave a review somewhere or recommend it to a fellow booklover. Reviews and word-of-mouth recommendations are the best way to introduce new readers to one of my books for the first time. No joke. These things make a difference. It doesn't have to be much. Even something like *This book* **ROCKS** would be enough.

I'd also like to hear from you. You can usually find me hanging out at one of the social media places below, as well as my website. Tell me what your reading experience was like, or just say HI. I don't bite (unless you're covered in caramel – then all bets are off).

https://www.dlhammons.com

https://www.facebook.com/DLHammonsauthor

https://www.threads.net/@dl_1956

https://www.goodreads.com/DLHammons

Inst

JERK

The Next Taggart McGill Mystery

COMING

SPRING 2024